THE OTHER AMERICANS

THE OTHER AMERICANS

Laila Lalami

BLOOMSBURY CIRCUS
LONDON · OXFORD · NEW YORK · NEW DELHI · SYDNEY

BLOOMSBURY CIRCUS
Bloomsbury Publishing Plc
50 Bedford Square, London, WC1B 3DP, UK

BLOOMSBURY, BLOOMSBURY CIRCUS and the Bloomsbury
Circus logo are trademarks of Bloomsbury Publishing Plc

First published in 2019 in the USA by Pantheon Books, a
division of Penguin Random House LLC, New York
First published in Great Britain 2019

A catalogue record for this book is available from the British Library

ISBN: HB: 978-1-5266-0670-9; TPB: 978-1-5266-0669-3;
eBook: 978-1-5266-0668-6

2 4 6 8 10 9 7 5 3 1

Printed and bound in Great Britain by CPI Group (UK) Ltd,
Croydon CR0 4YY

FSC
www.fsc.org

MIX
Paper from
responsible sources
FSC® C020471

To find out more about our authors and books visit www.bloomsbury.com
and sign up for our newsletters

For A. and S.

THE OTHER AMERICANS

Nora

My father was killed on a spring night four years ago, while I sat in the corner booth of a new bistro in Oakland. Whenever I think about that moment, these two contradictory images come to me: my father struggling for breath on the cracked asphalt, and me drinking champagne with my roommate, Margo. We were celebrating because Margo had received a grant from the Jerome Foundation to work on a new chamber piece, her second big commission that year. We'd ordered steamed mussels and shared an entrée and lingered late into the night. The waiter was trying to convince us to get the chocolate mousse for dessert when my phone rang.

I have no clear memory of what happened next. I must have told Margo the news. We must have paid the bill, put on our coats, walked the five blocks back to our apartment. A bag was packed, somehow. But I do remember driving home on the 5 freeway, in the foggy darkness that cloaked almond groves and orange orchards, all the while dreaming up alternate explanations: perhaps the sheriff's department had misidentified the body, or the hospital had swapped my father's records with someone else's. These possibilities were far-fetched, I knew, and yet I clung to them as I drove. Under my headlights, I could see only twenty feet ahead. But the fog lifted at dawn, and by the time I reached the Mojave, the sun was out and the sky a brazen blue.

All I could hear when I stepped into my parents' house were my heels on the travertine floor. There was a copy of *Reader's Digest* on the console, a set of keys on a yellow wrist coil, and a pair of sunglasses with a missing lens. One of the framed photos on the hallway wall was askew. In the living room, my mother sat on the sofa, staring at the cordless phone in her hand as though she couldn't remember how to use it. "Mom," I called, but she didn't look up. It was as if she couldn't hear me. She was still in the white shirt and black gi from her karate class the night before. Across the ottoman, the jacket of her uniform lay in a heap, the dragon appliquéd on its back a startling red.

It seemed to me then that my father was still with us—in the half-empty packet of Marlboros on the windowsill, the frayed slippers under the coffee table, the tooth marks on the pencil that stuck out from the book of crossword puzzles. Any moment now, he would walk in, smelling of coffee and hamburgers, saying, You won't believe what a customer told me this morning, and then, seeing me standing by the armchair, call out, Nora! When did you get here? His eyes would gleam with delight, he would kiss me on the cheeks, the stubble on his chin would tickle me, and I would say, Now. I just got here now.

But the doorway remained empty, and pain kicked me in the stomach. "I don't understand," I said, though what I meant was that I didn't believe. Disbelief had been the only constant since I'd heard the news. "I just talked to him yesterday."

My mother stirred, finally. She turned to me, and I saw that her eyes were rimmed with red and her lips cracked. "You talked to him?" she said, not without surprise. "What did he say?"

From the hallway came the rattle of the mailbox slot and the thump of the mail as it hit the floor. In its wicker basket, the cat raised its head, then went back to sleep.

"What did he say?" she asked again.

"Nothing. He said he wanted to chat with me for a bit, but I had to go teach and I wanted to get a cup of coffee in the few minutes I had left on my break. I told him I'd call him back later." My hand flew to my mouth. I could have talked to him one more time, heard the care in his voice, and yet I had squandered the chance. And all for some bitter coffee in a paper cup, hastily consumed before confronting a class of bored prep-school kids making their way through *The Odyssey*.

A motorcycle roared up the street and the windows shuddered. Nervously I undid the folding clasp on my watch and clicked it back in place. Then a grim silence fell on the room again. "What was Dad doing at the restaurant so late?" I asked. "Doesn't Marty usually close up?"

"He wanted to install new lights he bought, so he told Marty to go home."

And then what? He must have locked up the restaurant and walked out. Maybe he was jiggling his keys in his hands, the way he always did when he was lost in thought, or maybe he was distracted by a text on his cell phone. Either way, he didn't hear or see the car barreling down on him until it was too late. Had he suffered? Had he called out for help? How long had he lain on the asphalt before his breath ran out? Unbidden, a memory came to me of a summer party at the neighbors' house when I was four years old. They'd recently remodeled their backyard, and were showing off their new barbecue pit and seating nook to my parents. My sister ditched me; she was ten and wanted to play with the older kids. I started chasing after a pair of dragonflies, but just as my fingers closed around one of them, I fell into the pool. The water was icy and tasted like almonds. It drew me to the bottom with such force that I felt I would never draw another breath again. I was in the pool for only an instant before my father dove in after me, but in that instant my limbs froze, my chest burned, my heart nearly stopped. That pain came back to me now. "Something doesn't seem right," I said after a moment. "The one time Dad stays for close, he gets run over and killed?"

I realized too late that I had said the wrong thing, or used the wrong word. My mother began to weep. Loud, unguarded sobs that made her face flush and her shoulders heave. I crossed the living room, moved the rolled-up prayer mat out of the way, and sat beside her, holding her so close that I could feel her tremors. Everything about this moment felt strange to me—being in this house on a weekday in spring, wearing my shoes indoors, even comforting my mother as she cried. In my family, my father was the consoler. It was to him I came first whenever something bad happened to me, whether it was scraping my knee on the monkey bars when I was eight, or losing another composer competition just a month earlier.

My mother wiped her nose with a crumpled tissue. "I knew something was wrong when I came back from your sister's house. I went there to drop off karate patches for the children, and she asked me to stay for dinner. Then I came home, and he wasn't here."

Yet the armchair where my father usually sat still bore the imprint of his body. It was as if he were only in the next room.

"What did the police say?" I asked. "Do they have a lead?"

"No. The detective just asked a lot of questions. Did he have money troubles, did he use drugs, did he gamble, did he have enemies. Like that. I said no."

I remember being puzzled by these questions, which were so different from those that swirled around in my head: who was driving the car and how did they hit him and why did they flee the scene? Then my gaze was drawn to the window. Outside, two blackbirds landed one after the other on the electric wire. The neighbor across the street was deflating the giant Easter bunny that had sat for weeks in his front yard, gathering dust. It stared back with grotesque eyes as its white ears collapsed under his shoes. The wind whipped the flag on the pole, and the sun beat down without mercy.

Jeremy

Back then I was struggling with insomnia, and I would go to the gym right when it opened, at five a.m. The doctor had told me that regular exercise would help. She told me a lot of things would help. Hot baths. Blackout curtains. Reading. Chamomile. I took long baths, I read before bed, I drank cup after cup of chamomile, but most nights I still lay awake, listening to the clock on the bedside table ticking in the silence. I'd tell myself, If you fall asleep now, you could still get four hours of sleep, or three hours, or two. As if I could reason myself into sleeping. Then, a little before five, I'd get up and head to Desert Fitness.

That morning, I had finished my cardio and was doing my crunches when Fierro came in. The gym was mostly empty at that time, so I was glad for the company, though he wouldn't stop talking about his ex. This was right after he and Mary separated, and I think he was still in denial about it. His chattering made me lose count, and I had to stop and start twice before I was sure I'd completed my set. Fifty regular, fifty reverse, fifty double, fifty bicycle. I had another twenty minutes before I had to leave for work, but just to be safe, I skipped the biceps curls and went to the bench press. I liked to take my time when I lifted weights. Still do. I set myself up with two hundred and fifty pounds and settled down on the bench but, without so much as asking for permission, Fierro added fifteen pounds on each side of my barbell. "What're you doing?" I asked.

"Dude, come on. No point in doing it if you're not doing it right." He stood behind the bench, ready to spot me. Waiting, really. He was in a gray One Shot, One Kill shirt, with the short sleeves rolled up to show off his muscles.

"Doing it like you, you mean."

He leaned to the left, giving me his good ear. "What's that?"

"Never mind," I said. I could argue with Fierro, or I could start lifting and get to work on time. I started lifting.

"Anyway," he said, "last night I found out Mary didn't change the spark plugs on the Mustang, even though I reminded her about it three times. She's going to ruin that car. Dude, take a break if you need one."

I could feel beads of sweat on my forehead, but I pressed on. I didn't want to give Fierro the satisfaction. We could be competitive with each other about certain things, going back to our days in the Marines. A blonde in a black leotard walked in and Fierro's eyes instinctively tracked her all the way to the locker-room doors. He sucked on his teeth. "So I told Mary I wouldn't sign the divorce papers until she gave me the keys." He said this like he was proud of it, like he'd finally taken a stand.

"Isn't it her car, though?" I asked. I'd ridden in that Mustang a few times, after Fierro and I came back from Iraq. I'd sit in the back, sipping on whiskey from my flask, while Mary drove us to wherever we were going, a bar or a club. Whenever she turned or changed lanes, a silver-plated angel ornament swung from its chain on the rearview mirror. I remember one time, she was talking about the bachelorette party she'd gone to while she was in Vegas with her friends from work when Fierro interrupted her. You never told me about no bachelorette party, he said. That was one of their earliest fights, and the fighting had never stopped, even after they'd split up.

"*Her* car? Who put the down payment on it? Who replaced those crappy hubcaps with chrome wheels? Who installed redline tires just this last summer?" Fierro turned his thumb, crooked because of an old fracture, to his chest. "It was me. I did it." Now he put his hands over the barbell. "Come on, Gorecki. Take a break."

"I'm fine," I said. I didn't have much time for a break. If I was late to work, Vasco would chew me out. For a while now, he'd been waiting for me to slip up, just so he could say he needed to look at the schedule again and why didn't I take a different shift? I couldn't figure out why the guy hated me so much. I finished my last few reps in silence, then sat up on the bench to catch my breath. My shirt was soaked and stuck to my chest. "Didn't you tell me she was seeing someone?" I asked.

"What's that? Man, the music is so loud in here."

"You told me Mary was seeing some guy."

"Yeah."

"So she's not coming back. Just sign the damn papers already."

"Fuck, no. She thinks she can just move on. Erase the past like it never happened. Like *I* never happened. Well, she's wrong." He added twenty-five more pounds on each side of the barbell and sat down to do his reps, lifting in a steady rhythm, breathing in and out effortlessly.

I wiped my face with my towel and watched him for a minute. He'd been spending a lot more time at the gym since he'd separated from Mary. Sometimes, he worked out twice a day. "So my sister is having a barbecue," I said. "Wanna come with?"

"Sure. If it's okay with her."

"Of course it's okay. I don't want to go alone. You'd be doing me a favor, really."

"All right. When?"

"Day after tomorrow."

Ten minutes later, I was in my Jeep, the engine rattling in the quiet of the morning. The rising sun colored the sky a rusty red and as I drove down the 62, I lowered the window so I could feel the last of the cool morning air. Lights came on in coffee shops and diners like eyes blinking open. At the station, I changed into my uniform and rushed to the conference room, only to find I was the last one there and the sergeant's briefing had already started. I settled into a chair and avoided eye contact with Vasco, who was halfway through reading the previous night's reports in his monotone voice.

"Stabbing on the 5500 block of Shadow Mountain Road. The suspect was upset that his mother was moving out to go live with a man she'd just met. He pulled out a knife and slashed the boyfriend's arms three times. Dog attack on the 3200 block of Bermuda Ave. The owner had repeatedly been warned about his pit bull, but he let it loose in the yard and it jumped over the fence and attacked the neighbors' kid. Fatal hit-and-run on the 8300 block of Chemehuevi, corner with Highway 62. Nothing yet on the runaway car. Tagging at the high school overnight. Second incident this week. That's about it." As he gathered his papers into a file folder, he looked around the room at all the deputies. "One last thing. There's been a lot of chatter on social media about the Bowden incident. People see ten seconds of cell-phone footage and they think they know what happened. Don't pay attention to that. We're not here to be distracted by what people say online. We're here to do our job. Stay focused."

Vasco must have been in a rush because he left the conference room without commenting about my tardiness. Must be my lucky day, I thought. My shift was pretty quiet, too: a noise disturbance; a parked vehicle check; a dropped 911 call that turned out to be a butt dial; Marci Jamison once again trying to report her Ativan and Percocet stolen so she could get a replacement prescription. As I changed out of my uniform at the end of the day, I found myself making a mental list of everything I still had to do that night. Read for my ethnic studies class. Go over my history text to prepare for my final. Turn in my English paper by email. On my way out of the station, I walked past the dry-erase board where active cases were listed. One name made me stop. Guerraoui.

Efraín

I saw it happen. I wish I hadn't, because it only brought me trouble. And I really wish I hadn't told Marisela about it. That night, I was riding my bicycle on the 62, heading home after work, when the chain fell off my back gear. We used to have a car when we lived in Arizona, a Toyota Corolla we bought for $875 from one of the ushers at our church, but it broke down after we moved here and we couldn't afford to repair it or buy another one. We lost $875, just like that. Sometimes, Marisela complains that people come to this country to get ahead, and all we're doing is getting behind. I'm doing the best I can, I tell her, I can't do more than that. What I don't tell her is that we'd get ahead if we didn't have her two sisters in Torreón to support. And the bicycle isn't so bad—I got it for free from Enrique, and I can ride it almost anywhere. The only problem is the chain.

That's what happened that night. I had to stop when the chain fell off. I pulled up to the sidewalk, not far from where the 62 meets Chemehuevi Way, and turned the bicycle upside down. Getting a chain back on its gear is easy enough, but it was dark and I'm farsighted, so I couldn't see what I was doing. I don't usually carry my glasses with me because I don't need them, not for the carpet-cleaning service I work for during the day, or for washing linens at the motel in the evening. I got down on my knees and started draping the chain by feel, getting it back on the gear one link at a time. It took a while, and when I finally got it done, my hands were dirty. I raised myself up carefully, trying not to get any grease on my pants, holding my arms away from me, as if I were groping for something in the dark. That's when I heard a car speeding toward the intersection and then a dull sound. *Bump.* Like that. I looked up, and the car was already making a turn onto the side street. The old man rolled off the hood and landed facedown in the gutter. And the car didn't even stop. It went on as if it had only hit a can or a plastic bottle.

"You should call the police," Marisela said.

I walked past her to the kitchen sink and squeezed dish soap on my hands, trying to work the grease off. "Did you forget what happened to Araceli?" I said. Araceli lived down the street from us in Tucson. A plump woman with big hair and a cackling laugh. She called the police to report a neighbor who was beating his wife, and when they came to take her statement, they found out she didn't have her papers. Before she knew what was happening to her, Immigration was at her door. California is different from Arizona, at least that's what people say, the laws are different here. But how could I take a chance like that?

"So you just left?" Marisela said, her hand on her cheek. In the bright light of our kitchen, the freckles across the bridge of her nose looked darker. Twelve years we've been married, and those freckles still get me. I couldn't lie to her. I looked away, kept scrubbing my hands. She came closer, and when she spoke again her voice rose with astonishment. "You left him there?"

Well, no. Not exactly. I pulled out my phone from my pocket, getting grease all over the keypad before I realized that the call could be traced. So I looked at the buildings on that stretch of the 62, trying to decide where I could go for help. There was a diner with a bright sign, but all the lights inside were off, except for the one that flashed CLOSED in red and blue. The bowling arcade next door was open late, though, and I started down the pavement, until I noticed a jogger coming up to the intersection. A woman in running shorts, her blond hair in a ponytail, her ears covered by headphones. She couldn't have heard anything, but she was about to cross the highway at Chemehuevi. She would find the old man on the other side and she would call the police. I got on my bike and went home. "So you didn't help him?" Marisela asked.

"There wasn't anything I could do," I said, wiping my hands with a paper towel. Traces of grease still stuck underneath my fingernails. I walked past her to the bedroom, where I took off my uniform. The children were asleep in the bed under the window, and I moved quietly so that I wouldn't rouse them. Elena was eight at the time, and Daniel was six. Both citizens, I want to be clear about that. Everything I did was for them. Or didn't do, you might say.

I picked up a fresh towel from the pile on the bed, and stepped into the bathroom for a shower. The water was warm and I closed my eyes, but the first image that came to me was of the old man, his face sunken against the gutter, one of his knees twisted beneath the other at a peculiar angle, an arm tucked under his chest as if to support his weight. I saw new details, now that my eyes were closed, things I hadn't noticed in the shock of the moment. On the electric pole behind the man was an advertisement, printed on yellow paper and pinned at eye level. Five feet below that notice, the old man's hair was a shock of white, and the bright green of his shirt stood out against the gray asphalt.

I opened my eyes under the water. No, I told myself, I hadn't witnessed the accident. What I had really seen was a man falling to the ground and a white car speeding away in the night, and I wasn't even sure about the color. It could be white, or maybe it was silver. But I really didn't know what make or model it was, and I didn't catch the license plate number. So you see, there wasn't anything I could do. All I saw was a man falling to the ground.

Nora

I took a shower, wiped the steam from the mirror, and in the damp glass I saw that I looked different. Expectant. I couldn't quite believe that life would go on now without my father, that by the next morning the sun would rise, my mother would sit at the kitchen table, the cat would nibble at its food, the neighbor would lean on her walker as she made her way down the street. The last time I had been home was for Thanksgiving. Only five months had passed and yet I couldn't remember much about that visit. There had been a board game or two after the big meal, a movie at Cinema 6, a hike with my father at the national park in Joshua Tree, but I couldn't recall anything particular about those four days. They were just four ordinary days.

It took me a long while to get dressed. I put on a dress, a belt, my watch, but with each item my thoughts would wander before I remembered to button, strap, or clasp, so that by the time I came out of my bedroom, my hair was almost dry. I was crossing the entryway toward the kitchen when the front door flew open. Salma, Tareq, and their twins walked in, the adults carrying grocery bags and the eight-year-olds clutching their tablets. "Aunt Nora," Zaid called, and ran to hug me, while Aida quietly put her arms around my waist and squeezed.

I held them, surprised, as I still am sometimes, by how much they had grown since I had last seen them. And there were other small changes, too. The psoriasis spots on Aida's elbows had gotten bigger, I noticed, and Zaid had a temporary Captain America tattoo on the back of his hand. Once, my father and I were watching the kids splash around in the inflatable pool on a warm spring day and he asked me, What is dearer to the heart than a child? I thought about it for a minute, then gave up. What? I asked. A grandchild, he said. Now he would never see his grandchildren again, never build a Lego spaceship with Zaid or teach Aida how to do crossword puzzles.

"When did you get here?" my sister asked, dropping the grocery bags to the floor.

"Early this morning," I said.

Salma looked startlingly pale, and her polka-dot shirt and black pants were so big on her that I wondered if she was ill, but the thought drifted from me as she came closer. The minute we embraced, she began to cry. I found myself comforting her, just as I had comforted my mother earlier that day. Salma's husband stood beside us, waiting, but as the moment stretched he asked the twins to go to the living room and brought a box of Kleenex from the guest bathroom.

"I'm sorry I had to tell you by text," Salma said. "You weren't picking up your cell phone."

"I was eating dinner," I said. "I didn't hear it ring and I didn't see your text. It was Mom who told me." The memory still stunned me: while my father lay on the pavement, his life slipping out of him, I'd been out celebrating with Margo.

"Did you get the coffee?" my mother asked. She was standing in the doorway. Her eyes were small and her cheeks webbed with pink veins.

"Yes, Mama," Salma said.

I picked up one of the paper bags and followed my mother and sister into the kitchen. On the wall above the spice rack was a framed collage of black beans in the shape of a tree, which I'd made in the second grade. Each branch was labeled with a name. Daddy. Mommy. Salma. Nora. I was the last bough on the right. On the stainless-steel refrigerator were half a dozen pictures of Salma's twins and a magnetic dry-erase calendar with no appointments marked on it. From the little desk by the window, where bills and magazines were stacked, Tareq pulled out a piece of paper and a black marker. "What are you writing?" Salma asked him.

"A sign for the diner." He held it up. "We can tape it to the door." In block letters, he had written THE PANTRY IS CLOSED DUE TO A DEATH IN THE FAMLY.

"You're missing the *i*," I said.

Tareq turned the paper around so he could see for himself. "It's just a sign," he said with a shrug. "It doesn't matter."

"It matters. Dad wouldn't like it. He's very touchy about things like that." I glanced at my sister. "You remember how he reprinted all the menus because there was a typo in the steak special? He said customers would notice and think his restaurant was run by an idiot."

"I remember."

Tareq added a tiny *i*, barely visible between the *m* and the *l*. "There," he said. "Fixed." Then he took the restaurant keys and stepped out through the kitchen door. I leaned against the counter and watched my mother. She was scooping coffee grounds, evening out each spoonful before she poured it into the coffeemaker. Her movements were careful and precise, as if a great deal depended on this task. "I've been thinking about something," I said. "The cops said they found him by the gutter on Chemehuevi Way. That means whoever hit him had to swerve all the way to the side of the road to hit him, right?"

"That's why they think it's a drunk driver," Salma said. Often when she spoke to me, she could sound condescending, whether or not that was her intention. She must have realized it this time, though, because she quickly added, "Or it could be one of those Marines rushing to make it to the base at Twentynine Palms on time. They drive like maniacs when they're late."

My mother closed the coffeemaker lid with a snap and, with her back turned to me, began folding the grocery paper bags into rectangles, stacking them on the counter. I took that as a signal that I had to stop asking her about the accident. She had already told me all she knew.

In what remained of the afternoon, we worked in silence. From the glass cabinet, we took out cups and saucers for the coffee, and the little blue glasses for the tea. We washed mint leaves and unwrapped the snacks that Salma had brought. Whenever the phone rang, one of us answered it and gave directions to the house. In a little while, Tareq returned from the restaurant and set the keys back on the counter. "Who will take care of bookkeeping?" he asked.

I looked up from the napkins I had been folding. "What book-keeping?"

"Who's going to sort out payroll? Handle payments to suppliers? With the diner closed, everything's going to run a little behind."

"Are you seriously asking about money at a time like this?"

"Nora," Salma said, her tone reproachful.

"What? You heard him."

"These are not unreasonable questions. Not all of us can be like you, with your head in the clouds."

Your head in the clouds. The idiom rang like an echo in my life. It had started when I was nine or ten, so absorbed in reading my books that I didn't hear my name when I was called to the dinner table. "You have your head in the clouds," my mother would say, often with affection. A few years later, when I helped out at the restaurant after school, the remark turned into a bitter reprimand. "You gave out the wrong change. You have your head in the clouds," my mother complained. And later yet, when I decided against medical school, it became an accusation. "You're going to ruin your life, benti. You have your head in the clouds!"

Having my head in the clouds was my way of surviving. This realization came to me early, on my first day at Yucca Mesa Elementary, when Mrs. Nielsen cheerfully read the children's names on the roster, but could not bring herself to say "Nora Zhor Guerraoui." Twice she started on the middle name and stopped, frowning at the consonant cluster. The class grew silent, united in its curiosity about the word that had made the teacher falter. Then Mrs. Nielsen lowered her reading glasses over her nose and peered at me. "What an unusual name. Where are you from?" At recess, the kids fanned out and gathered again in small groups—military kids, church kids, trailer-park kids, hippie kids—groups in which I knew no one and no one knew me. I stayed behind by the blue wall that bordered the swings, and watched from a distance. In the cafeteria, I ate the zaalouk my mother had put in my lunchbox, while the other girls at my table whispered among themselves. Then Brittany Cutler, a pretty blonde with plaited hair and a toothy smile, turned to me and asked, "What are you eating?"

I looked up, immensely grateful for a chance to finally talk to someone. "Eggplant."

"It looks like poop."

The other girls tittered, and for the rest of the day they called me a poop-eater. At story time, we all gathered around Mrs. Nielsen to hear her read from "Rapunzel," but nobody wanted to sit next to me. Later, Mrs. Nielsen started playing "Twinkle, Twinkle, Little Star" on the xylophone and asked us if we recognized the tune. I said, "It's the purple and green song!" to which Mrs. Nielsen replied, "No, sweetie, the star twinkles, it's not purple or green. You really need to learn your colors." I didn't know how to tell her that I already knew my colors, that I was talking about how the music looked, the shapes and shades the notes made. So when my father came to pick me up after school, I ran across the blacktop and into his arms as though he were a savior. He dried my tears, took me home, and let me have Oreos before dinner.

But the next day I still had to go to school. I learned the alphabet, learned the pledge of allegiance, learned to stay out of the way of bullies. In class, I was quiet. At lunch, I sat alone. The silence cloaked me with safety, but it betrayed me a few months later, when Mrs. Nielsen became convinced I had a learning disability. She called my mother into the classroom one sunny morning in May and used words like *severe mutism, social anxiety, oppositional behavior.* The terms failed to elicit a flicker of recognition from my mother. After a moment, Mrs. Nielsen's voice dropped to a whisper. "There's something wrong with your daughter," she said. I sat on a yellow mat in the corner, playing, listening, waiting for my mother to say, "There's nothing wrong with my daughter." But she only nodded slowly, as if she agreed with the teacher.

When my father came home that night and found out what had happened, he said the teacher was a fool. "Hmara," he called her, a word he reserved for the television anchors with whom he argued during the eight o'clock news. Then he reached into the fridge for a beer and started sorting through the bills on the kitchen counter. I watched my mother's face for a reaction. It was immediate. "And you know more than the teacher?"

"I know more about my daughter."

"Salma didn't have this problem in kindergarten. She was first in class, always."

"There is no problem, Maryam."

"If she doesn't speak, she has to repeat the year. That's what the teacher said."

"No, she doesn't." He ruffled my hair. "Nor-eini, try to speak in class, okay?"

But the teacher's threat, relayed and amplified by my mother, was indelible in my mind. Not speaking meant that I would have to repeat, and repeating meant that I wouldn't have to see Brittany Cutler or her acolytes every day. So I stayed in kindergarten another year. I learned the alphabet again and the pledge of allegiance again, though this time there was Sonya Mukherjee, a girl who was just as quiet as me, a girl who didn't fit in with the others, either. By the time I started the first grade, I had one friend.

Still, it wasn't until middle school that I fell in with my own tribe—music nerds. Two summers earlier, having noticed my talk of music and colors, my father had enrolled me in piano classes with Mrs. Winslow, a neighbor who had retired to the desert after years of teaching music at USC. She gave a name to how I saw the world. *Synesthesia.* And with that word came the realization that there was nothing wrong with me, that I shared this way of experiencing sound with many others, some of them musicians. At the audition for band class, I played Minuet in G, and was immediately given a spot. Sonya, too, earned a place, playing the flute. And there were other good kids in the band. Lily and Jeremy and Manuel and Jamie. Kids whose first instinct wasn't to ask "What are you?" but "What do you play?" Pinned to the wall above the teacher's desk was a poster that asked: DID YOU PRACTICE YESTERDAY? ARE YOU PRACTICING TODAY? WILL YOU PRACTICE TOMORROW? The strict discipline and long rehearsals he imposed on us bound us together. And I didn't even have to talk much—I only had to play.

One day the jazz band was invited to perform at the Summer Festival in Palm Springs. Walking across the stage to the piano, I did what my teacher had advised. Pretend you're only playing for one person.

That way you won't be so nervous. I glanced at my father, who sat in the front row, leaning his head just so, waiting. Then I closed my eyes, and began to play. As my fingers moved on the keys, I felt as if I were speaking to my bandmates, calling to Manuel on the drums or answering a question from Lily on the bass. The talk between us deepened, and I became so immersed in our many-colored conversation that when it was over I was nearly startled by the rousing applause from the audience. I remember feeling happy that night, and whole.

Yet the sense of being different never completely went away. The fault lines usually appeared when I was asked what church I went to, or when my mother spoke to me in the school parking lot, or when the history teacher asked a random question about the Middle East and all eyes turned to me for an answer. It didn't help that my parents weren't getting along and that there was constant squabbling at home. Every time a door was slammed or a dish was smashed, I locked myself in my room and listened to music. I dreamed of growing up, going to college, escaping the desert. "Why do you always have your head in the clouds?" my mother would ask.

All at once I felt alert to the smell of the coffee brewing in the pot, the starch of the napkin in my hand, the weight of my body against the kitchen counter. "I don't have my head in the clouds," I said. "I just think that today isn't a good day to be talking about money."

"We're not talking about money," Salma said. "We're talking about Baba's restaurant, which he cared about immensely, as you yourself pointed out a little while ago."

"That's not what I meant."

"Well, what did you mean, then?"

"It would be good if your husband was a bit more sensitive, that's all."

"He was only trying to help."

The doorbell rang, startling me. Salma went to answer it, her bracelets jingling on her wrist at a steady pace, as though she were keeping time. With a growing ache in my chest, I finished folding the napkins. Only a day in this house and already the arguments had started. I didn't understand why people were visiting the house so soon; it could have waited until after the funeral. I didn't want to hear the story, told again and again to each new visitor, of how my father had been found unconscious on the pavement by a schoolteacher out on her nightly run. The paramedics arrived only minutes later, but it was too late, he was already dead. I didn't want to be asked where I was when it happened, or how I heard the news. I grew tired of shaking hands with my sister's friends, tired of hearing their hushed voices. After a while, I retreated to the deck.

Jeremy

When I got to her house, the front door was open. I could hear the din of overlapping conversations inside, some of them in a language that felt familiar to me but that I couldn't understand. There were several pairs of shoes lined up at the entrance, and I wondered if I should take mine off as well, but what if she wasn't even here? Framed photographs hung along the hallway, including one from our high school jazz band. It occurred to me that I had never been inside her house before, and yet for ten years my likeness had waited for me on the wall.

In the living room, I found myself in a crowd of strangers, all of them standing in small clusters, drinking tea from tiny blue glasses. Her mother sat on the sofa, absorbed in a conversation with an old man in a black jacket and a white skullcap. The phone rang in the kitchen. Someone called out for a glass of water and an Advil. The house was loud and stuffy and I felt out of place. I had come straight from the police station, and now I wasn't so sure it was a good idea. Then I saw her on the deck.

I walked through the glass doors, relieved to be out of the crowd if nothing else. It was just after dusk, the sky turning from blue to black. Along the wooden fence, bundles of red Indian paintbrush glowed like the embers of a dying fire. The floorboards creaked under my shoes. "Nora," I called. At the sound of my voice, she turned around. Her hair was long and black and fell about her shoulders. Her eyes were as I remembered them, dark and direct. She was wearing a green dress cinched at the waist with a narrow belt. In the yellow light that came from the living room, her skin looked golden. "I'm sorry for your loss."

She looked at me wordlessly, and for a moment I had the horrifying thought that she didn't remember me and that I shouldn't have come at all. But then she crossed the deck, her bare feet light and silent on the wooden slats, and hugged me. Warmly, I thought later that night as I sat in a bath. "Thank you for coming, Jeremy," she said. When she stepped back, her gaze was drawn to the living room. A sudden wail soared, and a chorus of bereaved voices rose in comfort. She looked at me again, this time with despair. "Would you mind—could you stay for a bit?"

"Sure, of course." I sat beside her on the wooden bench. But for all my certainty about coming to see her, I had prepared nothing else to say. I settled on something simple. "Your father was a good man."

"Thank you for saying that," she said, and touched my arm lightly.

"I remember when we had afternoon rehearsals, he'd come and listen to us. To you. None of the other parents did that."

She crossed her legs—they were long and brown, and her toenails were painted red. I forced myself to look away, patted my pocket, tried to remember how many cigarettes I'd had that day. Fewer than five. My new one-day limit. "Do you mind if I smoke?"

"No, go ahead."

I lit a cigarette and blew the smoke away from her, but the wind was against me. For a week now, fierce Santa Anas had been sweeping across the valley, bringing with them heat, dust, and the calls of wild animals from the mountains. Between gusts of wind, a low murmur drifted out from the living room.

"How did you hear about my dad?"

"One of my colleagues is working the case."

"You're a detective?"

"Sheriff's deputy. You sound surprised."

"I thought maybe you would end up a teacher or something. You always turned in the best paper in AP English."

But that was my only AP class. The truth was, I hadn't been a great student in high school. Always distracted, the teachers said. It wasn't distraction, though, it was exhaustion. I worked after school, took care of my sister, and stayed up most nights until my father came home. Nothing the teachers talked about in class seemed all that important by comparison. In AP English, at least, we got to read novels, and I'd always loved reading. I took a drag from my cigarette and tried to picture myself the way Nora had, in a classroom with kids, but the image seemed incongruous to me. The path my life had taken was the only one I could imagine for myself now. "I guess we don't always end up where we expect," I said. "What about you?"

"I'm a musician. A composer."

"See now, that makes sense." What could be more natural than Nora at the piano? She was always a minute or two early to music class, a minute or two late in leaving. Played every tune perfectly the first time around, then had to wait for the rest of us to catch up. "Is there someplace I can hear your music?"

"Not really." She hesitated. "I mean, I've recorded a few pieces you can find online, but I don't have orchestra commissions or a record deal or anything like that. I work as a substitute teacher to pay the bills. So."

Without knowing why, I felt I had to stave off the disappointment I heard in her voice. "I'm sure you'll get one soon."

"That makes one of us," she said with a chuckle.

We were quiet for a long moment, though the silence was not uncomfortable. Sitting together in the dark, we could see everything inside the house. It made the moment feel intimate, as if we were sharing something secret, or even illicit. In the kitchen, her sister put a fresh kettle on the stove, then said something to two women standing at the counter. An elderly couple walked into the living room, carrying Pyrex dishes covered with aluminum foil. The phone rang three times before someone went to answer it. "Are you waiting for those people to leave?" I asked.

"It's been such a horrible day, I can't bear talking to anyone."

"Who are they?"

"The man sitting next to my mom is my uncle. He brought a friend of his from the mosque out in Los Angeles, to help her arrange the funeral. The couple drinking coffee in the kitchen are our neighbors. And the others are friends of my sister's, for the most part."

In the piñon pine, an owl hooted. Nora brought her knees to her chest and gathered her arms around them. "I can't cry," she said.

"I didn't either after my mom died. Not for a while, anyway." I stubbed out my cigarette.

"Can I bum one off you? You're tempting me."

When I flicked the lighter for her, I noticed a tattooed inscription on the inside of her wrist, but I couldn't make out the words. It was too dark and her hands were shaking. "This is probably no consolation," I said, "but Coleman—the detective who's working the case—she's really good. She'll find the bastard who did this."

"She hasn't told us anything. My dad gets run over half a block from the restaurant and she can't rustle up any leads. Nothing."

"She will. It's just going to take a little time."

"I knew this would happen."

"How do you mean?"

"I knew something terrible would happen. You remember his business was arsoned after September 11th? They never found out who did it. And then he put up a huge flag outside his restaurant, like he had to prove he was one of the good ones. I told him over and over that he should sell. But he refused, he loved it here. God only knows why."

It seemed to me that she was talking to herself, arguing with the past as though she could alter it. As though the past could ever be altered. That was how I had felt, too, when my mother died. Late one afternoon, I came home from baseball practice, still basking in the coach's praise of my swing, still aroused by the sight of Maddie Clarke in a miniskirt cheering me from the stands, still smiling at the teasing jokes of my teammates, to find my mother passed out in the hallway, her purse slung across her chest, the day's mail in her hand. I scrambled for the phone, all the while struggling to remember the first-aid class I'd taken two years earlier, in the seventh grade. Was I supposed to look for a pulse? Move her or leave her on her side like that? Carefully, I turned her on her back, tapped her cheeks, unbuttoned her collar. Somehow I managed to find a pulse, but I couldn't wake her and neither could the paramedics when they arrived. By the time my father and sister had caught up with me at the Hi-Desert Medical Center, she was dead. Pulmonary embolism. To this day I can still remember, with a clarity that startles me, my father standing in a colorless hospital hallway, telling the doctor that there must be some mistake, that all she had was a little cough.

But there was no mistake; she was gone. She wasn't there when I returned to our dark and empty house later that night. She didn't call my name from her bedroom, didn't ask, What are you still doing up? You'd better go to sleep, it's a school night. In the morning, she wasn't leaning against the kitchen counter, sipping from her cup of coffee, looking out of the window at the new day. She didn't say, Did you forget to take the trash out last night? Because I smell something. She didn't ruffle my hair and ask if I slept well. I didn't sleep at all, either that night or many, many others to come. Her absence was too heavy to be surrendered to dreams.

For the funeral, my aunts Aura and Estella drove down from El Monte and my uncle Paul flew in from Oregon. They bought me a black suit and helped me with my tie and told me stories I hadn't heard before, stories about how my mother had won second place in a dance contest at the Orange County fair; how she had hives when she sat for her teaching-credential exam; how she could play any tune on the violin by ear, any tune at all, no matter how difficult; how she'd traveled all the way to Sonora three weeks after giving birth to Ashley, just to help out a cousin who'd gotten into trouble. These stories were meant to be comforting, but in truth they were excruciating. I wished all the family would leave. Then they left, the house was empty again, and I wished they had stayed. At school, nothing made sense. My bandmates gave me a condolence card they had all signed, but I had missed the spring recital, and I felt left out of the conversations they had about it. Some of the boys on the baseball team came up to me to say they were sorry for my loss, but at lunch they all stayed away, as if my grief were contagious. And when I came home, my father was sitting in the dark, drinking and staring into space. The silence was so profound, so unrelenting, that Ashley went to eat dinner with the Johnsons, a rowdy family that lived two doors down from us.

"Dad, should we just have cereal for dinner?" I asked.

"Whatever you think," my father said.

To fill the silence in the living room while I did my homework, I turned on the television. The sound was oddly comforting, even though it made it more difficult for me to concentrate. I kept reading and rereading the same three or four lines in my textbook as my mind wandered to distant days when my mother was alive and healthy. She would never again watch me play ball with the team I'd worked so hard to join, never again expertly correct my intonation on the guitar, never again pretend to be amused by one of my stupid jokes. I hadn't realized how close we were until she died.

Then Ashley began to follow the Johnsons to their church, where they ran a popular Bible study on Tuesdays and Thursdays. She would return home on those nights with a satiated look on her face that I was sure couldn't have been solely the result of the meal that was served beforehand. Although both of my parents had been regular church-goers, they didn't force Scripture into every conversation, or leaflet the neighborhood, or roll their eyes at evolution the way the Johnsons did. But now my father didn't even bother leaving the house on Sunday.

"Dad, should I make mac and cheese?" I asked.

"Whatever you think," my father said.

I started to come home early so I could make dinner. I missed practice too many times and by the start of my sophomore year I was dropped from the baseball team. In September, when al-Qaeda flew planes into the World Trade Center in New York, my father sat up in the easy chair and for the first time started to pay attention to the television. From then on Fox News was on at such high volumes that I retreated to my bedroom, ostensibly to do my homework, though most of the time I just read a book or played my guitar. My grades dropped.

But my cooking improved. Almost every night, I had a main dish and a side on the dinner table by seven. My father ate whatever I put in front of him, but Ashley was always rushing to get to the Johnsons'. She never finished her plate, so I finished it for her. I gained a lot of weight, and a lot of it in the wrong places. When I walked down the hallways at school, it seemed to me that everyone was staring at the man boobs growing under my shirt. Now if I tried to say hello to Mad-die Clarke, she replied with a disgusted grunt. Only months before I had been a head taller than the other boys, but now I was visible in a way that, strangely, made me feel invisible. My days became a blur of mechanical motions: get up, go to school, go home, make dinner, go to sleep, start over.

Before my mother's death, my plan had been to go to university to study speech pathology. As a child, I'd suffered from an articulation disorder that had required several months of therapy, and I still remembered how empowering it had felt to overcome it. And, having grown up with a mother who taught second-language learners, I thought that a career helping kids would be a good fit for me. But in December of my senior year, when I received an acceptance letter from the state school, my enthusiasm had dimmed and I wasn't so sure speech pathology was right for me anymore.

"Dad, what do you think I should do?" I asked.

"Whatever you think," my father said.

It was hard for me to escape the feeling that I had become my own parent. I did the grocery shopping, the cooking, and the laundry. When Ashley got her period, I was the one who went to the store with her to buy tampons. Because my father was now frequently short on cash, I found a part-time job at the ice-cream parlor, but there was never enough money to go around, and each month I had to figure out which bill to pay and which to skip. But just this once, I wanted my father to guide me, talk to me, help me sort out my future. And if he couldn't do that, then the least he could do would be to show up. Just show up. For each public performance of the Yucca Valley High School jazz band, I would leave a flyer on the refrigerator, with the date and place circled in highlighter. When I walked onto the stage with my guitar, I would scan the back of the auditorium, hoping to catch a glimpse of my father. But he never came, unlike Nora's. Even at this moment, I could recall the intense envy I felt whenever I saw Mr. Guerraoui in the front row. His eyes were full of pride, something I never experienced with my dad.

I glanced at Nora. The tip of her cigarette had grown heavy with ash.

"Careful," I said. "You'll get burned."

She looked at her cigarette as if she didn't know how it got there. In that slight movement of her arm, the ash scattered over the back of her hand. She brushed it off, then looked once more toward the living room. The crowd had finally thinned; only a handful of people remained. She stood up. "Thank you again for coming, Jeremy." She walked me back through the house to the front door.

This time, when I passed by the picture on the hallway wall, I didn't stop.

Maryam

I was trying to stay awake, so I switched on the radio and looked for Claudia Corbett's show on KDGL. Usually, she's on at lunchtime, and I listen to her while I'm peeling potatoes or chopping parsley, but the show is so popular that they rebroadcast it again at ten p.m. That night, a young woman was calling in to say she had gotten married just six months ago, but she and her husband were already fighting because he wanted to move to Portland to be a nature photographer, and she wanted to stay at her job with an insurance company in Salt Lake City, and neither one of them would change their minds. "Listen," Claudia told her sharply, the way she does sometimes, when callers start to ramble and refuse to face the obvious, "nobody said that marriage was easy. Marriage is work."

When we moved to America thirty-five years ago, many things took me by surprise, like gun shops next to barbershops, freeways that tangled like yarn, people who knocked on your door to talk about Jesus, twenty different kinds of milk at the grocery store, signs that said DON'T EVEN THINK ABOUT PARKING HERE. I remember pointing them out to Driss: they even have signs that tell you what you can't think! But above all, I was surprised by the talk shows, the way Americans loved to confess on television. Men talked about their affairs or addictions or gambling problems, women talked about their weight or plastic surgeries or the children they had outside marriage; even teenagers had something to say, mostly about how terrible their parents were—and all of it like it was a normal thing. I couldn't stop watching. The television sat on top of the supply cabinet in the back of the donut shop, and while I was washing dishes or mopping floors, I would

watch *Sally* or *Donahue,* which in those days were on in the middle of
the afternoon, when the shop was quiet. My brother had told me that
watching television would help me improve my English, and I will say
I learned a lot of new words, like *paternity test* and *artificial insemina-
tion* and *AIDS epidemic,* but my trouble was pronunciation, how easy
it was to say "tree" when I meant "three," or "udder" when I meant
"other." I needed a lot of practice. In Casablanca, I had my two sisters,
three uncles, and eight cousins, but here in California, my brother
was the only family I had, and he lived a hundred and thirty miles
away. I hadn't realized how far that was until we went from seeing him
every day to seeing him only once a month, and sometimes not even
that often. For me, that was the hardest thing about living in America,
being so far away, it was like being orphaned.

One day we went to the Stater Brothers on the 62. We had been
living in the Mojave for about nine months by then, but this was our
first winter here and we weren't used to the cold, so I bundled up
Salma in a green wool coat I'd bought for her at the Goodwill before
we went to the store. She sat in the shopping cart, which was another
thing that was new to me in America, but I let her, she liked the feeling of rolling around the store in the cart, and I didn't see the harm in
it. Looking through the coupons we'd clipped from the newspaper, I
found a discount we could apply to a can of Hunt's diced tomatoes, but
I couldn't see the brand anywhere on the shelf. "I'm sure they have
it," Driss said. He was like that, he always had faith, even about silly
little things, so while he looked for the can, I waited, shivering in my
denim jacket. Then a woman pushed her cart past us, and in her wake
I caught the scent of rose water. Instantly, I was back in Casablanca
with my sisters, putting our hair in rollers and trying on different colors of lipstick, looking at our reflections in the dresser mirror, where a
picture of Shadia was tucked into the frame, her hair in an elaborate
bouffant we were trying to replicate. The radio was on, we were waiting for the DJ to play the Bee Gees, our friends were coming by later
to watch an Egyptian movie starring Roshdy Abadha.

I don't know why I did this, but I followed the woman down the
aisle and along the refrigerated section, where she got milk and but-
ter and eggs and juice, enough for a big family, and then to the corner

display, where she picked out one of the new *E.T.* lunchboxes, with the alien and the little boy touching fingers and the light glowing between them. The woman had long brown hair, almost the same shade as mine, only she wore hers parted down the middle, and I remember that her coat had those huge shoulder pads that were becoming popular. She went into a new aisle, and I watched as she tried to choose a brand of baking flour from the dozens that sat on the shelf. "Hello," I said. The woman turned around, her eyebrows lifting, her lips stretching into a tentative smile. My name is Maryam, I wanted to tell her. What is yours? Do you live nearby? What do you do? Do you have children? I have one daughter, she is three years old. Would you like to have tea with me someday? Are you baking a cake? I know a great recipe. You shouldn't use Star Flour, though, it's not good for cakes. But when I opened my mouth again, nothing came out, my heart was beating too fast inside my chest.

"Yes?" she said. "Can I help you?"

"This is not good floor."

"What?"

Later, I would learn to sound out words in my head before I spoke them, the way I had been taught to do at school, when we recited the poems of al-Khansa' or al-Mutanabbi, and our teachers would not tolerate a missing inflection or an incorrect agreement, but that day all I felt was the betrayal of a foreign tongue. "This," I said, "is not good floor."

She looked at the ground. "I don't understand."

"Too thick."

"Lady, I have no idea whatchu tryin' to say."

Only now that I was close to her did I see that she had a beauty mark on her upper lip, just like my youngest sister, which I hadn't expected, and I stared at her even more intently. But I had already mangled what I'd tried to say and I was afraid to make it worse, so I pointed to the flour and rubbed my belly and smiled in a way I hoped made my meaning clear. She shook her head and laughed, displaying crooked teeth yellowed by coffee, then put a box of instant baking mix in her cart and walked off. Standing next to the canisters of frosting, I started crying. That's where Driss found me later, crying next to the frosting. "What's wrong?" he asked, taking my hand. I didn't know how to explain to him that nothing was wrong, and yet everything was wrong. Salma was watching me from the cart, and I quickly dried my face, I didn't want to upset her, especially after she brandished the can of Hunt's diced tomatoes like a prize. A consolation prize. "Where's the coupon?" Driss asked me.

I didn't have it, I'd dropped it somewhere along the way, when I'd followed the woman from aisle to aisle, so I retraced my steps, but I couldn't find the little envelope where we saved all our coupons. It had taken us weeks to clip that many, and now Driss was annoyed because we would have to pay more for our groceries, and he bickered with me about it while we waited in the checkout line. We had to be extremely careful with money back then, because we had just started our business. We worked hard in those early years, we worked very hard, and maybe we should have worked on our marriage, too, like Claudia Corbett said. Listening to her that night in the car, I was thinking that we should try again, stop arguing about everything, learn to forgive ourselves, and especially each other, for our mistakes, but when I walked in, Driss wasn't home. Usually, he was in his lounge chair doing his crossword puzzles, that was how *he* improved his English, he was obsessed with finding all the answers, and hardly ever looked up when I walked past him on my way to the kitchen. But as I said, that night the chair was empty, and he didn't pick up the phone when I called him, so I called Salma instead. It was nine forty. I remember the time because I was looking at the clock on the microwave while I talked to her, and she told me not to worry, maybe he was having car trouble or his cell phone was turned off. An hour later, the police came.

Nora

In sleep, I was lost to a world my father still inhabited. We were together in a bright room and the air smelled of the sprig of wormwood with which he flavored his mint tea. He was doing his crosswords, chewing on his pen cap as he considered each clue. Three letters, Nora. The father of all things, the king of all things. Any ideas? War, I said without looking up from my piano. Aha! Thank you, Nor-eini. Then I opened my eyes, and the walls of my bedroom closed in on me, their bright white an assault on my senses. A weight settled on my shoulders like an unwelcome coat. Waking up was the hardest time of the day now, when I remembered he was gone.

I turned to my side, curled myself up into a ball. Staring from above the dresser was a younger version of me, in a picture of the jazz band taken just before the junior-year recital. Black dress, hair in a severe bun, lips in an impatient pout. How eager I had been to leave home! And yet what wouldn't I give now for another day here with him. I closed my eyes again, hoping to reenter the dream, but it was useless, I was wide awake. After getting dressed, I put some Coltrane on the stereo, and sat on my bed to send an email to the headmaster at Bay Prep. At the time, I was substituting for an English teacher who was on maternity leave, but I'd left Oakland immediately after hearing about the accident, so I composed a note to the headmaster, explaining what had happened and saying I hoped I would work for him again soon. He would replace me, I knew, and it would be tough to find stable work like that. Then I heard voices down the hallway.

When I walked into the living room later, I found Detective Coleman sitting on the leather sofa, her legs crossed at the ankles, a file folder on her lap. She had dark eyes and long lashes that jutted out like pine needles. A small scar cut across her right eyebrow. My mother had a framed photo in her hand, which she was showing to the detective. "This was in 1980, before we moved to California."

"Hello," I said, and the detective stood up to shake my hand.

But the moment Coleman sat down again, my mother continued, "This is my husband, Driss, and this is me. That's our daughter Salma between us. She was two. And this—Nora, how do you say, the tower that warns the ships?"

"Lighthouse."

"Right. That's the lighthouse of Casablanca behind us."

"You moved here from Morocco, Mrs. Guerraoui?" Coleman asked.

"Yes, in 1981. It's a long story."

"Would you like something to drink, Detective?" I asked.

"Coffee, if you have any. But please don't make it on my behalf."

I went into the kitchen, tossed out the coffee, and started a fresh pot. Over the years, I had heard the story of the old country many times from my father; I couldn't bear to listen to it now. "It was a Saturday," he would say. That was how he always started the story. "It was a Saturday. The Saturday before finals week." I think he liked that story because it had the easily discernible arc of the American Dream: Immigrant Crosses Ocean, Starts a Business, Becomes a Success.

He told the story from time to time, just to remind himself that everything turned out fine for him. But all that changed one September morning. At least for me, it did. I remember that the smell of smoke reached me first. I was fiddling with the car radio, trying to find a station that wasn't playing commercials. Next to me, my father drummed his fingers on the steering wheel, waiting for the light to change. "Just put NPR on," he said. But I was sick of the news. That was why I'd insisted on going to work with him that Saturday morning—I couldn't bear the news any longer. I settled on a station that played classical music, leaned back in my seat, and let the colors wash over me. Then I smelled smoke. When my father made a left onto the 62, I saw a gray plume rising in the distance. I thought it was a burning car or a propane tank, but as we got closer, I realized the smoke was coming from the shop.

We turned onto Kickapoo Trail to find Aladdin Donuts burning like a stack of hay. In a single motion, my father jumped out of the station wagon and pulled out his cell phone, just as Mr. Melendez at the 7-Eleven across the street came running toward us. "I called 911," he said. He told us he'd been changing the paper in his cash register when he heard the sound of screeching tires. He'd thought nothing of it until the smell of smoke came drifting in through the doorway, a mix of gasoline, ash, melting plastic, and caramelizing syrup. Years later, a whiff of smoke, even if only from a beachside barbecue, can still conjure up my memories of the arson. Standing beside my father that day, I watched the flames lap at the store sign until the glass frame cracked. In the distance, a cacophony of sirens rose, ending in a deafening roar as the firefighters drew up to the lot. Under the spray of their hoses, the smoke turned a cloudy white that made my eyes water and my nostrils burn.

It was a junior officer from the San Bernardino County Fire Department who found the cause of the fire: a brick wrapped in a rag that had been doused in accelerant. "Homemade," the officer said.

"I know," my father replied. He had seen this kind of thing before, he said, in the Casablanca protests of 1981. He shook his head in disbelief. I think he was just realizing that he had moved six thousand miles for safety, only to find that he was not safe at all.

When we returned home, we found my mother where we had left her at six in the morning, sitting on the sofa with one foot tucked under her, watching CNN, where footage of the twin towers burning in New York still played in an endless loop. "What happened?" she asked, standing up.

My father told her.

I walked past them to my bedroom, where I peeled off the T-shirt and jeans that now reeked of smoke. But even after I showered, I couldn't get rid of the smell of soot. My hair was redolent with it. From the living room came the soundtrack of my life—my parents arguing with each other. "We should go back," my mother was saying.

"Go where?"

"Home. Casa."

"We can't go back, Maryam."

"Of course, we can." Morocco had changed, my mother insisted, things were different now. But my father didn't think this was true. Besides, the Mojave had grown on him; he couldn't imagine living in a big city like Casablanca anymore.

"We'll move to Marrakesh, you've always liked it there."

"But what about Nora? She's still in school. No, no. We can't move."

Even after I walked back into the living room, they continued talking about me as if I weren't there. They argued for days. And the more they argued, the more my mother turned to her Qur'an. She had found solace in it after the attacks, reading it to calm herself every morning after listening to the stream of tragedies on the news. At the dinner table, she would often quote from the holy book in her perfect Arabic enunciation, which none of us could ever hope to replicate. And she'd started praying again. She had never before shown much of an interest in religion so, even as he accommodated them, these changes took my father by surprise. But when he came home one evening to find all of his beer in the trash, he went to bed without speaking to her.

Thus began an eight-month period that I sometimes thought of as the Cold War. Every morning, my mother would take the beer out of the fridge, pour it down the sink, and toss the bottles into the trash bins, and every evening my father would bring home another six-pack. When he installed a separate fridge in the garage, she stuffed it with meat and vegetables. He complained he was not free in his own home; she said she did not feel safe in it. He went out more; she took up karate.

The fighting began to diffuse after the insurance settlement came in, and my father used the money to buy an old diner. It was called the Pantry. What could be more American than that? "Everything will be fine now," he promised her. "You'll see." This was how the Cold War ended, and an uneasy peace returned to our home. But one blowback of the almost year-long conflict was that I couldn't live in that home any longer; my parents' endless fighting made it impossible. I thought of college as a safe haven; I was desperate to leave.

By the time I returned with the coffee tray, my mother had put the photograph back on the mantelpiece, wedging it between a color picture of Salma and Tareq at their wedding and framed handprints of the twins. A different portrait of my father had been taken out of its frame and now sat on the coffee table, in front of Coleman. "Do you have children, Detective?" my mother was asking.

"Yes," Coleman said. "A boy. Miles."

"Salma is a dentist. She's great with kids."

I poured a cup of coffee for the detective. "Miles, after Miles Davis?"

"No, Miles Aiken. My husband loves basketball."

Coleman took a sip of her coffee and waited for me to sit down before she opened her notebook. "Mrs. Guerraoui, the autopsy confirmed that your husband was the victim of a hit-and-run motor vehicle accident. He suffered multiple injuries, both from the immediate impact to the right side of his body and from hitting the pavement afterward: a broken hip, five broken ribs, a punctured lung, bleeding in the head. It appears he was crossing Highway 62 at Chemehuevi, probably walking to where he was parked, when he was struck by a car or truck traveling east on the highway, landing him back on the north side of Chemehuevi. The medical examiner said that the extent of his injuries suggest that he died almost instantly. The time of death is estimated at about nine thirty p.m. on April 28th."

The scene I had imagined, and which I was helpless to stop from unfolding every time I thought about the accident, came into sharper focus. Yet the new details only deepened my anguish. I didn't know he had landed on his head or that his lung had been punctured. How long had it taken for him to die? Did he measure time breath by breath, waiting for someone to come help him? A fresh pain shot through me, so raw it made me want to scream.

Coleman grew quiet. She was giving us time to absorb the news, I think. At the other end of the sofa the cat raised its nose in the air, detected a scent, then trotted out of the living room after it.

"Ya lateef," my mother whispered, "ya lateef."

"I should also mention," Coleman said, "that Highway Patrol

would normally take over at this point, but I'm already three days into the investigation, and they asked if we could see it through."

My mother glanced at me, a look of mild relief in her eyes; she wouldn't have to meet or talk to someone new. From her file folder, Coleman pulled out another paper, and I noticed that her nails were bitten to the quick. It was a habit I had battled all through grade school and only conquered during middle school. The taste of the special polish I used to apply to my nails to make myself stop biting them came back to me now. Strong. Bitter. Lingering.

"I also have a preliminary report from CSU," Coleman said.

I felt a surge of hope. Television shows had taught me that there were always clues in the crime scene, the autopsy, the lab report. I expected to hear about fingerprints, DNA evidence, shoe impressions, a cigarette butt carelessly tossed out of a window, a tire mark on the asphalt, a strand of hair retrieved with a pair of tweezers from the gutter. Instead, Coleman spoke of car paint. "Forensics recovered microscopic paint chips from the victim's clothing, likely from the vehicle that struck him. White, it looks like."

"How common is white as a color?" I asked.

"Very common, I'm afraid. For most car models."

"So this is like looking for a needle in a haystack."

Coleman's face softened. "I wouldn't go that far. We have to wait for the full lab report. Once they test the chips, they will be able to confirm the color, and maybe tell me more about their origin."

"What about witnesses?" my mother asked. "Maybe someone saw something."

"No, Mrs. Guerraoui. We canvassed the homes and businesses near the crime scene, but we haven't found anyone who's seen anything. I will continue to look. I will also put out a call for help in the *Hi-Desert Star.* That's what the picture is for," she said, tapping the photograph that my mother had taken out of its frame and left on the coffee table.

I remembered how well Jeremy Gorecki had spoken of this detective and, yes, she seemed very nice, and it was kind of her to come to the house when I'd called the police station for an update. Still, it didn't seem that much was happening with the investigation. Three days had passed and in that time the killer could have hidden his car, painted it, disposed of it. Hell, he'd probably done all three. A tidal wave of grief washed over me and for a moment I felt unable to speak. Nothing about what happened made any sense. My father had often outrun disaster—the protests in Casablanca had moved him to California; the arson had made it possible for him to buy a diner. But now disaster had finally caught up with him.

Coleman closed her notebook and tucked her pen in her shirt pocket. "Thank you for the photo," she said.

My mother reached for the pot. "More coffee?"

"No, thank you, Mrs. Guerraoui. I'd better get going."

"Should I call you again tomorrow?" I asked.

"You can. But I will call you if I have any news."

I walked the detective to the door and watched as she backed out of the driveway in her cruiser. Gusts of wind blew dust and dirt across the road. In the distance, a coyote's bark turned into a howl.

Driss

It was a Saturday. The Saturday before finals week. I needed a break from Kant and Schopenhauer, so I went to have coffee with my friend Brahim at a little patisserie in downtown Casablanca, near the Arab League Park. Brahim and I had met a couple of years earlier, at the publication party for the winter edition of the magazine *Lamalif*. We both had poems in that issue. Mine was terrible, I don't mind saying that now, but his showed promise. He published a few more, he was thinking about doing a collection. For me, though, poetry was nothing more than a hobby, my mind was on other things: Maryam and I had a baby girl, and I needed to finish graduate school if I wanted to get a better teaching job.

What Brahim and I talked about that day, I can hardly remember. It was just an ordinary day, although nothing about that year had been ordinary—the war in the Sahara was dragging into its sixth year, the price of flour and oil had increased catastrophically, and labor unions had called for a general strike. Hardly a week went by that spring when someone didn't organize a protest against the government. But I do remember we weren't talking about politics, because we were preoccupied with our exams, hoping we'd pass all our subjects in the first session so we could have the rest of the summer to ourselves. We sipped our coffees, both of us taking it black and chasing it with water. We said goodbye to one another outside the café, and went our separate ways. It was already half past one, I realized suddenly, and I was late for lunch. My wife wouldn't like it. I was walking down the Rue Gouraud when an old woman called out to me from an apartment window three floors above. "What are you doing out, my son?" she asked as she pulled her shutters closed. "Go home, there's trouble."

"Where, Auntie?" I asked.

She pointed toward the Boulevard Hassan I. Only half-believing the old woman, I ducked into the next building and went up to the roof to check for myself. Standing in the middle of television antennas, I saw army tanks driving down the boulevard in a column, headed toward a mass of protesters at the intersection. In the distance, plumes of black smoke rose in the sky. A terrible, familiar fear settled over me. How was I going to get home? Perhaps, I thought, I could walk back toward the Arab League Park and try to catch a bus or find a taxi. I crossed the length of the roof to see if the Rue d'Alger was still safe, but found instead that a Jeep with red and green stripes was idling on the pavement. Abruptly it sped up and struck two teenage boys who were running away from the boulevard, then swerved off and chased after another teen. A girl. She couldn't have been more than fifteen or sixteen. From the other end of the street, a police van drew up to her, cornering her next to a pharmacy with a crescent neon sign. Then a policeman jumped out of the Jeep and started beating her with a truncheon. Blood pooled around her head like a halo.

This is it, I remember thinking. This is the end of the regime. How could it survive when it was killing its own children in broad daylight? But just as the thought crystallized in my mind, one of the policemen spotted me on the roof, raised his gun, and aimed. Even from a height of four floors, I could see the black barrel pointed at me. I sank to my knees, realizing only by its sibilant sound that the bullet had missed me. With my back against the wall, I waited for the thump of police boots on the stairway. All afternoon I waited. Even as night fell, I waited. I could still hear the sirens of police cars. Tires screeching. Glass breaking. People screaming. The wind in the palm trees.

Dawn brought with it a strange silence. I went down the stairway, walked across the empty lobby, down the street with its smashed storefronts, past the bloodied corpse that still lay under the flickering neon sign, and went home, where I found Maryam beside herself with worry. All night she had stayed up listening, too, hoping to hear footsteps, yet fearing they were the wrong ones. She hadn't known if I was alive or dead and she'd been too afraid to go to the police. If I'd been arrested, asking the police about me would do no good; they would not acknowledge it. And if I hadn't been, asking them about me might be used as evidence that I'd taken part in the protest. "I wasn't arrested," I said, taking her hand, trying my best to comfort her. "I'm fine."

But when I told her about the policeman who'd pointed a gun at me, she panicked.

"Are you sure you weren't followed?" Her gaze shifted to the door.

"No," I said. "No, I don't think so."

Still, our fear didn't dissipate, and by the afternoon we heard from Brahim's sister that he had been arrested. No one knew where he was being held. Others in our circle of graduate students had also been swept up. It was a matter of time before they would be forced to give up the names of supposed accomplices. Maryam's relief that I had been spared the same fate turned into a vow: she would never go through this ordeal again. Her older brother lived in Culver City and had once offered to sponsor us for visas to the United States.

She said she wanted to leave.

We landed at Los Angeles International a few months later, only to find the Golden State in the middle of a recession. After she'd dropped out of college, my wife had worked as a receptionist in a doctor's office in Casablanca, but here in California no one was hiring, especially not a new immigrant with a shaky grasp of English pronunciation. And I was a graduate student in philosophy; all I knew was how to pontificate about Sartre or Lévinas. But I came from a long line of bakers—my father and grandfather ran neighborhood ovens all their lives—and when I heard from Maryam's brother about a donut shop in the Mojave that was up for sale, I said we should try to buy it.

"You?" Maryam asked. She couldn't believe that the graduate student who spoke so fervently about the plight of workers laboring under the boot of capitalists suddenly wanted to start a business. I told her we had nothing to lose but the futon we'd been sleeping on since we landed. Besides, I pointed out, I wasn't the one who'd been desperate to move here. We had to do something.

Before leaving Casablanca, we had sold my car, her jewelry, and all our belongings, but that only added up to a few thousand dollars, so we borrowed the rest from her brother and sank everything into the shop, which we renamed Aladdin Donuts. I repainted the walls, fixed rickety chairs, and replaced the light fixtures. The menu above the counter listed some items I wasn't sure I could reproduce: apple fritters, cinnamon rolls, bear claws. I tore it down and decided to sell only donuts and coffee. Donuts were not that different from our sfenj, and I experimented with the dough until it became as soft as the one I had grown up with.

For the first year, Maryam and I slept with Salma between us on an air mattress we laid out in the utility room. I baked and worked the cash register, and Maryam cleaned and handled the bookkeeping. Every penny that did not go toward bills or supplies went to pay her brother back for the money we had borrowed. On Fridays, we went to senior centers, police stations, local schools, construction sites, bringing samples in pink boxes that bore the logo of our shop. People who tasted my special honey glaze raved about it to their friends. Word began to spread. The shop turned a profit. We were able to move into a proper apartment and, three years later, into a house. Nora was born. Maryam quit the shop to take care of the girls. That was how we came to this country.

Efraín

Marisela was waiting up for me, with the newspaper spread out on the kitchen table. I thought it was *La Prensa,* which she buys from Kasa Market sometimes, but when I sat down across from her with my plate and soda, I saw that it was the *Hi-Desert Star.* I kept my eyes on my food. I just wanted to enjoy my torta de carnitas. I deserved that, at least, after the rough day I'd had. Enrique and I got lost for an hour in Landers, trying to find the duplex we were supposed to clean, and when we finally got there, the lady of the house was mad at us and followed us from room to room while we shampooed the carpets, making us go over the same dirty spots, even though the stains were old and wouldn't come out. Then she tried to use a coupon to pay, and Enrique had to tell her three times that those coupons were for Rob's Carpet Cleaning and we worked for Ron's Steam Cleaning and Upholstery. The delay pushed all our other appointments back and in the evening when we returned the van, Ron called us careless and stupid and lazy. All I wanted now was some peace.

But my wife nudged the paper toward me.

"I don't read English," I said, irritation bubbling up in my voice, although the truth is that I can read some, enough to fill out a job application or make sense of the notices pinned on the corkboard at the grocery store. HOUSE FOR RENT. CAR FOR SALE. JANITOR NEEDED.

"It's about the accident," she said, tapping her index finger on an article to draw my attention to it. Marisela took an English class some years ago, before the children were born, and now that they're in school she goes to the library with them on Saturdays and sits beside them while they read, so she's getting better and better. She's the one who talks to the landlord when there's a leak in the bathroom or if we're behind on the rent. "It says the police is asking for the public's help with the case. Look. Right here."

"I don't have my reading glasses," I said.

Marisela pulled them out from her apron pocket and set them in front of me on the table. At the time of these events, she was working for a senior-care center, bathing and grooming people who had forgotten how to do it for themselves. That job changed her. It gave even the smallest of her gestures a disarming patience.

I pushed the reading glasses off to the side. "Later," I said, and took a bite of my torta. But it didn't taste right. Even though it had been wrapped in aluminum foil and kept on the stove warmer, the bolillo had soaked up the sauce and the meat was dry. It seemed to me the day's frustrations would never end. "What is this?" I asked.

"They're looking for witnesses."

I had told her a million times that I wasn't a witness. I didn't see the accident. All I saw was the man falling to the ground, it wasn't the same thing. I split the bolillo open and, pushing aside the onions and chiles, poked at the meat with my knife. "Did you use pork?"

"It says the victim lived in Yucca Valley."

"You know I don't like it when you use beef in the tortas. It doesn't taste the same."

"He was sixty-one years old. And he was a father and a grandfather."

She said this just to make me look at the newspaper, and finally I put on my reading glasses. In the photograph, an old man with a wide forehead and curly white hair reclined in an armchair, smiling at someone out of the frame. On his lap was a paper plate with a crumpled napkin and a half-eaten piece of chocolate cake. It was the kind of picture you might take at Christmas or a birthday party, when the house is full of family and friends and everyone is dancing and having a good time. The caption said Driss Guerraoui. What a strange name, I remember thinking. "Where is he from?" I asked.

Marisela leaned closer, and read the article again. "It doesn't say."

He couldn't have been American, that much I knew. He had to have been an immigrant like me. And Guerraoui sounded like Guerrero, but it wasn't a Spanish name. With my knife, I flipped the bread back on the meat. "This isn't pork," I said.

"It is. I just trimmed all the fat," Marisela said.

That was another thing that had changed since she'd started working for the senior-care home. She wanted us to eat "healthy" things. No more chicharrones while we watched television. No ice cream after dinner. Only one spoon of sugar in our morning coffee. But now that she was trimming fat from my carnitas, she might as well have been trimming joy from my life.

"Do you want some more sauce?" she asked, patting my hand. "I can add more sauce."

She took my plate to the counter and brought it back a few minutes later. I took another bite. The meat was moist now, but still it didn't taste the same. So much depends on the little things. If I had turned left at the fork in the road that morning, Enrique and I wouldn't have been late to our first appointment, the lady of the house wouldn't have been so angry, we would have kept our schedule, the boss wouldn't have called us lazy. But I drove, and Enrique read the map; that was always our arrangement. When he glanced at the street signs and said, Go left, I went left. Another little thing: if I'd taken the Saturday night shift instead of the Sunday night shift at the motel, I wouldn't have been traveling down the 62 on the night of the accident. I would never have laid eyes on this man, this Guerraoui. I wouldn't even know his name.

"They're looking for anyone who might have seen the runaway car," Marisela said.

"I told you, I didn't see it."

"You said it was white."

"I said it could be white, but really I'm not sure. And even if I was, I'm not talking to the police. I can't take that chance."

If I thought that would stop my wife, I was wrong.

"Amor," she said, nudging the paper toward me again, "it says you can call anonymously. On this hotline."

I should never have told her about the accident.

Jeremy

At the end of my shift the next day, I found myself at the Joshua Tree jail for another meth arrest, this time a middle-aged woman whose neighbor called the police when he found her sitting on the roof of his shed. While the paperwork was being processed, I went to get some water from the storage room, where canned beans, powdered milk, and bags of rice and pasta were stacked in columns that reached the ceiling. The overhead lights cast an unsteady glow over the gray concrete floors, and the only sound I could hear were metal doors closing somewhere down the hallway. The jail always unsettled me, no matter how often I came inside. I tossed the paper cup in the trashcan and hurried out to the front office, where I found Stratton booking a new suspect. Fierro.

I stepped inside the office. "Lomeli," I called.

"Yeah?"

"What's this guy in for?"

"Criminal threats. Destruction of property." Lomeli adjusted his reading glasses over his nose and looked at the form, running his finger down the page until he reached the appropriate line. "Smashed his ex-wife's car. Says here it's a Mustang coupe. Broke the windows, took a bat to the siding, slashed the tires."

"Jesus."

"Must've been something." With a glance at the booking counter, Lomeli whistled, whether in admiration or disapproval, I couldn't tell. Lomeli himself had been divorced three times, a fact I had trouble reconciling with the romance novels stacked on his desk, their spines labeled YUCCA VALLEY LIBRARY. "You know this guy?" he asked.

"We served together in Iraq."

Lomeli's eyes widened.

I wasn't the only vet at that station—Stratton had served in the Gulf War, Villegas had been in Bosnia, and one of our dispatchers had deployed to New Orleans after Katrina—but somehow I never quite fit in with the others. I didn't go out for drinks with them after work, didn't forward their chain emails, didn't find Vasco's jokes funny. And now one of my buddies was under arrest. I had seen Fierro just the day before, at my sister's barbecue. He'd seemed fine then, chatted with the other guests, played with the kids, flirted with one of Ashley's co-workers, a pretty redhead with a freckled face and pouty lips. By the time we left, he was all smiles and jokes. But now, this.

"He'll be taken to West Valley," Lomeli said after a minute.

"You can't keep him here?"

"I don't have room."

I stepped back into the hallway and walked up to the booking counter, where Stratton was fingerprinting Fierro. Next to the payphone was a list of bail bondsmen, and underneath it were boxes of blue latex gloves. A notice taped to the far wall said IF YOU THINK YOU MAY BE PREGNANT AND WANT AN ABORTION, TALK TO THE HOLDING NURSE. "Are you on any medications?" Stratton asked, handing Fierro a wet wipe for the ink.

"For what?"

"Diabetes, heart condition, that sort of thing. Something you're required to take."

"No, sir." Fierro's hair fell in greasy strands over his face. He flicked it away, like a diver who's finally come up for air, and his eyes caught mine. "Hey," he said, and broke into a smile.

"What the fuck, man?"

"She's just making a big deal over nothing."

"Nothing, huh? That's what you think this is?"

"Gorecki, you know this guy?" Stratton asked.

"Sometimes I wish I didn't."

"It's my car. *My* car. There's no law says I can't trash it." He spoke as though the truth of this was incontrovertible and soon enough everyone else around him would come to see it, too. How different he was now from the man—the boy, really—he'd been when we'd met at boot camp. MCRD in San Diego. We'd arrived by bus, still drowsy with sleep, still dreaming of glory, when the voice of the drill instructor delivered us to the new day. From now on, he said, the only words out of your mouths are Yes, sir or No, sir. Do you understand?

We lined up on the deck and were told what to do. Stand with your feet at 45-degree angles. Look straight ahead. Read the Uniform Code of Military Justice. As we marched toward the building a gust of wind blew and my paperwork flew out of my hand. I ran after it. A single page landed on Fierro's chest and he peeled it off and handed it back to me. For this, the DI screamed at us to get back in line, his voice so high he sounded like a rooster gone mad. What had he done, he bellowed, to get yet another batch of stupid boots like these two knuckleheads right here? What on God's green earth had he done? How was he supposed to make Marines out of us?

I was so used to silence and neglect that the DI's voice felt like a stab to the chest. I wanted to run back to the bus, go back to the house on Valley View Drive, with its crushing but dependable indifference. Yet Fierro took the yelling uncomplainingly, his angry eyes trained on something in the distance. In our bunks that first night, bunks we'd been forced to make and remake until everyone could do it in under one minute, I felt compelled to whisper an apology for getting him into trouble with the DI, but Fierro shrugged and said it was nothing his father hadn't done before. When we found out that we were both from small towns only twenty miles apart in the Mojave, it was enough to make friends out of us, in that unquestioning way when you are eighteen and far from home. Even when things got tough, when the DIs rammed their Smokey Bear covers into our faces or called us bitches and faggots and cocksuckers, Fierro took the abuse without complaint. But all this was before Camp Taqaddum, before Ramadi.

By the time we came back from the war, almost five years later, his restraint had disappeared. He'd become a talker, a prankster, a braggart. I remember going out drinking with him at the Joshua Tree Saloon, a few weeks after we'd returned home, and he wouldn't stop talking. It was a cold night in January and the air was threatening snow, but when we left the bar, we were still in the T-shirts we had on when we'd come in at two in the afternoon. Even though I didn't feel cold, I was shaking so much I dropped my car keys. I was on my knees looking for them in the dirt when the headlights of a sheriff's car blinded me. I failed the sobriety test, but Fierro struck up a conversation with the officer, told him we'd been in Iraq, and asked if he might let me off with a warning and a promise that I would call a cab. I should've been grateful when the officer said yes, and yet all I felt was rage—and I didn't even know why. Something about that cop, with his receding hair, his pitying eyes, his sagging belly, made me want to punch him. I couldn't have foreseen that someday I'd end up a cop myself, or that Fierro would land in jail.

Now Stratton led Fierro to the holding cell and locked the doors. The metal bars had recently been painted a cheerful blue and I stood against them, watching him. I didn't know how to help him, how to tidy up this mess he'd made. "Don't worry, this'll blow over soon," he said with a grin. "And meantime I got to meet Deputy Gorecki, all official and shit."

"Yeah, well. Take a good look, asshole. Make sure it's the last time I see you here."

Nora

Then it was my turn. I stepped into the gray light of the viewing room, but kept my gaze averted until the last moment. Once I looked at the coffin, my father's death would become real and unalterable; I would have to accept it. The casket was made of varnished wood, but free of any designs or embellishments. Inside it, a white burial shroud cloaked my father's body. His face was pale, his right cheek bruised, his lips tightly shut. "What did you want to tell me that day?" I whispered. It was rare for him to call in the middle of a workday, but not so rare as to have caused me any alarm. The extent of my loss was barely starting to reveal itself to me in that airless room, with the mortuary men behind me speaking in hushed voices. I stood beside the coffin with my heart aching inside my chest until it was time to leave.

Outside, the sun was so bright I had to shield my eyes with my hand. Sparrows came in a flutter of wings to settle on a eucalyptus tree at the edge of the parking lot. A man in a brown suit stood next to the hearse, its back doors gaping open like the maw of a hungry beast. My sister and her family were already in their Escalade, but my mother was waiting for me beside my car. When I put my key in the ignition, music from the classical station blared, replacing the silence with a crescendo of violins. I shut it off.

In the sudden silence, my mother said, "It's not supposed to be like this."

For my mother, things were forever not the way they were supposed to be. She had left her country with her family, but she still longed for everything else she hadn't been able to bring with her. She missed her old house, her childhood friends, the call for prayers at dawn. No matter how extravagant a meal she cooked, she found it wanting—an ingredient was always missing or the flavor just wasn't right. My sister's wedding sent her into paroxysms of nostalgia that transformed our house into a bazaar filled with henna patterns, embroidered belts, brass trays, a litter to carry the bride and groom. My mother had to leave many traditions behind and the more time passed, the more they mattered to her.

Even in death. The way we were handling the funeral seemed wrong to her. She was aghast at the fact that my father's body had lain in the morgue for four days before he was released to us. Make haste in taking the dead to the grave, she said, over and over, though there was nothing Salma or I could do about it; we had to wait for the autopsy to be done and for the paperwork to be completed. When we'd arrived at the mortuary that morning, my mother seemed surprised to find only three employees waiting for us.

"How is it supposed to be?" I asked.

"They should do the prayer here, at the mosque. Bring him inside and pray for him. And then your uncle and Tareq lead, how do you say, the walk to the cemetery?"

"The funeral procession?"

"Right. They lead the funeral procession, and we go the next day to visit the grave." She gave me an accusing look, as if I had plotted this new affront to tradition. "But they don't do it this way here."

All of a sudden I realized I had never known anyone who died, had no experience whatsoever with death. I had nothing to compare it to, unlike her. Before she'd turned twenty, she'd lost both of her parents and an aunt. Their pictures sat on the dresser in her bedroom, along with photos of all the family in Casablanca. "I'm sorry, Mom."

My phone buzzed with a text from my friend Elise. *Thinking of you today*, she said. None of my friends from the Bay Area were coming to the funeral. Elise was teaching and could not get away; Anissa was on a reporting trip to Texas and could not get away; and Margo was at a music festival in Pittsburgh and could not get away. I tried to swallow my disappointment, though it kept rising like bile. I think I was starting to apprehend how clarifying death could be: it made everyone around me disappear. Perhaps they were afraid of intruding on my

grief or saying the wrong thing, so instead they sent brief notes of condolence and asked what they could do. A question I couldn't answer.

In the rearview mirror, I noticed that the hearse had pulled out of
its spot. I hadn't seen the coffin being loaded, and the lapse gave me
a strange feeling of guilt, as if I'd let my father down. "They should've
given us some kind of signal," I said as I eased out of my space and followed my sister's Escalade. It barely cleared the metal gate of the mortuary of the Islamic Center before it sped toward the freeway entrance
at Vermont Avenue. It was the first week of May and the jacaranda
trees were starting to bloom, their sparse blossoms a bright shade of
violet. The sidewalks were packed with vendors and pedestrians. At
the on-ramp, a truck had just rear-ended a convertible in the right
lane, and traffic was slowly merging left. "Your father hated freeways,"
my mother said as she watched the commotion. "When we first moved
to California, he wanted me to drive him everywhere. I worried all the
time about the accidents."

"Is that why he never wanted to move out of the desert?"

"He didn't like L.A. It's full of crazy drivers."

"You know what's ironic, Mom? The 62 is three times as deadly as
the average road in California. I didn't know that until this week. So
we could have lived in L.A. or anywhere else and he would have been
safer there. And we'd have been away from all those hicks."

"But he liked the desert. When he was a boy, he used to go to Marrakesh every spring to visit his grandmother. And he loved hiking in
Joshua Tree, you know that."

"Joshua Tree isn't Yucca Valley."

"It's ten miles away."

"Might as well be a hundred."

We were already at the East L.A. interchange, negotiating the
switch to the 60. It was a little after eleven in the morning and the freeway was clear, with cars whizzing by at speeds that made my mother
clutch the handle above the passenger door. In the cup holder, my
phone buzzed again with a new message. I picked it up.

"Nora, you're driving."

"It's okay." I glanced at the screen—it was another text of condolence. I dropped the phone back in its place. Even now, a month after

Max had told me he needed to figure out what he wanted to do, my heart still seized whenever I received a text. I wanted so much to hear his voice, hear him say that he loved me, that everything would be all right. And I think, too, a part of me held out some hope that he would choose me over his wife.

"You want me to read the text to you?"

"Sorry? Oh, sure."

My mother picked up the phone. "It's from Andrea. *I'm sorry I couldn't be there today, but* . . . How do I get the rest?"

"You need to unlock the phone."

"Give me the password."

"It's okay, I'll just read it later. We're getting close now."

I followed my sister's car into Rose Hills Memorial, then down perfectly manicured lanes toward the Cedar Crest Lawn section. A row of oak trees sprouting new leaves bordered the parking lot. Beyond it, the lawn sloped into a valley, all of it a deep shade of green, in spite of the drought that had plagued the state for months. "This place is so big," my mother whispered, looking at the burial grounds that seemed to stretch endlessly around us. Then she put her face in her hands and began to weep. I reached across the seat divider and touched her knee. The strange thing was that I'd always cried easily—watching *Little House on the Prairie* or listening to Umm Kulthum. Now I had a ball in my throat and my chest hurt, but my eyes were dry. What was happening to me? Why couldn't I grieve like the rest of my family?

I stayed with my mother until she was ready to step out of the car. Tareq and Salma were already waiting, he in a black suit and she in a blue shirt and an ankle-length skirt. The twins were in the prim clothes they usually wore for school recitals. But from head to toe, my mother was in widow's white. The color of absence. The color of mourning. We all started down the path toward the gravesite and the sound of our footsteps cut through the vast silence of that part of the cemetery. On the grounds, a gardener stopped pulling weeds to stare at us.

Salma turned to me. "Did you remember to bring a scarf?"

"Yes, of course." I rummaged through my purse, but couldn't find it. "I think I left it in the car. I'll go back."

She pulled a blue scarf from her own purse.

"You brought an extra one?" I asked.

"Just in case."

A small group of people was waiting at the gravesite—my aunt and uncle from Culver City, two cousins, some friends of Salma and Tareq's, and three or four people I didn't know. A gaping hole in the ground waited, too. Then the coffin arrived, and the imam faced east, cupped his ears with his hands, and called the faithful to prayer. God is great, he chanted. God is great. At these words, my uncle and Tareq gathered with the other men in the front, and I had to stay in the back with my mother, my sister, and all the other women.

In the name of God, most Compassionate, most Merciful, the imam began. His voice was a beautiful baritone, but as he recited the Fatiha it rose to nearly an F, a greenish blue. The ritual words, once as familiar to me as a lullaby, did not come easily—the last time I had gone to prayers was for Eid services when I was sixteen years old. The outing had ended with another argument between my parents, in the car on the way back.

The sight of a cleric in robes praying over him would not have moved my father. But he would have liked Rose Hills, I decided. There were willow trees everywhere, the air was brisk and clear, and beneath my feet the ground felt soft. Bluebirds chased one another across the lawn. It was a good place to rest for a while. The voice of the imam brought me back to the present moment: he chanted a prayer for the Prophet, a prayer for the dead, and a prayer for the living.

Then the coffin was lowered into the grave, and my father was gone.

Driss

This is what happened. Eid fell in mid-December that year, and Maryam wanted the whole family to go to the mosque in Riverside for morning services. Take the girls if you want, I said, but why would I go? I'm an atheist. She doesn't like it when I use that word, especially when her brother visits us from Los Angeles, but it's the truth. Sometimes, I hear her apologizing to him in the driveway, telling him that I don't mean it, that I just say these things to get a rise out of him. But of course I mean it. I don't pretend to be someone I'm not. And yet I agreed to go that day, because Maryam insisted, and Salma was home from college for winter break, and I wanted to keep everyone happy.

Holiday services started at seven in the morning, but by six thirty you could hardly find parking. I had to circle the lot several times before I found a spot, and that put me in a bad mood. Maryam led the way on the concrete path, our daughters followed, and I lagged behind, trying to finish my cigarette before we went inside. At the entrance, a handsome boy, perhaps ten or eleven years old, held an orange bucket labeled EID DONATIONS. A tithe isn't a donation, I wanted to say, one is a tax and the other is a gift, but no one else seemed to mind it. People lined up to put their money in. Maryam had prepared the check at home and sealed it in an envelope, but as she let it drop into the bucket, the boy called out to Nora. "Sister," he said. "Cover your legs. You're indecent."

Indecent! For a moment, I thought I'd misheard him. Did he even know what the word meant? I was glad when Nora turned on him. "What did you just say?" she asked, her lips breaking into a puzzled smile.

"Cover your legs, sister."

"Who do you think you are, kid?"

"Your brother in faith," he said gravely. Then he nodded to thank a lady who'd placed a crisp $50 bill in the orange bucket. People walked past us, dressed in Eid clothes. No two outfits looked the same: men in suits and thobes and dashikis, women in flowing robes and shalwar kameezes and bright-colored tunics. My daughter was in a black skirt that fell below the knees, but it had not been enough for this miniature cleric. It was very crowded, and I could hear impatient car horns in the parking lot. An old man circled around us so he could get inside.

"We're going to be late," Maryam said as she pulled our daughters toward the women's section.

I had finished my cigarette by then, but stayed behind, watching the boy. He had curly hair, a small nose, skin the color of sand. Except for his green eyes, he could have passed for my son. His face glowed with a confidence that unsettled me. "What's your name?" I asked him.

"Qasim."

"And how old are you?"

"Eleven."

Just as I thought. So young, and yet so sure. I had been like that, once. I had recited the Qur'an at the msid, hardened my knees on the straw mats of our neighborhood mosque, kept the fast not just in Ramadan, but for a few days in Shawaal and Sha'baan as well. These rituals consoled me; they told me that the world was what it was because of sin, whether its manifestations were seductive or repellent, and all I needed to do was resist it. There was a mathematical elegance to faith like this: believe in God, follow His rules, and you will be rewarded; disbelieve, disobey, and you will be punished. But one day Mr. Fathi, my middle-school religion teacher, told the class about the seven stages of hell. I was familiar enough with the rivers of fire and fountains of pus and blood that awaited sinners, but that day the lesson was about how these people would find no respite even after their bodies burned—their skin would grow back only to burn anew. That made me think of Mr. Nguyen, who had a burn scar along his left arm, the result of a confrontation with French settlers during the war in his country. I loved Mr. Nguyen, as did the rest of the class, because he made algebra seem like child's play. That was the closest thing to a miracle I had ever witnessed. So I asked Mr. Fathi whether his friend Mr. Nguyen would burn in hell, too, with all the other unbelievers. Instead of an answer, I was given a whack on the head and told not to interrupt the lesson again. I was only a couple of years older than this boy, Qasim. My doubts were born that day. Over the years they grew, until one day they were all I had.

"Do you think," I asked the boy, "that maybe your faith has other things to worry about than my daughter's legs?"

Qasim only gave me a sad look, as though I had personally disappointed him, and had failed in raising my daughter, somehow. Inside the mosque, the last call to prayer rose, and he turned to go, but I wouldn't let him. "Tell me," I said, holding him back by the wrist. He didn't want to argue, and perhaps my hold on him was too strong, because he gave a whimper.

An old man I hadn't noticed before appeared suddenly before me. It was the imam. He had dark hair, a carefully trimmed beard, the same green eyes as Qasim. He started quoting the Qur'an to me. ("Tell the believing women not to reveal their adornment except for that which is apparent.") I counter-quoted. ("Tell the believing men to avert their gaze.") He claimed veiling was required by tradition; I insisted that tradition tells us only the Prophet's wives covered. He warned that women ought not to tempt men in the mosque; I mocked the men who would be so easily distracted from their worship. Finally, he said he had to go inside, that we could discuss this some other time, because right now he had a prayer to lead.

I lit a fresh cigarette and waited until Maryam and the girls came out. In the car on the way back, I told my wife what happened, but instead of taking my side, she complained that I had embarrassed her in front of the congregation. I was stunned. "But you don't even know these people," I said. "And I'm your husband."

"I know Mrs. Hammadi, but you just had to start—"

"Okay, but that's it. You don't know anyone else."

"—arguing with the imam like you know better than him."

"Of course, I know better. I don't need him to tell me right from wrong."

"That skirt was too sheer, I told Nora before we—"

"Oh, no, no, no. Don't make this to be her fault. You're the one who—"

"—left the house. Why doesn't she ever listen to me?"

"—dragged us all out here. And for what?"

In the backseat, Nora put on her headphones and stared out of the window. My wife and I continued bickering for a while, dredging up old arguments and using them against each other, but when I turned onto the 62, I was struck silent by the view. It was a cold, clear day in December, and there was snow on the peaks of the Little San Bernardino Mountains. The valley was a blanket of high grass and mesquite and yucca, slowly warming up under the morning sun, and after the road dipped and rose and turned, we reached the first grove of Joshua trees. How hard the believers make it to get into heaven, I thought, when they have all this right here.

Coleman

I remember this case well. It was the first homicide I investigated after I transferred here from Washington, D.C., in the spring of 2014. I'm from New York, originally, but D.C. is where I grew up, where I went to school, and where I worked for fifteen years, so it was a difficult move for me. Even more so for Miles. I could see it in his eyes when we asked him about his day while we ate dinner. He'd jab at his potatoes with a fork, answer our questions with yes or no, or sometimes just a shrug, then lock himself in his room to play video games. Miles used to be a sweet kid, you could even say a mama's boy, but he wouldn't let me kiss him good night anymore. Moving away from home is hard on a kid, I knew that, but it's not as if it didn't happen every day in this country. Hell, in the world. How did other people do it? That's what I wanted to know.

It wasn't even my idea to move out here, to the middle of the desert. It was Ray's, after he was offered district manager at Enterprise in Palm Springs. He'd waited so long for a promotion, watched so many others with less experience get ahead, that he knew if he didn't take this offer, another one might not come along. And it worked out well for him—he made more money, we could afford a bigger house, there was no snow to shovel in the winter, he could root for the Lakers. You would think he would've taken it a little easy, being manager and all, but he worked even harder. Every night, he studied his sales statements, going down each column with a little ruler so he wouldn't miss a zero or a comma. Ray has always been comfortable with numbers; they've never disappointed him, never held any mystery or complication. Sometimes, going through his sales, he talked to himself.

Meanwhile, Miles was in his room, sulking.

So my work came as a relief to me. I don't mean that it was pleasant. Having to witness a family's grief is never pleasant, but I had some experience with it. I could compartmentalize it. I could try to solve the case, give the family some closure, even if I didn't have much to work with at first. No usable tire marks. No debris from the vehicle. No surveillance cameras anywhere near that intersection. The only witness a jogger who found the body after the impact. Autopsy didn't turn up any drugs or alcohol. The victim had no money troubles or history of gambling, so he seemed like a pretty boring guy—at least, until I went through some of the texts on his cell phone, but even those didn't add up to a lead. My hopes were pinned on three microscopic paint chips that CSU recovered from the victim's clothing. That's it. That's all I had.

Which meant I had to talk to Murphy. I didn't have any complaints about his work, not exactly, it's just that the way he went about it made me a little uncomfortable. He was used to doing things a certain way. He'd been in the Crime Lab for something like forty years. He could've retired if he wanted to, but instead there he was, week in, week out, in a white lab coat with his name embroidered on the breast pocket like a real doctor. And I couldn't say anything about it because I knew how it would play with the sergeant—like I couldn't take the heat or like I was asking for special treatment. I was still new at the station. Murphy's been here since Noah built his ark.

Anyway, I went to see Murphy about the paint chips. His office had a huge window, so he got a lot of natural light for his cactuses. Or cacti, Murphy called them. The potted plants sat on opposite ends of a polished wood shelf, and in between there was a stereo system that played classical music at low volume. Framed art posters hung on the far wall. In the corner, he had a little coffee station, with an espresso machine, cups, saucers, napkins. And he also had a hot plate, which of course was a fire hazard, but, like I said, he's been here forty years. Really, he treated the place more like a living room than an office. The door was open, but I gave a little knock. "Murphy. You got an update for me?"

"Erica!" he said with a smile. He always called me by my first name, which I wasn't used to, and which made me pause.

"Anything on those paint chips you sent out to San Bernardino?"

"They usually take a few days. Would you like some coffee?"

"I just had some, thanks. Can you just check if they're back?"

"Red is a great color on you," he said with a glance at my chest. Immediately, I regretted leaving my jacket at my desk.

"Can you check?"

"Remind me the name?"

"Guerraoui. Hit-and-run on April 28."

He finally turned back to his computer and looked for the report. "You're in luck," he said. "They just posted it in this morning. FTIR says the paint is actually silver."

"Silver?"

"Silver. Looks like it came from a vehicle manufactured by Ford between 1992 and 1998."

"Any idea on the model?"

"Taurus, Crown Vic, Mustang, Explorer. Take your pick." The printer on his desk whirred as the report came out. He handed it to me. "They used it all over the place."

"I thought you said I was in luck."

"Could be worse."

I didn't see how. The day before, I'd asked Sergeant Vasco for a recanvass, but he said he couldn't spare any deputies at the moment. This isn't Metro P.D., he said, we don't have the same resources here. It was like he was testing me, trying to see if I could close this case without help from his uniforms, and the strange thing is that the hurdles he put up made me even more committed. I didn't have to prove myself to someone like him, not with my record at Metro, and yet that's exactly what I found myself doing.

"You sure you don't want coffee?" Murphy asked. "I just got a new batch of Ethiopian."

"Is this your family?" I said, raising my chin toward the framed photo of a blonde woman and a blue-eyed kid with their arms around each other. I was trying to shame Murphy a little bit, point out that a sixty-some-year-old married guy shouldn't be acting like this.

"Yes, that's my son. And that's my sister," he said. "My ex moved to Seattle four years ago, so my sister is helping me raise him."

Well. I stuffed my hands in my pocket, did a little math in my head. "He looks about the same age as my son," I said, careful to leave the surprise out of my voice.

"How old is yours?"

"He just turned thirteen. He's in the seventh grade."

"What school?"

"La Contenta. Yours?"

"Same." He looked me in the eye for the first time, and smiled. He had a full head of salt-and-pepper hair, a bit on the long side, but combed back neatly behind his ears. "Maybe they know each other," he said.

"I doubt it." Miles hadn't made any friends; that was part of why he resented us for moving out here. "It's a big school."

"That it is," he said. "Does your son like baseball? We have a standing game on Saturdays in the community park. He'd be welcome anytime."

"Oh," I said, a little taken aback. I had tried to strike up a conversation with the moms at Miles's school, and they'd seemed friendly enough, but their interest had cooled when they found out I couldn't chaperone the seventh-grade field trip or volunteer at the spring book fair or cover a table at the fundraising picnic. Several of them were stay-at-home moms and the rest had nine-to-five jobs, so they could arrange these activities around their schedules. But I couldn't, not with my line of work. When I suggested Ray could take my place, they looked baffled. *Why would a man want to do the bake sale?* Of course, they didn't come out and say it like that; they just went ahead and did the bake sale without telling him about it. "Thanks, Murphy. I'll tell Miles about the game."

"Okay. And I'll let you know if we find anything more on that paint. Sometimes it takes them a few days to narrow it down to a specific model."

Leaving Murphy's office that morning, I took the long way back to my desk. I didn't want to run into the sergeant and have him ask me for an update unless I had something solid to give him. All I had were three paint chips, one of which the forensics lab in San Bernardino had already dissolved into gas. Nothing more than thin air.

Jeremy

It was a pretty little house with two Adirondack chairs out front, a wind chime hanging from the eaves, and a wooden rail fence surrounding the yard. Fierro used to call it The Ranch. Time to go back to The Ranch, he'd say when we went bowling. He'd make it sound like he was sorry to have to go so soon, even though his eyes smiled with anticipation at being with his new wife, in their new house. In the driveway now was a silver Mustang coupe, every inch of it smashed, dented, or scratched. A side mirror sat in a pool of shattered glass, reflecting the moonlight. The name FIERRO had been recently peeled off the mailbox, leaving its ghost outlined in gray tracks. I walked up the little concrete path and knocked on the front door.

From the other side came the sound of someone flipping up the peephole, looking, hesitating. Finally, the door opened. "What're you doing here?" Mary asked. Under her red hair, her eyes were red. She was in a white tank top that showed the tattoo on her upper arm. *Death before dishonor.* She'd gotten it as a welcome-home surprise for Fierro, a celebration of his Bronze Star, but he'd hated it. Asked her why she'd ruin her beautiful skin like that.

"You okay?"

"No, I'm not okay." Her voice cut like glass.

"Sorry. That was a stupid thing to say."

"He scared the shit out of me, trashed my car, and the whole time he was laughing about it. He couldn't even let me have this one thing, this one little thing. Fucking asshole."

I'd never heard her curse. She was one of those girls who said fudge and shoot and darnit, and whenever anyone around her cussed, she'd blush for them. Fierro had been so charmed by this, he'd proposed to her on the last day of his second R&R. Wait until you get back, Sergeant Fletcher told him when he heard about it, don't make the same mistake I did. But Fierro wouldn't listen, he was crazy about her. She was nineteen, enrolled in cosmetology school, dreaming of working on a Hollywood set someday. This is the girl I'm gonna marry, he said. And he did.

"I'm sorry, Mary." I was trying to think of a graceful way to ask her to drop her complaint, see if she could accept some kind of payment for the car, but when I touched her arm, she pulled back from me with fear in her eyes. I was startled, and took a step back from the threshold myself. Something about the way she looked at me made me feel tainted, as if Fierro's crime said something about me, too. But just because we'd been in the Marines together didn't mean we were the same. Whatever troubled Fierro had started long before he'd gone to war. Surely she knew that. Still, the look in her eyes stopped me from bringing this up. "Listen," I said after a minute. "Change the locks."

"Yeah, I know. Locksmith left an hour ago."

"And get a dog."

"That's it? That's your advice? Why don't you tell him to leave me the hell alone? If you really wanted to help, that's what you'd do. Keep him away from me."

"I already told him this, Mary. He wouldn't listen." Again, I felt the heat of her rage. I saw how badly I had miscalculated, coming here to try to fix things. I was only making them worse.

A gust of dry wind blew across the street and a piece of glass fell from a window of the Mustang and crashed on the driveway. Mary glanced at it, then fixed her green eyes on me again. "You know, if someone had told me five years ago that you'd be the one with a steady job and going to college, I wouldn't have believed it."

I wanted to tell her that I wouldn't have believed it, either. Five years ago, Fierro had landed a job in security at the Indian casino in Morongo, while I had to get by on roofing work whenever I could find it. Five years ago, I'd gotten so drunk at their wedding that I'd thrown up in the water fountain where rose petals had been set to float. Five years ago, I couldn't have put a name to the bridesmaid I woke up with the next day at the Travelodge, her blond hair a tangle of ornate pins and glitter against my chest. I lost a year, maybe a year and a half, like that, just drifting, trying to fill the hole in me that I thought the war had left, until I realized it was the same hole I had gone into the Marines to fill in the first place. I was living with my sister at the time, and she kept telling me to go to church and stop drinking so much. Promise me, she begged, promise me. I'd kept half of that promise. Some weeks later, I was driving back from a roofing job when I noticed a billboard advertisement for the police academy in San Bernardino.

Maybe that feeling of being out of place would eventually clear up for Fierro, just as it had for me. But he needed to work at it. "He can get better," I said.

"Yeah, well. Good luck with that. I tried. I'm done trying."

And with this, she pushed the door closed.

Nora

In my memory, the cafeteria at Yucca Mesa Elementary was immense, but that evening it seemed small and cramped. This was an illusion, of course, because the cafeteria hadn't changed; I had. Folding chairs had been set up in a dozen neat rows, but nearly half the seats were already taken, and sweaters and scarves marked the spaces that were being saved. In the center aisle, an old man in a Dodgers cap was mounting his camera on a tripod. I followed my mother down to the front row, where Salma sat alone, staring at her cell phone. We kissed each other on the cheeks. "Where's Tareq?" my mother asked Salma.

"Emergency tooth repair."

"Oh, no," I said. "It's too bad he'll miss the play."

"That's how it is when you run a practice," my sister said coolly.

I turned my attention to the program booklet. *Sleeping Beauty,* the title said in gold lettering. I skipped past the director's introduction, the donors' list, the appeals for fundraising for next year's performance, and looked for the twins' names on the cast list. Aida and Zaid were to play night watchmen. "Do they have any lines?" I asked.

"No."

"How come?"

Salma shrugged.

"Well, I'm looking forward to it anyway," I said. "I've never seen them in a school performance." From behind the curtain came the shrill sound of a microphone being hooked up to a power source. The air-conditioning unit stopped and, a moment later, started again. Back when I went to school here, there was no AC, just an oversized fan that whirred painfully from above. I had to sit backstage in whatever costume Mrs. Fleming had sewn for the play, sweating under its weight, scratching my skin in places where it met the cheap fabric, waiting for my cue. Even though I ended up with the same parts every year, I liked performing in plays because it was the closest thing I'd found to reading a book. Books were better, of course. In books, I could be more than the mute sidekick; I could be the hero. "It's already ten past six," I said, looking at my watch.

"Do you have somewhere else you need to be?" my sister asked sharply.

The testiness in her voice had been there since my father's will had been delivered to the house by a courier from the lawyer's office. The will had been drawn up many years ago and we all knew what it said: legalese about splitting my father's assets between his spouse and children. What none of us had expected was a life insurance policy worth $250,000. Its sole beneficiary was me.

The din in the cafeteria rose. A cell phone rang, then another. In the back, chairs scraped against the floor. "I don't understand," Salma said. "I just don't understand. What did I ever do to him?"

"Nothing," my mother replied. "This is not your fault."

"Nor is it mine," I said, looking at my mother, but she didn't acknowledge me; her eyes were fixed on my sister.

"Have you thought about what you're going to do?" Salma asked me.

"About what?"

"What do you think? About all that money he left you."

"Since when do you care so much about money? Or is this Tareq talking?"

"This isn't about money."

"What is it about, then?"

The houselights dimmed, and the audience grew quiet. Salma turned to face me. "I'm the one who stayed here. I'm the one who stuck with dental school. I'm the one who took care of him when he had cataract surgery. I did everything he wanted me to do while you were"—she waved her hands in the air—"*gallivanting* at music festivals. And then he leaves it all to you. You can't even hold down a real job!"

The insult was still ringing in my ears when an old woman in the row behind us cleared her throat pointedly. I lowered my voice to ask, "Do you really want to talk about this here?"

"What does it matter where we talk about it?"

"He didn't leave everything to me. You and Mom still have the business."

"Yes, it was quite thoughtful of him not to take that away."

I glanced at my mother, hoping for some kind of support, or at least some sympathy. Instead, she put her hand on Salma's knee, as if to beg for her forgiveness. "Your father never told me he changed his will. I wouldn't have let him if I knew."

"Well, he did it anyway," Salma said. "Nora was always his favorite."

So much anger in her voice. So much resentment. But how had our father disfavored her? Had he not read to her from the same books, taken her to the same parks, played the same board games with her? Had he not driven thirty miles to Palm Springs every Sunday morning and waited two hours to drive her back when she took that SAT prep course in high school? Had he not paid for dentistry school? For that wedding in Orange County? Had he not watched her twins whenever she needed to be away on a conference? Had he loved her any less?

"Listen," I said, "I didn't ask for any of this." My voice was muffled by the sound of the piano overture.

The woman in the row behind us leaned closer. "Sshhh," she hissed.

"So what if you didn't ask for it?" Salma said. "You expect me to feel sorry for you? And why do you always have to bring Tareq into everything?"

"How many times do I have to say it? *I didn't know about the insurance.* I just don't understand why you're so mad at me when I had nothing to do with it. And yes, Tareq is always putting—"

A cold hand landed on my shoulder, startling me. "Either be quiet or take it outside," the woman said. With her side braid and dark eyes, she looked like an older version of Mrs. Nielsen, my kindergarten teacher. "Get your hand off me," I said.

The curtains parted. A king and queen stood on the stage, admiring their infant princess in her cradle. I was so unsettled by the blame in my sister's voice that I found it difficult to pay much attention to the play. It didn't help that the costumes were poorly made and that the children wore too much makeup. While bestowing her gifts on Aurora, one of the three fairies sneezed, sending green glitter flying everywhere but on the cradle. At least the action was moving quickly. In forty-five minutes, the princess had been cursed, pricked by a spindle, enchanted, and put in chambers. Aida and Zaid finally appeared as night watchmen, who dozed as the prince made his way past them to the princess's room. A kiss, a broken curse, and the audience erupted in applause.

As soon as the curtains closed, I turned to my sister again, but Salma ignored me and began to make her way out to the blacktop. I could see that she wanted me to correct what had happened, but even if I could, it would not undo the choice our father had made, nor what it said about us: that he thought she could manage without his help, and that I couldn't. But she believed it meant something else altogether: that he cared less about her than about me. Outside, the sky was a hazy orange and the air felt heavy with heat. Salma stood by the swings, her eyes filled with an envy that silenced me.

Envy was not something I expected from someone as accomplished as my sister, and yet it was there. It had been there, really, since the day I found out I'd been accepted at Stanford. Salma had gone to the state school in San Bernardino and, after receiving poor scores on her MCAT, went to Loma Linda School of Dentistry, which had seemed like a fine place to her, until my admissions letter arrived. She was quiet for days. My mother, on the other hand, wouldn't stop talking about it. She told her brother and his family, her new friends from mosque, the neighbors from up and down the street. Everything I said or did she suddenly deemed brilliant. Having her approval was an entirely new feeling for me, and it was perhaps because of it that I decided to study pre-med in college. But three years later, when I called home to say that I had changed my mind about medical school and that I would be applying to the graduate program in music at Mills College instead, the news was greeted with horror by my mother, and ridicule by my sister. My mother couldn't believe that all those years of calculus and biology and chemistry had led to chamber quartets and jazz ensembles. "Don't do this," she warned me. "You're going to ruin your life."

"Mom, calm down. You're acting like I got pregnant or something."

"Pregnant! Why do you say this? What have you been doing at school?"

"Nothing. I'm just saying it's a graduate degree, not a life sentence."

"You have your head in the clouds!"

Meanwhile, Salma had just become engaged to Tareq Darwish, a fellow dentistry student whose parents had emigrated from Syria in the 1970s. She and Tareq were planning to open a joint dental practice, a fact that my mother held up that day, and every day thereafter, as the kind of behavior to be expected of a child for whom parents had *given up everything*. I called my sister and asked her to talk some sense into our mother, but she only laughed. "Wait," she said. "Music? Seriously? Oh, Nora."

My father alone offered something besides derision. He listened to my music, and over my mother's objections, sent me small checks from time to time. Now he had set aside some money for me, and that had caused my sister's envy to flare up like a bad rash. She could barely look at me as we stood in the middle of the chattering crowd. I should go back to Oakland, I thought, I've been here long enough. I have a composition to finish, friends to see, my own life waiting for me in the Bay Area. Then the twins came running across the schoolyard toward us. "Did you like it, Aunt Nora?" Aida asked me.

"It was great," I said. "I've never seen a better royal guard. High five."

"What about me?" Zaid asked.

"No one can fake sleep as well as you. High five again."

The children stood between their mother and grandmother, their faces lit with a joy I hadn't seen since I'd returned home. I offered to take pictures. Through the viewfinder, I noticed that Aida's hair had darkened, its shade now closer to mine. I was about to remark on this when Salma took the children's hands and told them it was time to go. "Good night," she said stiffly, and led them away to her car.

In the Prius on the way back, I listened to my mother say, for what seemed like the tenth time that day, that she hadn't known about the life insurance. "I don't know when he bought it," she said. "He must have paid for it from the business account."

"Do you blame me for this, too, Mom?"

"I don't blame you. I worry about you. About your future."

My mother said this with resignation, as though it were her charge in life to be saddled with me. This happened every time I returned home. We'd spend a few peaceful hours in each other's company and then the détente would end and the comments would start, all of them variations on the theme of her disappointment in me. Why don't you find a better job? Why don't you apply to law school? Why don't you move back here if you're not going to law school and you can't find a better job? Did I tell you that Mrs. Hammadi's daughter is getting married? Are you wearing that to dinner? White isn't a good color for you, you know, it makes you look darker. Did you watch the video that Tareq put up on YouTube? His keynote address to the American Periodontal Association was watched by 313 people. Can you believe it? And the big one, the one that came up with increasing frequency as the years passed: When are you getting married?

Nothing but unconditional surrender would have satisfied my mother. Because of this, I had learned to deploy my own set of loaded questions. Why did you quit college after you got married? Why did you move us to the middle of the desert? Why, oh why, did you vote for George W. Bush? Why do you call a three-week-old embryo a baby? Surely you know the difference—you wanted to be a doctor. Yes, you told me about Mrs. Hammadi's daughter three times. Did she get married three times? Did you watch my piano performance at the San Francisco Botanical Gardens? It's also on YouTube. And how many times do I have to tell you? I don't want to get married.

These battles never ended in a clear victory. The best I could hope for was a return to the status quo, which usually happened right before I had to leave again. Now my father's will had opened a new front in the conflict with my mother, and this time Salma was involved in the hostilities as well. But I felt too weak to fight. I couldn't bear to spend another day in the house. Before going to bed that night, I filled up my car with gas, packed my bag, and zipped my laptop into its case. I would leave for Oakland first thing in the morning, I decided.

And yet when it was time to go, I couldn't face the thought of returning to my apartment, either. Going back to that life meant I had put my father's death behind me, that I had moved past it somehow, and I hadn't. So I asked my mother for the key to the cabin in Joshua Tree. Maybe "cabin" was too fancy a term for it. Though it sat on an acre of land, it was a simple one-room shack, with large windows and a slanted roof, built by a homesteader in the 1940s. One day, driving back from the national park, my father had seen a FOR SALE sign on the side of the road and called to make an offer—without consulting my mother. He said it was a steal at $25,000 and a fantastic investment; she called it a dump and a waste of money. He said he'd renovate it and rent it out; she retorted that no tourists would ever want to stay there. Every time the two of them talked they quarreled, and the cabin gave them a fresh subject of contention. My mother handed me the key reluctantly, all the while trying to talk me out of it. The cabin was too small. The swamp cooler didn't work well. It might be too hot there during the day. And it could get cold at night. Sometimes there were coyotes.

I didn't care. It was just for a few days, I told her. All the way to the cabin, I thought about my father. He had driven on this stretch of the 62 every day. Here was the gas station where he stopped for refills, the used books store where he picked out his paperbacks, the liquor store where he bought his beer. Already, life went on without him.

When I got to the cabin, I found that the front door wouldn't open. The key got stuck. With some effort, I pulled it out and went back to the car. Remembering a trick my father had taught me, I rummaged through the glove compartment for a pencil, with which I colored the teeth of the key until they were dark with graphite. Then I tried the lock again. This time, the door creaked open. The smell of dust and musk immediately made me sneeze.

The place was barely furnished. Under the window sat a gray sofa, its cushions stained and pilling. There was a small kitchen, with two stools at the counter, and a Formica-topped table with an unsteady leg. A stone fireplace separated the living area from the queen-size bed. The bathroom was the only private space. I opened the kitchen door and stepped into the backyard. There were several yuccas, a Joshua tree, and two garden chairs, caked with dust and weighted with stones to prevent their tumbling over in the desert wind. Here and there were tools my father had bought with the intent of landscaping, but by the looks of the yard he had never used.

I walked back through the house to the front porch, where the swamp cooler hung. A turtledove had built its nest on top of it and now the bird turned its head toward me, as if daring me to disturb its peace. We stared at each other for a moment. "All right, little mama," I told her, palms raised in defense. "We can share." Slowly, I slid my hand behind the metal box and turned on the water valve. All the while the turtledove kept watching me. I stepped back, drenched in sweat, and went inside.

I wanted to call Detective Coleman to ask for news, but it was early yet, and so I kept myself busy cleaning house. I scrubbed the sinks, wiped the windowpanes, swept the floors. The bookcase took a while to dust, as I sat on the floor leafing through the paperbacks that lined it. Spy novels. Mysteries. Thrillers. Was that what my father came here to do all those weekends when he said he was renovating? Or were these books meant for the tourists?

By the time I was done cleaning, it was the middle of the day and I felt suddenly exhausted. I went to sleep in my clothes. Again, I dreamed about him. We were in a train station, filled with travelers rushing about, dragging their roller suitcases behind. The creaking of the wheels came from every direction, making it difficult to hear him, though he was standing right beside me. Hurry, Nor-eini. Hurry. We're going to be late. When we went downstairs to our platform, I saw that we were not in a train station at all, but at a port. The ocean was cobalt blue and stretched before us endlessly. We managed to fit into a small boat with our bags. My father began to paddle, working his oar expertly, but I had trouble with mine. This way, Nora, he said. Look. Hold it this way. But the wooden handle kept slipping out of my hands.

I woke up in a sweat, my clothes sticking to me and the smell of household cleaner in my nostrils. After taking a shower, I glanced at the clock. It was finally time to call Detective Coleman. "We're still investigating," she said when I reached her. There were 251 silver

Fords in town, she told me, and it would take some time to figure out which one was involved in the accident—and that was assuming that the car belonged to a local, not a tourist.

"Has anyone come forward? A witness?"

"No, no one yet."

I tried to steel myself against more disappointment, but it came anyway. I would call Coleman again tomorrow, I thought. Perhaps tomorrow there would be some news.

Maryam

For a long time after my husband died, I felt as if I were caught in a heavy fog, unable to see my way forward, or even to perceive much of what was going on around me, the arrangements that my daughters were making, often without consulting me I should say, so that when I did speak, it was only to agree with a decision that had already been made. And yet that Thursday night, I forced myself to come out of the haze, put on some fresh clothes, and go see *Sleeping Beauty* at the elementary school. I did it for the sake of my grandchildren, who were only eight years old at the time; they didn't know much about life, and therefore nothing at all about death. I walked into the school cafeteria thinking we would have a normal evening as a family, but my son-in-law wasn't there, he had an emergency at the office, and my daughters started arguing about my husband's will. They couldn't even wait to get home to do it, they were yelling at each other in front of everyone, deaf to my pleas to lower their voices, and after a while I gave up, folded my hands in my lap, closed my eyes, and recited the Surat al-Nas, over and over again. I was so relieved to see the curtains part, and the king and queen appear onstage, that I started applauding like a madwoman.

When I was young, I was easily enchanted by new friends, new places, new ideas, but later the magic would wear off and I would see things for what they were. Other people were different, like my friend Karima Ait-Yaacoub, who was the voice of the student movement at the university in Casablanca, and I would say its face as well, because they put her on all the posters, after she went to prison. She was arrested early on, I think it was in 1979, they put her in Derb Moulay Cherif, which you may have heard of, perhaps, it was such a famous prison, if one can say that prisons are famous, maybe there is a better word for that kind of fame. Afterward, her husband was left to plead her case in and out of court, until he got himself arrested, too, distributing flyers for another protest, so that their children had to be taken out of school and sent to live with their grandmother in Midelt. I didn't want that life for Driss and me.

After our friend Brahim was arrested, I told Driss we should move to California, but he disagreed with me. He was still in thrall to his Marxist ideas, and couldn't see how foolish he was, placing his future in the hands of others. I am not proud of what I did next, though I had no other choice, how else was I going to convince him that he was putting his family at grave risk and that we needed to leave right away? When he came home from work the next day, I met him at the door. "The moqaddam was here," I said, wiping my hands on my apron.

"What did he want?"

"He said there had been a car break-in down the street, so we should be careful where we park the Renault at night, but after I thanked him and was about to close the door, he started asking me questions about you. How you were doing these days, whether you took your exams, what your plans were."

"Exams were canceled, he must know that," Driss said with a frown. He pulled a cigarette from his packet of Casa Sport and peered at me anxiously. "You think he wants to report me?"

"Why else would he come here, asking all these questions?"

Driss walked past me to the balcony, where he sat smoking and thinking until the muezzin called the evening prayer, the streetlights turned on, and the neighbors began telling their children that it was time to come home.

All I ever wanted was to keep my family together. And we were, for several years after we came to this country, because Driss and I spent eighteen hours a day together, working at the donut shop, and as a result we grew very close, there were many moments when we could read each other's mind or finish each other's sentences. At night, we would tell Salma stories until she went to sleep, then we'd practice phrases from our English book, call my brother on the phone, compose letters to my sisters, gossip about our customers. But when

I got pregnant with Nora, I was diagnosed with preeclampsia, probably caused by my blood pressure, which unfortunately is very high, Driss used to say it's because I eat too much salt, but of course it's also genetic, my mother suffered from it, too. The doctor ordered bed rest for the remainder of my pregnancy, imagine, no housework, no walking, not even to take Salma to school, no exercise of any kind.

I can still recall how long and lonely those six months were, being confined to my room all day, almost like being in a prison cell, especially because I am an active person, I enjoy doing things, not lying in bed, knitting or sleeping. I couldn't even watch my afternoon talk shows because I had flashing lights in my vision, and the television made them worse. Every night, I waited for my husband to come home. "Talk to me, Driss," I would say. "How was your day?"

But all he wanted to do after a long day at work, followed by cooking and cleaning at home, was to have some rest himself. Night after night, he would sit in his armchair, close his eyes, and say, "I'm too tired to talk."

After I gave birth, I expected things would go back to the way they were before, but Nora cried all the time, and it wasn't for the usual reasons, she didn't have colic, she wasn't hungry, her diaper wasn't dirty. She could be in her crib, sleeping or playing, and suddenly she would start wailing, I could never figure out what was wrong with her. Eventually, I gave up working at the shop. I'm not saying I regret staying at home, how could I, my daughters are the light of my life, it's just that I thought after all these sacrifices, at least my family would be close, but it surprised me to discover that my daughters lived in their own worlds.

Maybe it was their age difference. By the time Nora was old enough to play with dolls and toy trucks, Salma had already moved on to Clue and Monopoly. Or maybe it was their personalities. Nora loved to listen to music alone in her room, but Salma was always with her friends from the volleyball team. They didn't even look like sisters, because Salma has light skin, like her father, and Nora is dark like me. As the years passed, I spent most of my time alone, while my husband was at work, one daughter at practice, the other with her music. We were like a thrift-store tea set, there was always one piece missing.

After Driss died, Nora came back home, which was a comfort to me, because I couldn't stand being alone in the house, and I let her take care of all the small things, like mailing out payments to the mortuary, going to the dry cleaners to pick up a suit her father had dropped off a week before the accident, driving his car home from the street where he had parked it. In between all these errands, she would go into the master bedroom, run her fingers on the bristles of her father's hairbrush, open the closet and smell the sleeves of his jackets, or take one off its hanger and wrap herself in it. That was how I found her the day before the school play, sitting on the bed, wearing her father's suit jacket, staring at her feet. "Nora," I said, but she didn't hear me, I had to touch her shoulder before she noticed me standing there beside her.

She looked lost, and in a way, she *was* lost. She always had her head in the clouds, that one, and I think this was why her father left her a bit of money, to help her make a fresh start, maybe choose a better career this time, though of course the money only upset her sister, and caused them to have this terrible argument in the school cafeteria. I could hardly pay attention to the play that night, my heart was aching from hearing my daughters fight, like strangers rather than sisters, and I slowly let myself sink into the fog again, that hazy place where Driss and I were still young, still together, still a family.

Efraín

Elena was going to play one of the good fairies, and she was excited because she had to wear a blond wig. I could see it in the way she was looking at herself in the dresser mirror, tilting her head a little, smiling at her own reflection. Only eight years old, and already mimicking the women she saw on television. As soon as Marisela finished pinning the wig on her, she teetered forward on the chair, trying to reach the plastic clip-on earrings that sat on top of the dresser, between the bottle of cologne and my pain-relief ointment. "Why are you wearing a wig?" I asked from the bed. Elena's hair was black and glossy, and it was also long enough that it fell halfway down her back. It was perfect for the part, I thought. "Can't the good fairy have black hair?"

"Fairies have blond hair, Papá," Elena said.

"Is that true?" I asked Marisela. I had seen *Sleeping Beauty* once, on television, but I couldn't remember much about the story other than the princess falls asleep for one hundred years. I had been getting so little rest lately, I almost wished I could sleep that long myself.

"Fairies are supposed to have hats," Marisela said, "but the teacher ran out of them, so she gave us the wig instead." She smoothed a sheer pink cape over Elena's shoulders and turned to me. "Are you ready?"

"Yes." I took Daniel's hand and followed Marisela and Elena out of the apartment. The walk to school takes about fifteen minutes, and when the desert wind blows, those fifteen minutes can be unpleasant, but that afternoon there was only a soft, cooling breeze. I could feel the day's tedium and irritation lifting from me, replaced by the simple pleasure of being with my wife and children. Elena had only one line, which she'd practiced so often that all of us knew it by heart—"Little princess, I give you the gift of grace"—but it was punctuated by a wave of the magic wand. That was her favorite part, waving her magic wand.

The performance was taking place in the school's cafeteria. As soon as we took our seats, I leafed through the program booklet, looking for the good fairy with the blond wig. There were two dozen names on the cast list, but I found her easily enough: Elena Aceves Mendez. I felt a small thrill, because I had never seen my surname printed on anything other than my ID papers. I remember pointing it out to Marisela.

"We should save the program," she said with a smile.

Daniel pulled my sleeve and asked when the show was starting; that boy has always had trouble sitting still. While Marisela tried to distract him with a game of cat's cradle, I went back to the program. That was when I noticed the name I had been trying so desperately to erase from my mind. It appeared twice on the cast list, as if to double my shame. Aida Guerraoui Darwish. Zaid Guerraoui Darwish. I closed the program booklet, but nothing seemed right after that. The performance started late, two women in the front row argued loudly with each other, and when the moment came for my daughter to lift her magic wand and bestow her gift on the princess, she sneezed and dropped her wand. The evening I had looked forward to all week, thinking it might bring me joy, or at least some distraction, turned into a kind of purgatory. I had to sit in that darkened cafeteria, burdened by the feeling that the Guerraoui family was also sitting somewhere nearby, waiting for their children to appear. Night watchmen, both.

I told myself that it was just a coincidence—this town is small and there are only two grade schools, so the old man's grandchildren were bound to attend one or the other—but that didn't help. I felt I had been robbed of what little peace I had, and strangely this made me think of Alonso. He was the son of my mother's sister, born only a day before me, so that we grew up more like brothers than cousins. We even looked like brothers: we had the same cloudy eyes, the same widow's peak, the same small nose lost in a wide face. One night, when we were thirteen, Alonso and I left school at the usual time, but instead of going home with me, he went to help a friend of ours move house. It took longer than he expected, and later Alonso found himself waiting for the last bus in an unfamiliar neighborhood. Two street urchins, little more than children, came out of the shadows and asked for his money. When Alonso laughed and said no, they pulled out a switchblade and slashed the left side of his face. He ended up losing his left ear. After that, he was different. All his goodwill disappeared, he became full of self-pity. You couldn't talk about anything, a girl you wished to court, a job you wanted to have, a trip you dreamed of making someday, without Alonso rattling off a sad list of everything that could go wrong. And whenever we were alone together, he always stared at my left ear, as if he envied me for it.

That was the feeling I had now. I envied all the people around me in the cafeteria, everyone who hadn't seen the accident on the 62. More than anything, I wanted their ignorance, their innocence, their peace of mind, because I knew I had lost those things for good. After the performance, when it was time for us to go, I left the program booklet behind on the chair. It cost me a great deal to do that, but I did it. I couldn't take the chance that Marisela would see the old man's name in it and tell me yet again that I needed to do the right thing. What I couldn't get her to understand was that I was already doing the right thing. For us.

Jeremy

I pulled into the parking lot of the detention center in West Valley and sat in my Jeep, with the keys still in the ignition. At the café across the street, lightbulbs glowed, trapped inside the barred windows. Two people came out and chatted on the sidewalk for a few minutes before heading off in different directions. There was time yet to turn back. Go home. Let Fierro sit in jail and learn a lesson. No one would blame me for that. But in an unsettling way, I knew I was only stalling; I knew I would turn off the engine and go inside and fill out the forms.

An hour later, Fierro came out of central holding. There were shadows under his eyes and his skin was pale, but his eyes were as piercing as ever. Because of a backlog of cases, he hadn't been brought before a judge until the day before, when bail was set, so he'd spent four nights at West Valley. At the counter, he signed his name on a form and was handed a Ziploc bag that contained his keys and wallet. If he was surprised to see me waiting, he gave no indication. Without pausing to shake hands, he walked past me through the double doors and stood outside for a minute, trying to find his bearings. It was late in the afternoon. A pair of birds chased each other from perch to perch on the eucalyptus trees. The smell of coffee and meat drifted from the restaurant across the street. "Let's get outta here," he said. Only when we got inside the Jeep did he seem to relax. "Thanks for posting my bail."

On the radio the traffic report had started, but I turned the volume all the way down so he could hear me. "You're welcome. But here comes the fine print."

"What's that?"

"You're going to therapy."

Fierro was buckling his seat belt, but he stopped midair. "Fuck, no."

"No?"

"I'm not dealing with the VA again." He clicked his seat belt into place. "They made me wait five months for my new hearing aid, and I still can't get it to work right."

"This isn't through the VA. It's through the community center. A support group for people with anger-management issues. I heard about it from Stratton. One of his buddies runs it."

"You want me to go to therapy with a fucking amateur?"

"He's not an amateur, you dumb fuck. He has a master's degree, he knows what he's doing, and he's supposed to be really good. Hell, I'll even go with you, all right?"

"I'm not going to sit around with a bunch of people moaning and bitching about their feelings. Can we just get out of this place already?"

I started the car and eased out of the parking lot onto the street. At the first light, I pulled out a Marlboro from my pack. It was my third cigarette of the day. Or maybe my fourth. Anyway, I was making progress. It couldn't be harder to quit than liquor and I'd never looked back once I'd set my mind to it. I took a deep drag, savoring my cigarette all the more because I wouldn't have another one again that day. Fierro lowered the passenger-side window to let out the smoke. "That stuff'll kill ya," he said.

"All men must die."

"All men must serve," he said with a grin. After a moment, he turned to me again. "But, seriously, how can you put those toxins in your body? I don't get it."

"Clean-living tips from Dr. Fierro. What else you got for me?"

"Just that." He sniffed. "And stay away from crazy bitches."

We were about to get on the 10. I waited until I'd merged onto the freeway before I spoke again. "She's probably going to file a restraining order against you."

"Who, Mary? I wasn't planning on seeing her."

"I hope you mean that, man. You need to leave her alone. For good this time."

"I already signed the divorce papers."

"Is that true?"

"Why would I lie? I did it right after I smashed that damn car."

"All right. Good. First session is next Thursday, by the way."

"You serious about this support group bullshit?"

"'Course I'm serious. You need help."

"Dude, when you start to nag, you sound just like Mary. You know that?"

"Yeah, well. Maybe you should've listened to her."

For the rest of the drive home Fierro remained quiet. Even when we drove past the windmills, he didn't make his usual joke. Q: How do windmills feel about renewable energy? A: They're big fans! When we got to his apartment building, he flipped down the passenger-side mirror and ran his hands through his greasy hair, smoothing it down. At Camp Taqaddum, he used to stand in front of the small mirror in the showers and wrap a bandanna around his head, pulling it all the way to his eyebrows. It was the only way to keep the sweat from running down his face in a continuous stream when we were out on patrol. We went on dozens of them together, lost a buddy in them, but it wasn't a patrol that got us. It was an escort run, just a week before the end of our last tour, when we were told to take an Iraqi minister by the name of Dr. Jaber to a meeting on the west side of Ramadi. He was in charge of restoring parts of the electricity grid that had been destroyed during the invasion, but in the eight months he had been meeting with American contractors they had yet to agree on a plan. It was a Monday morning in May, I remember, the temperature already reaching the high nineties, though no one in our unit minded it. We were eager to get through our final few shifts and much of our conversation while we waited for the minister was about what we'd do once we were back stateside. Go to bars. Meet girls. Swim in a pool. Forget all that, Hec said. I want to move someplace where it rains and where I never have to see anyone.

After the meeting, we drove Dr. Jaber back on Route Michigan. The road ahead was white with sunlight. Sitting at the turret, I squinted against the glare, even through my Ray-Bans. From somewhere down the street came the creaking of a bread cart and the laughter of children. And then, just like that, I was flying ten feet into the air, my rifle spinning out of my arms, a piece of shrapnel lodged in my back. Everything went black. The next thing I remember was the taste of gravel dust in my mouth and Fierro screaming at the top of his lungs: *I got you, Gorecki, I got you.* He hoisted me over his back and carried me out of the ditch where I'd landed. Only later, when I woke up at the clinic, did I learn that he had a blown eardrum.

He flipped the passenger-side mirror closed. "Wanna get a drink?"

"Not tonight."

"What? I smell that bad?"

"A shower wouldn't kill you. But no, I'm just tired."

"All right. Thanks again, dude."

I pulled out of the lot and headed home. A heaviness had settled on me, the kind that I knew would keep me up all night. Maybe I should go on a hike, I thought. Tire myself out. Clear my mind. I drove past my street corner and continued down the highway toward the national park. I was waiting at a red light when I saw Nora walk into McLean's.

Nora

I had gone to the cabin to escape squabbles with my family, but the cabin presented a challenge of its own: it was so quiet that it seemed to me I could hear the beating of my own heart. I wasn't used to the desert, at least not anymore, and after a while I got into my car and went looking for a place to get a drink. I'd never been inside McLean's, and it surprised me to see how busy it was at barely six in the evening. I took a seat at the bar. A couple of tourists in hiking clothes and wide-brimmed hats were huddled over a single menu, debating whether to get plain or garlic fries. Three seats down, a man in blue overalls was scratching at a lottery ticket with a house key. Across from me, a couple of bearded men were conversing quietly over their beers. The bartender was mixing cocktails and didn't look up when I tried to catch his eye.

"Nora," a voice called from behind.

I swiveled on the barstool and my purse fell out of my lap, spilling its contents—keys, mace, some change, a tube of lipstick I didn't remember buying, an enameled pill box, my cell phone. It was a fantastic mess and Jeremy Gorecki stood over it, embarrassed. "I'm sorry," he said, picking up my things from the floor. "I didn't mean to startle you like that."

"It's okay." I took the purse from him and zipped it up. "What are you doing here?"

"I was about to get some dinner. Want to get a table?"

"I was only getting a drink. Or hoping to anyway." I glanced at the bartender, who was refilling a beer for one of the old men and paid me no notice. "All right."

I slid off the stool and followed Jeremy to a table by the window. In a T-shirt and jeans, he looked younger than he had in the button-down shirt and pants he wore when he came to the house. As a matter of fact, he was a year younger, I realized; I'd been held back that one year in kindergarten. When he motioned to the waitress, she came over right away, pulling out her notepad from her apron. She was a blonde, busty woman in a tank top and black jeans, and spoke with a smoker's gravelly voice. "What can I get you, hon?" she asked him sweetly. He opened his palm toward me.

"Could I have a gin and tonic, please?" I asked.

"Sure thing. Anything to eat?"

"No, just the drink. Thank you."

"I'll have the burger, medium, with fries," he said. "And a glass of water."

"Coming right up, hon."

The waitress left. I slipped my purse off my shoulder and hung it on the arm of my chair.

"How are you holding up?"

A question I had been asked by my roommate and friends a few times already, and for which I still had no answer. Since my father's death, it was as if my life had stopped and I remained stuck in the same moment, the same place. "I'm not," I said with a shrug.

"I'm so sorry, Nora. I know how devastating this is."

There was so much kindness in his voice. For a moment, my eyes pricked and it seemed as though tears were finally coming, but somehow the feeling passed. I rested my chin on the heel of my hand and looked out of the window for a while. The sky was the color of peach. Cars passed now and then on the highway. A delivery truck pulled up in the middle lane and the driver climbed out to deliver a package. How odd, at this late hour. "He left me all this money," I said, turning to look at Jeremy. "Can you believe it? Me, the fuck-up."

"You're not a fuck-up."

"You don't know that."

"I know fuck-ups. Trust me."

The waitress came back. "Here's your gin and tonic. And here's your hamburger, hon. Ketchup and mustard are right there. Can I get you two anything else?"

"No, I think we're good," he said.

"You didn't want a beer with your burger?" I asked.

He squeezed ketchup on the side of his plate. "I don't drink."

"At all?"

"No." After a moment of hesitation, he said, "I get really bad insomnia. It was taking five or six drinks to get me to sleep, and after a while even that many weren't enough. I didn't like where I was headed, so I stopped."

"And the insomnia is gone?"

"Well, no. It comes and goes."

I stirred the ice with the little black straw and took a big sip, all the while watching him. He sat with his back straight and ate quickly, though nothing about his composure suggested he was in a rush. It was so strange running into him at McLean's. I hadn't thought of him in ten years, and now I'd seen him twice in a week. It struck me that this was yet another consequence of death, that it disturbed long-established patterns, even something as insignificant as this. Outside, the delivery truck was gone, leaving a clear view of the strip mall across the street. A woman was closing up the nail salon, testing the locks with both hands before walking away to her car. "Isn't that where the ice-cream parlor was?" I asked, pointing to the salon.

"They tore it down a couple of years ago and rebuilt the whole thing."

"I used to go there with Sonya Mukherjee after Spanish class." In high school, Sonya and I had few friends. We were the only girls in the jazz band; we had last names that teachers always shortened to an initial; we celebrated holidays that were not listed on the school calendar; we were cast as the Magi in the Christmas play every year, despite our protestations that we were girls, always the Magi, with flowing white scarves covering our long hair, and robes dissimulating our budding breasts and hips. We were both thought to be Muslim and Sonya often had to say, No, no, I'm Hindu. Then in September of our sophomore year, two planes were flown into the World Trade Center and strangely that distinction seemed to matter less, not more. We were both called the same names. Ragheads. Talibans. Sometimes, raghead talibans. In Spanish class, at least, we got to be brown kids among other brown kids, an anonymity we craved all the more for its new rarity. After an hour of conjugating verbs—*yo me voy, me fui, me iba, me iria, me ire*—we often went to get ice cream.

"I remember," he said.

"You were in Spanish, too?"

"No, I worked at the ice-cream parlor two days a week."

"Right. Sorry." An image came back to me now, blurry and yet also solid, of Jeremy Gorecki standing at the cash register in a white polo shirt and red apron, waiting to ring up our orders. I felt the heat rising to my cheeks and was conscious of him noticing it. For a moment, I was quiet, thinking about those long-gone days. Whatever happened to Sonya? She had gotten into NYU and sent enthusiastic emails for the first few weeks, but I hadn't heard from her in years. I'd have to look her up someday.

"I remember one time you and Sonya got into such a giggling fit you knocked down the spoon rack. The whole place was a mess."

"For the record, Officer, it was the cup display, and we got kicked out for that."

"Yeah, sure."

"But *you* never got into trouble."

"'Course I did."

"Like what?"

"Kid stuff. I can't think of anything specific right now."

"Because there wasn't any," I said with a smile. Oh, God, I thought, I'm flirting with him. But it was a distraction from the intolerable fact of loss and the constant feeling of grief. His face was familiar—he had the same blue eyes, the same prominent nose—yet adulthood had made it new again. And the last ten years had clearly left their mark. There was a new hardness around his jawline, tempered by the early signs of crow's-feet at the corners of his eyes.

I finished my drink and motioned to the waitress that I wanted another one.

"What's it say?" he asked, looking at the tattoo on my wrist.

"It's Latin. 'A voice crying out.'"

He reached across the table and touched the inside of my wrist, then turned my hand toward the light to get a better look. "Any reason?"

"I went to a rally out in the Bay Area when I was in college. Remember the law that would've made felons out of undocumented immigrants? Back in '06?" He seemed on the verge of saying something about the rally, or the law, but instead he drew back his hand and waited for me to finish the story. "Anyway. When the police ordered us to disperse, I couldn't find a way out and I got arrested. They put me in zip ties and had me sit on the curb while they waited for transport. It was my first protest, and I couldn't believe I was getting arrested. All of a sudden it dawned on me that I'd need to be bailed out, my mom would find out, I'd have an arrest record. I kept telling myself I was fine with that, but the truth was, I was scared. Terrified, really. I was sitting there with my head on my knees when one of them asked me how old I was. I said nineteen. He asked where I went to school. I said Stanford. And then he cut off my ties and said, 'Go home, kid, and mind your own business.' I was so relieved to be let go, I didn't think to tell him that this *was* my business. Everyone's business."

"I'm sure he knew you weren't much of a menace to society. And he probably hated being there as much as you hated getting arrested."

The waitress brought a fresh G&T. I stirred the ice in my glass and took a sip. The juniper spirit was doing its work; my stomach felt warm and the knot between my shoulder blades was starting to loosen. I was glad to have run into Jeremy, it was better to have company than to drink alone. "So you like being a cop?" I asked.

"There are good days and bad days."

"Do I sense some disappointment in our hero?"

"Well, you teach high school, right? I'm guessing it's kind of like that. Sometimes it's fantastically rewarding, other times it's horrible. But the pay is great and I have a good schedule. Three days on, three days off. I fixed it so I can go to school on my days off. Do you want some of my fries?" He slid his plate to the center of the table.

"No, thanks. I'm not hungry. What kind of school?"

"Copper Canyon. I'm about to transfer to UC."

"Didn't you get into Cal State?"

"I dropped out after a semester and enlisted."

"Wait, what?"

"I joined the Marines."

"Wow." After a minute, I asked, "Where did you serve?"

"Iraq."

It had seemed strange enough that Jeremy was a police officer, but it struck me as utterly peculiar that he'd been in the Marines. Across the expanse of the table, I looked at him with new eyes. The long fingers that had once gracefully stretched across guitar strings to play an F sharp had held an automatic rifle and pointed it at people in another country, a country that had done no harm to his. The eye that had once winked in mischief as he passed notes in class had calmly observed human targets through a riflescope. The voice that had softened as he told me he'd joined the Marines had barked instructions over a headset or a bullhorn. In our desert town, there were Marine flags on houses and yellow ribbons on cars. The grocery store was festooned with banners that said WELCOME TO OUR TROOPS. Most of the kids in our high school sat for the ASVAB. So it shouldn't have surprised me so much that Jeremy had enlisted, and yet it did. I couldn't reconcile the memories I had of the stuttering boy in grade school with the reality that he was an agent of the state. "But why?" I asked.

"I wanted to study speech pathology, but when I got to Cal State I hated my classes and didn't do well in them. I felt like a complete stranger on that campus. Like I didn't belong. I was just, I don't know, not going anywhere with school. And we were at war. It seemed like the right thing to do."

"Invading Iraq was the right thing to do?"

"That's not what I meant," he said quickly. "I just meant, I'd always wanted to serve. My grandfather was a medic in World War II, and my dad was in the Army Reserve for a while, too. I was eighteen, I guess I wanted to be a part of something bigger, like them."

An awkward silence fell on the table.

"You sure you don't want any fries?" he asked after a minute.

"I'm sure. Thanks."

I touched the charm of my necklace, my father's gift to me for my high school graduation, and which I'd pulled out of the jewelry box in my bedroom the first night I got back, a protective talisman in the shape of a hand. I felt worn out all of a sudden and wanted desperately to be alone, to return to my grief, in solitude and without interruption. Beads of water had formed on my glass of gin and the black napkin underneath was soggy. Two tables down from us, an older woman pulled out a red lace fan from her purse and cooled herself with it. At the back of the restaurant, the waitress was refilling saltshakers, nodding along with the song that played on the stereo. Only when she noticed my insistent stare did she finally bring the check.

"I got it," Jeremy said.

"No, it's all right." I put money down and he did, too, pulling a bill from his wallet and walking out of the restaurant behind me. Outside, the last rays of sunlight painted the white blooms of yucca shrubs a deep orange. It was very quiet.

"You really shouldn't be driving, Nora."

"I'll be fine." I crossed the parking lot to my car, and he followed.

"Why don't you let me drive you home?"

"There's no need. I'm just going three or four miles."

"Nora."

"What?"

"I can't let you drive. You're, what, five-foot-three and a hundred-and-ten, a hundred-and-fifteen? You had two drinks in less than an hour and you didn't eat anything."

Hearing all this spelled out made me feel exposed. Vulnerable. All I wanted was to be alone again. I got in my car, but he held the door open with one hand. A familiar fear settled in the pit of my stomach. "I'm fine," I said, my voice turning uneven. "Really."

"Come on, Nora. Let me drive you. You can get your car tomorrow."

I got out of the Prius after a moment and followed him, holding my purse against my chest like a shield. He eased his Jeep onto the 62 and was heading toward my parents' house when I asked him to turn around and gave him directions to the cabin. "So you'll be in town for a while, then?" he asked.

"For now," I said, not wanting to explain that I couldn't stay at the house with my mother and that I needed time to think through what I was going to do next.

Five minutes later we pulled up to the cabin. My mother was sitting on the porch, waiting. Great, I thought. Just great. All of my energy went into looking sober and alert. "Thanks for the ride," I said and got out without waiting for an answer.

My mother stood up, her hands on her chest. "What happened?"

"Nothing, Mom. The battery in my key went out. I couldn't get the door to open."

"I told you not to buy a hybrid. They're not reliable."

"Okay. You were right." A meaningless concession to avert an escalation.

Inside the cabin the smell of mint tea hung in the air. A stack of Tupperware containers, each filled with a different dish—grilled peppers, chicken with carrots, a fruit salad—sat on the kitchen counter. The realization that my mother had been inside the cabin finished sobering me up. "What's this?" I asked, pointing to the Tupperware.

"You called Triple A?"

"I'll call them tomorrow."

"And who was that man? He looks familiar."

"What's all this, Mom?"

"I brought you something to eat."

"You didn't have to." I dropped my purse on the sofa. That was when I noticed the flower arrangement on the mantelpiece. Some years ago, my mother had taken up arts and crafts and spent most of her afternoons working on one project or another. Her latest hobby was dry-flower arrangements; this particular incarnation involved pink and white roses laid out in the shape of a heart. A heart! On the other end of the mantelpiece three black vases stood like sentinels. "Mom. There's really no need for any of this. I can take care of myself. And besides, I'm not staying long."

"But this place is so empty. You don't like the dry flowers?"

"No, they're pretty. Very pretty."

"Then why don't you like them?"

"It's just not my sort of thing."

"Your sister loves the one I made for her."

Of course she did.

My mother went to the mantelpiece and switched the vases and the flower arrangement around, then stepped back to assess. "Better?"

I sank into the sofa, defeated.

Jeremy

We barely spoke on the drive to the cabin, but the silence between us was different now. Everything had changed. I took my time turning the Jeep around, watching until she went inside. How good it had felt, talking to her about the old days. How beautiful she had looked, sitting by the window at McLean's with the last light of the day on her. And how warm her eyes had been, before she'd found out I'd fought in Iraq, before she'd been forced to ride with me, before she'd seen her mother waiting on the porch. Nothing would be the same again.

This was how it had felt, too, ten years ago, at the field trip to the Dorothy Chandler Pavilion. Mr. Mitchell had organized it as a reward to the jazz band after our performance of "Coconut Champagne" at the district-wide concert. I was excited to go, mostly because it meant getting out of town and skipping the other classes. But the trip was scheduled for the day after my mother's birthday. March 13. Though it had been three years since her passing, March 13 was still an agony. My father had started drinking at breakfast. I had my driver's license by then, but he refused to give me the wheel when it was time to go to the cemetery to visit her grave, so I sat in the passenger seat, keeping a watchful eye on the road while Ashley sat in the back, picking at her nail polish. Afterward, we went to a taco joint my mother had once declared the only authentic Mexican restaurant in the Mojave. When we returned home, my father dropped us off at the door and said he needed to run to the Home Depot to get some electrical wire and a couple of light-switch plates. "Be back in an hour," he said. But he didn't come back in an hour. Or two. Or five. I made dinner, checked that Ashley had done her homework, and insisted that she go to bed by ten. Around midnight, I called the police, then the hospital, but no one had arrested a Mark Gorecki or admitted him to the emergency room. It was three in the morning when I finally heard the garage door open. I turned off my bedside lamp and tried to go to sleep, facing the wall. Sitting in the music room that Friday morning, waiting for Mr. Mitchell to take attendance and collect permission slips for the field trip, my only focus was to stay awake long enough to make it onto the school bus.

"Fanning," Mr. Mitchell called. "Gorecki. Guerraoui. Henderson. Lorenzo."

I rummaged through my backpack for the permission slip with the counterfeit signature. I routinely signed all my school paperwork as well as Ashley's, but it was only when I walked up to the desk that I realized I didn't have the $15 fee. At breakfast that morning, I'd been too angry to even look at my father, let alone ask him for anything. "Mr. Mitchell," I mumbled, "I'm sorry, I forgot."

Mr. Mitchell shuffled some papers and said he needed a minute to sort it out. I walked back to my seat, trying to suppress my embarrassment, while Jonathan Atkins repeated, in a boo-hoo-hoo voice, *Mr. Mitchell, I'm sorry, I forgot.* I was delirious with sleeplessness; I couldn't think of a retort. And Atkins was on the wrestling team, his shoulders as lean and strong as one of those action figures I still kept in a storage bin in the garage. Not someone I could start a fight with. I was staring at my Chuck Taylors when Nora leaned across the space between our seats and whispered, "Ignore that guy, he's an idiot." I looked up, but she was already zipping her backpack. We were about to leave.

At the Dorothy Chandler Pavilion, while my bandmates admired the bronze sculpture of a peace dove or played in the dancing water fountain, I started to worry about lunch; I didn't have money for that, either. With utter lack of solidarity, my stomach started growling. I was famished. When the others went to order food, I stayed behind, walking along the side of the building, where the names of donors were etched on granite slabs. At the end of the walkway was a giant magnolia tree, and just below it, across the street, was the new Disney

Hall. I stood there awhile, wondering who could have designed such a monstrosity. Then I heard my name.

"Do you want some lunch?" Nora asked. There were two sandwiches, two drinks, and two chocolate cups on her tray. My stomach replied for me. I felt embarrassed, but she acted like she hadn't noticed. We sat with our legs crossed Indian style, with the tray on the ground between us. I had known her since we were kids, and yet I had never really seen her. Now I found myself looking at her, really looking at her. Her eyes were dark and willful. Her nose was graceful, her smile generous. She glanced over my shoulder at Disney Hall. "You like Frank Gehry?" she asked.

"That's the architect? This thing looks like he smashed a can with his shoe. I could've done that for Disney and saved them millions."

She laughed. I liked the sound of her laughter.

"I love it, actually," she said after a moment. "It's different from all the buildings around here. Gehry designed the Bilbao, too. I want to see that someday. Have you ever been to Spain?"

"I've never been out of the country. We went to Mexico once, but I was, like, nine months old. It doesn't count." I reached for the second half of my sandwich. "You probably travel a lot."

"Not really. We couldn't go to Morocco when I was little because my dad was afraid he'd get arrested, and then later when we finally went, all we did was go from house to house, visiting relatives. We didn't go to museums or monuments or anything." After a moment she said, "But I saw acrobats at the market in Marrakesh."

She asked what books I read, what shows I watched, and she really listened when I answered. We didn't have the same taste. I loved *The Simpsons;* she never watched it. I devoured the *Harry Potter* books; she'd given up on them after the first two. She raved about Zora Neale Hurston; I hadn't read her. We agreed on Mark Twain and *The Princess Bride,* but about nothing else in between. She had long hair in which her earrings got tangled every time she shook her head. I had an urge to reach across the tray and untangle them for her.

Then Sonya Mukherjee came to find us; the matinee was about to start. "Come on, you guys. Everybody's already inside." Nora stood up and held out a hand to help me off the ground. That morning she had been just another girl, but by the time I'd raised myself off my knees she was the only girl. For weeks afterward, I felt tethered to her. It was her face I looked for first when I got to school, her smile I tried to draw when I made a joke, her body I hoped to brush against when we were in line. I spent my time waiting for first-period English and fifth-period music, bookends to endless days of boredom, but I could never find another moment with her. She was always rushing from one place to another, as though she couldn't wait to leave this town forever.

Then we graduated and faded out of each other's lives. When I saw the name Guerraoui on the case board at the police station, I felt as if I'd received a notice that had been lost in the mail. It reminded me of Nora's kindness that day on the field trip, which was why I had gone to her house to offer condolences. But tonight at McLean's was something else. This time *she* had looked at me differently. Something might have started between us. But then the war came up and she'd turned fierce. Righteous, even. In a way, I found it touching. No one had argued with me like this ten years ago. When I'd told my old man that I'd dropped out of college for the Marines, he'd struggled to get out of his chair, already drunk at four in the afternoon, and when he was steady on his feet he clapped an arm on my shoulder, and told me he was proud of me.

Anderson

The lady detective came into the bowling alley around noon, when I was still hoovering the carpet on the concourse. I used to have a guy who did this, emptied the trash, too, and cleaned the bathrooms, but I had to let him go, so I did the hoovering myself, or sometimes A.J. did it for me. The little lady stood against the bright light from the entrance, and at first I couldn't see her face, only her figure. I turned off the vacuum cleaner with a kick. "Can I help you?" I asked. I could tell she wasn't here for a game, she was dressed all formal like, in a business suit, and she carried a notepad in her hand. As she stepped out of the light, she unclipped a police badge from her belt, and that's when I realized she was here about the hit-and-run with the guy next door.

What happened was a terrible accident. We need a lot more lighting and signals along the highway. You could drive for miles out here without coming across a single lamppost or a stoplight. Some people don't remember this, but the intersection of the 62 and Old Woman Springs Road used to be called "Crash Corner" because of how often accidents happened there. Gruesome ones, too, with body parts mangled into car parts right there in the middle of the road. The state put in a special sign and a left-turn lane, but the crashes kept happening at that intersection until they installed a light signal. That was in 1973, the year I opened my bowling alley. A long time ago.

See, my wife had come into a bit of money from her grandmother in Sacramento, and we were trying to figure out how to use it. Back then, there wasn't a whole lot to do in a town like ours—that's what gave me the idea to open a bowling arcade. A lot of sweat went into it.

I bought the land, found an architect, got the permits, hired a contrac-tor, the whole thing. You should've seen how many people showed up for the grand opening. I remember it was the week before Christmas and Helen, that's my wife, she put up a ten-foot Douglas fir on the con-course, all trimmed with lights and smelling like heaven. To this day, whenever I smell Christmas trees, I think about the grand opening. It made the front page of the *Hi-Desert Star.*

Helen was a little ball of energy, always looking for ways to grow our business. She came up with themes for our specials, got us a good deal on advertising with the local radio station, convinced some of our friends from church to start a bowling league. We did really well for a few years. But after A.J. was born, she lost interest in running the bowling alley and wanted to spend all her time with the baby. Even after he started school, she didn't want to go back to work. She was always waiting on him hand and foot. I warned her, I said, "You're spoiling that boy, Helen," but she waved me off, said I was being too harsh on him. She didn't get involved with the business again until after A.J. went off to college in Fullerton.

By then, though, there was another bowling place a few miles down the highway, and the movie theater, and the drive-in, and all of those bars and restaurants. People had more options for what to do on a Friday night. And Helen wasn't the same, either. She started getting the shakes on the left side of her body. Resting tremors, the doctors called them. Still, we managed to make a decent living. We worked for ourselves, we had no complaints. The Muslim guy moved in next door in 2002, I think it was. He bought the place from old Mrs. Swenson, who used to run it as a greasy spoon, hot dogs and burgers and such, and later he turned it into a full-service diner. What happened to him was a terrible accident. And to be honest, it's a matter of time before it'll happen to somebody else because that crosswalk gets so dark at night. Like I said, we need to have some lighting on the road and maybe even a stoplight.

The lady detective walked down the concourse toward me, and introduced herself as Detective Coleman. A black woman, about forty years old, with hair cropped very short, like a man. I don't know why women do that sort of thing, it's not attractive at all. Anyway, she said she was investigating the hit-and-run that took place half a block down from the bowling alley. I could tell straightaway that she wasn't from around here, but I couldn't trace her accent. "Were you working on Sunday, Mr. Baker?" she asked me.

"Sure," I said. "Same as any other Sunday."

She wrote down my name in her little notebook, and started asking me all kinds of questions, like what time I open and close, if I'd seen anything unusual or suspicious, anything at all. I thought about it while I unplugged the vacuum-cleaner cord and wound it firmly around the hook in the back. "It was just a regular night," I said.

"Do you have any security cameras?" she asked.

I almost laughed. "This isn't Chicago," I said. "We're a quiet little town. We don't really need that kind of thing here."

"So, no cameras?"

"No."

She was quiet for a minute, I could see she was disappointed by my answers. "What about your customers?" she asked. "Any chance I could talk to them? Someone might've seen something."

The accident had happened on a Sunday night, which is usually a busy night for us, and we're closed on Mondays, so by Tuesday morning, when she was asking me all these questions, I honestly couldn't remember who had been there. "I don't keep tabs on my customers, you know."

"Maybe I could look through your receipts from that night?"

I stuffed my hands in my pockets, jiggled the change in them. "Is that legal?"

"It is, if you let me."

I wasn't convinced, but she had asked nicely and I've never minded helping the police. They have a tough job to do, sometimes, a thankless job. "All right," I said. "Just give me a minute." I rolled the vacuum cleaner into the utility closet and walked to my office in the back. She followed close behind. "What time were you looking for?" I asked her over my shoulder.

"No specific time. Anyone who came here that night."

I sat at my desk and looked through the blue plastic organizer by the computer. I'm not a young man anymore, and even a small task like hoovering the carpet can get me winded, so I pulled out my hand-kerchief and wiped down the sweat from my forehead while I sifted through the papers. There were a lot of cash receipts from that Sunday night, but I found six or seven credit card slips and handed them to the lady detective. She took a picture of each one with her phone. "We really need to have a stoplight at that crosswalk," I told her.

"Hmm-hmm."

"You should tell your boss about it."

"I'm afraid that's not in the purview of his work."

"Beg your pardon?"

"That's something for the city council to decide."

"Right. I was just saying, is all."

She slipped her cell phone in her pocket. "What about your employees?"

"You mean Betty?" I said. She worked the cash register, but unless she was making a sale she was always on her phone, playing Soli-taire. She wouldn't have seen anything. "She doesn't start until three. You're welcome to try her then."

"All right," Coleman said, handing me her card. "If you recall any-thing else, Mr. Baker, please give me a call."

We walked back through the concourse area together. The light above lane 3 flickered, which meant I had to check the wiring again, a nuisance I'd been dealing with for weeks. At the entrance, I opened the door for Coleman, then stood behind the glass, watching as she went back to her car. I'd only ever seen lady detectives on TV shows before.

Nora

From the nest above the swamp cooler came the cooing of the turtledove. It had woken me up earlier that morning and now I lay in bed, watching a spider climb the window screen, the sky behind it a brilliant blue. The spider moved with elegance and without hurry, unconcerned about the past or the future, one as immaterial as the other. Time was passing—nine days now—but I felt stuck, as if I'd only just heard that my father had died. In the Muslim tradition, the period of mourning lasts forty days. Why forty? Moses spent forty days without bread or water before receiving the covenant on Mount Sinai. Between his baptism and his return to Galilee, Jesus was forty days in the wilderness, resisting temptation. Muhammad was forty years old when he secluded himself in the cave at Hira, and Gabriel appeared to him. Forty was a potent number, a promise that ease would come after hardship, that good tidings would follow bad. But my grief would not end in forty days. Or forty weeks. Or ever, it seemed. All I had left of my father were memories, each as fragile as a wisp of smoke.

I thought about his last visit to me, the previous spring, when he'd come to watch me perform at the Botanical Gardens. He'd worn a pin-striped suit and a black tie and, looking at his reflection in the full-length mirror in the hallway of my apartment, he had said, "Noreini, wait." I was already at the door, the folder with my music tucked under my arm, my hand halfway to the light switch. "Wait, Nor-eini." My father took off his jacket and, sitting on my piano bench, brushed his shoes until they shone. He wanted to look his best for the performance. Come to think of it, he always wanted to look his best when he

ventured out of his work clothes, as if any trip into the wider world—
the whiter world—was a test he might not pass someday, if he wasn't
careful. At the Botanical Gardens, he'd asked a passerby for a photo of
us standing by the marquee with my name on it. Where was that picture now? In the drawer under my bedroom window? Or somewhere
on the desk I shared with Margo? I'd have to look for it when I got
back. I needed to get back to my new piece, too; I wanted to finish it
in time for fall fellowship deadlines.

Then the cabin phone rang, startling me. It was an old-fashioned
landline phone and its sound was urgent and bothersome. I dragged
myself out of bed to pick it up, holding the receiver close with one
hand, and working with the other to untangle the cord. The line crack-
led. "Can I speak to Mr. Guerrari?" a man asked. His voice was high-
pitched, almost feminine in tone, and he spoke with a European accent
I couldn't place.

"Guerraoui," I corrected, my heart skipping a beat.

"Sorry, it's hard to make out the handwriting on this order. I only
have the carbon copy in front of me. Is Mr. Guerraoui home?"

"No, he's not here. He passed away."

There was a moment of shocked silence on the other end of the
line. In that time, I relived my disbelief at the news of my father's
death, the sight of him in his burial shroud, how cold his skin had
been when I'd touched it, the grief and anger that took turns inside
my heart.

"I'm—I'm sorry," the man said. "I didn't know. I called the cell
phone number he left me, but it went to voicemail, and no one ever
answered this one until today."

"He didn't give you the house number?"

"No. Just this one." After a moment, the man drew his breath
again. "Who should I talk to about getting paid for the balance?"

"What balance? I'm sorry, who did you say you were?"

"The balance on the engagement ring he ordered in April. This is
Maurice from Maurice and Dana's Designs."

I had trouble parsing the phrase *engagement ring*. It didn't seem
to belong to a language I could speak or understand, and that feeling

persisted even after I wrote down the address for the jewelry shop, drove to Palm Springs to find it, and was buzzed inside by Maurice. I was clinging to the possibility that there was some kind of misunderstanding, that my father had meant "anniversary ring," even though my mother had developed an allergy to detergent some years ago and couldn't wear rings of any kind. "I'm here about the ring," I said, nearly out of breath as I walked into the shop.

Maurice nodded thoughtfully and his eyes misted over, as if he were about to grieve with me. He was very short—his waist barely reached the top of the glass counter that separated us—and he wore gold rings on the last two fingers of each hand. From a file folder by the cash register he retrieved the receipt and showed it to me. The words *engagement ring* jumped out from the first line. "And he ordered this ring from you himself?"

"Yes," Maurice said. "He was very clear about what he wanted. Something elegant and timeless. He didn't like anything we had here, so we had to custom-order it. That's why it took so long."

I tried to picture my father standing right where I was, looking at all the rings on display in this shop. Nothing here had been good enough for his lover, his love, his soon-to-be-fiancée. No, this couldn't be true. It seemed to me as if Maurice were talking about some other man, a stranger. Because how could my father have done something like this? Did my mother know he was getting ready to leave her? Nothing about the last few days suggested that she knew about an affair. "Who's the ring for?" I asked. "Do you know the woman's name?"

"No, I'm sorry. He came in alone. I've never had a situation like this come up before." Maurice watched me for a moment, and then he cleared his throat. "So. About the balance. Your father put down half, and half was due on delivery." He placed the jewelry box in front of me. A diamond solitaire. Princess cut. The inside of the ring bore three words, three precious words, etched in cursive. "The total comes to $3,250."

"I can't pay for this. I'm sorry, I just can't."

"But I can't sell this ring to anyone else, not when it's already inscribed. What am I supposed to do?"

"I don't know." I pushed the jewelry box across the glass counter and walked out of the shop. Standing in the parking lot for a moment, I wondered if the phone call my father made to me on the day he died might have been about this. Was he going to prepare me for what he was about to do? From behind came the sound of hurried footsteps.

"Miss," Maurice called out. "Wait."

But I got into my car and left. As I drove back to Yucca Valley, I thought again about the Cold War between my parents, the long silences that followed, silences I had mistaken for peace. Instead, the rift between them had deepened. Now I remembered that, the previous October, Salma had invited my parents for a weekend in Lake Tahoe, but at the last minute my father had begged off, saying he had too much work to do. And on Thanksgiving, he'd disappeared for a couple of hours and no one had been able to reach him. But if those were signs of an affair, I hadn't noticed them.

Who was the woman? How long had he been seeing her? Did he bring her to the cabin? Did he sleep with her in that big bed, the bed where I had been sleeping not two hours before? All the certainties I'd once had about him vanished. I was overwhelmed by feelings I couldn't quite put into words yet. In my haze, the only thing I could feel clearly was the weight of his secret; it was mine to carry now. I couldn't tell my mother about it, because it would only compound her grief, and I couldn't trust my sister with it, because she told my mother everything.

Driss

I know how this looks. A woman like her, young enough to be my daughter. But it wasn't cheap or crude like that. I didn't chase after her, I didn't make promises. And it wasn't love at first sight, either. There was no thunderbolt, no magic moment. It happened slowly, day by day. She came into the restaurant one Sunday morning, took a seat at the counter, and ordered the breakfast special. Because of the wide-brimmed straw hat she hung on the back of her chair, I thought she was a tourist, here for the weekend, but when I brought her the eggs and hash browns she'd ordered, she asked me if I knew whether the hardware store two blocks up from the restaurant was open on Sundays. She needed to buy paint for her floorboards.

The next week, she was back. We started talking. I found out she was from San Ysidro, a couple miles north of the border with Mexico, and until recently had worked as a bartender, but after an acrimonious separation from a man she had been with since high school, she'd decided to start over. Move to the desert. Open a vintage store. Growing up, she'd always shopped at thrift stores or at the Goodwill and, as a result, had learned to spot stylish, inexpensive clothes. "I have an eye for what other people miss," she said. And I could see she had good taste, from the linen dress she had on, the red kerchief around her neck, the leather-strapped watch on her wrist. But what really drew me to her was the ease of her smile.

She'd leased a commercial space near the antique stores on the 62, in that little stretch where tourists and beatniks always stopped on their way to concerts in Pioneertown. She was working on refurbishing the place, getting ready for the grand opening. I knew what that was like, starting a business in a new town, so I tried to help. I went with her to see the space, gave her my opinion about local contractors, who could be trusted and who couldn't, who was punctual and who was on desert time. She considered my advice, took some of it and discarded some, but she always listened to what I had to say. I had forgotten what that was like. Being listened to, I mean. Her name was Beatrice.

I won't ask you to understand what happened. I just want you to imagine it. We were standing in the middle of the store, with the morning light streaming in from the windows, and we were talking about the wallpaper. In several places, especially by the front and back doors, it was stained or peeling, so I recommended a local contractor for the tedious job of stripping and repainting. Beatrice ran her hand over the paper, which had a pattern of pink vines on a light green background. "You're right that it should go," she said, "but I will keep it here, in the alcove." In that little nook, she said, the wallpaper was still in its original condition, and would be the perfect background against which to display antique hair accessories and costume jewelry. I scribbled the name of the contractor on the back of my business card and handed it to her. When she took it from me, our eyes met and she smiled. That is the moment I always go back to when I try to unwind what happened between us.

I'm sixty-one years old now, a grandfather already. Maryam and I were married more than half our lives, and I thought we would spend the other half together. We argued a lot, especially in the last few years, but that wasn't why we grew so far apart. The truth is that we were always different, from the beginning. We met in 1978, at a UNEM meeting at the university in Casablanca, but I had been there because I wanted an end to government corruption, better schools, fair wages, things like that, whereas she'd come to find a friend who'd borrowed a textbook from her and never returned it. I was driven by a sense of optimism, which I don't think Maryam ever really shared; she was more the pragmatic sort. When the police arrested Brahim and Karima and others like them, I wanted to stay in Casablanca and continue the fight, but Maryam wanted us to move here.

Always, we had to do what she wanted. She couldn't compromise. Once, I remember, when we were still newlyweds, we went to the fabric market to shop for curtains. Our apartment was on the ground floor of a converted colonial house, but it faced commercial buildings on all sides, and it got very little sunlight. We agreed on sheer curtains because they would let in what little light there was, give us some privacy, and wouldn't be expensive. The shopkeeper unrolled sample after sample, while Maryam assailed him with questions: how much is this one, how much is that one, are you seriously asking for this much, do you have this in other colors. Then she picked out damask curtains. "But this will block the light," I said.

"It's such a pretty pattern," she replied.

I tried to imagine our living room with those curtains, and I couldn't. On the weekends, I liked to sit by the window and read the newspapers, but with these curtains I knew I'd have to sit on the balcony or go to a café just to get through the morning news. "You like something with a pattern?" I spread out the fabric samples on the counter. "Then how about this lace? It has a pattern."

"I don't like lace."

"No lace. Let's try cotton, then. It'll let in some light."

But Maryam didn't like any of the fabrics I chose, so in the end I gave in. We bought the curtains she liked and went home. I got the ladder and brought out my tools, but every time I drilled a hole, she'd tell me the rod needed to move a little higher or a little lower. When the curtains were finally up, we had five holes in the wall and the rod slanted on the left. I don't know why I'm remembering this, so many years later, it's such a small thing. Maybe it's because I'm trying to understand what happened myself. All I know is that life is short. Without realizing it, I had been traveling down the road from birth to death with the wrong companion. But now I had found the right one, and I didn't want to give her up.

Coleman

The victim's daughter came into the office, her eyes telegraphing that she had some news. It took her a while to get to it, and maybe I should've been more patient with her, but I was having a rough morning. I'd just found out that Miles was flunking math, which was infuriating to me because it had been his best subject when we lived in D.C. Now he had two Ds in pre-algebra. Meanwhile, the PTA ladies had asked if *given my line of work* I could chaperone for the seventh-grade dance, but I had to say no because I had a district meeting that night. I was pretty sure I had blown my last chance with them. I would never be admitted to their tribe. And to make things worse, Vasco was pressing me about this hit-and-run. He was getting bad press about a police-beating incident earlier that spring, and he was desperate for some good news. All of this is to say that I had a lot on my mind when Nora Guerraoui came to speak to me that morning. She shifted in her seat, drained the glass of water she'd asked for, clicked and unclicked the clasp of her bracelet watch. I thought about the pile of paperwork on my desk, all those silver Fords waiting to be checked and cross-checked. "What can I do for you, Ms. Guerraoui?"

"Please, just call me Nora."

"What can I do for you?"

More fiddling with her watch. Another minute passed. "So I came across some information?"

"All right." Let this be good, I thought.

"I don't know if it's relevant to the case."

"Why don't you tell me what it is? We can decide if it's relevant later."

"My dad was having an affair."

Oh, that.

"You don't seem surprised."

"These things happen."

"But you knew?"

"Yes."

"How?"

"Texts on his cell phone."

"It wasn't locked?"

"No."

"Well, that's dumb."

Love ain't smart, I wanted to say. I'd seen it before, people doing the dumbest things you can imagine, out of love or lust or whatever you wanted to call it, all along thinking they were going to get away with it because they were special. And thank God for that, or they'd never get caught.

"Who is this woman?"

"I can't say."

"Why?"

"Safety. Privacy. Plus, I have a duty to preserve the integrity of this investigation." A knock on the conference-room window made me look up. It was Murphy, holding up a bottle of cold lemonade. *Want one?* his lips mouthed. I shook my head no, though my throat felt dry. The weekend before, I'd driven Miles to the baseball game Murphy had told me about, in the community park. Murphy was there with his son, Brandon. I didn't know if he had prepared Brandon beforehand, but that kid went right up to Miles and started talking to him. Miles had grown about a foot over the previous year, and that had made him awkward, almost like his brain hadn't caught up with his body. His voice had grown deeper, too, and he wasn't used to the sound of it, which might have had something to do with his being so quiet all the time. But he followed Brandon to the field, and the more time passed, the more loose-limbed he got. After a while, Murphy came to sit next to me on the stands. We talked for a bit. That's all we did. We just talked. But leaving the field, I felt a little weird about the whole thing.

You sure? Murphy mouthed from the other side of the office window, holding up the lemonade again. I nodded. *Yes, I'm sure.*

"Is that woman involved?"

"No," I said. The woman in question—remarkably young, unremarkably pretty—had a solid alibi. She'd cut herself that night while trimming her plants and had been getting two stitches in the ER at the time of the accident. When I interviewed her, all she could talk about was how the old man loved her, how he was going to leave his wife for her, how they were getting ready to move in together. I couldn't see a motive. It was a dead end, as far as I was concerned.

"Please tell me her name."

"I can't do that." I could tell she was going to try finding out anyhow, which I couldn't blame her for, but I didn't want this to get messy. "Nora," I said, as gently as I could, "what difference would it make if you knew? It wouldn't change anything about what happened. It's better not to know."

"Better for whom? It's not better for me, I can tell you that."

"I'm sorry."

"Who is she?"

"I can't say."

"But if it's true that she's not involved, what harm is there in telling me her name?"

"I've already explained why I can't do that." She was trying to get me into an argument, maybe coax me into saying more, but I resisted. Again she clicked and unclicked her bracelet watch, it was a nervous tic. "And still no new witnesses?" she asked.

"No, not yet."

"Something isn't right. If this was just an accident, why didn't the driver stay at the scene and wait for the police? Why didn't anyone see anything?"

"That's what I'm trying to find out."

"What if I offered a reward? Would that help?"

Sometimes it helped, sometimes it created noise. People who were hoping for a reward could get creative with details. But it was going to take me weeks to check all those silver Fords, and a reward would speed things up considerably. This was my chance to turn things around. "How much were you thinking?" I asked.

"Twenty-five thousand dollars? Is that enough?"

That's a lot for a teacher, I thought. At least, I thought she was a teacher. Her mother hadn't been too specific on that, she'd been too busy telling me about the other daughter, the dentist. When Miles was still a baby, Ray and I had wanted to have another child, but we were both focused on our careers and it never worked out. Then we got a little too old to try. So I didn't know what it was like to have two children, especially two daughters. The dynamics of it, I mean. Maybe the mother couldn't help being prouder of the dentist with the successful practice and the adorable twins. I was just an observer myself, but I couldn't help comparing the two daughters as well. Only the younger one was calling me every day, asking about the case. At first, this had irritated me, but now I found myself warming up to her. She was trying to help. "Twenty-five thousand is fantastic," I said, unable to repress a smile, in spite of the circumstances. "We'll have to make a formal announcement in the paper and on the radio. We can even print some posters."

Nora

To share details of my father's life with a stranger went against every instinct I had, and yet I did it, hoping that, in return, the detective would give me a clue that might unlock the mystery of his affair. Even if it was just a name. After all, names can tell stories. If she was a Fatima, say, then maybe my father had met her through his Moroccan friends in Los Angeles. If she was a Jennifer, then she was almost certainly decades younger than him, and he'd probably met her at a bar or the gym. If she was a Guadalupe, then I'd wager he'd tried to impress her with his fluency in Castilian Spanish. But no matter how directly or indirectly I asked about the woman, Coleman remained unmoved.

By the time I walked out of the police station, it was early afternoon and a dry, hot wind was blowing from the east. It whipped my hair violently against my face, so that I had to gather strands of it in my hands just to see my way through the parking lot. My mouth tasted like dust. I got into my car, switched on the ignition, and waited for the AC to kick in. Across the lot, two sheriff's deputies stood together under the shade of a palm tree, smoking and talking, seemingly unbothered by the heat and the wind. I watched them for a moment, then stepped out of the car and went back into the station. "Could I speak to Deputy Gorecki?" I asked the receptionist.

She brushed her fringe out of her eyes. "Who should I say is asking?"

"Nora."

"Last name?"

"Guerraoui. G-u-e-r-r-a-o-u-i."

She looked defeated, but recovered somehow and told me to have a seat. The television screen in the lobby showed the local news, with the sound turned off and the closed-captioning turned on: the town council had met to review requests for funding for next year; electric-line repairs would be blocking part of Yucca Trail all day tomorrow; the Marine Corps would hold a live-fire exercise in Johnson Valley. Then it was commercials. I was on the verge of leaving when the door opened and Jeremy came out, a speck of mustard at the corner of his mouth. "I didn't mean to interrupt your lunch," I said.

"No worries," he said, running the back of his hand across his mouth. "Is everything all right?"

I nodded, even though nothing was all right. In his uniform, he looked tall and imposing, an impression that was reinforced by all the things he carried—gun, baton, pepper spray, taser, and whatever else hung on his belt. In a strange way, this made what I had to say to him seem like a confession. "I just wanted to apologize about the other night at McLean's. You were right, I shouldn't have tried to drive."

"It's okay."

"No, it's not. I could've gotten into an accident and hurt someone."

"You were in a lot of pain."

I had been. I still was. And the pain was complicated now by the realization that my father had a secret life, that for weeks or months or even years, he'd lied and tricked and cheated. He was the person I trusted most in the world, and now I was learning that I didn't really know him. I should never have picked up that damn phone in the cabin, I thought, I should've let it ring. I felt dizzy with loss.

"Do you want to get a cup of coffee?" Jeremy asked, touching my arm.

I was tempted to unburden myself right then and there, tell him everything I'd just found out, and my frustrations with what I still didn't know. Behind the glass window, the receptionist was looking at her forms, but listening carefully. The elevator doors opened and a man with a police badge clipped to his belt came out, glancing at us as he walked past. "Thanks," I said, steadying myself. "But I really should go."

"Take care," he called as I went down the steps to the glass doors.

Outside, the wind had grown even more violent. It rattled the windows of my car and swept sand and palm fronds across the highway, but even so it took me only a few minutes to get back to the cabin. The big bed was the first thing I saw when I came inside. How long had my father been carrying on his affair? How could he have done this to my mother, after thirty-seven years? For the first time, I began to think of him not as the father who had walked me to my piano class every Thursday, but as the man who sneaked out to the cabin every chance he got. I couldn't bear the thought of sleeping on the mattress where that woman had slept or touching the bedding she'd used. I turned around and walked out.

This time, I drove to the furniture store, where I bought a new mattress, paying the extra fee to have it delivered the same day. Then I stopped by Walmart for new pillows, sheets, and towels. I was in the throes of a manic energy, as though by purging a few artifacts from the cabin, I could disguise the ruins I'd excavated. Yet afterward, when all the remains of his affair had been cleared, I sat alone in the cabin, and I still couldn't forget what I'd learned about him.

I pulled out my laptop and did something it had never once occurred to me to do: I Googled him. His name appeared in a business listing for the restaurant, dating back to when he bought it. Briefly he was quoted in a *Hi-Desert Star* article from 2010, after a winter storm had uprooted a palm tree and left debris on the highway near his business. And he had an account with an ancestry website; it seemed he had been researching his family's history for some time, tracing it from Casablanca to a tribe in the Chaouia. That's what I'd been doing, too, digging through his past.

But it wasn't just my father's life that I was seeing under a new light, it was mine as well. In my first year at Stanford, I'd joined a jazz ensemble that met in the basement of a church half a mile from campus. One day, walking out of rehearsal with the trumpet player, we ran into a friend of his, a tall, lanky junior with brown hair and an easy smile. His name was Beckett Burke. He'd graduated from Harvard-Westlake, regularly spent winter vacation in Switzerland and spring break in Costa Rica, and was planning to work for an organization that offered contraceptive services and infant immunization in Uganda. The mere mention of these countries, which Beckett did offhandedly as he ordered from the à la carte menu of the Peruvian restaurant he led me to on our first date, nearly took my breath away. When, a couple of weeks later, he took me to his apartment and relieved me of my virginity, I did not mind, or yet know I should mind, that the sex was rushed and unenjoyable. I was flattered that he was interested in me and proud to stand beside him at parties, absorbing his effortless cool as if by osmosis. With his hand on my back, he introduced me as "the lovely Nora Guerraoui" and the sound of my name on his lips, even with his exaggeratedly rolled *r*'s, thrilled me. What did a sophisticated boy like him, a boy who already knew exactly what he wanted to do with his life—aid management in developing countries—ever want with me?

I could not think of a satisfying answer to that question, which was why I started to arrange my life around his. Beckett didn't like poetry, so I stopped going to the spoken-word performances that had become the highlight of my week and instead followed him to the indie theater where hip new movies played. On Sunday mornings, he liked to drink coffee and read the *New York Times,* so I bought my own subscription. Sometimes, on Sunday afternoons and after much cajoling, he would agree to go on a hike with me, but it was usually brief because he complained incessantly about the weather; it was always too hot or too cold or too rainy or too buggy. When Beckett started to cancel dates or set them up at the last minute, I blamed his busy schedule. When he forgot to call me, I blamed myself for being dull. Only when I saw him walking down Arboretum Avenue with Margarita Semprevivo, his arm around her tiny waist, did I finally understand that he had moved on to "the lovely Rita."

Of course, there was nothing unusual about what happened. People break up all the time, for all sorts of reasons. But the cheating had so damaged my ability to trust that it took me fifteen months to start dating again. Sameer Hanim was about as different from Beckett as it was possible to be in a place like Stanford. He had grown up in a small town in Ohio, attended a science magnet school, had perfect SAT scores, but couldn't tell you what Puligny-Montrachet was or where Eton was located or why sports socks didn't go with dress shoes. Like me, he had been pressured into his field of study—software engineering, in his case—by a mother whose own ambitions had been deferred and denied. What he really wanted to do was make animation. The sketches that hung in the apartment he shared with two other engineering students would not have been out of place in an art exhibit, or at least it seemed so to my untrained eye. He was a shy, quiet boy who loved spending Saturday afternoons watching old television series or browsing comic-book stores.

And yet when we were out at dinner and a pretty girl walked by, his eyes would always follow after her. What was it about me that failed to hold his attention? The question consumed me and I became obsessed with finding the correct answer. I got a new haircut, bought trendy clothes, spent hours reading Frank Miller and Alan Moore and Jim Starlin so I could keep up with conversations about comics. With each new change, Sameer's attention would settle for a few days, and then we'd be at a party, and I'd notice him staring at someone else. In the end, he cheated on me, too, with a white girl from his algorithms class. Later, they started a software company together.

Even Max, my current mistake, was the same. The only difference was that instead of cheating on me, he had cheated with me. Either way, I had never been enough. I had always been found wanting. For years, I'd told myself that all this was just bad luck or that I had terrible taste in men. But now I wondered if it was something deeper: my father cheated, and I loved men who cheated.

Maryam

Time passed, yet I still found myself reaching for two glasses when I made mint tea in the morning, or looking for my husband's socks when I folded the laundry, or wanting him to hand me a fresh towel when I stepped out of the shower. These little moments were painful, they reminded me that I was no longer his wife, that I was his widow now, a state of being I was still trying to accept. But life has to be faced, even when it can't be accepted, and after I received a second phone call from the restaurant manager, asking me when we planned to reopen, by which he meant something else, of course—he meant that the staff had bills to pay and families to support—I realized I could no longer delay the inevitable. I had to go to work.

At five thirty the next morning, when I pulled into the parking lot of the Pantry, I found the cook already waiting for me, smoking a cigarette by the dumpsters. My husband had warned him not to do that, because Mr. Baker, the owner of the bowling alley next door, often complained about the risk of fire, so I told José to put the cigarette out, and he stubbed it under his shoe and followed me inside, not speaking to me until after the first customers came in. An old man took a seat at the counter, reading his Bible as he waited for coffee; a family of four settled into one of the booths by the window, their children arguing over packs of crayons; and a couple in matching Kings caps huddled in the corner, staring at their phones, but then I looked at the table in the back of the diner, and instead of Driss doing his crosswords or reading the newspaper, there was only an empty chair.

"Coffee, Mrs. Guerraoui?" Marty asked me. Despite what people think, my name isn't Maryam Guerraoui, it's Maryam Bouziane, but so

many women in this country take on their husbands' names that I had
long ago given up explaining that we were different. Marty was the
first employee my husband had hired at the donut shop, a young man
barely out of high school back then, and now he had bifocals dangling
from a retainer around his neck, yet even he didn't know, or perhaps
didn't remember, my true name.

"Thank you," I said, and took the cup of coffee from him. After he
walked away, I remained at the counter for a while, trying to will my
body to carry out the duties that lay ahead. I had to clear the box of old
lightbulbs Driss had left in the hallway, order napkins and toilet paper,
decide whether we were going to put up Memorial Day decorations
this year, and then try to find them. But in the end, I couldn't face any
of this, and I carried my coffee to the cash register and slumped in the
chair behind it. I could do this much at least, I could make change for
customers, hand out mints, or give packs of crayons to the children.

Outside, a young couple in hiking jackets and boots got out of a
dusty car and stood in the parking lot, checking their tires as if for a
leak, then came into the diner, barely glancing at me as they walked
past, and found a table for themselves. In a few weeks, the spring season would be over, the tourists would be gone, and the town would
return to its empty self. Perhaps then I wouldn't be needed at the
diner.

But had I ever been truly needed? My husband had bought this
restaurant in spite of my objections and, perhaps because of our arguments about it, he rarely called on me to help. I came here only if he
was short-staffed, when one of the workers was sick, or if it was a busy
weekend. Maybe if I had been more involved, I might have been with
him the night of the accident, I might have seen the car, or heard it
coming, and maybe even warned him to get out of the way.

Footsteps made me look up. It was a young man in blue hospital
scrubs, his beard neatly trimmed and his hair pulled into a ponytail, he
was probably from the medical office two blocks from the restaurant.
"I saw the notice in the newspaper," he said as he handed me the bill
and his money. "I'm sorry for your loss."

"Thank you," I said. My voice sounded like a stranger's. I couldn't
bring myself to say more, talk to this man the way my husband would

have, ask him how everything tasted, or how work was these days, or was he enjoying the nice weather. From the framed article on the wall, Driss looked on with a smile, a stack of blueberry pancakes and a cup of coffee before him on the counter. DINING IN THE DESERT, the headline said. My husband was proud of that article; it helped ease some of his frustrations, the humiliations he had to suffer through sometimes, working in a restaurant and waiting on people.

"Did they catch the guy who did it?" the customer asked me.

"No," I said as I handed him his change.

"Well, I hope they do. People drive way too fast on the highway, it's really dangerous. We need some kind of light or a signal at that intersection. Maybe you could raise this at the next city council meeting?"

He waited for me to say something more, turn my husband's death into a public cause, rally others around it, but pain is a private business, it would be too difficult for me to talk about it in front of others, let alone strangers at the city council meeting. I had noticed this before about Americans—they always want to take action, they have a hard time staying still, or allowing themselves to feel uncomfortable emotions—so when I shook my head no, the man seemed disappointed in me, and after a moment he left, the door jingling as it closed behind him.

Jeremy

Fierro was waiting for me outside his apartment building, in jeans and a T-shirt, his USMC baseball cap pulled so low I couldn't see his eyes. In the car, he turned up the volume on the radio when Metallica came on, but I didn't complain, even though all that crying and hollering about being a rebel gave me a headache, and later when he went on a rant about the Dodgers' losing streak, I just nodded along. Whatever it took to get the guy the support he needed. I'd sent an email to Hec, an old buddy of ours from Charlie company, because I'd remembered he was in a group like this, up in Oregon, and he'd said it had helped him some. I was hoping it would help Fierro, too.

A folding sign outside the community center told us that the anger-management support group met inside the gym. Flyers advertising summer swim classes for kids, ballroom dancing for seniors, and a family-movie night hung on the wall next to the double doors. Most of the chairs were already taken by the time Fierro and I walked in and joined the circle around the facilitator. His name was Rossi. He wore a bright yellow shirt that stretched tightly over his pectorals, and he spoke with a thunderous voice that I had not expected from a member of the therapeutic professions. "Who would like to share tonight?" he asked.

Immediately a hand shot in the air. It belonged to a middle-aged man whose knee bounced up and down like the needle of a sewing machine. "Hi, I'm Doug. I had a really bad week. My daughter invited a bunch of her friends over for a board game and they were loud. I came downstairs to get a drink. I wanted to tell them to be quiet, but I didn't want to interfere because my wife had warned me to stay out of their way. Plus, she was already mad at me because she says I never help around the house. Which isn't true. I mean, I run the vacuum and I empty the dishwasher sometimes. Anyway, I couldn't say anything to my daughter and her friends, but it's like, I couldn't take the noise, either. So I just stood there, in the kitchen, feeling like I might explode."

A woman in a nurse's uniform who was slouching in her chair, arms crossed, sat up suddenly. "It happens to me, too. I'm Adriana, by the way. Sometimes I just want to scream when my kids ask me to take them to the park or the movies. I can't go out looking like this." She uncrossed her arms then, and I saw that her left hand was missing its ring and pinky fingers. "But I know I can't say anything, because it'll only make them think that my ex-boyfriend was right about me. About my temper, I mean. I'm in so much pain all the time. That's what they don't understand."

I could practically feel the heat of Fierro's disdain radiating from him. Maybe this wasn't such a good idea, I thought. Maybe I should've insisted that he go through the VA, even though they wouldn't offer him the private counseling he wanted and would just send him home with another prescription for Paxil or Zoloft or Wellbutrin. But then Fierro did something I didn't expect: he raised his hand.

"Ah," Rossi said. "We have a new member tonight. Please, introduce yourself."

"My name is Bryan Fierro. It's hard to find someone to talk to sometimes, so I 'preciate you all having me here. My problem is, I can't sleep. I don't mean, like, occasional insomnia, everyone gets that sometimes. What I mean is, I never get more than three or four hours of sleep, ever, no matter what I do. Been going on for years. I've tried everything. You name it, I've tried it. Even chamomile tea. You know how fucked up a guy is when he starts drinking a tea he can't even spell. Nothing works. I stay up all night and think. Like, I think myself into circles."

I looked at Fierro only once—when the word *insomnia* came out of his mouth—then stared at my shoes until it was over.

"Anger can cause all kinds of problems," Rossi said. "And insomnia is certainly one of them. Lack of sleep can lead to exhaustion, which can lead to poor decision-making, which in turn leads to even more anger. It's an ugly chain reaction. You may want to talk to your doctor about getting a sleeping aid. Without proper rest, it's harder to make good choices, explore the source of your anger, and try to control it."

"Right," Fierro said, nodding. "Right."

An older man with tattooed arms raised his hand to speak. He worked for Home Depot, he said, and had been put on probation at work because he'd had an outburst with a customer over an order of window shades. Another guy, a long-haul truck driver, said he missed his wife while he was gone, but as soon as he came back home they'd fight until it was time for him to leave again.

Finally, the wall clock chimed nine o'clock and the session was over. I waited until Fierro and I had left the community center and were alone in my car before I turned to him. "You think that stunt you pulled in there was funny?"

He thumped me lightly on the arm. "Kind of. Admit it, it was funny."

"You can be such an asshole sometimes."

"I told you it'd be a bunch of pussies talking about their feelings."

"Try calling them that to their faces, see what happens."

"Dude. Relax, it's not a big deal."

"Everything's always a joke to you."

Fierro leaned in. "What's that?"

"You heard me. So don't act like you didn't."

"Come on, don't make such a big deal out of it. I won't do it next time."

"There won't be a next time," I said, starting the car and backing out of my parking spot. I was getting tired of his antics. If he didn't want to get help, I wasn't going to make him. Let him do whatever the hell he wanted. I turned the dial on the radio, changing stations. I was looking for the news, but the folk and country station came first and I settled on that instead. My father had been in a folk band before he met my mother, and I'd grown up listening to that music at home—that was how I'd become interested in playing guitar.

Fierro took off his cap and ran his fingers through his hair. "I liked those people. Seriously."

But that was the trouble. I could never be sure he was serious. "Yeah, whatever."

"And the group leader, what's-his-name, he was nice."

"Rossi."

"Seems like a good guy."

"He is. You're really going to be back next week?"

"I said I would, and I will. Wanna go bowling?"

"It's getting late."

"Dude. It's only nine."

I thought for a minute. "Let's go to Desert Arcade."

"Nah. That place is lame."

"You want to go bowling or not?"

I drove down the highway until I saw the bright new sign for the Pantry—so bright you could see it from a block away—but the restaurant was already closed by the time we pulled into the parking lot. Only the bowling alley next door was open. I didn't know why I'd wanted to come here or what I was hoping for, exactly, but ever since I'd seen Nora at McLean's, I'd been under the grip of nostalgia.

"It's pretty empty," Fierro said when we walked into the arcade.

And it wasn't hard to see why: the carpet was threadbare, the lighting was bland, the video game consoles were old. But there were ten perfectly polished lanes and plenty of room to play. I went up to the counter, and old Mr. Baker put away his newspaper and stood up. I'd gone to high school with his son, A.J., but I could tell he didn't recognize me; I looked different without all that weight I'd once carried.

Fierro and I ordered a couple of games and rental shoes, then walked across the concourse to lane 2. Three lanes down from us, a family of five was halfway through their game. They were in matching shirts—green jerseys with white trim on the side and a league name embroidered on the back. *The Pin Pushers.* They were laughing at some private joke, excited at the evening that lay ahead. We started bowling. It was '80s night and I hummed along with songs I'd first heard when I was in grade school, but Fierro said he didn't know half of them. He'd grown up in Havana, Texas, and only moved with his mother to Desert Hot Springs when his parents split up. "They didn't have music in Havana?" I said. "I thought you guys liked to mambo."

"We didn't even have a radio," he said. "My dad was looking for things to sell to pay for his heroin, and when he found out I was hiding the radio under my bed, he took it from me and beat me up. I was eight years old. First thing my mom did when we finally moved out to California was buy us a stereo."

He told me stories like this all the time. At least I have some good memories of the old man, I thought. My father was a drunk now, and a belligerent one at that, but he'd once been a decent father and a good husband. Helping with homework, running to the store for milk, showing up at PTA meetings. On Saturdays, he would get up early and make breakfast for the whole family—not just pancakes, but eggs and bacon and potatoes and fresh orange juice—after which we would all gather in the living room in our pajamas to watch a movie. But that last weekend, in the middle of a repeat of *Freaky Friday*, my mother had started to cough and couldn't stop. I said we should call the doctor, but my father thought she'd put too much hot sauce on her eggs; he patted her knee and told her to drink some water. Two days later she died, and our family fell apart like a house of cards.

Now my sister lived only five miles from me, but our encounters were uncomfortable, which was one reason I'd asked Fierro to come with me to her barbecue the previous weekend. We'd sat under string lights on her deck, enjoying our grilled chicken and potato salad, and then she'd asked me how I was sleeping. When I told her I might have to go back on Ambien again, she'd turned it into a recruiting opportunity. Gave me a diagnosis of what ailed me and how I could fix it. All of which led to an invitation to one of her Bible study groups. Meanwhile, my dad sat in the big lawn chair, drinking and holding forth on the war in Iraq. He'd served in the Army Reserve, did a brief stint as an equipment-repair technician in Kuwait during Desert Storm, and somehow that made him an expert. But he'd never had to see intestines hanging like garlands from a pomegranate tree, never had to break down someone's door at three a.m., never had to hold a gun on a mother while the males of the household were rounded up, never had to put a tourniquet on what was left of Sanger's arm, never had to walk past the bodies left behind on the street, their eyes and noses and mouths obliterated by militias from one faction or another. Talking about the fallen came more easily to those who hadn't witnessed the falling. So we'd had another one of our arguments, him insisting that Saddam was a threat to our freedoms, that we'd liberated the country from a tyrant, that we'd helped the women, and me asking him what Saddam had to do with our freedoms, where those WMDs were, and how those bombs were working out for the women. These arguments had long ago become rehearsed. Circular, even. It didn't matter what I said, my father would always return to the same point. *Saddam was a bad guy, we're the good guys.* The two of us weren't fighting about the war, we were fighting about something else, something that had lain unspoken between us for many years.

"Bam!" Fierro said. He'd just scored his first strike of the game. "You're going down, dude." He sat in a swivel chair, spreading his legs in a self-satisfied way, and took a swig from his Coke.

"We'll see about that," I said with a laugh. I picked up a ball and, coming up to the foul line in stride, released it and hit eight pins.

"We should get us some of 'em bowling shirts," Fierro said with a glance at the family in the lane nearby. "We could be *The Deadly Pins.* Wait, no. *The Mortal Pins!* How's that?"

I picked up another ball and went back to the line. I knew before I threw it that I'd hit the last two pins and score a spare. The thing about Fierro was, he was a good player, but he was easily distracted. He missed two easy shots because he kept chattering. I beat him handily.

After the game, I drove him back to Desert Hot Springs. The moon had already risen and the streets were empty and quiet, but there was some kind of outdoor celebration in his apartment complex, with loud music playing and kids splashing in the pool. He eyed the partiers wearily, then got out of the car and reached through the open window to shake my hand. "See you next week, brother."

I got back on the highway, taking my time going home. Under my headlights, the yellow lines that marked the edge of the lane passed ceaselessly. I'd turned in my final paper for the spring semester, and

I had hours and hours to kill before I could hope to fall asleep. Dolly Parton's "Do I Ever Cross Your Mind" came on the radio and, whether because of the mood it set or because of my bout of nostalgia, I found myself thinking again about that dinner with Nora, going over every detail as if to sear it in my mind.

Efraín

After the old man robbed me of the pleasure of watching my daughter's performance in the school play, he invaded my dreams. Nearly every night, I returned to that little stretch of the 62, my hands covered with grease, and watched his body roll off the hood of the car and land on the pavement. I thought of him now as Guerrero. Merciless in his campaign against me. Early in the morning, when I shaved by the yellow light above the bathroom mirror, he bumped against me and made me cut myself. In the van, while Enrique read the map, Guerrero was in the back, sabotaging our equipment by poking a hole in the carpet-cleaning hose or raiding our food supplies. I couldn't find my Inca Kola when I opened my lunchbox, even though I had put it there myself. "You can have some of mine," Enrique said, handing me his can. A button was missing on his uniform shirt and I wondered if that, too, was Guerrero's doing.

Part of me, the part that had coolly measured the cost of calling the police and decided it was too high, knew that this was all in my head. It wasn't the first time I had nicked myself while shaving, the carpet-cleaning hose was very old, Marisela had replaced my soda with water when my back was turned. But another part of me scrupulously tracked all the mishaps and setbacks I had suffered since the night of the accident and held up the tally to me at every opportunity. The longer I refused to come forward, the longer the list grew.

It surprised me that my memory of the accident did not dull with time, but became clearer instead. Now I was certain, or nearly certain, that the car that struck Guerrero was silver and that, whatever make or model it was, it had a long hood. And there was a sticker on the rear side window, round and red, an advertisement of some kind. Perhaps memory is not merely the preservation of a moment in the mind, but the process of repeatedly returning to it, carefully breaking it up in parts and assembling them again until we can make sense of what we remember. Several times a day, I returned to that moment on the highway, seeing it differently each time, as if it had been cast under a new light.

I didn't tell my wife about the new details that had come to me, and she didn't mention the accident on Saturday night when, exhausted from work and lack of sleep, I lay down on the sofa with my head on her lap. All I wanted was to forget, and yet my mind was diligently working on the opposite, forcing me back to that night on the 62. It was as though I were stuck in time, forced to relive, again and again, what had happened that night. Marisela seemed to have made her peace with my silence, because she stroked my hair while she watched Don Francisco on *Sábado Gigante*, and didn't ask me any questions.

Nor did she bring up the accident on Sunday morning when we took the children to church. From his pulpit beneath the stained-glass windows, the priest spoke of the sacrament of penance, quoting from the Book of Psalms: "Then I acknowledged my sin to you and did not cover up my iniquity." Oh, I knew what he meant. Confess, and your guilt will be forgiven.

But I had committed no crime, so why should I feel guilty?

And yet I did. It was guilt that weighed so heavily on me, and that made me revisit the accident so often over the past few days. I wanted desperately to be free of it, but walking back home, with Daniel's hand in mine and Elena skipping over the lines on the sidewalk, I wondered whether forgiveness was worth all the things it could cost me. As we waited to cross the road, Marisela gave me a funny look. "What is it?" I asked.

"Your socks," she said.

I looked down and saw that one sock was blue and the other was black.

"I noticed when we were in church," she said with a little laugh. "But I couldn't say anything then."

My God, how I loved her smile. It was what had attracted my

attention the first time I had seen her, on a crowded bus in Torreón, many years ago. She was smiling politely at something the conductor had said. In spite of the summer heat, she was in a long-sleeved black dress and shoes, and her hair was plaited in a severe braid on the side. It took a week before I ran into her again, and another before I caught on that she was a widow. But she barely acknowledged me, she was still wrapped up in memories of her dead husband, and I realized that I would have to compete with him for my happiness. My cousin Alonso, as usual, said there was no hope. "Nine months and she's still wearing black," he said. "He must have been some man."

"Whose side are you on?" I asked.

It only made me more determined to talk to her. By asking around, I found out that she had two sisters who owned a hair salon in the neighborhood. Half sisters, I should say. They were much older, but neither of them was married or had a family. Instead, the two old crones had recast themselves as protectors of the beautiful Marisela. If I wanted a proper introduction, I would have to go through them. I was not rich or handsome, but I had been saving up for years to go north, and I suppose they saw this as a sign of ambition—something that Marisela's first husband had apparently lacked. They made the introduction, and I was able to court Marisela. This is why I can never complain that we send them money every month, even though we have so little of it ourselves. But now another dead man was troubling my peace, and this time there were no magical stepsisters to save me.

Nora

A day passed, then another. I tried to go back to the routine of ordinary life, but I was unprepared for the brutality with which it greeted me. When I checked my email, I found two rejections, one from the Pacific Music Festival and the other from Banff. The PMF note was boilerplate, but the judges at Banff had written that my composition was "too cerebral" and "didn't quite fit our aesthetic." Every time I tried to parse what this meant, I came up with nothing. I had no idea what the judges were trying to say. What purpose did such criticism serve? I couldn't do anything with it.

For several weeks before my father's death, I had been working on a series of jazz pieces inspired by my first trip to Morocco, when my parents had taken my sister and me to meet their relatives. My great-grandmother was still alive at the time, and we had taken the train from Casablanca to Marrakesh to visit her. We arrived at dusk and, walking through the throngs of food vendors and snake charmers and fortune-tellers on the Jamaat el-Fna, we'd stopped to watch a troupe of acrobats performing. Some of them were teens roughly my age, but others were much younger. All were barefoot and moved with an agility I had never witnessed before. They jumped and cartwheeled and backflipped until, rolling in twos and threes, they landed in a perfect pyramid. We were jostled by the crowd, and my parents and sister moved on, heading toward the north side of the square, but I stayed where I was, transfixed by the pattern of the acrobats' movements. Each boy performed alone, yet in community with the others. It was that moment I was trying to capture in music, years later.

The rejection from Banff wasn't unusual and, in any case, it was for a piece that was still under consideration by several other festivals, but it had found me in a state of such intense grief that it shattered me. All of my insecurities seeped out at once. I hadn't trained at a conservatory, hadn't apprenticed with a renowned soloist, hadn't attracted the attention of a good mentor, hadn't played gigs at the Fillmore or the Blue Note. In the jazz bands or chamber orchestras I'd performed with over the years, I was often the only woman, the odd one out. And I liked to write in different traditions, jazz and classical, which meant that my place in the music world was not quite settled. Perhaps it would never be.

That evening, alone in the cabin, I opened Sibelius on my laptop, and it was as if I were looking at someone else's notations. I couldn't get the judges' words out of my head. My work was too cerebral. Too out there. Too something or other. I don't know how long I sat on that old sofa, an hour or two or three, but the composition stopped exciting me or inspiring me or even making any sense to me. Maybe I needed to get rid of it. Erase it and start over. My cursor was poised over the Delete button when I heard a car pull up the driveway. A moment later, there was a knock at the door.

The sun was setting, and in its orange glow Jeremy's eyes looked green rather than blue. He was in hiking pants and boots, and he jingled his keys nervously. "I was on my way to Hidden Valley," he said, "and I wondered if you wanted to come."

"Now? It's past seven."

"The heat's finally breaking. And there's a full moon tonight."

The sky was the color of a ripe apricot. Soon it would be night, the cabin would be cast in even deeper silence, and I would be alone again, facing my score. Above the swamp cooler the turtledove cooed. We both turned to look. "She's got eggs in there," I said.

"Or he does."

"How can you tell it's a male?"

"I can't, I just know they take turns incubating."

So that was why the nest was never empty. I had begun to wonder how the poor dove fed itself if it was sitting in there all the time. Now it tilted its head sideways and stared at us with curiosity. "Come inside while I get my shoes," I said.

The cabin was barely furnished. The sofa, the chair, the coffee table—these were solid and comfortable, but they held no history and revealed nothing about me. There were no mementoes on the shelves, no family pictures on the wall. I closed Sibelius before Jeremy could ask about my music. "My mom made that," I said when I saw him looking at the ridiculous arrangement of dried flowers above the fireplace. I finished tying my shoelaces and stood up. "I don't know if I have a water bottle," I said, walking to the kitchenette and opening and closing cabinets at random.

"I have one in the car."

"Flashlight?"

"I have that, too."

In the car, I lowered my window and let the wind whip through, its hum a stand-in for conversation. The town lights sparkled in the desert, but once we drove into the national park, darkness wrapped itself around us. In the distance were giant boulders and, everywhere on the plain beneath them, Joshua trees. I had always loved the oaks and pines and redwoods of the Bay Area, with their long and leafy limbs, but I had missed the desert trees: stout, prickly, wild-armed, and yet utterly fragile. It was only after I had left my hometown that I had really taken the full measure of how rare they were.

When we got to Hidden Valley, we found the metal gate locked. A sign said that the trail was closed after sunset. But Jeremy parked the car on the side of the road, got out, and hopped easily over the gate. "You coming?" he called. We started walking. Though the moon was still low in the sky, it was bright enough that there was no need for a flashlight. An owl flew overhead, its wings so quiet that we didn't see the bird until it was ten feet past us.

"It's nice that the park is so quiet," I said.

"That's why I prefer summers here. No tourists, just locals."

"Like me?" I asked with a chuckle.

"Like you."

For a while, we walked in silence, the only sound the crunching of the dirt underneath our shoes. The rhythm of it was calming, and I took a deep breath. The air smelled faintly of sage.

Half a mile down the trail, Jeremy pointed to a boulder formation. "There's a good view from up there."

"Let's see it, then."

He went first, calling out any slippery spots when he came to them, but I matched his pace easily. Somehow my body had retained the memory of scaling these rocks dozens of times as a child. At the top we sat down, our legs stretched before us, and watched the valley beneath. The moonlight silvered the landscape, softening its features in places and in others casting them in harsh angles. It was peaceful, but beneath the silence, I knew, life still pulsed in all its beauty and violence. Bats fed, owls hunted, lizards crawled out of their holes. I wondered whether there would ever be a time when I would be at peace, when my heart would not feel as though lead had been cast inside it. In the past, I had found in music a refuge from my sorrows and disappointments, but now I wasn't sure it could be, not when it could be reduced by a panel of judges to a few dismissive words. "Do you still play music?" I asked.

"No, not since high school. I don't even know where my guitar is. Probably somewhere in my dad's garage."

"Remember when we went on a field trip to see the L.A. Phil?"

"Of course. Senior year."

"It was the first time I'd seen a Frank Gehry building. First time I'd been in a concert hall, even. I sat next to a woman in a satin gown and gloves who kept pointing out to her husband all the people she knew in the audience. She said she was excited to hear Massenet. That the Philharmonic played him too rarely. But afterward she said she didn't like the performance because the conducting had been rebarbative. Rebarbative! It was a word I'd only ever seen in books. I'd never heard anyone say it. I thought everyone in big cities talked like that. I couldn't wait to go to college."

"I remember that day," he said softly. "We ate lunch together."

"We did?" From the way he looked at me, it seemed the moment held some significance, but I couldn't tell what it was. How strange the work of memory, I thought. What some people remembered and others forgot.

After a moment, he asked, "Was Stanford like you thought it would be?"

"Yes and no," I said. Only the buildings were exactly as advertised

in the brochure; everything else about the place was different, beginning with the people. I was the only Arab in my high school, but now
there were people from many different backgrounds in my dorm,
and that made me feel less alone. Still, whenever I opened my mouth,
I singled myself out as a country bumpkin. Once, in freshman comp, I
answered a question about architectural design by talking about the
"bow arts." *Beaux Arts,* my professor corrected with an amused laugh,
the x *is pronounced* z, *and the* t *and the* s *are silent.* It seemed to me I
would never wash off the trace of the countryside from my speech, my
clothes, myself. But eventually I adjusted, and even learned to enjoy
everything the city had to offer. "I'd dreamed about it for so long," I
said, "that it was bound not to be the way I imagined it."

From a cluster of shrubs in the distance came the *rat-a-tat* of a
cactus wren. I glanced over Jeremy's shoulder in the direction of the
sound and when it stopped I saw that his eyes were fixed on me. A
flicker of desire in them. Without knowing why, I wanted to blow it
out. Snuff it before it had a chance to start kindling. "Have you ever
heard of Max Bloemhof?"

"No. Who's he?"

"He wrote a great book about apartheid in South Africa, called
Before Night Comes. Some people think of it as a modern classic. He
also wrote *We Ourselves,* about Northern Ireland. Not as good, but it
was a huge bestseller."

"Wait, I think I know who you're talking about. I saw him on *The
Daily Show* once."

"That's him. I met him at an artists' colony in upstate New York. I
didn't know anyone there, but he sat next to me one night and talked
to me and made me feel at ease. He asked what I was working on, and
then when he heard the chamber piece I'd just finished, he said I was
the most talented musician he'd ever heard at the residency. I guess I
was flattered by his attention. And later, he said I was the love of his
life, that he couldn't live without me." I wrapped my arms around my
knees and rested my chin on them. My throat felt dry.

"But . . ." Jeremy prompted.

"He was married. He said he was already separated, it was a matter of time before he divorced, he had to be careful because of his

kids. But he never broke it off. Three weeks ago, I told him he had to choose. And I guess he did choose, because I haven't heard from him since."

There, it was done. Now he would let go of the past, stop thinking of me as the girl at the ice-cream parlor, or the girl at the concert hall, or whatever other fiction he had spun about me. I stood up and rubbed my hands, dislodging specks of dirt from my palms. When I had climbed up the boulder, I hadn't expected to be talking about Max, and now I suddenly wished I hadn't. Something about Jeremy had made me want to open up—if only to push him away. Eager to put the moment behind me, I began to make my way down.

"Nora, wait."

The sound of his voice made me turn, and I slid down the boulder, scraping my arm in all its length and landing on my knees in the dirt. He called my name again as he climbed down toward me. Holding my arm to the moonlight, he looked at the scrape. "We should go back," he said.

"We're more than halfway through."

He ran his fingers along the scrape, but they came out dry.

"See," I said, trying not to wince. I had come to do this hike and now I wanted to finish it. "Let's just go." Twenty minutes later, we came to the final bend in the loop. A desiccated tree with bone-colored branches sat in a cluster of chuparosa bushes. Instantly I was flooded with memories. "My dad used to bring my sister and me here when we were kids. We'd race to see who could make it to the highest branch." The tree was just as tall as it had been when I was a child, but the desert had stripped its boughs of their moisture and color. "I don't think I've ever seen it at night, though. The branches look so gnarly. Terrifying, really."

"What do you have to be so scared of?"

"Ghosts," I said. "They won't leave me alone."

When I looked up, I found him watching me. He put his hand on my cheek, and after a moment his lips touched mine. How easy it was to lean into him. How good it felt to be wanted. He wrapped his arms around me and drew me so close that we almost lost our balance.

Jeremy

When we got back to the car, I held her arm to the moonlight, and saw that the skin was scraped all the way from her elbow to her wrist. I pulled out my first-aid kit from the trunk and sat on the bumper while I rummaged inside it for disinfectant wipes. The air had cooled; across the road a jackrabbit hopped out of the bushes. I cleaned the scrape quickly, so it wouldn't sting too much, then spread antibiotic ointment on it before covering it with a bandage. "Do you always drive around with a medical kit, rescuing women?" she asked me teasingly.

"I had it here for my last camping trip," I said. "Does it hurt still?"

She shook her head, and her earrings got tangled in her hair again, their silver catching the light. But I could do now what I had been too scared to do at seventeen—I brushed her hair away from her face and untangled the earrings one by one. She was watching me. Her eyes were so dark, her gaze so penetrating, that I felt as if all my secrets were bare to her. Because I had missed my mark in the past and because I wasn't sure I would get another chance, I drew her to me, kissed her again, whispered in her ear. She hesitated, then gave a nod.

I drove out of the park with one hand on the steering wheel and the other on her knee. Moonlight across the windshield. Patsy Cline on the radio. By the time I got to the convenience store, the clerk was getting ready to lock up. "Come on, man," I said. "It'll just take a minute." The clerk shook his head. He was a little man with yellow glasses and thin lips that wanted to yield nothing. I held the sliding door open with my hand and he narrowed his eyes at me. "Sir, step back," he said. "We're closing." The security guard came over—a big guy with tattoos on his neck and scars on his arms. He took one look at me and told the clerk to let me in.

But when I got back to the car with the condoms, she wasn't there. The air was knocked out of me. I really thought she was gone, until I stepped back up to the curb and saw her all the way on the other side of the parking lot. I walked over and stood next to her. "Look," she said, and pointed across the highway at the open desert. A bighorn sheep. I had never seen one this close to town, this far from a herd. I took her hand in mine and waited. The bighorn was grazing in a patch of dry grass, and after a moment it stopped and stared at us. A ram with dark fur and a beautiful set of long, curly horns. Ears that twitched when a car drove past on the highway. Then it turned around and went away at a trot, its hindquarters white and soft like the inside of a cut pear.

The cabin was blistering hot when we came back. Nora turned the swamp cooler back on, opened a window, and went to the kitchen for water. Leaning against the counter, I listened to the hum of the fridge, the ticking of the clock, the clinking of the ice in her glass of water. Wait, I told myself. Give her time. After the air had cooled, after she'd taken off her shoes, after she'd poured another glass of water, I put out my hand and she took it.

And then we were standing by her bed. It wasn't my scars she touched first when I took off my shirt, or the tattoo I'd gotten just before I'd shipped out. It was my eyelids, my brows, my cheekbones, as though she were only seeing the old me. Her fingers were so light. When she slipped off her shirt, I noticed a beauty mark on the swell of her left breast, just above the scalloped line of her bra. It was one of those halter tops and I fumbled like a teenager trying to find the clasp. "It's here," she said and unhooked it from the front.

Whatever awkwardness I felt dissipated when she put her arms around me. My hands found the curves of her breasts, her hips, her thighs. What were ten years? Nothing. A heartbeat. The blink of an eye. We were still at the concert hall, the sunlight was still pouring in through the branches of the magnolia tree, she was still stirring the ice in her soda with a red straw, she was still smiling at me. She hadn't yet been called away to see the show, hadn't yet walked across the stage at graduation and continued walking—out of town, out of my life. That

I lay in bed with her now seemed to me a small miracle. I kissed the base of her throat and slid down, taking her nipples one after the other into my mouth. On her navel was a piercing but no ring, and I kissed the tiny little dot, sliding slowly down. When I tasted her she coiled her fingers into my hair with an urgency that thrilled me. With my eyes closed, I could indulge in the fantasy that all this had happened before and that it would happen again and again. How easy it was to let myself believe this when she guided me into her.

Afterward, she lay in my arms, the heft of her body against mine a comfort I hadn't known I needed. Immediately I felt myself drifting to sleep, but was brought back from the edge of slumber when she went into the bathroom. Minutes passed. From outside came the call of an animal in pain, perhaps a rabbit caught in the wire fence that bordered the backyard. But when I heard the sound again, I realized it was coming from the bathroom. I knocked on the door, but she wouldn't answer. I called her name. Still she wouldn't answer.

Nora

What was it about him that had tempted me? A friend from years ago, barely distinguishable in my memory from others in the high school band, yet so different now that he almost seemed like a new person. But he was a good listener, had sought me out, tried to console me, and perhaps that was all it took. Was this, too, a part of grief? Just as the question formed in my mind, something loosened in my heart, and the tears came. They flowed so fast it was as if a dam had been broken inside me. I muffled the sobs with my hand, but he must have heard me, because there was a knock on the door and a moment later the knob turned and he was inside the bathroom. I bit my lip, though it only made the tears come faster. "It's okay," I managed to say after a minute. "You can go now."

"I'm not going to leave you like this."

For a long while, he stood in the bathroom, holding me. When the tears finally stopped, he got a glass of water from the kitchen and waited for me to drink it. I felt relieved by my outburst, it had been a long time coming, yet embarrassed that it had happened in front of Jeremy. I looked around the bathroom for a shirt or a robe, but there was only a hand towel hanging from the bar on the wall. As if sensing this, he put his arms around me again.

"Why him?" I whispered. "Why?"

"There is no why," he said softly. Then he took my hand and led me back through the mess of discarded clothes and rumpled sheets on the floor. "Come back to bed."

My eyes were swollen, my nose was stuffy, my face flushed. How sexy, I thought. What am I doing here? What is *he* doing here? He should have left by now. But he lay beside me, his fingers tracing circles on my back. There is no why, he'd said. There was no reason, no explanation, no deeper meaning. Just bad luck. I listened to the beating of his heart in his chest. What a fragile thing a heart was. So easy to fool. To break. To stop on impact in a darkened intersection. "There has to be a why," I said.

"Not necessarily." He'd been raised Catholic, he said, and was taught that sin was punished and virtue rewarded. Good things happened to good people, bad things to bad people. Even when his mother died, he'd continued to believe this because another thing he'd been taught was that adversity was a test. But then he went to war, and lost all belief. One minute this guy Sanger was telling him about the kind of roof shingles he wanted for his house back in Jackson Hole and the next he had no hands to wave in the air anymore. "I couldn't understand it. I couldn't figure out why he'd been maimed and I still had my hands, even though I was standing right next to him. That's when I started to realize that some things couldn't be explained. It was just chance. It couldn't be argued with. There's no reason or order to it."

This wasn't enough for me. To believe that my father's death was just an unfortunate accident meant that I would have to forget everything else I knew about my hometown. Discount the arson, erase the small insults, untether the hit-and-run from the time and place in which it happened. I couldn't.

Outside, a mockingbird trilled. "It's getting late," he said. "Try to get some sleep."

But I couldn't sleep, and he held me until the curtain grayed with dawn and the roosters in the neighbor's yard began calling to one another. Then he got up and got dressed and came to say goodbye to me, kneeling by the side of the bed like a man at prayer.

Efraín

I was leaving Kasa Market the following week, my arms weighed down by groceries and my thoughts on the game I wanted to watch once I got home, when Guerrero stuck his foot out and made me trip. I landed in front of the notice board, limes and lemons rolling all around me, chips crumbling to pieces in their bag. I pushed myself up, and there was his picture, on a poster. We stood together, he and I, staring at his likeness and at the number beneath it, so big I didn't need my glasses to read it. Twenty-five thousand dollars. Imagine what you could do with that much money. All you have to do is call. "I'm not going to call," I said, bending down to pick up two limes from beneath the candy rack. By some miracle, the carton of eggs looked undisturbed, but when I opened it to check, I found that one was broken. "See what you made me do?" I asked.

This is nothing, he said with a laugh.

I didn't know if he meant that an egg was nothing or that he could do a lot more to me than make me trip and fall at the grocery store. I thought of asking him bluntly whether he was threatening me, but I was afraid of what he might say in return. I wasn't prepared for a fight. In the end, I ignored him, and continued picking up my groceries from the floor. I had to pull myself together. This was all in my head anyway. I needed to get home to my wife and children, try to go to bed early, get some rest for a change.

Look. This is the detective's name. Write it down.

There was an uneasy stillness in the air. Somewhere in the store, a baby began to wail and could not be comforted by its mother. I gathered all my items and stood up, rubbing soreness from my knees. I was trying to decide if I should go back and tell the cashier that I needed a new carton, or just go home and have Marisela ask me why I couldn't be trusted to bring home six unbroken eggs, when a teenage girl walked past me, giving me a wary look as she stepped out of the store. I had seen that look before, cast on misfits, maniacs, and madmen, warning them to stay away, as if what troubled them was a leprosy, contagious and incurable. Listen, I wanted to tell the girl, I'm not crazy. But the door had already closed behind her.

Write down the detective's name. You can decide later what you want to do.

I put the carton with the broken egg in my grocery bag and left the market. In the parking lot, I noticed a car with a long hood, just like the one that had struck Guerrero—a Ford, it turned out, only this one was blue, instead of silver—and this fresh detail, especially at this particular moment, added to my anger and frustration. I was starting to realize that the more I tried to forget what happened that night on the highway, the more I came across reminders of it.

At home, I didn't eat dinner, ignored the children's pleas to join them in a game, lay on the sofa all evening, watching but not following the fútbol match on the screen. I feared what Marisela would say if I told her what had been happening to me, and yet I was not sure I could keep it to myself, either.

Tell her about the reward. Tell her.

I shook my head no. I had a good notion what my wife would say if I told her about the money. "See?" she would say. "It's a sign that you should call. Tell the police what happened." I had enough voices swirling around in my head as it was.

How daring this Guerrero had become. He had burst into my home, made himself comfortable on the corner chair, inserted himself into a conversation between Marisela and me. It reminded me of the old days, when I was still courting her. Back then, she would often lapse into long silences, her thoughts drifting to her first husband, dead only a year after they were married. Once or twice she even called me by his name—Ernesto. "There are plenty of beautiful girls in Torreón," my cousin Alonso said, staring at my left ear. "Why are you still pining after this one?" But I didn't give up, and look at us now. Twelve years, two kids.

After she put the children to bed, Marisela asked if I wanted to eat dinner now. "I saved you a plate," she said.

"Maybe later. I'm not hungry right now."

She came to sit beside me on the sofa. "Who's winning?"

I hadn't paid attention to the match, and now I couldn't answer. The light from the television screen colored the living room in shades of green and red and blue. Years ago, I had waited out her dead husband. Worn him out until he left. Surely I could do the same with Guerrero.

Coleman

At home, all I heard for the next week was Brandon this or Brandon that. "Brandon thinks the Dodgers suck this year." "Brandon invited me to go to the drive-in on Saturday." "Brandon let me borrow the new *Call of Duty.*" It wasn't much of a conversation, but at least Miles was talking to us now, he wasn't shuttered up in his room all the time. He even volunteered to make waffles for breakfast, with strawberries and whipped cream, which he hadn't done since we'd moved to California. "See?" Ray said as he loaded up the dishwasher afterward. "He just needed a little time to adjust. Like I told you, baby. He's fine." But I was still worried about his grades, so after breakfast that Saturday morning, I told Miles that if he planned to go to the drive-in with Brandon, he had to come to the library with me for a couple of hours. I wanted him to get away from his video games and do a set of problems from the new math workbook we'd bought for him. "Fine," he grumbled, then stared at his phone the whole way to the library. When we got out of the car, he slammed the door so hard I thought it might go off its hinges. "I told you before not to do that," I said.

"You can't tell me what to do."

"Of course, I can. I just did."

"You're not my mom."

This hurt me so much, I could hardly breathe. Miles was an infant when Ray and I met, at a Fourth of July party given by one of my colleagues at Metro, a forensic pathologist who lived in Bethesda, Maryland. I got lost on the way there and by the time I arrived the only seats available in the backyard were next to Sharon from H.R. or next to Ray and the baby. It was an easy choice. The minute I sat down,

Miles raised his chubby little arms up for me to hold him—and I did. Like I said, he was a mama's boy. Later on, I found out that Ray's ex-wife had decided shortly after giving birth that she had no interest in either marriage or motherhood, and had freed herself of both by filing for divorce and moving to Florida. My marriage to Ray hasn't always been easy, either—we've had our share of tough times, especially after we bought our place in D.C. and money was tight for a while—but I've never had any doubt about Miles. He wasn't my blood, but he was mine all the same. The way he smiled just before he made a winning move on the chessboard, that was me. The persistence he showed whenever he tried to solve a puzzle, that was me, too. I saw myself in him every day. Our bond, woven moment by loving moment for thirteen years, was strong. Yet now, glaring at me on the sidewalk, he was trying to break it. I couldn't understand what had caused him to disown me, or why he'd chosen this particular moment to do it. "Why are you saying this?" I asked, my voice dropping to a whisper.

"Because it's true."

"It's not true. Why are you talking like this? What's going on?"

"Nothing."

"Well, something's going on." I put my hand on his cheek and when he raised his eyes to me, I saw that he was fighting tears. My poor, sweet son. "Tell me, baby. What happened?"

"Brandon says we can't go to the movies."

"He said that? When?"

"He just texted me."

"So maybe his plans changed. Why are you so upset? You can go next week."

"No, he's going with Sam."

"Which one is Sam? The one with the red hair?"

He shrugged and got all quiet again. I wondered if this was about race, the other kids were white, but whenever I had seen Miles with Brandon, the two of them seemed to get along well. It's a terrible thing to watch your child suffer, a terrible thing. It made me feel helpless. There was nothing I could do to make my son's pain go away. I couldn't even comfort him with a hug, because we were standing outside the library and it might embarrass him and make things worse between us.

"Tell you what," I said. "Why don't you work on your math, and then Dad will take you to the drive-in tonight? You can get popcorn and those Sour Patch Kids you like so much."

He shrugged.

"Is that a yes? Say yes, it'll be fun."

"Yeah, maybe."

We went inside, found a spot between an old man in a baseball cap reading one of those *Left Behind* books and a teenage girl leafing through brochures for the community college. Miles started a set of problems in his workbook, and I pulled out my laptop. The $25,000 reward that Nora Guerraoui had offered had been announced in the *Hi-Desert Star* and on KDGL three days earlier, and I'd put up posters everywhere I could think of, including the bus stop and the grocery stores, but I didn't have any serious takers yet, just the usual white noise that comes with any announcement of a monetary reward. I wrote another email to Vasco, asking yet again if I could have that recanvass. Someone had to have seen something. I just needed to find them.

By the time we left the library, it was the middle of the afternoon and the air had cooled considerably. The arthritis in my elbow joints flared when the weather changed abruptly like this, and I buttoned my jacket against the wind. I wondered if we might be getting a thunderstorm later, which would mean no movie at the drive-in, and I looked up worriedly at the gray sky. That's when I spotted the security cameras mounted on the eaves of the library building.

Nora

The call from Detective Coleman came while I was in the grocery aisle of the Stater Brothers. I can still recall every detail of that moment. A special on red seedless grapes was blaring from the loudspeaker, a woman was cradling her infant as she bagged navel oranges, two retirees were arguing over how many bananas they should buy, and I was picking out medjool dates. Sweet, chewy, locally produced. They came from palms a USDA botanist brought to the Coachella Valley in the 1920s from the oasis of Boudenib, in Morocco. The trees took root easily in California, and soon an industry developed around them. Now you could walk into any supermarket in the United States and buy dates that once grew only in the shade of the Atlas Mountains. I'd placed two boxes in my shopping cart and was wheeling it toward the leafy greens when my cell phone rang.

I left the cart where it was. Ten minutes later I pulled into the driveway of my parents' house, where I picked up my mother. With the glare of the midday sun scrambling the road before me like a Hockney collage, I drove down the 62 toward the police station. A helicopter droned in the sky, heading toward the Marine base. "You're going too fast," my mother said, reaching for the handle above her window. Only then did I notice that my knuckles had whitened from gripping the steering wheel. I lifted my foot off the pedal. We passed a string of motels and fast-food joints, a tall crane on which a man in uniform was doing some work, and finally the stretch of trendy boutiques and organic restaurants that made up the town of Joshua Tree. The police station was just a couple of miles past Park Boulevard, in an orange and white building next to the courthouse.

At the station, Detective Coleman walked us through the main office, where deputies, some in uniform and others in plainclothes, sat at their cubicles. From somewhere came the sound of a printer jamming, people talking, a phone ringing—all the ordinary signs of a workplace on a Tuesday morning. And yet I felt my skin break into goose bumps, as though I were someplace alien or dangerous. The room was small, and the window shade hung sideways, casting a slanted light over the furniture. Four chairs were arranged around a table that was covered with round tracks left behind by cups and glasses. "Would you like some coffee? Or maybe some water?" the detective asked us.

"No, thanks," I said.

"Water," my mother said.

For heaven's sake, this wasn't a social call. But I held back from saying anything because it would only cause further delays. Detective Coleman walked out and returned a moment later with a cup of water. "Please," I said. "Just tell us who it is."

Coleman put a manila file folder on the table and sat down. "The driver of the vehicle that struck your father was Anderson Baker. He's given us a full statement and turned in the keys to his car. It's a silver Ford Crown Vic, 1992 model."

"Wait. Anderson Baker, who owns the bowling alley?"

"Yes."

I turned to my mother, who sat slumped in her chair with her hand over her mouth. When she drew her breath again, she spoke at a clipped pace, her voice full of frustration at her pronunciation, which always got worse when she became emotional. "That man was always trying to start trouble. He said our customers took up all the parking spots and he didn't have any spaces left for his business. My husband bought the special signs, you know, with the name on them . . ."

"Custom parking signs," I offered.

"Right. But the tourists coming from Joshua Tree, they don't pay attention. They just park wherever they can. So Baker was angry."

I knew about the trouble with Baker only in the broadest of terms. One of the things I had been relieved about when I left home at eighteen was that I didn't need to hear about the family business—no more talk of shift schedules, food orders, late deliveries, trash pickup, or sewer-line repairs. When I spoke on the phone with my father, I didn't ask him about his restaurant, and if he mentioned it, it was usually in connection with some new idea he wanted to try, like these custom parking signs. The lot had twenty-three spaces, thirteen of which belonged to the Pantry and ten to Desert Bowling Arcade. The custom signs were meant to clear up any ambiguity about space, but obviously that hadn't worked. I turned to Coleman. "What my mom is trying to say is, this is premeditated."

"I understand what she's saying," Coleman said levelly. She opened the manila file folder on the table. "In his affidavit, Mr. Baker states that it was very dark out that night and there is no signal light at the intersection of Highway 62 and Chemehuevi Way. He said he didn't know it was your father he'd hit until he read about it in the newspaper."

"Who did he think he hit?"

"A coyote."

"So he left my father out to die?" I asked. "If it was just an accident," I said, my voice rising, "then why didn't he turn himself in right away? Why did he wait until you found him?"

"He said he was worried about losing his license. He lives all the way out in Landers and he needs his car to get to his place of business."

"That's a load of bullshit." I couldn't tell if Coleman believed Baker's lies; she gave no verbal hint of her views, and her face retained the careful composure of an experienced investigator. After a moment, I asked, "What are you charging him with?"

"The D.A. makes that decision."

"Okay. But what are the charges?"

"Felony hit-and-run."

"That's it? He killed my dad." The words came out in a helpless croak. It seemed to me as if the past I had left behind years ago had suddenly come crowding up against me and might choke me if I wasn't careful. "Do you know," I said, "I went to high school with Baker's son, Anderson Junior. A.J., everyone called him. Nasty kid. One time he wrote *raghead* on my locker."

My mother turned to me. "When?"

"Sophomore year."

"You never told me."

"What would you have done if I had told you?"

Across the table Coleman shifted in her seat. With her thumbnail, she scratched at the scar on her eyebrow. It was an old wound, but the skin still looked pink in places. "I'm sorry," she said, her voice completely different now, "but what happened to you in high school is probably not relevant to this hit-and-run case."

"What *is* relevant? The fact that Baker was fighting with my dad?"

"How long has this dispute been going on?" Coleman asked.

I waited for my mother to answer. The truth was, there hadn't always been a dispute, or whatever it was Coleman wanted to call it. There was a time when we got along. In 2002, when my father had just bought the Pantry, I had gone into the bowling alley with him to meet Anderson Baker. It was just a little after dusk, but already half of the lanes were taken and it seemed they were getting ready for a busy night. Baker was talking to the cash-register clerk, but he turned around when we came in and smiled and shook hands with my father. He had been cordial, then. Distant, but cordial. There had been some talk early on about having food orders delivered to the arcade, but that had never led anywhere and the two businesses kept to themselves. All that changed a few years later.

"Since we expanded the restaurant," my mother said quietly.

"What happened was," I said, "a writer for *Los Angeles Magazine* came out here to do a feature about Joshua Tree, and she included the Pantry in her write-up. The article had a picture of my dad pouring coffee for a customer, and the restaurant quickly got popular with tourists. My dad ended up buying the little dry cleaner's shop next door, and he got the three parking spaces that came with it, too. I guess that's when the trouble with Baker started. Right, Mom? When he expanded."

"All right," Coleman said, "I will look into it. But I should also mention that Mr. Baker made no attempt to fix the dent on his car, which is consistent with his contention that it was just an accident."

"It was no accident. You heard what my mom said."

"I will look into it," Coleman said again, closing her file folder.

"Did any witnesses come forward?"

"I'm afraid not."

"Can I ask you something about the investigation?"

"Sure."

"How did you find out it was Baker?"

"I told you about my son?"

"Yes. Miles, right?"

"That's right. I was at the library with him on Saturday, helping him with his math homework, and I noticed their security cameras. The accident took place at the intersection of Highway 62 and Cheme-huevi, but the location of the body suggests that the driver took a left turn. If he did that, he would've had the option of making a right on Martinez Trail, which runs parallel to the highway and sometimes can be faster. It's a popular shortcut. But he would've been captured on the library's cameras. Only twenty-eight cars drove by between nine thirty and ten thirty p.m. And just three were silver Fords. It was a matter of checking out each one."

"So he would've gotten away with it if he hadn't taken a shortcut?"

"But he did," Coleman said. "And now we have a confession."

"All right," I said. "Thank you so much, Detective Coleman. Thank you."

I followed my mother out of the police station. Neither of us spoke. I was trying to put a name to the feeling that filled my heart now that the driver had been identified, but I found that I couldn't. It wasn't relief, though there was some of that. It wasn't closure, though there was some of that, too. It was a different kind of pain. Outside, the mid-day sun beat down with such force that a wisp of steam rose from the pavement. I called my sister to tell her what we had just learned, but she didn't pick up. I left her a voicemail asking her to please call me, that I had some news.

As I drove my mother home, I reviewed everything the detective had said about the murder. That's how I thought of it now, as a mur-der. I had feared all along that it would be, and it came to me then that what had made me linger in town past the funeral wasn't just the fog of grief, it was the presentiment that my father had been killed in cold blood.

"Red light," my mother warned. "Slow down."

"Sorry," I said as I came to an abrupt stop. I turned to look at my mother. "Did something happen recently with Baker?"

"What do you mean?"

"I mean, something that could have prompted this. They'd been arguing about something or other since Dad expanded, right? So why now?"

My mother thought for a minute. "There was the thing with the Land Rover."

"What thing with the Land Rover?"

"Green light."

The story came out in pieces and it took two or three tellings for all of its details to settle into place. Afterward, I pulled into the driveway of my parents' house. My childhood home, with its little porch and its overgrown sage bush and the screen that never quite fit into the doorjamb. For the first time since I'd heard that my father was dead, my mind began to function again. The aimless fury that had trailed me since I'd left town at eighteen had found a purpose: I would make sure that Anderson Baker was brought to justice. I just wasn't sure how yet.

Driss

I remember that the park rangers had to put up a sign on the highway warning visitors that campsites at Joshua Tree were booked. The town was packed with hikers, bike riders, families from Los Angeles and San Diego who wanted out of the big city for Presidents' Day weekend. Business had been a little slow that winter, so I was thrilled to see several parties waiting at the Pantry, spilling out from the entrance onto the sidewalk. A young woman in a bohemian shirt came in to ask if she could order a mimosa while she waited. Not for the first time, I wondered whether I should apply for an alcohol license, try to appeal to the kind of people who had been coming to the Mojave lately. I was working the cash register when Anderson Baker burst in. "Who here has a Land Rover Defender?" he asked. "It's in one of my spots."

"Just a minute," I said. I was making change for an elderly couple, both of them after-church regulars. When I was counting money, I couldn't talk, and Baker's interruption forced me to put the bills back in the register and start over.

"It's double-parked. It's taking up two spaces." He raised his fingers in a V, as if I didn't know what "double-parked" meant.

"Just a minute," I said again. I counted out the change and handed it to the couple, slamming the register drawer closed with my hip. "Thank you."

The couple stepped away, and Baker took their place. "Whose Land Rover is that?"

I craned my neck to look beyond his shoulder at the parking lot.

From where I stood, I could see only an old, dusty Buick and a blue truck covered with colorful stickers. A parking spot in the corner was still open, and anyway the bowling alley never got busy until after lunch. Before I could say anything, though, he snapped, "Well? Don't just stand there. Find out."

I didn't know what had set him off like this. Of course, we'd had disagreements in the past, but they'd been about serious things, like the noise during the remodeling I'd done a while back, or the smell from the sewer line that broke under the bathrooms of his arcade. Now he was upset about a parking space. His face turned pink as he glared at me, waiting for me to fix a problem I'd had no part in creating. "All right," I said, trying to calm him down. "Let me find out."

I picked up a pitcher of water and went to the first table—a family of four, still in hiking clothes, still smelling of campfire smoke. I refilled their glasses, asked how their chicken-fried steaks tasted, and whether they happened to drive a Land Rover. Then I moved on to the next table. But Baker wouldn't wait, he pushed past me into the middle of the diner, all six feet of him occupying the center aisle, and in a radio announcer's voice, he boomed, "Land Rover Defender. Gunmetal gray. Come move it now or I'll have it towed." Silence descended on the restaurant. Everyone looked up, but no one claimed the Land Rover. So Baker stormed out, leaving me to apologize, to bring extra crayons for the children and refill breadbaskets for the adults.

Our relationship had already become touchy, but that morning's argument turned it raw. Now I had to be watchful about everything: what parking spaces my customers used, how long the delivery truck sat idling when it brought soft drinks, whether the cook smoked cigarettes too close to the dumpster. I had the feeling that I was being watched constantly, that the slightest misstep on my part would cause another eruption. What could I do with a neighbor like that? How could I prevent him from finding fault when fault was all he was looking for?

These questions were so unsettling that I put them aside. Maybe I was letting what happened with the Land Rover blind me. Baker and I had been neighbors for a very long time, after all, and when a freak storm three years earlier had left debris all over the street, we'd worked together to clean it up. This was just a rough patch. Besides, he was getting old, which meant that sooner or later he would have to retire. I needed to keep all this in perspective. Be patient, I told myself. Be patient. Things will get better.

Nora

The charge against Anderson Baker was formally filed on a clear morning in May, with the air still crisp from a recent thunderstorm and the mountains in the distance outlined like a woodcut print. I drove to the arraignment at the Morongo Basin Courthouse in a state of febrile anticipation that was only heightened when, passing through the metal detector, I was pulled aside for a random pat-down. It had started years ago, this experience, and it was unavoidable. It didn't matter if it was a state-of-the-art machine at San Francisco International Airport or some rinky-dink contraption at a sports arena in Kern County, I was always pulled aside for the random pat-down. The local courthouse was no different. My mother had already gone through the process and was waiting for me on the other side. "Where's Salma?" I asked her as we embraced.

"In clinic."

"But this is very important. Couldn't she have rescheduled?"

"I don't know."

"Can you call her? It's only nine thirty. If she leaves now, she can still make it."

My mother hesitated. The argument between my sister and me at the children's school play had mortified her and she seemed reluctant to risk getting into another one here, at the courthouse. She didn't reply. Instead, she looked at the wall screen that showed the cases on the docket that day. "There," she said. "*Baker.* Courtroom M-2."

When we walked in, the only seats left were in the last row of pews. How strange, I thought, that the courtroom had pews. They gave the gallery a patrician air, but this impression was tempered by the white grid ceiling, which would not have looked out of place in an industrial warehouse. The room was windowless and brightly lit and, although there were attorneys and bailiffs and an audience, it was eerily quiet. The judge was already at the bench, shuffling papers, waiting for one defendant to be taken out and another brought in.

The old man who sat next to me looked up suddenly as a boy in a gray T-shirt was called up on a possession charge. The boy came forward, shoulders hunched, his arms white and skinny, a look of bewilderment on his face. The charges were read, and bail was set at $5,000. Most of the cases that morning were like this. Pot. Crystal meth. Sometimes heroin. Skirmishes in the endless war on drugs. I couldn't shake the feeling that my father's murder was buried under a rubble of cases that properly belonged elsewhere.

It was past eleven when Anderson Baker was finally brought into the courtroom. He was so tall—six foot three, six foot four—that I had no trouble seeing him from the last row. In a white linen shirt and beige pants, he looked as though he had spent the night at a wedding in Palm Springs and was just now coming home, no worse for the wear. He turned around and scanned the courtroom, his eyes settling on someone seated in the first row across the aisle. Mrs. Baker. A tall, thin woman, all sharp edges. On her lap was a sleeping girl, perhaps three or four years old, with a full head of blond curls. A granddaughter, presumably. And next to Mrs. Baker was A.J., her son. High school star wrestler, popular kid, vicious bully. He had gotten into some college out in Orange County, I couldn't remember which, and lived in the area. Now here he was, providing moral support to his father. On the other side of A.J. was a young brunette, probably his wife, and in the row behind her sat two middle-aged men I recognized as maintenance workers at Desert Bowling Arcade.

I began to realize how unprepared I was for this day in court. It hadn't even occurred to me to tell anyone at my father's restaurant about the arraignment, or to ask if they might like to come to court with us. Again, I felt a surge of irritation at my sister for not canceling her clinic appointments that morning. It was as if she were trying to send me a message: *You deal with this. I've done enough.* I knew, of course, that she was still angry about the life insurance money, but of all the ways to make a statement about it, she'd chosen the most hurtful to me, and the most damaging to the case. Because why would anyone care about a dead man if the only people present at the hearing were his wife and daughter? And how could anyone believe that someone like Baker was capable of premeditated killing when all his friends and family, the little girl and the pretty brunette included, were there for him?

Baker turned back to face the judge as the charge was read: one count of felony hit-and-run resulting in injury or death. "Do you have a lawyer, Mr. Baker?" the judge asked him.

"Caroline Perry, Your Honor."

"Mr. Baker, how do you plead?"

"Not guilty."

I had read somewhere that most defendants entered not guilty pleas at arraignments, so this answer was to be expected, but I worried that the presence in the courtroom of so many people who supported Baker gave additional credibility to his plea. The judge rested his chin on the heel of his hand and waited for the lawyer to speak.

"Your Honor," Caroline Perry began, "my client has no criminal record." The ease with which she spoke to the judge suggested that she knew him or had argued cases before him in the past. In just a few broad strokes, she drew a flattering portrait of the man standing beside her: Anderson Baker was a business owner with strong ties to the community; he was a native of the Mojave whose family all lived within a few miles of one another; he was seventy-eight years old and had owned a home here for forty-five of those years; and he was a veteran of the Vietnam War. "Your Honor, this accident was very unfortunate, but the evidence will show that my client believed he hit a wild animal; he had no knowledge that he hit a human being. This was a tragic mistake, not a crime."

Was this a harbinger of what would happen when the case went to trial? The jury would be hearing two stories about what happened on the night of April 28, one told by the prosecutor and one told by the defense attorney. It didn't really matter which one was true, it only mattered which one the jury found more convincing. And I could already see that Baker's attorney was a good storyteller. She could neither retract Baker's confession nor deny the overwhelming physical evidence—the extent of my father's injuries, the paint chips recovered by the forensics team, the three-foot dent on the Crown Vic. So she had chosen to focus on awareness: Baker didn't *know* he had killed a man.

But a coyote weighed, what, thirty or forty pounds? How could Anderson Baker have possibly mistaken the impact of a small animal for that of a hundred-and-seventy-pound man? The case seemed so clear-cut to me that I had to swallow the protest that was rising in my throat, and wait for the prosecutor to speak.

The assistant D.A. was a small, chubby man by the name of Thomas J. Frazier (the J. stood for Jefferson). He seemed to be in his early thirties, and either new to his job or completely overworked, because he had to sort through his papers for a few excruciating minutes before he was ready to address the judge. "Your Honor, given the age of the defendant, the state is not opposed to bail."

"All right. Bail is set at $10,000."

I turned to my mother in disbelief. "Mom, I think that's it. It's over."

"What do you mean, it's over?"

"I mean, it's done. He can post bail and be out before dinner."

"He'll be free?"

Free, yes. I buried my face in my hands. Perhaps if I had done a better job of explaining to Coleman and the D.A. the threat that Anderson Baker posed to my father, we might have seen a more serious charge. Or if Salma had come today and brought the twins with her, the outcome of the bond hearing might have been a little different. I was overwhelmed with the feeling that I had failed my father somehow. He hadn't even been mentioned in the proceedings; the focus had been on Baker's history and Baker's service and Baker's family, and so he'd received the benefit of the doubt. But if the roles had been reversed on the night of April 28, and Mohammed Driss Guerraoui had killed a man he'd been fighting with for many years, would he have been charged only with a count of hit-and-run? Would the D.A. have so readily agreed to bail? Growing up in this town, I had long ago learned that the savagery of a man named Mohammed was rarely questioned, but his humanity always had to be proven.

"We should go," my mother said.

All around us people were shuffling in and out of seats. I stood up as if in a daze and followed my mother through the swinging doors. In spite of the air conditioning, the place felt hot. The hallway was loud and crowded and as I stepped aside to let someone through to the courtroom I found myself face to face with A.J. He looked the same as he had in high school, tall and blond, except that his face had filled out over the last ten years. In his crisp black suit and red tie, he could have passed for a businessman who had come here for a minor transgression, a traffic-ticket challenge or a hunting-permit violation, but the effect was contradicted by the presence of his mother, who carried the sleeping toddler in her arms, and the young woman who was rummaging through her purse. "A.J., honey," she said, "I can't find my keys."

But A.J. didn't hear her; he was staring at me. Then he detached himself from the group and crossed the hallway. "Nora," he called.

Jeremy

"So what did you say?" I asked. I was leaning against the kitchen counter, watching her stir a stew in the pot. Three silver bracelets jingled on her wrist with each turn of the wooden spoon. She was still in the white blouse and gray pants she'd worn that morning to court and her hair was tied in a bun. Such a different look on her. So formal. Severe, even. I'd wanted to take her to dinner that night, but she said she wasn't in a mood to go out, and suggested that we eat here, in the cabin.

"Nothing," she said. "I just stood there like an idiot. I was petrified. You remember what A.J. was like." She told me about the slur he'd written in blue marker on her locker. The principal had made him wash it off and apologize, but didn't suspend him; the school's wrestling team was competing that weekend.

The strange thing was that I could barely remember this particular incident; it had happened the year I'd lost my mother, when school was little more than a blur. The memories I had of Nora were from a later time. They were like little treasures I'd saved up in a box: how her skirt hiked up her legs when she sat down at the piano in music class; how she'd throw her head back and laugh when she and Sonya were at the ice-cream parlor together; that time she'd stood under my umbrella, her hair spilling over my arm while we waited for the school bus to take us to Big Bear Lake.

"And he wrote it without the second *a*," she said. "He couldn't even spell *raghead*."

It was a word I'd heard nearly every day when I was in Iraq. Hell, I'd used it myself. Around the chow table that kind of talk was common. Hajji. Camel jockey. Dune coon. Ali Baba. One guy in my platoon even called Iraqis monkeys and savages. Back then I had thought of this behavior, if I'd thought of it at all, as part of the war: we had to dehumanize the enemy in order to fight it. But now, hearing her talk about the slur on her locker, I felt shame overtake me, followed by a private rebellion. This wasn't the same thing, and I sure as hell wasn't like A.J. "I'm sorry," I said, touching her elbow, where the scrape from the other night had scabbed.

"I remember we had health class together once," she said. "The teacher was talking about genital warts and A.J. said, 'My mom gets them all the time.' I was kind of stunned, so I turned to look at him. He pointed to the corner of his mouth. 'She gets them right here,' he said. I laughed—I couldn't help it—I laughed. I said, 'That's not what genital means.' After that, he hated me even more. And then a few days after 9/11, he defaced my locker."

A memory surfaced. "He used to call me Jabba," I said.

"Jabba?"

"Like Jabba the Hut. Because I was fat." Even at a distance of many years, the insult still stung. I could still hear A.J.'s voice behind me in algebra class. *Hohohoho Jabba Jabba.*

"That's awful," she said. She turned the heat off and served the meat, potatoes, and carrots on a single plate.

"You're not eating?"

"I already had something, I'm not hungry." Carefully, she spooned the tomato sauce on top of the meat and set the plate on the table for me.

"Will you sit with me, then?"

She took the chair across from me and watched me eat. The sauce tasted familiar and yet different at the same time. I detected paprika, which I knew well enough, but also cumin, parsley, coriander. The meat was tender and came easily off the bone. "Amazing," I said. "You're a great cook."

"I like your optimism."

"Yeah?" I reached for her hand and kissed her palm.

"I didn't make it," she said with a smile. "I can't cook. Not anything like this, anyway. My mom made it. I had lunch with her after the hearing and she sent me home with more food."

"Well, it's tasty either way."

She took my fork and tried some of the stew for herself. "It *is* amazing. She should've been the one who started a restaurant." She handed me back the fork and rested her chin on her hand, once again lost in thoughts about the court hearing. "I can't believe I just stood there, speechless, while A.J. said how sorry he was for my loss and how this was just a tragic accident. That's what he called it, 'tragic.' And when he offered me his hand, I shook it. As if nothing had happened. As if he weren't on his way to bail out his father." Her eyes were dark and probing. With her hair wound in a tight bun like that, she could have passed for an officer of the court—a prosecutor or a defense attorney. "Meanwhile, his father is still trying to make it look like it was a random mistake. Like he just happened to run over and kill the man he'd been fighting with."

"You really think it was murder?"

"I know it was. I know it in my bones. And now he's out on bail. He could go out and do it all over again."

The image of Fierro at West Valley came to me suddenly. How eager he had been to leave the jail, how he hadn't even bothered to shake hands with me before he was out through the double doors. A strange uneasiness settled on me. I wiped my mouth with my napkin.

"You were right about Coleman, though. She's a good cop."

I gave a quick nod and went to the sink to wash my plate, looking out of the window at the backyard as I dried it. It was the third week of May; the days had grown long. In the yucca shrub beneath the window, bumblebees drunk on nectar flung themselves into new blooms. "Want to take a walk?" I asked.

"Sure. Let me change out of this, though."

When she came back, she was in a blue sundress, flat-heeled sandals, and all her jewelry was gone, save the necklace her father had given her. This was more like her, I thought, taking her hand. We walked the mile from the cabin to the main road. At the corner market, we bought fresh grapes and ate them on the way back. An old man walked by with his dog, touching the brim of his hat with a finger when he passed us. Two joggers ran on the other side of the road, kicking up dust in their wake.

It was dark by the time we returned to the cabin. The crickets had begun to sing. Under the pale halo of the porch light, one of the turtledoves was feeding its chicks. We watched it drop seeds into one hungry mouth, while the other called out for its share. The moonlight glinted off the wind chime that hung from the eaves. I kissed the back of her neck and took out the pins one by one from her hair, letting it fall about her shoulders.

I woke late the next morning, so late that for a minute I didn't know where I was. Then I saw her curled up beside me and closed my eyes again. It was a Friday; I had the day off. Ordinarily, I would have gone to the gym, done my laundry, run some errands, but now I lay next to her, in rumpled sheets that still smelled of sex, and waited until she stirred and seemed about to wake. In the kitchen I started the coffee and picked out a mug—YUCCA VALLEY LIBRARY, it said in yellow lettering. My family had once owned a set of these; my mom had bought them at a fundraiser.

"Morning," Nora said. She went to the swamp cooler and turned the dial up. "I can't believe how stuffy it feels already."

I added a drop of milk to the coffee I'd just poured myself and gave it to her, then pulled another mug from the cupboard. "It's not that hot," I said. "You just need new filter pads on that cooler." I sipped from my coffee and watched her. She was in a yellow tank top and black shorts, stretching and muffling a yawn. It still didn't seem real, us together like this. Like something I might have dreamed up when I was a kid. Even the order of things was different. "I can change them for you," I said after a minute.

"Don't worry about it."

"It's easy. It takes, like, thirty minutes."

"I'm sure you have better things to do."

"I really don't mind."

While she showered, I drove to the store to pick up new filter pads. It was a simple chore, I'd done it many times before. But this swamp cooler was a little more difficult because I had to work around the turtledove's nest, all while she—or was it he?—hovered worriedly around me. I unscrewed the panels and pulled out the pads; they were filled with dust, sand, and pollen. The metal braces that held them in place were old and rusty, but I managed to ease out the pads. By then the sun was fully out; I could feel beads of sweat traveling down my spine. With a brush I cleaned the trays, leaving a trail of dirt on the ground. Then I slid the new pads into place, the braces closing around them with a satisfying click.

I called to her to turn the cooler on and was glad to hear the motor starting with a roar. After tossing the old pads in the trash bins, I went back inside. I found her standing across from the vent, eyes closed and arms wide open, enjoying the cool air. "I might not move from this spot," she said. Her hair was down on her shoulders, the way I liked it, and under her white shirt her nipples looked brown and hard. In three quick steps I reached her and, with my hands still dark with dirt, drew her to me.

A.J.

Running a bowling alley means having to worry about two things. There's the mechanical part—the pinsetter machines, the sweeping bars, the ball returns—and then there's the people part. By far the hardest part of the job is dealing with people. I don't mean the staff. We had some good employees at Desert Arcade, including one guy who'd been with us since my dad opened for business in the 1970s. I mean the customers: parents who allowed their kids to wander down the lanes, idiots who pitched a second ball when the first one didn't come back, league bowlers who threw a fit when they didn't score a perfect game. The challenge was dealing with all of them without losing my temper or my smile. It was a struggle sometimes. But I had to help out my dad, who was seventy-eight years old and had trouble keeping up with his business.

Both of my parents were old. In fact, they'd given up trying to have a baby by the time I was born. My mom was forty-four when she had me, my dad forty-nine. It was a miracle, they said, having their prayers answered after so many years. Every miracle has a cost, though, that's what I've come to learn, and it's not always paid by those who owe it. When I was a little boy, people would stop my dad and me at the community park or the grocery store just to tell him how cute his grandson looked. "Look at those blond curls," they'd marvel. He would always correct them. "That's my son," he would say. At some point, he got tired of it. He stopped holding my hand when we went out, so it wouldn't invite questions or comments from total strangers. It was easier for him, I guess. Not for me.

My mom, on the other hand, she never cared what other people thought. Even though her age kept her out of the PTA's social circles, she volunteered in the school cafeteria at lunch and helped organize the Halloween carnival every year. We spent a lot of time together, especially on weekends when my dad was at the bowling alley for fourteen hours straight. I get my love of dogs from her. She's always had dogs, sometimes four or five at a time, all of them sable-and-white rough collies. They're a fantastic breed—smart, trainable, extremely devoted. When I was in middle school, my mom started breeding them and entering them in dog shows all over California. She and I would drive hundreds of miles to compete with one of them, and I got to see a lot of the state that way.

You'd think that spending so much time with my mom would have made it easier for me to talk to girls, but it didn't. My mom was old and plain and agreeable, and the girls at my school were young and pretty and looking for trouble. Whenever I tried to impress them, it backfired. They'd roll their eyes or laugh. Do you know what it does to a boy when a girl laughs at him? Every time it happened, I tried to think of something clever to say, but that only made it worse. And I really hated that everyone called me A.J., which wasn't my name, it was just a nickname that a teacher had given me in kindergarten, and somehow it stuck, even with my family. I spent most of my time with my dogs. They were less complicated than people.

Everything changed in freshman year. I'd always been a skinny kid, but I was pretty strong and flexible, and during tryouts Coach Johnson saw something in me. Natural ability, you could say. He put me on the wrestling team. There were fifteen of us across five weight classes, and already ranked second in the county even before I joined. What appealed to me about wrestling was the simplicity of it—you didn't kick a ball or use a racket or wear elaborate gear, and you didn't depend on someone else to help you score a point. You relied only on yourself, on your own ability. I fell in love with wrestling. Unless I was sitting in class or taking care of my dogs, I was training at the gym.

Coach Johnson taught me a lot, maybe more than anyone has ever taught me before or since. "Remember," he would say, "what you practice on the mat has to be practiced off the mat. Focus. Speed. Opportunity. FSO. You've got to be watchful, quick, and seize any chance you get, because life will rarely give you a second shot." We won all our matches that season, and got a statewide ranking for the first time in our school's history. Between my training, my diet, and the fact that I grew a foot during that year, I looked amazing. It sounds conceited to say it, but I don't know how else to put it: I looked amazing.

By the time I started sophomore year, it was the girls who tried to impress me, by decorating my locker or making playlists for my training runs. One day in biology, Mrs. Barron asked us to split into small groups for a new project she had for us, an illustrated booklet on cellular respiration. I hated group projects because of that awkward moment when everyone chose their friends and I was left scrambling for a partner. But right away someone tapped my shoulder. It was Neil Gilbert, a lame kid with oozing acne on his face. My secret nickname for him was Crater Face. "Wanna do the booklet together, A.J.?" he asked.

"I'm already doing it with Stacey," I said, and turned back and winked at Stacey Briggs. That was another thing about being on the wrestling team: it had given me some confidence.

"Yeah, we're working together," Stacey said, flashing me a smile. She wasn't quite as pretty as Maddie Clarke, the girl everyone had a crush on, but she had a great personality and was always up for anything. I used to call her Energizer Stacey. She lived up to it, too, because she did all the writing for the project. She made up a cast of characters for the story, like Hermione the Human, Petunia the Plant, Ginny the Glucose, Moaning Myrtle the Mitochondria, and I penciled all the illustrations and inked them in full color. It took me a week, but our project booklet looked like a graphic novel.

I spent a lot of time at Stacey's apartment because her parents were out of the picture and her brother Lee didn't mind that she brought me home. He liked that I was on the wrestling team, said that wrestling was part of Greek and Roman culture. "It's a civilized sport," he said as he stretched his legs on the coffee table, "not like some of that savage stuff you see nowadays." He was watching *Falling Down* on television. It was an early scene, when Michael Douglas walks into a convenience store to ask for change so he can make a phone call to his daughter, but the Korean clerk wants him to buy something first.

"Why doesn't that guy just give him the change?" Stacey asked as she sat down on the couch next to her brother.

"Because all they care about is money," Lee told her. "You kids want some popcorn?"

"Not me," I said.

"Oh, right. You can't eat junk food." And he went to the fridge and found me some carrots to munch on while we watched the movie.

It was nice to be around an adult who wasn't in AARP for a change, someone who didn't mind doing fun things with me. Sometimes, Lee would take us to concerts in Palm Springs or Riverside or even farther than that, in Orange County. Stacey and I broke up during senior year, but Lee Briggs and I remained friendly. He'd teach me things about Western culture, things I didn't learn in school, which was pretty neat. When I got to college in Fullerton, I even considered majoring in Classics, but the school closed down the department because of the state's budget cuts. It was a bullshit excuse, of course, because they didn't cut Asian-American studies or African-American studies or even Chicano studies. So I ended up majoring in business administration.

It worked out well, in the end, because I started my own business in Irvine. I would have stayed there for good if things had been different, but my mom had Parkinson's disease and, even though I tried to visit every Sunday, I knew the time would come when I would have to move back home. Her tremors were getting worse; she needed someone to help her with basic things like cooking and cleaning. And my dad, too, he needed help with his business, because he didn't have as many people working for him anymore. I was married by then and it wasn't easy convincing Annette to live in the middle of the desert. But that's what we do for family.

Moving back was a big adjustment. If you liked hiking and rock climbing, or if you were into weird art installations that popped up in the middle of nowhere, then this place was fine. But for someone like me, there were no driving ranges or department stores or even a decent multiplex. After a long day of work at the bowling alley, I still had energy I wanted to burn, and there were no wrestling gyms in town. There was so little to do, really. Which was why I was so surprised to see Nora Guerraoui here. Growing up in this place, all any of us ever wanted was to leave, and yet we both ended up coming back. I would never have guessed it.

Nora

It fell to me, then, to show that what happened on April 28 was not an accident. In order to trace a motive, I had to go back in time, not only to events that preceded that night, but to the very beginning, when my father bought the Pantry. The restaurant had been built in 1951, on land that belonged to Chemehuevi Indians, by Bill and Prudence Swenson, a pair of homesteaders from Corona. At the time, it was little more than a hamburger stand, serving travelers on their way to or from the Marine base that had recently opened in Twentynine Palms. But as the town grew, so did demand for places to eat. The Swensons added a few more items to the menu, built a full kitchen and dining area, and cleared the Joshua trees on the northern side of the building for a parking lot. Over the years, new businesses opened up all around them: Baker's bowling alley and Oglesby's dry cleaner next door, Kinney's tire shop and Linden's beauty salon across the highway. I don't think it's an exaggeration to say that when my father bought the restaurant from the retiring Swensons, he stood out like a tall weed in a clipped hedge. And perhaps he knew it, because he made himself small, and tried his best to keep the place exactly as it had been for decades.

But there came a time when he had to expand the dining room and update the kitchen appliances, and although this had been good for his business, it had led to tensions with Anderson Baker. When I pulled up to the restaurant's parking lot that morning, I noticed another change my father had made just before he died. He'd put up a huge new sign on the roof. You could see it from down the block. Was this what had triggered Baker's bout of anger? The sudden prominence? Yet my mother hadn't mentioned the sign when I'd asked her about recent disagreements. The only incident she'd pointed to was the fight about parking spaces a few weeks earlier, during Presidents' Day weekend.

Walking into the Pantry, I found Marty at the cash register, feeding a new roll of paper into the printer. At the sound of the door jingle, he looked up. "Morning, miss," he said. Even though I'd often told him to just call me by my first name, he always insisted on calling me Miss. He was attached to formalities like that.

"Morning. Everything okay today?" I asked, trying to sound assertive, yet cruelly aware of the inexperience in my voice.

"Everything's fine, miss."

"Great." I walked past him and took a seat at the counter. On the stool next to me, someone had left behind a copy of the *Los Angeles Times,* and I picked it up. The top stories were a fire in Angeles National Forest and the death at fifty-seven of a baseball star whose name I didn't recognize. Below the fold was news of a failed attempt at land preservation in the Mojave, and of a bomb attack in Syria that had left twenty-three people dead. I made a mental note to buy a copy of the *Hi-Desert Star* later that day, to see if Baker's arraignment had been covered.

"What can I get you today?" Veronica asked as she came to the other side of the counter. She was tall and thin, with hazel eyes and a small overbite that on her was not unattractive. She'd been working at the diner almost as long as Marty. The kind of waitress who could handle a party of ten with three screaming children without ever losing her patience, and was always chatty and cheerful, without making it seem like a job requirement.

"Could I have the cheese omelette?" I asked, folding the newspaper and putting it back where it had been. "And some iced tea, please."

She turned to the kitchen window to place the order. Then she brought me a glass of iced tea and set it on a napkin.

"Were you working on Presidents' Day, Veronica?" I asked.

"We don't get time off on holiday weekends." She tucked her hands into her apron. "I always have to figure out what to do with the kids, especially during spring break or in the summer. And it's worse now that I'm getting divorced. They have day camps over there at the community center, you know, but it's expensive. I have to leave them with my sister. She's on disability, so it's not easy for her to watch three kids, but at least they're with family."

"Right," I said and waited a moment to bring the conversation back to my line of thought. "I asked because a detective from the sheriff's department might come talk to you. Coleman is her name."

"Talk to me about what?"

"About what Anderson Baker did that day," I said, choosing my words carefully. "How he burst in here and started yelling at my dad about parking spaces. The ugly scene he made about that Land Rover. You remember that, don't you?"

In the kitchen, the cook dropped a batch of fries in hot oil. A few feet away, Marty rang up a customer at the cash register. "Yeah, I remember," Veronica said after a moment. "Baker came in just as I was about to go on my cigarette break." She brought the pitcher of iced tea again and topped off my glass, even though I had barely touched it. "When is that detective gonna come talk to me?"

"Soon, I hope. Any moment, really."

"That whore works for the sheriff's department."

"Wait. I'm sorry, who are you talking about?"

"The woman my husband left me for. She works for the sheriff's department. Answers the phone for them. I don't even know how he met her, he never said."

"I'm sorry."

"Fifteen years we were married. Can you believe it? Fifteen years. Three kids. One of them a cesarean. He cheated on me twice before and I took him back both times because he said it didn't mean nothing. And I thought, well, I'm the one he married, not them, so maybe he's right. But then he met that whore and he damn near lost his mind. Says she's his soulmate. I thought I was."

"I'm so sorry."

"Not your fault," Veronica said with a shrug.

I couldn't get away from stories of infidelity, it seemed. But I saw it differently now, my mistake. I remembered how it had felt to sit in the main house at the artist colony in upstate New York, surrounded by painters and writers and visual artists who were far more accomplished than I, wondering how on earth I had managed to get admitted into this place. I felt like an impostor; I was certain I would be discovered and thrown out. Then one night, the famous Max Bloemhof arrived and, seeing me curled up in an armchair with a copy of *Memory of Fire*, came right up to me and introduced himself. I remembered how it all began. How he asked about my music. How I'd sat at the grand piano and played a piece I'd just finished. How he'd looked at me. "Do you know," he said, "I once watched Brad Mehldau play this piano. He was sitting right where you are." He asked me to stop by his cottage sometime so he could give me a copy of his new book. The colony was on forty-two acres of land where horses and deer grazed, and for days I had stayed on the paved pathways, avoiding the fields for fear of ticks that carried Lyme disease. Yet that night, I took the shortcut to Max's studio, walking, almost running, through the green fields. I remembered how he opened the door, how I stepped across the threshold, knowing what would happen next. For months, I didn't allow myself to talk about the affair or think about his wife. Instead I waited, believing that our story would truly begin only after he left her and the messy details could be forgotten.

They weren't. In March, he came to my apartment with a bottle of champagne and a duffel bag. It was past ten o'clock and I was already in my pajamas, a pencil and a page of musical notations in my hand. "What happened?" I asked, alarmed to see him on my doorstep so late, and yet also excited—perhaps he'd finally made the leap he'd been promising me he would make. "I just got a Lannan," he said. It was his first big fellowship after years of scant attention from grant foundations. He'd once bitterly denounced the critics who served on judging committees as "a bunch of sheep" and "tasteless hacks," but now his eyes shone with happiness and the deep lines around his mouth faded. "Let's celebrate," he said as he walked into my apartment. Margo, who'd been reading a magazine on the sofa, shuffled past us to her bedroom. I took out the champagne flutes and watched Max wrestle with the bottle. The hair on his arms was very dark, and on his right wrist he wore an old wind-up watch that had a cracked glass front but kept the time unfailingly. "Evelyn is taking Isabella for a field trip overnight," he said, "and Ian is at a sleepover."

"So you can spend the night?"

"I can spend the night."

The champagne bottle popped, and Margo slammed her door shut. I put my work aside, drank the champagne, and listened to Max tell me about his fellowship plans. He would travel across the U.S. to conduct interviews with surviving Freedom Riders, in the hope that he could use selected quotes to weave together an oral history of their fight. "Kind of like Svetlana Alexievich, but more rigorous," he said, which irritated me no end. He did this a lot, I thought, sneered at other writers, particularly women. He didn't ask what piece I'd been working on when he arrived. In fact, except for the night we met, he'd rarely shown any genuine interest in my music. The next morning, while I was still in bed, my head pulsing with an incipient hangover, he got up and packed his bag. He was getting ready to return to his wife and kids and responsibilities, and I would be left behind. What was my place in all this? And the answer was as clear to me as if he'd spoken it himself: I was the bottle of champagne, the personal celebration. I raised myself on one elbow and told him he had to choose.

For weeks, I waited to hear from him, and would have waited even longer. So I hadn't expected what happened with Jeremy that night in Joshua Tree or the few nights since. I was unprepared for the eagerness with which he took me in his arms, the tenderness that was in his voice when he spoke to me. It stunned me that my body had moved on like this, that it had grasped on to life, insisted on whatever comfort it could find, even as my heart pined for the old world, the world as it was when my father was still in it. The time I spent with Jeremy was a private solace, a few hours when there was no fighting with my sister, no criticism from my mother, no disappointment in myself. I could just *be,* even if it was for only a short while. He was the grown-up version of the boy I had always known, kind and funny and warm, and yet I feared that beneath this easy familiarity lay disturbing secrets.

Whenever he came to see me, he tried to fix up little things around the cabin. One time he changed the air filter on the swamp cooler, another time he found a replacement bulb for the missing light above the stove. That morning, I caught him eyeing the unsteady chairs around the dining table. "You don't need to bother with that," I said. "It's not like I'm staying for good." But he insisted. "It'll only take a minute," he said. I was beginning to think he was trying to make up for something, though I had no idea what it was he'd done. And I didn't want to find out. I couldn't allow myself to be drawn into a relationship at such a fragile moment. All my attention was on the hit-and-run case.

"Want some toast on the side?" Veronica asked. She placed the cheese omelette in front of me on the counter and once again topped off my iced tea.

"No, thanks."

"Or maybe fresh biscuits?"

"This is just fine, thanks," I said. Then, remembering something else, I asked her, "So that big new sign outside, it went up the morning my dad died, right?"

"Right."

"I imagine there must've been a lot of noise? Or some kind of disruption?"

"I guess so, yeah."

"Was Baker upset about that?"

Veronica tilted her head, but didn't answer one way or another, and I thought it best not to push too much. She walked away to the other end of the counter, where the sugar dispensers sat, waiting to be refilled. I picked at my food as I watched the other diners through the mirror above the counter window. There was a time when I would have known some of the Pantry's customers or at least recognized them, but all I could see now was a roomful of strangers. Two construction workers in orange vests had finished their meals and sat with their arms hanging over the headrests, their faces turned toward the windows. A young couple pulled miniature containers of jam from the dispenser and made a pyramid out of them to amuse their toddler. A middle-aged man in a baseball cap, a toothpick hanging from his lip, was reading the newspaper. His glass was empty, but Marty hadn't noticed. I picked up the water pitcher and went to refill it.

Afterward, the pitcher still in my hand, I cast an appraising eye on the restaurant. The counter, which had been shiny new a few years ago, bore the unmistakable dullness of too many wipe-downs. There was a crater in the vinyl flooring at the entrance. Cracks ran through the grouting on the baseboard. The paint on the far wall, once an appealing pistachio color, had yellowed over the years and was peeling in places. The descriptions on the menu—calling the eggs "farm-fresh," the bacon "applewood smoked," the tomatoes "vine-ripe," the bread "Grandma's own"—were no longer au courant. A gash cut through the backrest of the last booth by the window. The plates were gray. The water glasses were scratched. The gumball machine was empty.

But the place was busy.

Perhaps this was what Baker had begrudged my father.

I put the pitcher of water back on the counter and walked around the corner to the back office, a tiny room with a high window and barely enough space for a desk, a chair, a filing cabinet. The air smelled of forbidden cigarettes and used books, a mix that immediately brought me memories of long afternoons spent reading on the deck, my father sitting beside me, smoking, despite the advice of his doctor. My mother was at the desk now, still in widow's white, hunched over a ledger of some sort. "Morning, Mom," I said. "Did you find that note?"

"Not yet," she said, taking off her reading glasses. "Look at this place, benti."

On the desk around her were mountains of papers. Files jutted against stapled records and paper-clipped receipts, rising in peaks and hollowing in valleys, the glass top of the desk buried beneath it all.

"What's going on here?"

"I don't know what your father was doing. Nothing is in order."

"That's not like him."

She shook her head and was quiet for a moment. Did she know *why* he had been so distracted lately? But nothing in her expression suggested it, and my heart ached for her. "I'm sure you'll have this in shape in no time, Mom."

"Maybe he threw it out."

"I hope not." The note in question was a handwritten piece of paper that had been taped to the door of the restaurant the day after the Land Rover incident. As soon as my mother had told me about it,

I said we needed to find it and turn it over to Detective Coleman. It could serve as evidence. "Let me look for it," I said.

"All right."

My mother went back to her ledger, and I started sifting through the papers on the desk. There were payments for paper napkins and drinking straws, orders of Styrofoam to-go containers, two prescriptions for an antihistamine, a copy of the AARP magazine, but no note. I rummaged through the desk drawers, leafed through books of crossword puzzles, and checked the pockets of the suit jacket that was hanging over the back of the desk chair. Finally, on the windowsill, beneath a half-empty box of matches, I found the folded note. It was a piece of lined paper on which Baker had written, in an arthritic penmanship, PARK IN YOUR SPACES ONLY! A strip of clear tape lined the top of the page, and the word *only* was underlined twice. The note wasn't signed, but to my eyes, it seemed incriminating. This was progress. "Here it is," I said, my voice rising with excitement.

My mother came to look over my shoulder. "That's good. Really good."

"Can you think of anything else we could show the detective?"

"No," she said after a minute. Then she went back to sit behind the desk. "But there's something I need to tell you."

"What is it?"

"Close the door."

I closed the door and stood against it, puzzled by the secrecy. "What is it?"

"We want to sell the restaurant."

"What are you talking about? Who is *we*?"

"Your sister and me. We want to sell."

My mother said this with a finality that stunned me. I came closer to the desk, facing the piles of paper I had been sorting through just a moment earlier. "How long have you two been talking about this? It's crazy you're having these conversations and then informing me of your decisions after the fact. Shouldn't we discuss this first?"

"The market is a little slow now," my mother said, folding her reading glasses and sitting back in her chair. "But I think we can find a buyer."

"Did you not hear what I said? We *can't* sell the restaurant."

"Why?"

"Because Dad wouldn't have wanted us to. You know this. Salma knows this."

"But *I* never wanted a restaurant. It was your father's idea. What I wanted was a coin laundry. No employees, no big expense, no waking up at five in the morning." She ticked off these items on the fingers of her left hand. It seemed to me she was falling back, almost with relief, into an old argument, and this time she would see it through. "But your father never listened to me. I don't want the restaurant and I don't want to see Baker going and coming. Every day, he's going and coming like nothing happened. I want to sell. And your sister, too. She said she needs the money."

"For heaven's sake, we can't sell. That would give Baker exactly what he's been after all this time. He wanted Dad out of here and you're letting him have his way. And what does Salma need the money for? Her practice is doing well."

I saw that I had finally scored a point, because my mother was speechless for a minute. She put her reading glasses into a tortoiseshell case and slipped it into her purse. "So you want to keep the restaurant?"

"Yes."

"Who's going to run it?"

"Marty can. He pretty much does, already."

"He's not family."

"So? It's a job, and he's good at it. This would only make it official."

"No. He can't do it alone. You want to do it?"

"But I have my own work, Mom."

"So why do you want to keep the restaurant? Go make your music. Salma and I talked to the realtor on Wednesday and he—"

"You already talked to a realtor? Mom, will you please just wait? Let me think about it. I have just as much say in this decision as the two of you. And we have to wait for the probate to be closed, anyway. That's going to take months."

"We can shut down the restaurant until probate is closed." And then, seeing my eyes widen with revolt, she said, "Okay. Fine. Think about it. Then we'll talk to the realtor."

It took all I had not to slam the door behind me as I left the office. The move to sell the restaurant had taken me by surprise, but it was the fact that my mother and sister had formed some kind of alliance behind my back that made it so devastating. Walking back through the restaurant toward the exit, I couldn't help but wonder what it would look like under new owners. Would they keep the dappled mirror over the counter? Or the metal sign by the back door that said COCA-COLA: GOOD WITH FOOD? Would Rafi and Marty and Veronica still have jobs? Would Baker still start arguments over parking spaces? I didn't like where any of this was leading. What I wanted more than anything, and this desire surprised me with its clarity, was for this place to stay exactly the same as it was when my father was alive.

Coleman

I was in the break room pouring myself a cup of coffee when Gorecki came in. It was a little after six in the morning, and I don't think either of us was ready for the sergeant's briefing, or even fully awake yet. He picked up a Dixie cup from the tall stack next to the sink and held it out to me like a beggar, rubbing sleep from his eyes. He was working on a college degree, in American history if I remember correctly, and this fact set him apart from the career deputies, and at times it even created some conflict, but I liked that he was kind of an outsider, like me. "How are you?" I asked as I filled his cup.

"Pretty good, actually. How about you?"

"Hanging in there," I said, and took a sip of my coffee. It tasted bitter and did nothing for my mood. The night before, while Miles was in the shower, I had gone through his Instagram account and found, mixed in with the selfies, desert landscapes, and artsy compositions, a shirtless picture of Brandon. It had been taken after a basketball game at school, with Brandon looking straight at the camera, smiling, his arm reaching as if to touch the person taking the photo: Miles. I had a sense of what was happening, but not how to talk about it with my son, much less with his father. "A little worried about Miles."

"His schoolwork, you mean? I thought you were helping him with that."

"I am," I said, catching myself. Gorecki waited for me to say more, but instead I asked about the sergeant. "How are things with Vasco?"

"He caught me reading a book during my shift the other day. Chewed me out." He shook his head slowly. "You'd think reading was illegal, the way he was acting."

"He's worried about appearances. There's a new article on Bowden." I tilted my head to indicate the newspaper that lay at the other end of the counter. Bowden was an unemployed plumber with a long rap sheet that included petty theft, possession, and assault. He was being served with an arrest warrant for another drug charge when he fled through the back door of his house, leading deputies on a car chase across unpaved streets in Twentynine Palms, down Highway 62, on to a tire shop in Yucca Valley, where they finally caught up with him. The *Los Angeles Times* had dug up cell phone footage showing Bowden lying on his stomach, his face against the asphalt, and a deputy repeatedly punching him in the head.

"Well, you made an arrest in that hit-and-run. Vasco's happy about that."

"Stroke of luck," I said, and immediately regretted the modesty in my voice. Humility had been drilled in me, as it was in most of the women I knew, and I found it hard to get rid of it, even though it was frequently mistaken for inability.

"That's not how Vasco made it sound," Gorecki said. "He called it good old-fashioned police work. Held you up as an example and said that's how you get shit done."

"It was the old man who owns the bowling alley. Not some hard-ass guy or anything."

"And you think it was just an accident?"

"Accidents are common on that highway," I said. The victim's daughter kept insisting that it was more than that, and it was true that the three-foot dent on the Crown Vic made Baker's coyote story less believable, but it was a huge leap from hit-and-run to murder. Vasco wasn't thrilled about the daughter's allegations—it meant he couldn't close the case—but I had a professional duty to investigate her claims, and I tried to look into them whenever I had some time.

My first stop had been to the Pantry, where the workers essentially confirmed the story that the Guerraoui family had told me: frictions that started out over dust and dirt from remodeling a few years ago had recently boiled over into arguments. But neither the restaurant manager nor the waitresses could recall specific criminal threats that Anderson Baker might have made against the victim. There was no

I'm gonna kill you or *You better watch your back* or even a measly *I'll make you regret it*, any of which could have been used to establish intent. "They just griped a lot," Marty Holtz, the manager, told me as he stood at the front desk, spraying Windex on plastic-covered menus and wiping them down with a paper towel. "They griped constantly, and about everything."

Meanwhile, at the bowling alley, the cashier, Betty Sanders, claimed that the problem hadn't started with the mess from remodeling, but a few months before that. "Thing is," she said, rubbing out excess lipstick with a tissue, "Mr. Baker had already talked to the dry cleaner next door about buying his shop when he retired. Then the Muslim guy comes in last minute and offers him a little more. Bought it from right under him. So."

"So Mr. Baker was angry."

"I wouldn't say angry," she said, suddenly aware of what the word might imply. "Just—disappointed, I guess."

I had the nagging feeling that I was missing something about the Guerraoui case, something I couldn't see because I wasn't familiar with this town and its people. At the end of my visit to the Pantry and Desert Arcade, I didn't know which version of the past I could trust, which story was supported by the facts and which had been reshaped to fit them, whether out of grief or out of malice.

Gorecki topped off his coffee and took a long sip. "You don't think it's odd that Mr. Baker didn't come forward before?"

"Not particularly." When given the choice between claiming responsibility for what they had done or avoiding it as long as possible, most people chose Door Number Two. At least, that had been my experience. The problem was that I had no witnesses to the crime and nothing that could be used to prove intent. Besides, from the beginning, Baker had been fully cooperative, even if his wife had been a little strange. When I went to interview him at home, she'd opened the door and stared at me with her mouth agape. Having a police investigator show up on your doorstep is an unsettling experience, maybe even frightening for some people, but with her it was more like a visceral fear. I had to wait outside in the heat while she went to get her husband.

Somewhere in the office a phone rang, and a door slammed shut. "You know," Gorecki said, "I went to school with the victim's daughter."

"Which one? The dentist?"

"The musician."

"You never mentioned it," I said. God, I hated small towns. I missed being at home, in D.C. "Does everyone know everyone else around here?"

"Pretty much."

When I worked for Metro P.D., my morning routine was so different. I would go into a little café next to my train stop and sit at the window with my coffee, just watching people come and go, all of them strangers to me, as I was to them. I never thought it was anything special, or that I'd miss it someday, but I did. Now I couldn't get to work without hearing town gossip.

Gorecki cleared his throat. "And Nora and I—we're also seeing each other."

"You *what*?" I didn't need this, not with the dispute with Baker, and not with the daughter insisting it was murder. The more I tried to keep this case neat and clean, the messier it got. "For how long?"

"It just happened."

"You have to disclose this to the sergeant."

"I know," he said, draining the last of his coffee. "That's gonna be a fun conversation."

"And quit asking me questions about the case. Did she tell you to ask me?"

"No." A second too late.

"Then why are you asking?"

"I was just curious, that's all."

"You know I can't say anything while the investigation is still open."

"And you didn't. So there's no harm." Then he tapped the folded newspaper on the counter, where images from the Bowden incident were splashed across the front page. "I better go. I have appearances to worry about, right?"

Nora

A couple of days after our argument at the restaurant, my mother asked me to go shopping with her in Palm Desert. We'd never performed the usual mother-daughter rituals together—no spa dates, no tea time, no rom-coms, no crafting or baking for us. Part of this was my fault, because when I was growing up I spent far too much time locked up in my room, listening to music, but the other part was that my sister genuinely enjoyed these outings with her and I never wanted to be a third wheel. My mother's invitation was therefore highly unusual, and I took it to mean that she was calling a truce after our skirmish about the sale of the Pantry.

Mercifully, it was a weekday, and Macy's was mostly empty. My mother seemed to be in good spirits, holding on to my arm as we walked around the department store. She bought a casserole dish and a set of stainless-steel measuring cups, but spent the better part of the morning helping me pick out some clothes. I had brought only a few things with me from Oakland, and needed a pair of pants, a few shirts, a couple of dresses. We were in the shoe section when it struck me that we were doing something completely ordinary, that we were returning to the mundane tasks that make up most of our existence. Standing in front of a display that advertised a 20 percent discount on summer shoes, I picked up a tan sandal with an ankle strap. "What do you think?" I asked.

"It won't go with your new pants," my mother said.

"No?" I put the sandal back on the table and held up a classic black pump with a high heel. "What about this?"

"That's much better."

A sales clerk who'd been watching from a few feet away came over, and I gave him both pairs of shoes. Then I sat down across from my mother. New strands of gray streaked through her hair and there were dark pools under her eyes. She was still in mourning, and would be for a long while yet. But how much did she really know about the man she was grieving? The question had been nagging at me ever since I'd received that phone call from the jewelry shop. "I've been wondering," I said. "Why exactly did Dad buy that cabin?"

"You know why. So he could rent it out."

"But he didn't rent out to tourists that often, did he?"

"In the beginning, he did. But there was always trouble. Someone would plug the toilet or burn something in the toaster oven or break dishes and not replace them. I warned your father about this, but of course he never listened."

Across the sales floor, a tall blonde was sipping an iced coffee as she went through the sales rack, methodically checking every pair in her size. What did my father's mistress look like? Was she young and pretty, the way I had imagined at first, or was she someone with more substance to her? Some wit or personality. She had to be someone special if he was breaking up his marriage over her. In which case, how could my mother not know about it? "So if Dad didn't rent out the cabin much, why did he keep it?" I asked.

My mother thought about this for a moment. When she spoke again, her voice was hoarse. "I think your father really liked being a landlord. No one in his family owned a house before. The cabin made him feel, I don't know, like he was successful." She rubbed her eyes with the palm of her hand.

So she had no idea what had been going on, and all I had accomplished with my fact-finding mission that morning was to stir up her grief. I shouldn't have asked, I thought. I looked away, desperate for another subject of conversation, and was relieved to see that the sales clerk was returning with the shoe boxes. I tried on the black pumps first.

"They look great on you," my mother said.

"You like them?"

"Yes. Are they comfortable? Walk around, see how you feel."

I took three hesitant steps; I wasn't used to high heels. "They look, uh, professional."

"Exactly," my mother said, clasping her hands. She was gazing at me with an expression I couldn't quite decipher and I looked at the shoes again, wondering if I'd missed something. "You know," she said after a minute, "it's not too late to go to law school."

"What?"

"You're young, Nora. Three years will go by quickly. And you can afford to go back to school now, with the life insurance money."

"What are you talking about, Mom? Why are you bringing this up again?"

"Because you would be a great lawyer, I'm sure of it. The neighbors told me yesterday that their daughter Jessica passed the bar exam. Remember how she used to ask you for help with her math homework? She couldn't finish it without you, and now look at her. A lawyer! She's going to work for a big firm in San Diego."

So this was why my mother had asked me to go shopping. Not because she wanted to spend time with me, but because she wanted to convince me to start a proper career, be more like Salma, or more like Jessica, or more like someone else. This was not a new conversation. We'd been having it in one form or another since I'd given up on medical school and decided to study music instead. The thought of having this argument again, sitting here in the shoe section at Macy's, was intolerable. *She* was intolerable.

Only a moment earlier, I'd been feeling sorry for my mother and betrayed by my father, but now everything shifted. Whatever else he did, he'd never wished me to be a different person. He wouldn't have staged an ambush like this or tried to convince me to give up on the only thing that gave meaning to my life. His love was free. But my mother's love was a war. It was fought every day for the sake of shaping me into somebody new, somebody better. Even if I had gone to medical school or law school or business school, she would have found something else in me that needed to be improved, and would have made it a point to tell me about it. What was even more infuriating was that my mother never behaved like this with my sister. Salma could do no wrong.

I kicked off the black pumps and tried on the tan sandals. They were comfortable, and would be perfect for summer. "I'm getting these," I said.

We drove back from Palm Desert in silence. Whatever lightness the day held had been dimmed by our argument; I couldn't wait to be alone again. I dropped my mother off at the house and with a quick goodbye wave headed back onto the highway. It was the middle of the afternoon now and the sidewalks were empty, but passing the party supply store where my father had bought me a piñata for my eighth birthday, I felt his absence anew. At the Stater Brothers, where I stopped for milk, the smell of his aftershave on a random customer nearly brought me to tears. Even when I walked into the cabin, the memory came back to me of a hike we had taken to Willow Hole together. I missed him.

Salma

The first thing you see when you wake up is the Pan Am bag hanging from your mother's shoulder. It is blue and white and has a hole in one corner. You're in your father's arms, still groggy with sleep, and as he carries you off the plane, you ask, "Is this where I go to school?" School is all you've been talking about for weeks, the carrot your parents dangled to get you to leave home. All you had to do was take the plane, they said, school would be at the other end. "Yes, here," your father says, but distractedly. At the gate, your uncle is waiting. He hoists you up, kisses you, rubs his unshaved chin against your cheek. He smells like cigarettes, and he laughs easily, like your father. Yet not like your father at all.

Your uncle and his wife live in Culver City. They have a foldout couch, a backyard with a lemon tree and a swing set, and two boys who pinch you when no one is looking. On their days off, the adults cook elaborate meals, drink mint tea, and talk for hours about the king and Ronald Reagan. They make the king sound like he's in the next room, and Reagan like he's in another house. The children are supposed to play outside, but most of the time you have no idea what your cousins are saying, so you mimic the way they walk, the way they laugh, and finally the way they talk. They dress you up in costumes and parade you around the yard. You become a perfect little ape.

In the spring, you move with your parents to a small town in the Mojave, where they buy a donut shop. The sun and the wind are impossible to escape. Within days, your skin burns, your lips chap, your hair grows two shades lighter. You ask about school again. "Maybe next year," your father says, casually. "Right now, you're too young."

Betrayal is still new to you, and hard to swallow. Leafing through the realtor magazines from the dispenser outside the shop, you pretend to read. Eventually you learn to recognize the letters that go with the pictures: h-o-m-e. You ask for more magazines. Your mother gets a library card, checks out five books at a time, and sticks you in a corner with them. She has a shop to run, trays to wash, floors to clean, and no time to play. But at night, when everything is quiet, she sings you lullabies in Arabic and lets you fall asleep with your head in her lap. You press your face against her belly, amazed at how warm it must have been inside. If only you could go back in there. One weekend, your uncle and his family come for a visit. When your cousins try to pinch you, you bite them.

The day finally arrives: you start school at Yucca Mesa Elementary. You already know your alphabet and raise your hand and answer correctly every time Mrs. Hamilton calls on you. You are not an ape anymore. Now you are a circus seal. In your repertoire, there are many tricks: you sing "I'm a Little Teacup"; you spell *girl* and *home* and *want*; you get an A on your first test. Your mother starts taking you everywhere with her. You say words like *semolina* and *delicatessen* without stumbling, ask where the zucchini is without giggling. You take after the Amazigh side of the family and every spring your hair grows lighter. Grocery-store clerks ask if you'd like a sticker, young lady. Bank clerks ask if you're excited about the Easter egg hunt. It will be years before you encounter the word *passing*.

Then all of a sudden, there is a crib in your parents' room, a stroller in the hallway, a yellow activity mat you're not allowed to touch. Your father coos over the new baby like she's something special, even though she can't add two and two, or tell the time, or win Scariest Pumpkin at the first-grade Halloween festival. She has dark skin and chubby legs and big eyes that seem to track you everywhere you go. When no one is looking, you pinch her. She cries inconsolably. Your mother wonders aloud what is wrong with that child.

You still speak Arabic, but you no longer dream in it.

You grow to be tall, almost six feet by the time you're in the ninth grade. You play volleyball, compete in the science fair, collect box tops for the school's fundraiser, correctly guess the number of jelly beans in the jar. You're never late, never sick, never rude. All your friends' parents love you. "Such a sensible girl," they say. One afternoon, while your family is at the neighbors' pool party, you run off with the other girls to try on makeup, and leave your sister behind. She falls into the deep end of the pool and nearly drowns. In that moment, you realize you're not a sensible girl, and immediately hide this fact from everyone.

The summer you turn twenty, while you're home from college, the king dies. His funeral is broadcast live on CNN and your parents watch in disbelief, as if they need proof that it really is happening. Two million people line up on the streets of the capital, hoping to catch a glimpse of the velvet-draped coffin as it makes its way from the royal palace to the mausoleum. Your father yells at the television: "Did you forget what he did?" Your mother shushes him and raises the volume on the set. Bill Clinton and Jacques Chirac are in attendance. So are Hosni Mubarak and Rifaat al-Assad. One by one, they praise the deceased monarch, call him a man of peace, a champion of tolerance. "Well," your father says, in a small voice, "I guess I can go visit my mother now."

A year later, when you finally travel to Casablanca with your family, you do not recognize your grandmother, nor does she recognize you. How is it possible to miss someone you don't remember? And yet you do. For the duration of your visit, you sit side by side with her, in companionable silence. When you do venture out, tourist guides ask you in English if you'd like a tour of the medina and, if you ignore them, they try again, this time in German. Bazaar clerks call you Miss, offer you mint tea, and charge you four times the price for every trinket. Boys standing at street corners whistle when you pass, then openly touch their groins.

After college, you go to dentistry school at Loma Linda. There, you meet a clear-eyed man who is never late, never sick, never rude. When he speaks Arabic, it is as if music is streaming from his mouth. Words like *zaytun* and *sukkar* and *habibet el-omr* sound like they're accompanied by a thirteen-string lute. You marry him, open a practice together, make your parents proud. "Why can't you be more like Salma?" your mother tells your sister, and each time she says this, you feel a special thrill.

Day after day, you stare at open mouths, smell rancid breath, scrape rot from cavities. Increasingly you have to spend your afternoons arguing with insurance companies about billing and payments. The whole thing gives you a headache. You take a Vicodin. You are no longer a trained seal. Now you are a bird. You float away, free. When your husband complains that the painkiller samples are disappearing fast, you say it's not your fault you had three root canals in one week. You haven't begun to order extra boxes of diazepam and he isn't suspicious yet.

But someday he will be, and you will have to meet his eyes across the dinner table, answer his questions, and agree to let him take over your surgeries. He will ask that you see a substance abuse specialist, but you will say you're fine. At least talk to someone, he will beg. Talk to your mother. The thought of your mother finding out about your habit is excruciating. Her approval is a prison you do not wish to escape. I'll see a specialist, you say, and never make the appointment. After he goes to bed, you sit on a lounge chair on the deck, and watch the view that the realtor said was unparalleled anywhere in the valley. You take another pill.

This is where the plane took you.

Nora

I can see now that there was an element of stubbornness in what I did next. But at the time, I felt I had no choice but to help manage the restaurant, because my mother abruptly stopped showing up to work. This might have been her way of forcing my hand on the sale, though it had the reverse effect: I stepped in for her. And it surprised me, too, how quickly all the little habits I had learned years ago came back. I wore closed-toe shoes, even in the heat, a comfortable pair of washable pants, and a polo shirt with the diner's name embroidered across the breast pocket. I folded silverware into napkins, refilled salt-and-pepper shakers, took over Veronica's tables whenever she went on her cigarette break, made sure the wait station had plates and cups and bowls, talked to customers, and tried to be cheerful about it. How are you this fine morning? Would you like some ketchup or mustard? Careful, that plate is very hot. What a beautiful baby.

After a few days working at the restaurant, I found that I could take care of all my duties and still have time to run to the store for supplies or to the bank for quarters and nickels. Still, I had forgotten how physically taxing food service was, how much my feet could swell or my arms ache from a single day's labor. How did Veronica do it? Or Rafi? By the end of my shift, when my only thought was of how long it would take me to get to the cabin and collapse on one of the porch chairs with a beer, they still looked as fresh as they had when they started their day.

But the best at this line of work was Marty. I could never keep up with him. He had his own set of habits, too, like carrying extra straws in his apron pocket so he wouldn't have to walk back to the wait station every time a customer asked for one. Without needing to be told, he changed the channel on the stereo when the music got too loud for an elderly couple, or lowered the shade when the afternoon sun streaming through the windows made a toddler squint. He knew several of our customers by name and talked to them like old friends. He would close the restaurant every night, and when I opened it in the morning, I would find that he had given me a head start by restocking the jam caddies or refilling the sugar dispensers.

Late one morning, while I was at the wait station with the paper napkins I had just bought on my run to Costco, Marty left the cash register and came to talk to me. "Miss Guerraoui," he said, taking off his glasses and letting them dangle from their retainer, "are you taking over from your mother?"

"I'm just trying to help out."

"I see."

"If I missed something, let me know."

"As a matter of fact, there is something."

"What is it?"

"Your father promised me a raise last year, but we had to replace the freezer and he told me it had to wait. Then a couple of months ago, he ordered that fancy new sign you see outside, so I brought up the raise again and he said he'd do it. But then he passed away and now, who knows what's happening?" He swept his hand in a gesture that took in the entire restaurant. "I'm not even sure who's in charge around here."

I swallowed. "I'm in charge."

"So you're gonna give me that raise your father promised? Twenty-one dollars an hour, that's what we agreed on. Twenty-one."

"That makes sense," I said cautiously. "I'll talk to my mom about it."

Marty gave me a disappointed smile, as if he suspected all along that this would be the answer, and went back to the cash register. I retreated to the back office, wondering how I would bring this up to my mother. I had a good notion of what she might say—that this was my problem now, she never wanted to have a restaurant, we should sell this place as soon as possible. It would set off another argument about the future. Then again, every conversation with my mother ended in an argument about the future.

For the past few days, I had been thinking of how best to use the insurance settlement my father had left me. It was an enormous amount of money, and I had already used some of it to pay off my student loans, but it wasn't enough to buy the restaurant outright. If I wanted to keep it, I would have to buy out my sister and somehow convince my mother to hold on to her share. And there were other expenses I had to consider as well: the back door of the diner needed a new lock, the dining room could use another coat of paint, and the menus had to be updated. Holding on to the restaurant meant having employees and keeping track of timecards and deciding on raises and a million other responsibilities.

But if I agreed to sell, my share of the proceeds combined with what remained of the life insurance money would easily buy me four years in the Bay Area. Twice that long if I stayed in the Mojave. I would finally have the time and the means to work on my music. I could afford to travel to music festivals, take master classes if I wanted, or just stay home and work. It was an incredible gift that my father had given me. The only thing that made it less sweet was that Anderson Baker would succeed in running my father out of town. That, I couldn't accept. Even though selling the restaurant and walking away made plenty of sense, a part of me stubbornly wanted to hold on to it.

Jeremy

Aside from a couple of walks around the neighborhood, Nora said no whenever I asked her if she wanted to leave the cabin, go out for a meal or a movie with me. I didn't press her. Years in the service had taught me the value of patience. I'd learned to wait for an order, wait for a signal, wait for an air drop, wait for a pickup, wait for the bathroom, wait for the phone, wait for my deployment to end. So I considered it progress when she agreed to come to dinner at my house one night. I drove straight to the Stater Brothers after work to pick up a few groceries and was reducing the sauce for the chicken when the doorbell rang. She was wearing a red sundress with tiny straps that I immediately imagined sliding off her shoulders later. I stepped aside to let her in and closed the door behind us. She stood in my living room, taking it all in: the blue couch I'd inherited from Ashley and Tommy after they upgraded their furniture; the big stereo I'd bought with my combat pay and that no longer looked as impressive as it had when I returned home; the game controller on the floor. Her eye lingered on the Iraqi banknote pinned to the corkboard by the sliding door. I brought out the bouquet of peonies I'd bought for her. "What's the occasion?" she asked, with genuine surprise.

"They're in season," I said, suddenly too embarrassed to admit that I was trying to turn a homemade meal into a proper date. I kissed her, the bouquet squished between us, its sprigs of lavender and green berries brushing up against our necks. "Do you want to take them home, or should I put them in water?"

"Let's have them out. They smell so good."

I emptied a canister of spaghetti and filled it with water, then put the peonies in it. I set it on the counter, where we'd be able to see it from the dining room. "Are you hungry?"

"Famished."

"Good. I made a lot of food."

She stood against the counter, watching me. "Who taught you how to cook?"

"I taught myself, after my mom died." I held up a spoonful of the chicken sauce. "Here, have a taste."

Her eyes widened.

"Too much salt?"

"No. It's perfect."

I carried the dishes to the table. In the two years I'd lived in this house, I'd never used the dimmer on the light switch in my dining room, but now I lowered it to an intimate level before I sat down across from her. For the first time I saw her eat, no, *devour* all the food on her plate—the chicken, the side of potatoes, two pieces of the French bread I'd almost taken out of my cart at the store because I didn't think she'd eat it, the green beans, everything—and the more she ate the more she smiled and the more she smiled the happier I felt.

She told me about her day. A big group of women bikers had stopped by the restaurant for brunch, and the place had been so busy she'd had to get some folding chairs from the storage room, but afterward there was a long lull. She'd checked her email and found a personal rejection from a music festival in San Francisco, which thrilled her. I found this confusing, until she explained that she usually received form rejections, and getting a personal note with a few words of encouragement meant a great deal to her. It restored some of her confidence in her work. "What about you?" she asked.

"It was just an ordinary day," I said. I tried not to think about work, if I could help it. A woman in Twentynine Palms reported that her son had stabbed her Chihuahua and she feared he might do it again. When I got to the house, I found her in the front yard, cradling the dog in her arms like a baby, its hind legs wrapped in blue bandage. Her son was in his room listening to music, she said, or what he called music, and also he didn't have a job. She led the way inside, across an olive-green carpet covered with urine stains, to the son's bedroom. He jumped up the moment he saw me. "You called the cops on me?" he yelled. It took a good fifteen minutes to get his side of the story, which was that he had nothing to do with that fucking Chihuahua and that it had probably gotten cut by stepping on a razor the mother had left lying around. "Look around you, man. This house look clean to you?" he asked. The mother huffed, "A razor? I don't have a razor. I'm not the one who shaves in this house." While they argued, I watched and waited. It would have been hard not to notice the son's skinny arms, his dilated pupils, the twitching of his hands as he talked. Sure enough, a pat-down turned up a couple of ounces of crystal meth. But as soon as I arrested the kid, the mother turned on me. She begged and cried and threatened, then followed me to the cruiser with the Chihuahua whimpering in her arms. When I put the kid in the back, the dog suddenly revived and, baring its teeth and snapping its jaws, tried to lunge at me. I told the woman to restrain her Chihuahua, but instead she released it and it flew at the cruiser window, then went sliding down to the ground, scratching the siding. And still it didn't stop barking.

"Sounds kind of surreal," Nora said.

"That's how it is," I said. The surreal was ordinary and the ordinary was surreal. "Ready for some dessert?" I took the pan of chocolate brownies from the oven. I'd made them from a box, but I added a swirl of whipped cream to each plate before I brought them out to the table. Not too bad, I thought, and with a hint of vanilla, too. But she wasn't eating hers. "You don't like brownies?"

"I do, but I'm stuffed," she said, patting her stomach. "If I eat anything else, it might end up on my thighs."

I laughed, then I saw that she was serious. "Come over here for a minute," I said, pushing back my chair so she could sit on my lap. I held her close, running my hand along her legs and around her hips. "Your thighs are beautiful." I moved my hand to her chest. "But my favorite part of you is this."

"My breasts?"

"Your heart."

Our eyes met. She looked away. "Don't say things like that, Jeremy."

"Why?"

"It's going to make this complicated."

"This is already complicated."

Outside, the crickets were singing, a nighttime serenade I hadn't paid much attention to until now, as I waited for her to speak. When she finally looked at me, I saw that she was appraising me in a new way. Something was being decided in that moment between us. I rested my head in the crook of her neck, but the doorbell rang, and I had to go answer it.

"Dude. Where you been? You're late."

Fierro was on my doorstep in a T-shirt, jeans, and the baseball cap he usually wore to the gun range. I was irritated at him for interrupting my dinner, at myself for forgetting that I'd agreed to go with him, and again at him for reminding me of my commitment. "Shit. I totally forgot." Though I stood in the doorway, he walked past me, somehow alert to the smell of food and flowers and female presence. I followed him into the dining room, a strange knot forming in my chest. In one fluid motion, Nora stood up from the table and pulled up the strap of her dress, which had fallen down her shoulder.

"I didn't know you had company," Fierro said.

Nora smiled at Fierro and Fierro smiled at Nora and they both looked at me.

"Sorry," I said. "Nora, this is Bryan Fierro. Bryan, this is Nora Guerraoui."

"It's lovely to meet you," she said, offering her hand.

"Nice to meet you, too."

"That's a cool shirt."

"You like Kyuss?" Fierro said with a grin. "I love 'em. I saw Josh Homme in concert a couple of years ago in Palm Springs. He was fantastic. I wanna go again when he comes to Vegas in October."

"Maybe we can go to the range tomorrow night instead," I said.

"You ever seen Homme in concert?" Fierro asked.

"No," Nora said. "But I bet he's great."

"Dude. He's awesome."

"I read somewhere that he has a new band with John Paul Jones?"

"That's right, they did Coachella two years ago."

"Listen, man. We can go to the range tomorrow."

Fierro glanced at me with irritation. "They have the Tuesday night special. And I want to try out my new Glock."

"It's all right," Nora said, reaching for her purse. "I was just leaving."

But I didn't want her to leave. I wanted her to stay and talk to me and spend the night with me, holding on to me in her sleep. I wanted Fierro to leave and stop being so needy and get on with his life. As she made her way out, I followed, carefully closing the door after us. Outside, the weather had cooled; she shivered in her sundress.

"I'm sorry," I said. "I completely forgot he was coming."

"It's fine, really."

"You sure?"

"Positive."

"Oh, and Kyuss?"

She laughed. "What? I was trying to be nice."

I kissed her goodbye, then watched her get into her hybrid and pull silently out of the driveway. When I walked back inside, I found Fierro standing at the sink, eating a chicken drumstick he'd taken straight from the pan. I cleared the dinner plates and started loading the dishwasher, moving with practiced efficiency in my narrow kitchen.

Fierro turned away from the sink. "Dude. She's smokin' hot. Where'd you pick her up? I know it's not at the gym. I never seen her there before."

"I didn't pick her up. Let's go to Rod & Gun. I don't want to drive all the way out to Twentynine Palms tonight."

"She picked you up? Wow."

"Nobody picked anybody up. Rod & Gun?"

"Rod & Gun closes early. She Mexican?"

"No. Let's go to Pistol & Rifle, then."

"Huh. She kinda looks Mexican."

"She's not."

"What is she, then?"

"Moroccan."

"Moroccan," he repeated, as though it were a word he had never heard before. "Did you fuck her?"

Ordinarily, I would've said yes. I was not above bragging. In some deep, dark corner of myself, I was still a fat seventeen-year-old that none of the girls wanted—and somehow the opposite, too, a fit nineteen-year-old on home leave who all the girls suddenly noticed. Hell, yes, I would've said. I fucked her on this table right here. Twice. You should've seen the tits on this one, or that one gives fantastic head. But whatever it was I had with Nora was not the same. It was old, and yet it was new. It was muddled in a way that felt so different I didn't want to talk about her, least of all with Fierro. I turned away and started wiping down the countertops. "I can drive to the range. But wash your hands. I don't want your paw prints everywhere."

Fierro squeezed some dish soap into his hands and turned the tap on. With a glance over his shoulder, he said, "Tell me you weren't just sitting here talking to her about books or some shit. Tell me you fucked her."

I walked past him to the bedroom, where I unlocked the safe and took out my gun. When I turned around, Fierro was standing in the doorway. He grabbed on to the doorframe bar and did a set of five pull-ups, just for the hell of it. Then he dropped down, fixed his eyes on me, and broke into a wide smile. "You fucked her, didn't you? Good for you, dude." He thumped me on the arm. "Now let's go shoot some guns."

A lot of people wanted to take advantage of the Tuesday night special, it turned out; the range was so packed and we had to wait our turn. The fluorescent lights cast a yellow glare on the vinyl flooring and the smell of men and guns and synthetic gear hung in the air. From the loudspeaker came an announcement that a lane was available for Casey. Fierro cracked his knuckles while we waited, and I leaned back in my seat and thought about how readily Nora had offered to leave when she found out I was supposed to go to the gun range. The truth was, I couldn't picture her in a place like this, either.

"Did I tell you Johnnie got caught masturbating in the towel section last weekend?" Fierro said suddenly. "He got fired. Which means Dexter gets to be supervisor. Which means I get to be department manager."

"You got a promotion?"

"It just kinda happened. They could've picked Frank for the job, but they picked me. I don't really know why."

"Doesn't matter. When something good happens to you, go for it. Don't ask why. Just enjoy it. Congrats."

"Thanks, dude. 'Preciate it."

"See? That support group is helping you."

He made a little whistling sound, a strange mannerism he'd picked up from Fletcher. After a minute, he turned to me again. "Hey, did I tell you I heard from Sarge? He started a beekeeping business."

"Beekeeping?" I said, more out of surprise than interest.

"Yup. He's got a place near Waynesboro. Seems he's doing well."

Fierro really looked up to Sergeant Fletcher. I did, too, in the beginning. The first time I saw him, he was standing in the brightness of a January morning with his hands on his hips, waiting for us to get in formation. He had very delicate features—brown eyes, a small nose, perfect teeth—which seemed oddly out of place in a barracks full of men who did their best to look tough. At all times, he remained calm. He never got worked up, never even raised his voice. He was from Fairfax County, Virginia. The kind of place where kids grow up with fencing lessons, math tutors, trips to the botanical gardens. Doctor dad, lawyer mom. How someone like him had ended up in the Marines, no one knew. Something about a brawl at a country club when he was a senior in high school, but that sounded to me like nothing more than barracks gossip. He'd already served in Afghanistan and now here he was in Iraq, with three stripes on his right sleeve. In the beginning he seemed aloof, whether because of his upbringing or his experience, I wasn't sure. And it got worse when there was a reshuffling from the higher-ups and Lieutenant Carter was assigned to the platoon. The lieutenant was everything Fletcher wasn't: average-looking, funny, approachable, always willing to play *Halo* or *Call of Duty* with the men after they got back to base. And he never minded when he lost a game to a grunt.

One day the lieutenant announced we had to check on a safe house outside Ramadi. It turned out to be a farm, the land around it nearly barren, the only animals three thin goats obstinately grazing on a small patch of yellow grass. Sergeant Fletcher had a lot more experience, so when he suggested going in with the terp and two others to talk to the owner, the lieutenant agreed. The air was still and heavy with heat. The men waited, drinking from their CamelBaks now and then. After idling for thirty minutes, the Humvees grew so hot that it seemed a relief when the lieutenant gave the order to dismount and start the search. I found myself with Perez and Sanger, rounding the farmhouse toward the well. An old tractor sat on its side, wheels in the air, gathering dust. Here and there lay all manner of farm tools.

From a eucalyptus tree nearby came the sudden fluttering of bird wings. Out of instinct, I looked up. Then I felt my foot give in and the next thing I knew I was sliding down a dark hole, dragging dirt and tarp and branches down with me and landing over a body, the weight of my ballistic plate pinning it to the ground. But it wasn't a body, it was a man, alive and awake. I locked eyes with him, surprised to find my own fear reflected back at me. The smell of our sweat filled my nostrils. Even with Sanger and Perez shouting from above the hole, I heard the distinct click of the man's gun under me, followed, after a second that stretched into eternity, by the merciful sound of an empty barrel.

Everything else after that happened quickly—Sanger jumped into the hole, helped me put the suspect in cuffs, Perez called for Doc Jones—but all I could think of was that I could have died right then, before I'd turned twenty, before I'd had a chance to hike in the Grand Canyon or see the Empire State Building or ride in one of those glass elevators I'd always wanted to try. I had been in Iraq nineteen days. The thought that this would be my life for the foreseeable future had the brutal force of a revelation. Later, while Doc Jones checked my knee, I watched Sergeant Fletcher pull the lieutenant to the side. "Sir, there was no need to send the men in like that. The farmer was cooperating, he told us about the hideout."

"No harm done," the lieutenant said.

"Not this time."

"Next time, we'll wait for you to finish your palavers."

"Yes, sir," Sergeant Fletcher said, but the way he said it sounded more like a warning. *Don't make this mistake again, asshole.* The lieutenant looked away, fiddled with his headset, said we should be ready to mount up soon. Fletcher came over to where I sat on the dirt with Doc Jones. "How's that knee, Gorecki?"

"It's inflamed," Doc Jones answered. "I'll give him some Motrin, but he'll have to stay off it for a day or two."

"Looks like you earned yourself a little break," Fletcher said with a smile.

I nodded, though I couldn't shake the feeling that I owed my life to chance. An empty barrel. Nor could I forget that the lieutenant had put me in that hole. Everything I'd once liked about him irritated me now. His jokes. His games. How he made sure everyone in the platoon knew he'd graduated from Duke. There was no subtlety to his bragging, either. Another thing: the lieutenant loved to have the whole platoon stand in their gear in the sun while he pontificated about the day's briefs, no matter how straightforward they were. I found myself wishing that Sergeant Fletcher had been in charge. Fletcher was smart, cautious, took care of his men like they were his own children. Sometimes, I still caught myself thinking about him that way.

As a father.

Which made what happened later all the more painful.

We were finally called to lane 8. In my hands, the gun was cold and hard and familiar. More than once I hit the bull's-eye. I was a good shot, had always been. Back in boot camp, my score on marksmanship had given me the confidence that the grueling physical training had all but taken away. Nothing compared to the rush of adrenaline before the shot, the cool calm in the aftermath, the reliability of the exercise in a world that was so plainly unreliable.

In the car, Fierro said he liked his new Glock so much that maybe he'd get one for his younger brother for Christmas. We were quiet as we listened to the radio. He coughed into his hands a few times, said, Dude, I think I'm coming down with something. Then we were in the driveway, saying goodbye with a handshake and a shoulder bump, telling each other we'd talk again in a few days. When I walked back inside my house, the scent of peonies and chocolate greeted me in the hallway. I put my gun in the safe and went out again.

· · ·

At the cabin, the porch light was off. But I tried the knob; the door was unlocked. I found Nora asleep on the couch, one of her hands folded under her face. She looked peaceful and fragile all at once, and I had a little argument with myself whether I should wake her. Then I ran my thumb along the arch of her foot. She stirred, looked at me confusedly as I knelt beside her. "You shouldn't leave the door open like that. It's not safe."

"I must've fallen asleep," she said, sitting up in surprise. The strap of her dress slid down, revealing the swell of a breast. I leaned in to kiss her. Pages from her composition, which had been resting on her stomach, fell to the floor. Black pen marks snaked between the lines and along the margins of every page. She picked them up, stacked them on her lap, holding them as lovingly as she might a child. "So," she said, and by the way she inflected the word I knew what she was going to ask next. "You go shooting guns often?"

"I'm a cop, Nora."

"I know, but even if you weren't, you'd have a gun?"

"Probably."

"Why?"

"For protection."

"From what?"

"People who come into your house without knocking," I teased. She waited for me to say more, but I had a feeling that talk of guns might lead to talk of war, which I was trying to avoid, so I handed her the pages of sheet music that had fallen to the floor and changed the subject. "Can I hear this sometime?" I asked.

"You want to?"

I'd found two pieces of hers online, one a classical composition and the other one more jazzy and I'd liked them both, but they were from three years before, and I was curious about what she was working on now. "Yes, of course."

She hesitated. "It's not done yet."

"I don't mind."

She stretched and yawned, then went to the bathroom to brush her teeth. I stood in the doorway for a minute, then came to stand beside her. Around the sink the caulking I'd redone the day before was bright against the scuffed pink tiles. She hadn't wanted me to bother with it, but when I pointed out that bad caulking could damage the wall, she relented. I ran my finger along the lines of grout; they had dried and the sink looked better now. "So can we finish our conversation?" I asked.

"What conversation?"

"What we were talking about before Fierro showed up."

She looked at me through the mirror and the appraising gaze I'd noticed in her eyes earlier that evening returned. She rinsed her mouth, put her toothbrush in the plastic cup next to the tap, and stood still. Unmoving. Unyielding. I slid a finger under the strap of her dress and moved it off her shoulder. As I pressed my lips against her skin, a wave of sadness hit me; all I would ever get from her was this, nothing more. Already I could see how it would end. I should enjoy this while it lasts, I told myself.

But then she turned to face me. "You really want to hear that piece?" There was a note of challenge in her voice. She was asking me something else: she was asking if I was really prepared for the thing I said I wanted. Outside, the wind chime started clinking, disturbing the silence. The turtledove cooed in response.

"Yes," I said. "Of course."

She walked over to her laptop and scrolled through her files until she found the right one. While the music played, I sat on the couch and closed my eyes, moved not just by how beautiful the piece sounded, but by how easily Nora had opened her heart to me. She held nothing back, and it terrified me that someday she might expect the same of me.

Anderson

It was an accident. Of course, the daughter tried to make it seem like it was more than that, got some people all riled up about it, but she didn't live here and didn't know what it was like. It was just an accident. Unfortunate and unavoidable, like the lawyer said. I wasn't even going to hire a lawyer, but Helen insisted because she didn't trust the police, and I guess she was right. I was glad we had Miss Perry in our corner, she looked out for us, even though we could barely afford her fee. What I don't understand is, what was that guy doing crossing the intersection when it was so dark out? The problem here, what we really should be talking about, is we need signals and lighting on that highway. But it makes no sense accusing people about something that couldn't've been prevented. Accidents happen. Why is that so hard to understand?

After my lawyer told me about the daughter's crazy accusations, I thought about visiting the restaurant next door and having a word with that young lady, telling her how she was mistaken about the whole thing. Miss Perry talked me out of it, though, said it would only make it seem like I had done something wrong. And I hadn't. I was trying to do the right thing.

People were different, back in my day. I remember another accident, in '75 or '76, a couple of years after Helen and I opened our bowling alley, and it didn't end up like this. It happened on Family Night. The special ran on Thursday afternoons from three to six p.m., but we still called it Family Night, so it would fit with the other themes Helen posted on the board out front. One day, a family with six kids came in. "You might want to get two lanes," I said to the father. He had a thick mustache, the kind that was popular in those days, and he looked so young it was hard to believe he had six children. But he wouldn't hear of paying for two lanes. He and his wife took their little tribe to lane 8. It took them a long while to play their games, especially since the youngest kid looked about three years old, and afterward, their seating area looked like a pigsty. The seats were covered with potato chips, even though the sign at the front clearly said that no food was allowed in the bowling area.

I had two parties waiting in the concourse, so I told my porter Greg to hurry up and clean up after them. He was sweeping the floors when he hit the bumper rail with his broom. It went down and so he kicked it back up with his foot, not thinking much of it, but the bumper fell right back down and sliced through his shoe. Greg is a big, burly guy from Moreno Valley, and yet the pain was so bad he passed out. I ran to his side, helped him up, and Helen got him some ice water. We drove him to the hospital—back then, that was High Desert Memorial in Yucca Valley—and waited with him to see what the doctor would say. They didn't have the technology they have nowadays, though, and he lost two toes on his left foot. Greg was a champ, he went back to work a couple of weeks later. We put up new signs about keeping food off the bowling area, and we were strict about enforcing safety rules. But we understood when something was an accident. We didn't go around trying to blame other people for what happened.

This town has changed a lot since then. Hardesty's Groceries is gone, and so is Steeley's Sporting Goods. We have a Walmart and an Applebee's now. We even got a Starbucks. All kinds of people have been coming here. All kinds. I go to the store these days, I don't recognize anybody. Used to be I always ran into friends or neighbors or even acquaintances from church. Not anymore. And the changes are happening so fast. Ten years ago, you could still have some peace and quiet around here, but now you have lines of tourists, their cars idling, waiting to get into the national park, or getting rowdy in their Airbnbs, doing drugs or God knows what. Some people say I should be grateful for the business that the newcomers are bringing to the town, but the way I see it, they're changing this place and wanting me to be grateful for it. They didn't ask if we wanted them here, they just came.

Coleman

When I don't have all the evidence I need, I trace a story from the few details I have, and see if it holds up. Late one Sunday afternoon, after I found Miles sprawled on the couch again, staring longingly at his Instagram, I told him that he could invite his new friend to dinner. As soon as Brandon texted that he could come, Miles ran off to clean his room—made his bed, picked up his dirty laundry, brought out the trash. Then he took a thirty-minute shower. Of course, Ray didn't notice anything, his eyes were glued to the TV. The Lakers were playing that evening, and no passion compares to that of a fan who's switched allegiances. I peeled the potatoes, marinated the chicken, and set the table for four. Miles came back into the living room reeking of Old Spice, and I dropped a fork just to make Ray look up. But no. Lakers at 78, Nuggets at 75, going into the third quarter.

Brandon rang the doorbell promptly at seven. He was in an old T-shirt and frayed khakis, but he'd made some effort to brush his floppy hair into place with gel. His bike was set next to my car on the driveway, and I noticed that the bottle in the holder was covered with a sticker that said REAL MEN RIDE BIKES. "Thank you for inviting me, Mrs. Coleman," he said as he stepped inside.

"My pleasure," I said.

Ray paused the basketball game and got out of the easy chair to shake hands with our guest. "Hello, young man."

"This is Brandon," I said. "He's in the same grade as Miles."

"Uh-huh," Ray said, his eyes darting back to the TV screen.

Miles jostled past me. "Wanna play *Battlefield* on Xbox?" he asked, and whisked Brandon off to his room. A minute later, the door closed behind them, Ray was back in his chair, and I was alone again.

When I have something on my mind, I try to give my hands something to do, just to keep myself from going crazy, but I had already cleaned the house from top to bottom and was out of ideas. So I sat next to Ray on the couch, biting my nails, a habit I hadn't been able to break despite his constant nagging about it. When the basketball game was finally over, I dressed the salad and called the boys to the table. The Lakers had won, thankfully, and Ray was in a great mood. He picked up the lemonade pitcher and started filling everyone's glasses. "So, Brandon. You and Miles are in the same classes?" he asked.

"No, Mr. Coleman. We don't have any classes together. We're just in the same grade."

"Right, right. That's what I meant."

The boys started serving themselves from the grilled potato dish. Miles picked up the bottle of ketchup and, without being asked, moved the jar of mustard next to Brandon's plate.

"Did you grow up here, Brandon?" I asked.

"Yes, but I was born in Torrance. My mom was going to school near there and she only moved back here after she finished."

"What was she studying?" Ray asked.

"Dental hygiene," Brandon said, and then he and Miles started laughing at some inside joke. The moment one of them stopped, the other started.

It had been weeks since I'd heard Miles's laughter, and the sound gave me such pleasure that I chuckled along with them. "What's so funny?" I asked.

"Nothing, Mom," Miles said.

Well, at least I was back to being his mom. That was something, even if he was still distant and refused to explain the joke to me. To have been so close to him for thirteen years only to find myself unable to pierce this new shield he'd built around himself was painful to me. I pushed the chicken around on my plate and waited for Ray to say something, but he only shook his head slowly, in a knowing way.

Later that night, when we were getting ready for bed, I asked him what he thought about Brandon. "Well, it takes all kinds," he said. It was an irritating habit my husband had, resorting to folk wisdom when he didn't know what to say.

What if I told him that Brandon wasn't just a friend for Miles? A few years ago, Ray had stopped visiting his cousin in New York after she'd moved in with her girlfriend, even though he always denied that this was the reason. "She changed after she went to grad school," he would say, "that's all it is. Nothing more." And now he was pretending not to notice what was right in front of him, which was strange, because he was such an attentive father. It was making me doubt myself. Maybe there was nothing to notice. Maybe I was making too much of the little things. Miles was happy, that much I could see. Wasn't it all that mattered?

I went to work the next day feeling drained from lack of sleep. Sitting in the briefing room, I drank a big cup of coffee and tried to pay attention to the daily reports. Vasco was cheerful—he'd gotten some good press after rescuing an abandoned baby and it seemed the Bowden incident was finally receding from the news. As we walked out of the conference room, he asked me where I was on the hit-and-run case. I told him the truth: I hadn't been able to find solid evidence of intent, so the murder investigation was pretty much dead. "That's good," he said. "Time to move on."

I went back to my desk, answered some emails, and tried to catch up on paperwork. Down the hall, the espresso machine in Murphy's office screeched. Had he noticed anything with our boys? If he had, he showed no sign of it. When I'd run into him in the break room earlier that morning, he'd given me a friendly smile, but didn't talk to me. I was about to drive to the Subway for lunch when I got a call from the front office that someone was here to talk to me about the Guerraoui case. A witness.

The notice in the newspaper and the posters I'd left around town nearly a month earlier had yielded a few dozen calls, but they'd all been useless, and anyway the case was essentially closed now. So when I walked into the lobby, I was more irritated than excited, convinced that this would only be a waste of my time. Mr. Aceves stood up quickly, and his hat fell from his lap. Picking it up with his left hand, he offered me his right. Next to him was a tiny woman who introduced herself as his wife. "I can translate for him," she said.

"That won't be necessary," I said. "We have several people here who speak Spanish."

This came as a disappointment to the couple. I don't think they wanted to be separated. When I invited Mr. Aceves to the interview room, he limped behind me like a man being led to the gallows.

Efraín

We sat in a small gray room, with the window shades drawn. There was a videotape recorder, which made me nervous, but the deputy who was brought in to translate, a feo with curly hair and braces on his teeth, told me that this was normal. "El protocolo," he said, and asked if I wanted some water or coffee. I said no. I was eager to get it over with, describe what I had seen that night, and leave. So I told the story the way I remembered it. "I was riding my bicycle on the 62, heading home after work, when the chain fell off my back gear." I was speaking to Detective Coleman, who sat across from me, but I had to wait while the deputy translated.

It was a strange way to tell a story, pausing after every sentence, waiting to hear it spoken in another language, though in a strange way this made me more conscious of its details. After a while, I was even relieved that there was a videotape, because once my words were recorded I would finally be free to forget them. That was all I wanted now. To put all this behind me. I couldn't take Guerrero's meddling in my life anymore, or Marisela's silence over the past few weeks. Even though she'd stopped asking me about the accident, I knew she wanted me to talk to the police and I hated to see the disappointment in her eyes, day after day, when I said no. I wanted things to go back to the way they were before.

As soon as I reached the end of my story, the detective made me tell it again, this time interrupting me with questions that could get me to contradict myself—or at least, that's how it seemed to me, because she spoke to me in a combative way. "Wait, were you going east or west on Highway 62?"

"East," I said.

"How far were you from the intersection when you stopped?"

"About a hundred feet. Maybe a hundred and fifty."

"And what happened after the car hit Mr. Guerraoui?"

"Well, the car turned left on Chemehuevi, and as it did, the man rolled off the hood and fell down on the pavement."

"You didn't try to help him?"

"He wasn't moving," I said, glancing at the translator for help. "He wasn't moving at all. I was sure he was dead."

"You said earlier that the accident happened at nine thirty. But how did you know the time? You're not wearing a watch."

"No. But I leave work at about nine and I usually get home by ten. The intersection is about halfway between my work and my apartment, so I'm guessing it happened around nine thirty, but I could be wrong."

"And what color was the car?"

"Silver, I think."

"Make and model?"

"I'm not sure. I only saw the car from the side as it turned on Chemehuevi. But it was a sedan with a long hood. I think it might have been a Ford."

"Did you read about this in the newspaper, Mr. Aceves?"

"What newspaper? I didn't read anything about this. I just saw a car like it in the parking lot of Kasa Market."

"What about the sticker on the side window? What did it look like?"

"It was round and red, like an apple."

"Were there any passengers in this car?"

"I didn't see any passengers."

"What about the driver?"

"I didn't really see him."

"But it was a *him*?"

"I think so. He was wearing a baseball cap."

"And did he slow down?"

No, he didn't. I had told her this the first time, but she asked me again anyway, asked me to close my eyes and return to that night, see if the driver had paused at any time, either before or after striking Guerrero. I told her once more that the driver hadn't slowed down and hadn't stopped. If anything, he'd sped up. That's what had made me look up from my bicycle—the sound of the car speeding up.

"When did he speed up?"

"When?"

"Before or after hitting the victim?"

"Before."

"Are you sure about this?"

I had heard the car speeding up, then the sound of the impact. "Yes," I said. "He sped up before. Then after he hit the man, he took the turn and ran off again down Chemehuevi."

Again, she asked me to start over, tell the story from the beginning. By the time I stepped out of that room, it was well past lunchtime and I was exhausted. I wasn't even sure whether I had been of any help, because the detective refused to say. All she said was that someone from the district attorney's office would be in touch with me when the case went to trial.

When I came out to the lobby, Marisela stood up. "How was it?"

"It's done," I said. "Let's go."

I took her hand and hurried down the stairs to the glass doors. Marisela had taken the morning off from work to be with me, but as we came out into the sunlight I worried that I had only entangled her in this mess. I had spent weeks burdened by guilt and apprehension, and I still wasn't completely free of either. If the case went to trial, I would again have to remember the accident and talk about it in front of others, and if there was no trial, my name was somewhere in those police files now, where it could be found at the touch of a button. "What about the reward?" she asked, touching my arm.

"They said they have to check if the information I gave is correct."

Her face fell. Maybe she expected that I would walk out of the police station with one of those huge checks, the kind people get when they win the lottery, and now it was dawning on her that it would take a few days, maybe even a few weeks, to get the money. In the meantime, they would know where to find us. We walked the length of the parking lot, past the Morongo Basin courthouse, and up the street to the bus stop.

It was a cloudy day, but the heat was scorching. We sat together under the awning, sweating and waiting. Marisela took my hand and squeezed it. "Everything's going to work out," she said. She was trying to give me hope and, for once, I let myself believe her. Twenty-five thousand dollars was a lot of money, more than we'd ever had before. It was enough to start over in a new place, where the police wouldn't know where we lived. The highway stretched for miles ahead of us, leading out of the desert toward the ocean. All we had to do was take it.

Nora

I was helping Marty hang a Memorial Day banner on the front window of the restaurant when Detective Coleman called to tell me she had a witness, a motel worker who'd been riding his bicycle on the highway the night of April 28. He mentioned a red sticker on the rear side of Baker's window, a detail that had not been made public, and told her that the driver had sped up as he approached the intersection and again after the impact, which suggested that he was conscious he had hit someone, and should not have left the scene. This testimony was the first solid piece of evidence, she said, to show that the driver had been willfully reckless.

The word *solid* nearly took my breath away. My father's dead body, my mother's claims about Baker, the handwritten note about parking spaces—none of these had been solid enough. If it weren't for this witness, the case would have dissolved like ether. My eyes welled with tears, and I had to move away from the ladder and sit down on the curb to catch my breath. Now that I'd started crying, it happened all the time, even when I tried to resist it. Wiping my cheeks with the palm of my hand, I asked, "So now you have proof that Baker killed my dad?"

"Proof that he knew he'd hit the victim."

"But not that it was murder?"

"A murder charge requires a much higher standard of proof. I think the D.A. is looking at vehicular manslaughter."

"He doesn't believe the witness?"

"I don't know what he believes, I couldn't say. But it's worth remembering that there's no streetlight at that intersection and that

Mr. Baker is seventy-eight years old. Some people shouldn't be driving at that age."

I was quiet for a while, trying to process everything the detective had told me. A blue van came into the parking lot, trailing thick exhaust, and the driver sat with the engine running as he fiddled with something in the backseat. Behind me, the diner's door jingled and a woman came out, carrying leftovers in a Styrofoam container.

"Listen," Coleman said. "I understand your frustration, I do. But vehicular manslaughter is a very serious charge and we might not have gotten this far if it weren't for the reward you put up. You've done what you could."

The sun had risen above the palo verde tree on the side of the restaurant, and the light was on my face. For the past five weeks, each day had begun with the same two realizations, agonizing and immutable: my father was dead and his killer was free. But now, for the first time, I could allow myself to imagine a day when Baker would have to answer, at least in part, for what he did. "Will he go to jail?"

"Probably. But that really depends on the jury."

And, I thought, on the stories that the defense and prosecution told in court. "Can I at least meet this witness?" I asked. "I want to thank him for coming forward."

"I wouldn't advise it. I think it might be better to wait until after the trial."

"What about the reward?"

"If you sign the check, we'll make sure he gets it."

"All right," I said. "Thank you for everything, Detective."

I stood up and dusted myself off. Marty walked past me, carrying the stepladder, glancing one more time at the banner that said HAPPY MEMORIAL DAY in red, white, and blue. Underneath the greeting, in block letters, came the plea, or perhaps the admonishment, to remember those who had made the ultimate sacrifice. Soon, newspapers would run their annual celebrations of American soldiers, and politicians would take turns pandering to them. Meanwhile, the civilians who died in American wars would receive only silence. National memory was built from such erasures.

But private memory was nothing but a struggle against erasure. I wanted to make sure that my father wasn't forgotten. At the Pantry, I had kept everything exactly as it had been before he died. Already I was settling into a routine. In the mornings, I opened the restaurant and did whatever needed to be done—handled the cash register, restocked the bathrooms with paper towels, called the electric store for replacement bulbs for the kitchen. Usually, I ate lunch standing at the counter. In the afternoon, I went back to the cabin and took a nap, which was often interrupted by the sound of the turtledove teaching its chicks how to fly. Then I would make coffee and finally sit at the piano. In other words, I had been trying to hold on to the past at all cost. My mother knew better; she didn't try to fight her feelings of pain or fear, but accepted them as she might accept unwelcome visitors, knowing that someday, even if it was very far in the future, they would leave. It was a strength she derived from her deep faith, and in that moment I envied her for it. All I had were uncertainties.

Jeremy

Afterward Nora went to the bathroom. Without meaning to, I found myself listening, wondering if she had gone in there to cry. But in a moment, I heard the toilet flush, water running from the tap, and she was back in my bedroom, wearing one of my T-shirts. She stood looking at my bookshelves, tilting her head sideways so she could read the spines. Asimov. Bradbury. Butler. Clarke. Dick. During a severe bout of insomnia some months earlier I'd alphabetized all my books, music, and movies, and organized them by genre while I was at it. At the height of my sleeplessness, I could tear through three novels a week. Now I watched her run her finger over my Terry Gilliam DVDs, examine the papier-mâché lighthouse I'd made in grade school and never thrown away, no matter how often I'd moved. Then she pulled out a photo box from the shelf beside the bed. "Leave that," I said, raising myself on one elbow. "It's getting late."

Playfully, she lifted the box out of my reach.

"All right," I said after a minute. "Sit here, though." I patted the space next to me.

The photos were not in any particular order; I'd tossed them there after pooling together several rolls of photographs. She picked up the first one, a picture of me at Camp Taqaddum, and suddenly I was looking at myself through her eyes. An invader. An occupier. An imperialist. Labels I would have easily applied to myself if I were arguing with my father or with other vets, whether in person or in the online discussion forums I logged into late at night when I couldn't sleep, but that I had a hard time accepting from civilians, people far removed from the fog of war. She picked up the pictures one by one, and I saw myself waiting in the noontime heat again with ninety pounds of gear on me. Riding in a Humvee, my chinstrap so tight it was giving me a rash. Leaning against the barracks wall, my eyes bluer than ever in my sunburned face. Standing at a checkpoint with my weapon in my hands. "What does it say?" she asked, pointing to the big sign hanging from a light pole behind me.

"I don't know. That was an Iraqi sign, it wasn't one of ours. You don't read Arabic?"

"I never studied it, but I speak it just fine."

I offered up my palm. "Eedik, min fadlik."

"Listen to you! They taught you that in training?"

She gave me her hand and I made a show of kissing it. Then I whispered in her ear, "Keefik, ya sukkar?"

"They definitely didn't teach you that in training," she said with a chuckle.

"Our terp was kind of a player. He was always trying to sweet-talk a Sudanese woman who worked in the laundry facility."

"Terp?"

"Interpreter."

"Were there any women in your platoon?"

"No, but there were in others."

"Arabs?"

"One guy from Florida. Haydar. He's still in Iraq. He's an NCO now. Noncommissioned officer." I put my arm around her waist and she leaned against me, the heft of her almost like an armor itself.

"How old were you here?" It was a photo taken at chow, during our first tour. Fierro and I had big smiles on our faces and blueberry jam smeared across our teeth. Trying to be funny. We looked like idiots.

"Nineteen."

"Nineteen. My God." She stared at the photo for a long moment, then moved to another, where I stood with others in our unit, our M4s hanging from our shoulders. "What was it like, carrying that around?"

"You get used to it. You get used to anything, I guess. When they took it away after my deployment, it felt like they had taken away one of my arms. It took a while to learn how to walk around without it."

In the neighbor's yard, the dog barked. It was a German shepherd, a friendly pup that I'd played with before, but it still got nervous when it heard a noise, even if it was only the call of a bird or the roar of a car down the street. She picked up another photo, where we all stood around Sergeant Fletcher, squinting in the sunlight.

Enough of this, I thought. I closed the box, tossed it on the nightstand, and switched off the light. Then I turned to face the wall. In the dark I felt her tracing the scar on my back; it started on my flank and snaked up toward my shoulder, like a tree bending sideways against the wind. She ran her hand over the line of black dots that still opened from time to time, spitting out shrapnel. I knew this moment would come. I knew she would start asking questions about the war; all the women I'd been with did. I would give them the broadest outline of a story about my time in Iraq, and their eyes would widen with horror and they'd want to kiss me and make me feel better. It wasn't hard, it worked every time. There was something false about it, though. Even when I managed to hold on to them for more than a couple of months, the look in their eyes that said I was a hero would drive me away. But Nora didn't look at me with that kind of wonder. Long before I'd gone to war, war had come to her—a brick thrown in her father's window, a slur written on her locker. I wouldn't be able to satisfy her with the answers I'd given the others, and even if I could, I wasn't sure I wanted to. With her, I was less inclined to speak of the war in two voices, the wistful one I used with my buddies and the weary one I reserved for my dates. With her, everything felt mixed-up.

Outside, the dog barked again, though no unusual sound had interrupted the silence. The barking startled the crickets, but after a minute they started singing, and then an owl joined their song. I got up to close the window and adjusted and readjusted the blackout curtains until I got them just right. All the while, I avoided her gaze. "I think I'm gonna take a bath," I said. "That damn dog won't let me sleep."

I stepped into the bathroom and sat in the tub as it filled with water, nudging the lever handle toward the hottest setting with my foot. Being asked about the war meant having to remember it, and to remember the war was to relive it. It was one thing when the memories were involuntary, like that time I walked into a gas station in Riverside and caught a whiff of perfume on the clerk that took me so immediately to a crowded market square in Anbar that I nearly doubled over from the sensation, but to recall memories willfully was another thing entirely. The door creaked open and Nora stepped inside the bathroom and knelt by the side of the tub. She ran her finger on my tattoo, the scar on my side, the scratches she herself had left during our lovemaking. My body bore signs that I knew she wanted to decipher and piece together into a story, but it would always be an incomplete story. To tell her the whole of it was to risk her judgment, and I already judged myself every day. "Are you coming to bed?" she asked.

"In a minute," I said, avoiding her eyes.

After she stepped out of the bathroom, I stayed in the tub. Maybe I should stop thinking of my time in the war as a story and tell it to her the way I remembered it late at night when I couldn't sleep, in fragments, sometimes in order and sometimes out of order, stopping in places where the remembering got too close to the reliving. By now the bathwater had grown uncomfortably cold and I shivered as I dried myself. In the dark of the bedroom, I found her sitting on the bed, already dressed in the blue shirt and linen skirt she'd worn for dinner at the Italian restaurant we went to in Palm Springs. "You're leaving?" I asked.

"I figured you wanted to be alone," she said, slipping her feet into her shoes. She reached for her watch on the bedside table and stood up. The clasp clicked in the silence. "It's getting late, anyway."

"Don't go," I said, crossing the room toward her in the sliver of light. "Please. Stay."

I was naked and cold, and she looked at me for a moment before taking her shoes off and lying back on the bed. I nestled against her, draping my arm across her hip and tucking my knees against hers, soaking up the warmth of her. When I spoke, my voice was barely above a whisper. A month into our second tour, Sergeant Fletcher received some information about the whereabouts of a sniper who'd killed one of our guys and wounded four, a shooter so skilled that we were all speculating he must have been trained in the Iraqi military. The target was supposed to be hiding in an apartment building on the eastern side of Ramadi, and we rolled out at zero four hundred, when the neighborhood was shrouded in darkness and the air still cool. The first to dismount was Perez, whom we nicknamed Chewie because of his red hair and mustache, then the rest of us followed. We'd gone maybe nine or ten yards when Perez got blown up. All we could find of him later was a leg that landed on the hood of our Humvee, and his intestines hanging from a tree. The sergeant had us collect what we could into a bag, which would be shipped to Perez's family in Texas for the funeral.

A couple of days later, Sergeant Fletcher took us to see the informant who'd told him about the sniper's hiding place. His name was Badawi, a former clerk at the Ministry of Interior. He had a nice house, with blue trim on the windows and an addition above the kitchen that he was still building. There was a whiff of burned bread in the hallway—that was the smell I could still smell in my dreams—and the only people inside were Badawi's wife and children. Aside from making tea when we came to visit, the wife had never spoken to any of us. When Fletcher asked where her husband was, she said she didn't know, that he hadn't come home the night before. She was in a green housedress with a geometric pattern, and her hair was in a kerchief tied at the nape of her neck. Her kids sat on the floor, playing cards, the presence of Marines no longer a novelty to them, yet she could barely disguise her contempt for us. Her eyes were full of blame. Each question Fletcher asked, she answered with a clipped yes or no.

"Maybe she can't say anything in front of the kids," Fletcher said. He took her into the back room, and Fierro and I stayed behind, keeping an eye on the children. The game they played was unfamiliar to me, and I tried to figure out the rules by watching them. Not ten minutes later, the terp came out, walking past us to the front door.

"We done here?" Fierro asked.

"No, but the sergeant doesn't need me. That woman speaks English."

Fierro and I looked at each other, stunned. In the six months we'd been coming to this house to visit the informant, his wife had never given any indication that she understood us. Now I wondered what we might have said in her presence, whether it had any intelligence value, whether it might have been used against us. And there were other comments, too, comments about her, obscene things we were confident our English concealed. From the back room came the sound of a chair being dragged against the floor. "Sergeant?" I asked. But there was no answer: Fletcher had turned off his headset.

I went down the hallway, keeping the kids in my line of vision. Even with the sound of the nature documentary that was showing on television, I heard the pop clearly. I reached for the door, but it flew open and Fletcher came out, his body filling the frame. "What's going on?" I asked.

"She tried to reach for my sidearm."

Behind him, the woman lay on the floor, a bullet hole through her cheek, choking on her own blood. I walked into the room, yet her eyes didn't track me, they were fixed on a spot in the ceiling. A minute later, she stopped moving. We mounted up and left, but all the way back to camp I ran through the sequence of events that had started with the killing of Perez and ended with the killing of Badawi's wife. The story, or what I could make of it, had an arc that my instinct told me was wrong and, once we were alone in the barracks, I tried to ask Fierro about it.

"What the fuck does it matter?" he said.

"It doesn't bother you that she didn't have anything to do with this?"

"You don't know that."

"You don't know that she did, either."

"One of our guys is dead and you want me to worry about her? Go the fuck to sleep."

At chow the next morning I sat next to Fletcher, found a way to bring the conversation back to the night before, but he only shrugged and said the wife had gone crazy when he'd told her he'd find Badawi no matter how long it took, and that's when she'd reached for his weapon. "And you couldn't stop her?" I asked. "A tiny woman like her?"

"I *did* stop her," he said with a frown. "What's the matter with you, Gorecki? Take some time to think through what you just implied here. Think it through carefully; you might have a different perspective."

My perspective wouldn't have changed if I'd stayed where I'd been ordered to, in the living room with Fierro. I wouldn't have seen or heard anything. But I'd taken four inquisitive steps down the hallway, and those four steps made me doubt everything. Fletcher wasn't trying to win the war—that was something for the higher-ups to worry about. He cared only about protecting his men. And he wanted to avenge them, too. But my questions had clearly irritated him and I found out just how much when he posted me on shitter cleanup duty for three days. Three whole days. I remember pulling out the first tub, pouring fuel over it, and before striking the match to light it up, doubling over to puke.

"What was her name?" Nora asked. "The woman Fletcher killed."

"I don't know. He filed a report, but I never got to see it."

At some point while I was telling her the story, she'd turned around to face me. Somehow, she had removed all my pretenses. It was as if she had found the right key to unlock a rusty old safe, and the contents spilled out. But I couldn't tell if I had gone too far, told too much. We were quiet for a while. Eventually, she closed her eyes, and I held her until the morning, when she got up to go to work.

Nora

I was wrestling with the lock on the medicine cabinet in the storage room when Veronica walked in with a half-empty bag of Dixie cups. She tied it in a knot and hoisted it easily onto the top shelf, where it landed with a loud, crinkly sound that set my teeth on edge. My head was throbbing, and the lock wasn't cooperating. Veronica watched me for a minute and then, in a practiced gesture, readjusted the key and opened the medicine cabinet for me. "There," she said. "It gets stuck sometimes."

"Thanks," I said. Inside the cabinet were bottles of antiseptic, antibiotic ointment, and bandages of all sizes, but no painkillers. "We don't have any Ibuprofen?"

"We must've run out."

On the wall next to the cabinet was a framed picture of the Pantry staff, taken the day my father had opened for business, twelve years earlier. Marty, still with a full head of hair, held a menu, and a younger Veronica, looking prim in her new uniform, smiled shyly at the camera. From the kitchen came the clatter of glasses being loaded into the rack.

"Ask Rafi," Veronica said. Her tone suddenly turned vicious. "He's always helping himself to stuff around here. Maybe he took it." Then she pulled a pack of cigarettes and a lighter from her apron pocket and stepped out.

I slammed the medicine cabinet shut. Managing the restaurant these last few weeks had opened my eyes to all the petty grievances the workers nursed toward one another: Veronica didn't like Rafi, who had a crush on Renata, who was sleeping with José, who thought Marty was out to get him. I couldn't keep up. I walked back to the dining room, where a couple with three young children was being seated, the toddler screaming, refusing to sit in the high chair. My head throbbed.

I poured myself a cup of coffee and sat down at the counter to drink it. The night before, Jeremy and I had stayed up late talking, and I had gotten little sleep. I didn't know why I was spending so much time with him. He wasn't the sweet kid I knew in high school; he had fought in a brutal war, a war I hated. Hearing about the terrible things he had seen or done in Iraq made me feel implicated, something I hadn't grasped until it was too late. I didn't know how to navigate back to my state of ignorance. There was no map I could follow.

I was taking the trash out to the dumpster later that morning when I saw a blue station wagon pull up in front of Desert Arcade. The car had a broken taillight, a yellow ribbon decal on the back window, and a bumper sticker that said PROUD PARENT OF AN HONOR ROLL STUDENT. A family of four got out. Father, mother, two girls. "Mommy, can I get a Skittles from the machine?" the older girl asked. Her hair was plaited and pinned on top of her head, in a style that made her look like a milkmaid. The younger girl had dark hair and walked blindly behind, her eyes never leaving the comic book she was reading.

A happy family.

I was so drawn to them that when they went into the bowling alley, I followed. It took a moment for my eyes to adjust to Desert Arcade's dimly lit lobby. A floor-to-ceiling advertisement for Budweiser Beer was pasted on the far wall, though its colors had dulled with age and one of its corners was peeling. On the stereo, the chorus of a pop ballad I didn't recognize was playing at top volume. A huge flag hung over the front counter, where the family stood, waiting for bowling shoes. When they ambled away to their lane, the clerk turned to me. "Can I help you?"

The sound of a pin strike drew my gaze to the bowling area. In one of the farther lanes, two older men, their sunglasses resting on the visors of their baseball caps, were looking up at the screen for their scores. The family of four had just sat down in lane 5, and the father was entering names in the machine, while the mother helped the girls choose bowling balls.

"Can I help you?" the clerk said again.

I turned back to say no, that I was about to leave, but then I saw A.J. standing next to the concession stand at one end of the concourse. He was speaking on his cell phone, but his eyes were fixed on me. Did he work at the bowling alley now? He certainly looked it, in his black polo shirt and name tag. Perhaps he was taking over the business from his father, just as I was taking over the restaurant from my dad. My skin broke into goose bumps. It's just the air conditioning, I told myself, that's all it is. I wasn't sixteen anymore, A.J. didn't scare me.

"Can I help you?"

"Yes," I said. "Can I buy a game, please?"

"What size shoe?"

"Seven."

"Here you go. Lane 3."

I paid and took the red-and-blue bowling shoes to my lane. I didn't have socks, and the insoles of the shoes felt rough and scratchy. No matter. I tied the shoelaces and stood up. Nearly all the bowling balls on the rack were too heavy for me, but I chose one anyway, for its color, a deep red. Walking to the foul line, I threw the ball down the lane. It fell with a loud thud and ended up in the gutter. The next ball missed, too, and the one after that, but I persisted, and eventually I hit one pin.

"Nora."

I turned around to find A.J. standing not five feet from me. He fixed me with a stare that pinned me to the spot. Time stopped. It seemed to me as if we were in that school hallway again, me standing at my locker, the slur scribbled in blue, and him with his arm around Stacey Briggs. The other students walked hurriedly past on their way to class. No one came to my side, no word was spoken in my defense.

"You're doing it all wrong," A.J. said in a measured voice. "You need to straighten your wrist. Let me show you."

He picked up a bowling ball and placed it in my hands, maneuvering my fingertips into the holes, first my thumb, and then my ring and middle fingers. The resin was dry and as he pushed my fingers into the ball, it scraped my skin painfully. Fear and revulsion raced inside me. "The trick," he was saying as he gripped my hand and mimed swinging the ball, "is to keep your hand straight, otherwise when you pitch the ball, the arc is off." He was so close I could feel his hot breath against my neck. My pulse quickened. I managed to free myself from his grip and, with all the power I could muster, pitched the ball down the lane. It hit four pins.

"See? That's much better already," he said.

The sweeping bar cleared the fallen pins and reset those that remained. A.J. walked up to the foul line with a new ball, a blue fifteen-pounder. He raised it to his chest for a moment and then, with a fluid but powerful movement of the wrist, released it down the lane. The remaining pins fell in a clatter. He turned to me. "Like that." Then he smiled. "Enjoy the rest of your game."

I waited until he'd walked away, then went to the counter, turned in my shoes, and rushed back to the safety of the Pantry. My heart was beating so fast I had to sit on the wooden bench at the entrance. That was where Veronica found me a moment later. "I have something for you," she said, brandishing a bottle of Ibuprofen.

"You're a lifesaver," I said, taking it from her and walking to the counter for a tall glass of water.

"Rafi had it stashed in his cupboard."

"I'm sure he just forgot to put it back."

She gave me a look that said I was naïve, but maybe someday I'd come around.

A.J.

I couldn't wrestle in this town, not seriously anyway, so I ended up spending all my free time with my collies, Gordon and Annie. I walked them, played with them, taught them how to steer clear of rattlesnakes and scorpions, and sometimes after I got home from work, I took them out to my parents' backyard and trained them to gait properly. I was seriously considering showing them, the way my mom and I did when I was a kid. I'd loved traveling to different parts of California with her, taking care of the dogs, watching them compete. We made the perfect team: my mom would fill out the paperwork and talk to the handlers and breeders and judges, and I would groom the collies and keep them company until the show.

One time, we traveled all the way up to Fresno for an AKC competition. It was the farthest we'd gone from home, but we thought it was worth it because our dog Royal was doing so well that year that he had a good chance at winning first prize. A lot of people watch conformation shows on television and think that winning is about appearance, but the truth is that it's about much more than that. A dog can look great and never win, because aside from appearance and behavior, what the judges are really looking for is purity, the kind of traits that will be passed down the line to the offspring. Not that appearance doesn't matter. Of course it does. It was my job to make sure Royal looked perfect, that his fur was smooth and shiny, his ears clean, his teeth bright, all of that. When he won Best of Breed at the Fresno show, I felt as if I had won something myself, that's how much work I put into it.

But late that Sunday night, when we came back home, my dad was waiting up for us. I remember that David Letterman was on TV, and that the volume was cranked all the way up, because my dad was starting to lose some of his hearing.

"We won," I hollered, just so he could hear me over the sound of the Top 10 List, and held up Royal's first-place ribbon as if for proof.

My dad turned off the TV and struggled out of the armchair. He was a big guy, and he had to look down to meet my mom's eyes. "Do you know what time it is?" he asked her.

"We didn't leave Fresno until late," she said. She put down her purse on the coffee table and unzipped her fleece jacket, but didn't take it off. It was a cold night in February, and my dad hadn't turned on the heater. He was cheap like that.

"You told me you'd leave by four at the latest."

"Oh, I know. But there were so many people to meet after the show. One of the judges is from Ashland, and she said we should enter Royal in a show up there."

"Ashland. All the way in Oregon?"

"Yeah."

I came closer so I could show him the ribbon. It was blue and yellow and had the AKC logo on it. "We won first prize," I said.

Who knows what set him off? Maybe it was the sound of my voice, or the fact that Royal was jostling him, trying to take his seat on the armchair. "First prize, huh?" he said. "And how much did this cost?"

I had no idea. I glanced at my mom for help, but he put his heavy arm on my shoulder and, pushing Royal aside roughly, made me sit down in his armchair. On the coffee table was a yellow notepad filled with his scribblings, and he tore out a page from it and told me to write down the cost of everything we had spent that weekend: gas for the van, lodging at the dog hotel, our meals, the show fee, everything.

My mom hovered about, saying things like Come on, honey, not now, and Why don't we do this in the morning? But my dad waved her off and made me write down the numbers and add them. I wasn't very good at math, and it took me a while to finish.

"How are you planning to pay for this?" he said.

I couldn't understand why he was asking me these questions. I was thirteen years old, I didn't handle the money. "Mom," I said.

"*Mom,*" he mimicked. Then he turned on her. "All right, *Mom.* Do you have any idea how many shoe rentals and bowling games it takes to pay for the little weekend the two of you just had?"

"Come on, Anderson," she said. "Not now. We're tired."

"Oh, you're tired? How do you think I feel? I spent all day working, I couldn't even take a break because Greg called in sick, while you two were out there in Fresno, having a good time. Do you know how much I made today? And how much you spent?"

When he got into one of his tempers, it was useless arguing with him because he could go on for hours. If he ran out of arguments, he would go back to the first one and start over. This wasn't about the money. It wouldn't have mattered if we had spent $50 or $5,000, he would have made a scene, because my mom and I had done something together that made us happy, and he felt left out. We went to bed and the next morning everything was back to normal—until a few weeks later, when my mom and I went to another dog show, in San Diego. He saw a picture of us riding a roller-coaster by the seaside, and he flew into another rage. After a while, my mom got tired of it. She sold the few dogs she'd bred, and we stopped going to shows. She kept just two, Royal and Loyal.

By the time I moved back home, those two were getting old. Royal was blind in one eye and Loyal had arthritis, and I kept telling my mom that sooner or later she would have to put them down. Gordon and Annie were collies, too, but Annie had the blood of a champion. At thirteen months old, she had better conformation than Royal did at his best. That's what gave me the idea of entering her into dog shows. But I never got a chance to do that, on account of what happened that summer.

Jeremy

Nora had told me she was seriously considering taking over the Pantry from her mother, and even though I couldn't imagine her as a restaurant owner, or any kind of a business owner, I encouraged it. I drove with her to the Costco in Palm Springs when she needed to buy supplies for the diner. I helped her install a wooden chandelier in the cabin, an antique she had found at a thrift store, and offered to repaint her kitchen. I did anything I could to tie her to this town, and to me. Something had shifted that night when we were in my house. Everything I had once feared about love—the risk it required, the pain it could cause—seemed insignificant to me now. From the moment I had seen her standing on her parents' deck, lost like ten mislaid years, I had been willing to take the risk. And the pain that might still come my way was easy to push out of my mind when I took her in my arms.

Often, I reminded her about things she seemed to have forgotten: that she'd given a class presentation on heredity in Gregor Mendel's pea plants, which was interrupted by an earthquake drill; that she'd built the campfire on the overnight field trip to Whitewater Preserve; that she'd lied about sleeping at a friend's house the night a group of us had gone to Anaheim for a concert. But now I was also discovering new things about her: what she looked like at dawn, just before the light filtered through the window above us; how her voice softened when she talked to her mother on the phone, and hardened when she talked to her sister. She was smiling more easily, and more often, and for the first time in years I began to think about the future.

The only thing that could have made my life better would've been if my boss would stop being so difficult, and that, too, changed abruptly at the end of May. That morning, I hadn't heard my alarm and was fifteen minutes late to the briefing, which earned me a sarcastic "Thank you for joining us," from Vasco and three warrants to serve. The first two warrants were for drug possession and went without a hitch, but when I tried to serve the third, the perp took one look at me and went off through the back of the house. I chased after him, jumped over the wire fence, and ran into the desert for three hundred yards before I caught up to him. I slammed him to the ground and got on top of him. My knee was on his back as I cuffed him, my heart was racing, my gear felt like it had doubled in weight. It was high noon, a hundred and two degrees, and we were in a patch of empty land. How far did he think he could go? "Officer," he said. "Listen, I wasn't expecting a cop. I got spooked."

And all for petty theft. I did a full search, expecting to find pot or meth or even a weapon on this fool, but there was nothing. My uniform was covered in dirt and sand, and there was a big hole in the right leg of my pants. I wanted to book him and go back to the station to change, but there was a service call waiting for me nearby, a disturbance out in Joshua Tree, in that dusty section where old homesteader cabins sat next to trailers surrounded by chicken-wire fences and guarded by mean-looking mutts. When I pulled up to the address, I found an old man sitting on a porch chair, shirtless and with a Mountain Dew in hand. "Afternoon, Officer." He walked up to the cruiser window and stood so close that I could see the white hairs on his chest. "I'm the one that called. Name's Jim. Jim Novacek."

"What's the matter, Mr. Novacek?"

"Gorecki, huh," he said, looking at the nametag on my uniform. "You Polish?"

It was a hot day in the valley, even for May, and the air was thick with dust and sand. This kind of weather made people cranky, especially old people with nothing better to do—they called the police over the smallest little thing and then they wanted to chat. "What's the matter here, Mr. Novacek?"

"Like I told the lady on the phone, this neighborhood's not what it used to be. All those Mexicans everywhere now."

In the backseat, the suspect sucked his teeth in agreement.

This happened from time to time, people assuming things about me. Part of it was my last name, but the other part was my light skin. Once, in high school, Victor Alcala, a handsome kid who was popular with girls, started taunting me. Hey, Big Tits, he called across the hallway. What time is the concert tonight? I kept my eye on my locker, shuffled my notebooks, tried to ignore the laughter around me. Yet help came quickly, and from an unlikely source: Stacey Briggs hurled back a string of racist taunts so vicious that they left Victor speechless. He never bothered me again. And I never corrected Stacey, never told her I had more in common with Victor than she ever imagined.

"Mr. Novacek," I said, trying hard to keep my voice from rising. "You called for a noise disturbance, and I don't hear anything."

"It's coming from this dump over here." The old man pointed to the house next door. It had a flat roof and boarded-up windows. Garbage in the yard. A clothesline with no pins. An empty doghouse. "The mewling won't stop."

"It's a cat? You should've called animal control."

"But I see Mexican kids coming in and out of that house all day. Drinking and doing drugs and God only knows what. They probably tortured that poor cat in there. That's why I called the cops."

I got out of the cruiser and stood with my hands on my belt. Under my uniform, beads of sweat traveled down my spine, landing in that space just below my bulletproof vest. When would this day be over?

Then a soft mewling sound rose.

"You hear that?" the old man said.

"Yeah, I hear it."

I called it in. With one hand on my sidearm, I walked up to the house. There was no lock on the front door, just a bit of wire that looped through the knob hole and connected it to the doorframe. I unfastened the wire, but the door was heavy and I had to push hard until it gave in with a loud creak. The smell of dust, bird shit, and old newspaper made me want to gag. The house was so dark I felt as though I had fallen into an abyss. I turned on my flashlight and aimed it straight ahead. A small living room appeared, with a low ceiling and a brick fireplace. On the far wall, someone had spray-painted GO HOME in red block letters. There were crushed beer cans all over the floor.

Hypodermic needles. Cigarette butts. Playing cards. Except for an old couch with big holes where the seat cushions should've been, there was no furniture.

Then there was a movement, a faint rustling I might not have heard if I hadn't been standing still. I turned my flashlight on the couch and moved closer, my pulse quickening with anticipation. Deep in the hole was a heap of blue blankets, from which arose a tiny little fist. The milky smell of the infant was so strong in my nostrils now that I wondered why I hadn't noticed it sooner. I set the flashlight on the dirty wood floor and dropped to my knees. The baby's eyes were wide open and as soon as they landed on me the crying started, this time with the full force of expectation. I slid both of my hands inside the hole and brought out the blue bundle. Cradling the infant in my arms, I parted the blanket and was relieved to see no obvious sign of injury. A soiled diaper, though. The crying intensified. "Shsh," I whispered, "shsh, little buddy, it's okay." I gave him my index finger and immediately he grabbed it. Holding him close in my arms, I walked back out of the house, pushing the front door open wider with my leg. In the yard, the neighbor was waiting, squinting in the sunlight. "I'll be darned," he said.

I turned my back to the sun, so the baby would be in the shade, and radioed dispatch again. I couldn't remember what the procedure was in a case like this, I had to wait for instructions from the sergeant. But for once, Vasco was nice. "Stay put, Gorecki," he said. "We're sending help right away."

The moment the paramedic put his stethoscope on the baby's chest, he started to cry again, kicking his feet inside the blankets. "Heartbeat's good," the medic said with a smile. He was an older guy who dyed his hair and wore a thick layer of ChapStick, trying, I think, to hold on to what remained of his surfer looks. When he was finished taking the baby's vitals, he brought out a bottle of water. "He's got crystals in his diaper. He's completely dehydrated."

"How long do you think he's been in there?" I asked.

"Hard to say. If I had to guess, twenty-four hours. Maybe thirty six."

"Jesus."

Behind us, the neighbor was giving a statement to the detective, spelling out his last name carefully. "N-o-v-a-c-e-k." The suspect I'd almost forgotten about was still waiting in the back of the cruiser. Two deputies were checking the house one more time for evidence. And all the while, Sergeant Vasco was giving an interview to a reporter from the *Hi-Desert Star*. The next morning, his picture was on the front page of the newspaper, with the baby in his arms. "Police Rescue Abandoned Baby" the headline said.

He didn't ride my ass so much after that.

Maryam

Memory is an unreliable visitor. For a long while, I couldn't remember the name of the young man who had brought Nora to the cabin when her car key broke, although he looked familiar to me, and I knew I had seen him somewhere before. Then one day, while I was taking the recycling out to the garage, it all came back to me at once, not only his name, but his father's name, too. The summer before Nora went to college, I needed an electrician to fix the wiring on the garage door, and one of the mothers at school said that she had hired this man, Mark Gorecki, so I called him. He didn't just fix the garage door, he kept finding new things that needed to be done, like a three-way switch that didn't work, or a broken light fixture on the deck. He repaired everything perfectly, but I could smell beer on him at noon, and I didn't like that he had racked up a $300 bill by the time he was finished, so I never called him again, not even when the fan in the bedroom stopped working and we had to sleep with the windows open.

Coming back in from the garage, I went to the front hallway and stood looking at the framed photos on the wall, pictures from all the important moments in my family's life, and especially my daughters' lives, their birthdays and graduations and achievements. At length, I found the young man, standing in a suit that looked too small for him, in the middle of Nora's jazz band. Running my finger over the list at the bottom, I found his name: Jeremy Gorecki. It was nice of him to drive her back that day, I thought; waiting for Triple A in the heat would've been tough, especially since she was by herself.

I hadn't expected to see him again, but a few weeks later, while I was waiting in the express lane at the Stater Brothers, he came to stand behind me in line. At first, he didn't see me, he was texting on his phone, smiling at whoever he was talking to, and only after he finished his conversation did he put down his items on the conveyor belt, a canister of coffee, a pack of sugar, a box of condoms, and a blue-and-white carryall with a zipper pocket on one side. It was my carryall, the one I had used to bring Tupperwares of food to the cabin, and I had left it hanging on a nail in the kitchen, in case Nora needed it for groceries, but now here it was, in the hands of Jeremy Gorecki. I reached for the plastic divider and put it down on the conveyor belt between us.

"Thank you," he said, reflexively, but when he looked at me, I saw recognition come over him. I turned to look at the tabloids, their covers screaming about celebrities' addictions to drugs or affairs with the nanny, then pulled out a copy of *People*, just to give myself something to do, and made a show of reading it. "Mrs. Guerraoui?" he asked.

How strange it was to hear my husband's name in this stranger's mouth. What did he know about us, and why did he want to talk to me, here at the grocery store, with that box on the conveyor belt between us? To my relief, the line moved forward, and I stuffed the magazine back on the rack and pulled a few bills out of my wallet to pay for my groceries. I was planning to make stuffed bell peppers with lamb for my son-in-law—that was his favorite dish, he and Salma were coming to have dinner with me—but the thought of cooking an elaborate meal was far from my mind now. All I wanted was to get out of this place.

"Eleven eighty is your change," the cashier said. She took out two bills from the register, then stopped. "The change machine is broken, and I'm low on quarters and dimes."

"It's okay."

"You don't mind so many pennies?"

"No." I wanted her to hurry, but she counted the pennies slowly and carefully, whispering to herself so she wouldn't lose track.

Jeremy tried again. "Mrs. Guerraoui," he said. "Hello there." His voice was deep and clear, and I couldn't pretend any longer that I hadn't heard him.

"Oh," I said, feigning surprise, "hello." He was very tall, and I had to look up to meet his eyes, which were very blue against his tanned face, it was not an unpleasant face, though his lips had a purple tint that came from smoking, a terrible habit. On his upper arm was a tattoo, which is common enough in this town, you see them everywhere, especially on low-class people and criminals, although nowadays artists get them, too. My daughter has one, it's very tiny, it's usually hidden by her bracelets, but a tattoo on the arm is different, it makes a statement, it wants to be seen, perhaps that was what this young man wanted.

The cashier was still counting my change, while the store bagger, a teenage boy with braces on his teeth, finished putting away my groceries.

"Do you need help with that?" Jeremy asked, coming closer to me.

"I'm fine," I said, and quickly reached for the fabric tote and hoisted it up, but I had misjudged how heavy it was, and had trouble lifting it up over my shoulder.

"Here," he said, taking it off my hands easily. "Let me help you."

"Ma'am," the cashier said, "your change."

I took the two bills and the handful of pennies from her, and while I put them away in my wallet, she started scanning Jeremy's items, so that I had no choice but to wait for him to pay.

Afterward, we stepped out of the store together. It was a sunny morning in June, the heat was rising fast, and on the sidewalk two children ate ice creams, the chocolate melting and running down their shirts, not caring about the mess they were making, they were enjoying their cones. I started across the parking lot to my car, Jeremy walking beside me with my groceries, and the silence between us grew so long that I felt compelled to make polite chatter. "How is your father?" I asked. "Mark, right?"

"My father?" he said, glancing at me with surprise. "He's fine— I guess. I haven't seen him in a while."

"He fixed my garage door. A long time ago."

"Ah. He doesn't work much these days, though; he's getting old."

I didn't expect the rush of sadness that came over me when I heard this, perhaps it was the familiarity of it—after all I know something about how families can grow apart, and how hard it is to bring them together again. We made it to my car, and after Jeremy handed me my bag of groceries, I stood in the sun and watched him walk away, thinking we were no longer strangers, he and I.

Nora

A couple of weeks later, Salma invited me to her house for Father's Day. I didn't particularly want to see her, but she said that brunch would be followed by a visit to our father's grave at Rose Hills, which made it impossible for me to come up with a valid reason to skip one and not the other. With a mix of dread and resignation, I drove down Old Woman Springs Road, heading toward Landers, the little town where my sister and brother-in-law had moved a few years earlier. Their home was a 2,800-square-foot house with a transom on the front door and huge windows that faced east. Everything about it screamed money—the landscaping, the custom mailbox, the sign that warned SIMPSON SECURITY: ARMED RESPONSE. As it happened, the door had been left ajar, and I was halfway across the living room before I saw my brother-in-law. "It was open," I said.

"You don't have to explain," Tareq said mildly. "This is your home. You're welcome here anytime."

"Happy Father's Day," I said, giving him the greeting card I'd bought that morning at Walgreens. The stationery aisle had been packed with children young and old, and somehow I had managed to keep my composure until I saw a little girl, perhaps eight or nine years old, asking her older brother if he thought their dad would like the card she'd picked out. I had to sit in my car for a while after that, trying to collect myself before I could drive to my sister's house. "Where is everyone?"

"Thank you for this," Tareq said. He seemed genuinely pleased and held on to the card as we spoke. "Your mom's not here yet. The kids are playing, and Salma's out on the deck. Why don't you go talk to her? I'll bring you ladies some lemonade."

From the family room came the sound of a crash—a Jenga tower?—and the taunting laughter of Aida. I slid the glass door open and stepped outside. Under the shade of the umbrella, Salma sat on a lounge chair, so motionless that for a moment I thought she was sleeping. She was in a mint-green top and white linen pants, a vivid rendering of what *Orange Coast* magazine might have featured under Casual Weekend Wear, and her hair was in an elaborate updo that must have taken hours of practice. But when she looked up, I noticed deep bags under her eyes, which not even her carefully applied makeup could disguise. "Oh," she said. "You made it."

"Of course," I said, bending down to kiss her on the cheeks. "I can only stay for a couple of hours, though. I have to go back to work." I took the chair next to hers. My back hurt from having carried boxes of groceries earlier that morning, and I stretched my legs out and heaved a sigh of relief. A soft wind blew, rustling the leaves of the sage bushes that bordered the deck. Beyond it the lot sloped into a valley of Joshua trees, and, in the distance, giant red-rock formations. "What a great view you have here, Salma."

She smiled. "Yes, it's nice and clear today, too."

Maybe it was the satisfaction in her voice that grated on my ear, or maybe it was seeing her lounging like this, but instantly I found myself thinking about Baker's arraignment. Salma had made no effort to be in court, hadn't rescheduled her clinic appointments, hadn't even called me afterward to hear the details of the hearing. I was trying to think of a way to bring this up when the door slid open again and Tareq appeared, carrying a pitcher.

"I have a migraine," my sister told him, somewhat abruptly.

Tareq didn't reply. He stirred the lemonade with a metal spoon, bruised the mint leaves for a minute, then poured two glasses.

"The bright light can't be good for you," I said. "Maybe we should go inside."

"No, I like it out here." Turning to her husband again, she asked, "Can I get a pill?"

A raven landed near us and eyed the ground for any crumbs. Tareq waved it away. "Drink the lemonade," he said. "It should help."

"I'd rather have something." Her eyes were pleading.

"I'll leave you two to catch up."

I didn't know what to make of this exchange between them, or the tension that I sensed beneath their pleasantries. Why wouldn't he give her something for her migraine? "Are you all right?" I asked her after he left.

"I'm fine," she said.

For the first time, it occurred to me that the perfection my sister wore like an armor was starting to show some cracks. It could only be grief, I thought; grief had done this to her. All at once my irritation disappeared. I reached across the side table to touch her arm, and immediately she put her hand over her mouth to stifle a sob. "Oh, Salma," I said.

"I'm fine," she said again, and took a long sip of her lemonade. From the neighbor's yard came the rattle of a wire fence being opened, followed by the joyful barking of a dog. "Why do you have to leave so early anyway?" she asked.

"I told you, I have to go back to work."

"You mean the restaurant?"

"Yes."

"Nora, why are you doing this?" she asked me warily. "Mama doesn't want to run the restaurant anymore, and she shouldn't have to. She's getting on in years, you know. She just wants to retire."

"She can still retire. I can buy her share of the business so long as you keep yours." Then, warming up to my idea, I said, "We could be partners, you and I. The Guerraoui sisters. How about that?"

"That sounds nice, but then what? Who's going to run it?"

"You don't think I can?"

"It's not that. I just thought you wanted to write music."

"I *do* want to write music, but I'm also not letting Baker get away with murder and I'm not giving up on Dad's dream."

"It was *his* dream, Nora, not yours. You don't want to be living someone else's dream, trust me." Her voice brimmed with rage. She swiveled her legs off the ottoman and sat facing me, looking at me so intently that I thought she might grab me by the shoulders and shake me. "Look, if you're going to do something as crazy as writing music, you might as well commit to it. Get rid of the diner and go write the best goddamn music you can."

I was startled by her sudden passion. What could have caused it? And was it connected to the strain I had noticed earlier with her husband? These two made an ideal couple, or so I had always thought. "What's going on with you?" I asked, bewildered by the turn our conversation had taken.

My sister gazed at me, as if deciding whether to trust me with whatever troubled her. A horned lizard skittered across the deck, finding some shade under the twins' bicycles. The raven came back, taking a few hesitant steps toward the dining table. I waited. Salma seemed about to unburden herself, but the glass door slid open, and my mother appeared. She was out of widow's white, and the cobalt blue of her dress made her look much younger. In her hands was a tray laden with summer dishes—vegetable kebabs and calamari salad and grilled eggplant and cut watermelon. The twins followed behind, arguing about who had won the game. Tareq came out, too, carrying a pot of coffee. And just like that, the moment of intimacy between my sister and me was over.

We moved to the table, where Tareq opened his gifts, commenting nicely about each one with a few nice words. From Aida, he received an unwearable silk tie, in a pattern of blue stripes on a bright yellow background. ("Thank you, habibti. Yellow is my favorite color.") From Zaid, a fancy pen. ("I'll use it to write my prescriptions.") From Salma, a state-of-the-art audio system. ("I can't wait to try it out.") From my mother, a box of Belgian chocolates. ("These are my weakness.") And from me, the card I had given him earlier. ("You're so thoughtful.")

But for the rest of the day, I found myself in the throes of a deep melancholy. How rare it was for my sister and me to talk about anything, let alone about something intimate. And just as we were about to, the moment had passed.

Jeremy

At the end of June, I had to go to a two-day training session on de-escalation techniques that Vasco had ordered a few weeks earlier, when the Bowden incident was still on the front page of the *Los Angeles Times*. The training was taking place in San Bernardino and, rather than drive the fifty miles back and forth, I'd decided to stay in town with one of the other deputies. For two days, we sat in a classroom and were told very different things from what we'd been told at the academy: attempt to defuse a tense situation with words, not weapons; if the suspect is agitated, demonstrate empathy by paraphrasing his statement; do not become emotionally involved in the encounter; assess the outcome before resorting to force. At the end of each unit, though, the trainer insisted that we had to do all this while putting our own safety first.

At dawn on the third day I drove back home, going straight to the police station for my regular shift and afterward to the community center, where I met Fierro for his support group. I was bone tired, and went for the coffee that sat at the table under the wall clock, pouring myself a giant cup and hoping it would be enough to keep me awake through the evening's session. Fierro was in a foul mood. The promotion he'd been promised at the Walmart had not materialized, he told me, and he would remain sales associate for the foreseeable future. "Something else will come along," I said, though I wasn't sure I sounded convincing.

With a grunt, he leaned back in his chair, waiting for the moderator to arrive. But a few minutes before eight, we discovered that Rossi was out that night. His replacement was a frail-looking therapist named Dexter, who kept clicking and unclicking his ballpoint pen. "Who would like to start tonight?"

Doug, the bald-headed guy who always raised his hand first, talked about how agitated he was all the time, how he couldn't eat anything, what a tough day he'd had. After twenty minutes of his aimless chatter, Adriana, the nurse, got frustrated and interrupted him. "There are other people here," she said sharply.

"Now, now," Dexter replied, his palms raised. "Let's calm down."

"I *am* calm," she snapped.

Fierro was sitting with his arms crossed and his good ear cocked toward Adriana. "She didn't say nothing," he agreed. "She's calm."

Doug objected to being interrupted, Adriana asked what he thought would happen when he wouldn't shut up, and Fierro agreed with her again. It took Dexter a long while to regain control of the room. But then he called on someone different to speak, and that upset Doug, Adriana, and Fierro all at once. I tilted my wrist discreetly to look at my watch. There was so much I still had to do that night. Fill up with gas. Write a check for my car insurance. Run a load of laundry, I was out of clean socks. Suddenly I felt ten pairs of eyes locked on me, and realized I had missed something. "Sorry. What was that?"

"Would you like to share something about your anger?" Dexter asked.

Me, angry? Well, since he asked. I was angry that Vasco had been using that abandoned baby for PR advantage. I was angry that he'd sent us to a training session in San Bernardino just to make himself look good. I was angry that people were afraid of my uniform. Inside it, I was just like them, but they only saw me as a political prop or some movie fantasy, nothing in between. I was angry about the war. God, was I angry about the war. People were being killed while Bush was painting still lifes and Rumsfeld was writing books and Cheney just wouldn't fucking shut up. I was angry that I had to spend my evening here, listening to other angry people. "I'm just here for support," I said.

"He's with me," Fierro said, raising his hand, seemingly relieved that he finally got a chance to speak. He talked about the usual: his wife. How she had moved on, how she had a new life with somebody else, how he'd been left behind. Adriana nodded thoughtfully while he spoke, as if she understood or agreed with him. It seemed that this support group was helping him open up about himself, and I was glad he had stuck with it, but I wondered how Mary was doing now, too, and I made a mental note to call or visit her at the hair salon. I needed a haircut anyway.

At the end of the session, as we were putting the folding chairs back in the utility closet, Fierro asked when Rossi would be back. "I'm not sure," Dexter told him. "I think he might be moving out of state. But I'll be here."

It was dark when we stepped outside, and the air was muggy.

"I don't like this new guy," Fierro said as he pulled out his car keys.

"He's just getting to know everyone. I'm sure he'll be fine."

"I guess," Fierro said as we crossed the parking lot. "Wanna hit the bowling alley?"

"Not tonight."

"Come on, dude. Just a couple of games."

"No, I'm too tired."

"You didn't want to go last week, either."

"I've got a lot going on."

"How about a game of poker? My neighbors are playing tonight."

"No, man. I feel like I've been driving for three days straight. I'm exhausted."

"All right, then." We shook hands, and I got into my Jeep and pulled out of the parking lot onto the 62. My windshield was dusty and in the yellow glare of my headlights the road seemed hazy. Never mind filling up with gas, I thought, or writing a check for the insurance, or running the laundry. All of that could wait. What I really needed now was some care, and some sleep. I turned on the radio, settling on a classic rock station, and headed for the cabin.

All the lights were on in the house. You could see everything inside, as clearly as if you were in a movie theater: the flower arrangement on the mantelpiece, the shelves that strained under the weight of books, the antique wooden chandelier, a baseball cap hanging from the hat peg. The fresh coat of paint made the kitchen look new and it startled me that even Nora at the window looked new. After she told me about her encounter with A.J. at the bowling alley, I'd insisted she get a second bolt for the front door, and I still planned to fix the loose screen on the kitchen window. The sound of my tires on the driveway gravel made her look up from the sink, and she dried her hands and came to the door. "How was training?" she asked.

"It was long." I stepped across the threshold, took her in my arms, and kicked the door closed with my leg. All my worries shrank when I was with her. The loneliness I'd once taken for granted had disappeared from my life and in its place was something I hadn't experienced before, the feeling that our two solitudes had joined together. Everything receded from my attention—the humming of the swamp cooler, the cooing of the turtledove, the music on the stereo. She was all that mattered. In another moment, we moved to the bed, struggling with buttons and hooks and zippers. I was taking off her bra when she froze and pushed me away, screaming. "There's someone at the window."

She scrambled for the sheets to cover herself, but I grabbed her by the wrist and pulled her down to the floor beside me. Covering her mouth with my hand, I listened to the sounds that came from the back of the house—a chair falling, keys dropping, footsteps across the backyard. "Stay right here," I whispered, pulling up my pants. "Don't move."

I turned off the light, picked up one of the hiking sticks that slanted against a corner, and went to the front door. Outside, the light from the new moon was so scant that I could see only a few feet in any direction. I crept along the wall, past the swamp cooler with its birds' nest, and rounded the corner to the backyard. The sound of the wire fence being scaled made me run blindly toward it. Only when I was about six feet away did I get a good view of the Peeping Tom trying to climb it. I swung the hiking stick and landed it with all my force on his hip. There was a cry of pain and then he fell to the ground. I swung the stick a second time, but a familiar voice stopped me. "Dude. Take it easy. It's just me."

"What the fuck?"

In the darkness, Fierro's skin looked pale and his features seemed drawn as if by charcoal. He got up, rubbed the pain from his hip. "You swing that thing like a baseball bat. It hurts."

"The fuck you doing here?"

"You missed bowling night again."

"So you followed me?"

"I got curious where you've been going the last few weeks. You never want to hang out anymore." He dusted himself off and pulled his hoodie over his head. Then he made that whistling sound he'd picked up from Fletcher, shaking his head at some realization he should've had long ago. "I didn't know you liked hajji pussy so much."

I punched him so fast his head snapped back. "Stay away from her," I said.

He stumbled, let out a gasp, put his hand on his jaw, then steadied himself. "I'll go wherever the fuck I want."

I threw my fist again, but this time he was expecting me, and dodged it. He tried to land a punch, too, and we tumbled together to the ground, swinging and kicking at each other. The dirt scraped against my chest and I could feel specks of sand lodging themselves between my shoulder blades. Then my head hit something hard— a rock at the edge of the fence. There was nowhere else for me to go. I kneed him in the groin, then pushed myself up, straddled him, and began to pummel, not stopping even after I felt blood on my knuckles.

"Jeremy," Nora called. "Jeremy. Stop."

I pushed myself up and took a moment to catch my breath. The numbness cleared, and suddenly I felt the cut on my eyebrow and the ache in my hands. But aside from these, I felt good. Great, even. As though I'd been welcomed back to a familiar place.

"What happened?" she asked as she came closer.

She'd put on a pair of shorts and a white camisole, so thin that the outline of her breasts showed. I took a step forward, placing myself between Fierro and her.

"Are you okay?"

"I'm fine. Go back inside, baby."

Behind me, Fierro was struggling to get up.

"What's going on?" she said, craning her neck to look at him. "What's he doing here?"

"Go back inside."

"Tell me what's going on."

"*Inside.* Please." Her eyes traveled from Fierro to me, and back again. She seemed about to say something, then decided against it and walked back to the cabin. I watched until she had rounded the corner, then turned around. Fierro was still on the ground, his sweater halfway up his chest, his pants covered with dirt. With some effort, he stood up and dusted himself off. We looked at each other, taking the measure of what was happening, here in the dark and empty yard of an old cabin. Then he did something that stunned me: he started to cry.

"Come on, man," I said. "Get yourself together. You need to go."

But he was still sobbing. I'd never seen him like this. With the sleeve of his sweater, he wiped away tears and blood, streaking dirt across his eyes like camouflage. "Go where?" he said. "I got no one."

Slowly the anger leaked out of me, and guilt took its place. Guilt at having survived when others in my platoon had died, having my health when others had lost theirs, having found someone to love when others were alone. "Give me your keys," I said.

"Why?"

"Just give me your keys. And wait here."

When I walked back in, I found Nora standing behind the door. She'd put on a cardigan and held one of her arms in the other, half-hugging herself. "You're bleeding," she said. "That's it, I'm calling the cops."

"I *am* a cop. And I'm fine, baby. It's just a cut." I put my shirt back on and looked around for my keys.

"Tell me what the hell's going on."

"Later. Lock the door behind me."

I waited until I heard the deadbolt turn. Then I got Fierro into his old Chevy and took off with him. The windshield was covered with a layer of dust, and the smell of car exhaust drifted inside, mixing with the scent of our sweat and blood. How often had we ridden together, at night in the desert, scarred by fights we ourselves had started? And all the while thinking that it would be over once we returned home from the war.

When Fierro turned the light on in his apartment, a cockroach skittered across the white wall and disappeared behind the television. His packed ruck leaned against the wall. A tower of empty pizza boxes stood like an altar in one corner, surrounded by smashed beer cans. There was no furniture other than a futon and a coffee table. The whole apartment smelled like trash. "All right," he said, turning to me. "We made it back. You can go now."

"I'm not in a rush."

"Give me back my keys."

"Why don't we order something? I could use a bite."

"I'm not hungry." He took out a Bud Light from the fridge. On the door, a magnet that said WALLACE INSURANCE held down a piece of paper with a phone number on it. In loopy letters next to it was a name. Samantha. A girl he'd met at my sister's barbecue, taken on a date, and never heard from again. I scanned the kitchen counter. No glasses or knives in plain sight.

"Pizza or Chinese?" I asked.

"I don't care."

"Pizza it is."

While I placed the order, he put a bunch of paper towels under the tap and wiped the dirt and blood from his face. His right eye was closing fast and his left was turning blue. "I think I have a Coke somewhere in the fridge," he said. "Help yourself."

I found a bag of hash browns in the freezer, stuck behind two empty vodka bottles, and gave it to him. He held it to his eyes, one after the other. I could already feel a massive headache settling in, and the cut on my eyebrow throbbed. What I wouldn't do for a shower now. What I wouldn't do to be back in bed, away from all this. While we waited for the pizza to arrive, he opened another beer. "Remember Rodriguez?" he asked.

"Rodriguez from Texas?" I said.

"No, Rodriguez from New Jersey. I've never seen anyone drink as much Coke in my life. Dude could down three cans in an hour, easy."

"Well. Let me tell you a story about Rodriguez from New Jersey.

He was driving us on a recon, and he'd had so much Coke he had to take a piss. But he couldn't hold it. 'I gotta go,' he kept saying. 'I gotta go.' We found him a plastic bottle and he did his business, but when he tried to cap it he dropped it on the floor. We had to sit in a Humvee for three hours smelling his piss."

"Dumb fuck."

"I wonder what happened to him."

"Back in New Jersey, last I heard. Delivers sodas."

"No way."

"Dude. I swear it's true."

When the pizza arrived, we ate quickly, stacking the slices one on top of the other like hamburger buns. Then Fierro wiped his mouth with a napkin. "This is good."

"Yeah. Not bad for Domino's."

"No, I meant us. Here, like this."

"I can't be around all the time, man. I have my own life."

He watched me for a moment. "All right. Listen, I'm sorry I showed up at your girl's place. I wasn't trying to scare her, I really wasn't. I didn't know where you went, that's all. It's not like I'm some pervert or anything. Besides, you never talk about her. I didn't even know you were still seeing her. You've been avoiding me, like you're ashamed of me or something."

But I wasn't ashamed of Fierro, I was protective of Nora. That was why, from the beginning, I'd tried to keep the two of them apart. Maybe that had made things worse. "You need to get help. Medical help. I thought I could help you, but I can't."

"You don't have to worry about me."

"You've said that before, but here we are."

He shook his head slowly, like I didn't get it. "Sarge said I could stay with him for a while. Help him out with the bees."

"Fletcher called you?"

"No, I called him."

This felt like a punch in the gut. He knew how I felt about Fletcher, and yet he'd reached out to him, and brought it up at this particular moment. I was angry, but mostly I was tired, so very tired. I could see that he still wasn't ready to face whatever troubled him, that he was only trying to run away to a different place. He's made his choice, I thought. And I would make mine.

That was the last time I saw him, though I heard from him a few more times. The first time was about two months later, when I was working the Labor Day shift, and was alone at my desk. He told me he'd been learning a lot about bees, because Fletcher had 40,000 of them. Queens can lay as many as 1,500 eggs each day, drones are kicked out of the nest every fall, if a queen dies unexpectedly, worker bees can develop reproductive organs and lay a replacement queen. But he didn't like the Waynesboro area very much and complained that people in the South weren't as nice as he'd expected them to be. Another time, maybe eight months later, he called me in the middle of the night to ask if I wanted to meet him for drinks, he was only four hours away in Nevada. He was calling me from a pay phone near a freeway overpass, and the sound of traffic made it harder for him to hear me. I had to tell him twice that I couldn't go anywhere, I had to work early the next morning. I didn't ask what he was doing in Nevada.

The Marines had brought us together, two dumb kids from the desert, and although we'd fought side by side for years, in the end we'd come out just as we'd gone in: two different people. Now it was time for us to go our separate ways.

Nora

Somewhere on the Grapevine, a truck had crashed on the northbound side of the 5, spilling its cargo of toys and turning the freeway into an obstacle course of nerf guns, action figures, and assorted dolls. Traffic was blocked for miles. So it was almost midnight by the time I reached the 880 and glimpsed, with relief, the orange and green lights of Tribune Tower. I had worked there as an intern one summer, back when the *Oakland Tribune* still had its offices in the building. It was one of my favorite places in the city. My apartment was on the third floor of a pink Victorian house with no garage, no elevator, and no laundry room, and until recently I could afford it only because I had a roommate. That night when I came in, I found Margo in the hallway, still in her jacket, having just returned from a late dinner at her brother's house. "How are you holding up?" she asked as we hugged. "Let me help you with your bags."

"This is it," I said, dropping my duffel bag on the wood floor.

"I wish I'd been able to come down for the funeral." She hung her jacket in the coat closet. "I just couldn't get away."

"No, I understand." I put my keys in the bowl on the console and slipped off my shoes. Margo was studying my face, as if trying to decide whether to tell me something, and an uncomfortable silence fell between us. "All right," I said. "I'm going to turn in for the night."

Without switching on the light in my room, I took off my clothes and got into bed, covering myself with the blanket I had bought after Max complained that my apartment was too humid. The neon sign from the movie theater down the street lit the ceiling an intermittent red, and I turned to the wall, falling quickly into a heavy and dreamless sleep. I didn't stir until almost noon, when the sun was bright against the window shades. I had spent only a couple of months in the desert, but I had already grown accustomed to its open space and uninterrupted silence: the moment I opened my eyes, my room seemed cluttered, my bed too narrow, the street too loud.

When I walked out of my bedroom, I found Margo at the dining table with her laptop. She worked as a math tutor for a test-preparation company, and often her mornings were spent answering rescheduling requests from difficult parents. These requests she met with a midwesterner's patience, coupled with a freelancer's anxiety to get paid. Dvořák was on the stereo, a piano and violin piece that mercifully drowned out the hum of the street. After pouring myself a cup of coffee, I came to sit across from her at the table.

"How was it?" she asked. "Tell me everything."

In the texts and calls we'd exchanged since I'd left, I'd only shared with her the broadest outline of what had happened, but now I began filling in the picture, telling her about my mother's refusal to keep the restaurant, my attempt to run it even while the Bakers stayed next door, what had started with Jeremy and how it had ended. As I spoke, I felt something shifting, as if a spell I had been under for several weeks was finally broken. I had tried to fill the hole my father had left in my life by holding on to his things—his cabin, his diner, his secrets—and I saw clearly now that none of these could be a bulwark against death. Grief demanded surrender. I had to let go. I had to learn how to live with just the memories, nothing else.

But either I'd chattered for too long or Margo's capacity to console hadn't been deepened by the experience of death, because her eyes kept shifting. "I'm sorry," she said. After a suitable pause, she asked, "So you're back here for good?"

"That's the plan." The pile of mail she had saved was waiting for me, and I started idly sifting through it. A lot had accumulated in just nine weeks: bills, credit-card offers, magazines, mailers from art or music organizations.

"Because there's something I've been meaning to tell you."

I looked up from the junk mail. "What is it?"

"I'm moving out."

"What? Where to?"

"Fremont. Claire put a deposit on a place."

"You're moving in together?"

"Yeah," she said with a grin.

"Congrats." Margo and Claire had been together for nearly three years, and I really should've been happy for them, but sitting at the table that Sunday morning, all I could find when I searched my heart was the feeling of being unmoored. Lost. I had come back to Oakland thinking that I could live as I had before, but that was no longer possible. "When are you moving out?" I asked, unable to keep the note of desperation out of my voice.

"In ten days."

"That soon? You're not giving me much notice."

"But you've been gone so long, Nora. Claire and I expected to look for a while, but we just got lucky with this apartment. You should see it. Built-in bookshelves, crown molding, a backyard view. We knew lightning wasn't going to strike twice."

"That's great," I said. Quickly and savagely, I tore up credit-card offers, realtor mailers, a reminder for a doctor's appointment I'd already missed, a subscription renewal for the *New Yorker*, a sympathy card from the headmaster at Bay Prep, an invitation to my friend Anissa's housewarming party. And then, beneath the detritus of the life I wished I could have again, I found an envelope from Silverwood Music Center, with a note informing me that I'd been accepted for their summer festival. The curators wanted to include one of my pieces in an evening program featuring younger composers. "I just got into Silverwood," I said, my voice rising with excitement.

"Mazel tov!" Margo said. "Congratulations to us both, then. We're moving on to bigger and better things."

It was the kind of break I would read about in the trades every fall, a gushing article celebrating the arrival of a fresh new talent in American music, but that's all it ever was to me—a story, not something that actually happened, least of all to people like me. I wished I could've called my father to tell him the news—Can you believe it? I would've said. And I almost didn't apply!—and now I was seized with pain at the thought that he hadn't lived long enough to hear about this. I could have called my mother instead, but I knew that she was still upset with me. For years, we had been operating under a Don't Ask, Don't Tell policy about my sex life, and our mutual violation of that agreement while I was home—she asked, I told—had given her yet another reason to be disappointed in me. Why couldn't I be more like Salma, she moaned, find myself a nice Muslim doctor or engineer and marry him? Two days before, when I told her I was leaving town, she'd seemed relieved.

And I was, too. I was tired of fighting with my mother and fearful of where things were going with Jeremy. I had found solace with him, even moments of joy I hadn't known before, but we were so different that it was bound not to last, and the incident with Fierro had clarified for me just how much separated us. I couldn't get the fixed stare at the cabin window out of my mind. Whenever I tried to interpret the expression in Fierro's eyes, I couldn't decide whether it was disgust or desire, but both made me feel like I was nothing more than a body, or even a commodity. And trailing the memory of Fierro's stare was always another one: the way Jeremy had stood over his friend's beaten body, his chest heaving, his knuckles red with blood, the hint of a smile on his lips. It was the first time I had seen that side of him. "I'm sorry," he said when he came to see me the next day at the restaurant. "I'm sorry about what happened."

He leaned in to kiss me, but I pulled away from him. "Your friend was staring right at me," I said, my voice shaking.

"Don't be scared. I'm not going to let anything happen to you."

Such bravado, I thought. A promise that could never be made, much less kept. We were standing under the awning of the Pantry. The busboy came out of the side door with a trash bag, which he swung into the dumpster. I waited until he had gone back inside before I spoke again. "I feel so violated."

"I'm sorry," he said again.

"Why did he follow you to the cabin?"

"I don't know." He leaned against the stucco wall, thinking for a long moment about the question. On his right eyebrow was a cut that was partially covered by a Band-Aid and along his left jaw was a bruise that was still raw and pink. "I think maybe he feels like I've moved on, or past him, somehow."

"But that doesn't make any sense," I said. "Is there something you're not telling me?"

All at once the story poured out of him. Fierro had been going through a nasty divorce, he'd threatened his wife, smashed up her car, and got arrested. But Jeremy had bailed him out of the West Valley Detention Center and found him an anger-management group, which had helped—until it didn't.

"My God," I said. "And you go shooting guns with him. Guns, Jeremy. Guns. What will he do next?"

A white-haired woman with a cane walked out of the Pantry and we both moved aside to let her pass, but she must have heard the word *guns* because she continued staring at us as she crossed the parking lot. What a picture we must make, I thought, me in the dress I'd worn for my father's funeral and him in a police uniform and with his face beaten up. As I pushed a strand of hair away from my face, he suddenly noticed the bruise on my wrist.

"I didn't realize I'd grabbed you so hard." He put his hand on my waist, trying again to draw me closer, but I resisted. "I'm sorry, baby. I was just trying to protect you."

"I never asked you to protect me. I never asked for any of this."

The sun was high in the sky and, though we stood in the shade of the awning, the heat reached us, making us both uncomfortable. The radio transmitter on Jeremy's uniform buzzed and he listened to the dispatcher for a minute before turning down the volume and looking at me again. "I know you're scared, Nora, and I know you're upset. But don't do this. Don't blame me for something I didn't do. I have no control over him. I couldn't have known he'd show up at your place."

"You think ignorance and innocence are the same thing? You say you didn't know this would happen, but you're the one who bailed him out. He would never have shown up at my house if it weren't for you. You can't bring this violence all the way to my doorstep and not expect me to be repulsed."

The word made him flinch. He was quiet, his eyes hardening. "All this talk of innocence," he said. "And you messed around with a married guy for months. What does that make you?"

I couldn't believe he was using this against me. I should never have opened up to him, I thought, I had been a fool to make myself vulnerable like this. Anger brimmed inside me, threatening to spill at any moment. "This isn't really working," I said, trying hard to keep my voice even.

"Don't say that," he said, his tone different now. "We're good together. Let's talk about it tonight. I have to go back to work now."

But I didn't want to talk anymore. It seemed to me then that my relationship with Jeremy had been part of the impulse, born out of grief, to hold on to the past at all cost. A week after my father's death, a well-intentioned friend had posted on my Facebook page an article filled with advice for mourners: don't drink too much, don't make big financial decisions, don't jump into a relationship. As if grief were a business deal that could be successfully negotiated if one followed a few simple rules. I hadn't been able to do it, clearly.

Now, sitting at my dining table and holding the acceptance letter from Silverwood Music Festival in my hand, I was grateful to be back in Oakland. At least, I would always have my music. It was my consolation, my only hope, the answer to what I didn't understand and what I couldn't change.

I helped Margo pack up and move to Fremont and, because I couldn't face the prospect of more change, stayed in the apartment alone. I woke up in a devastatingly empty place every morning, and every morning I tried to convince myself that I had been right to return to the city. Often I caught myself thinking about the tenderness with which Jeremy held me, how he had made me feel less alone, but each time I forced myself to push these memories aside. It was better to make a clean cut now, try to put my life back together the way it had been before.

My piano piece came as a relief in those early days. Something about those twelve acrobats in Marrakesh had so moved me that I was still thinking about them years later and a continent away. They each performed a solitary act, and yet the effect would only be achieved when viewed in unison. I had never belonged to any tribe, and perhaps I would never be able to, but I could try to put that feeling in my music. I worked for hours on end, sometimes coming out into the dining room to find that night had fallen, and the breakfast dishes were still on the table. I'd reheat a frozen pizza, eat it standing at the sink, and return to the piano.

One morning in August, just before I had to leave for Silverwood, I went to the post office to fill out a hold-mail form. The walk was less than a mile, but along the way I noticed that the little store that sold Ethiopian coffee was expanding into a café, the Korean restaurant my friend Anissa and I had gone to for her birthday had been turned into a sushi bar, and the yoga studio had moved. As I waited for the light at the intersection, I thought about what else had changed over the summer: I didn't have to fill in applications for teaching jobs in the fall, I was featured in a major music festival, I lived by myself.

Then the light turned red, but instead of crossing, I continued another three blocks toward La Coccinelle. I'm just going to walk past it, I told myself. Nothing more. It would be good to take a longer morning stroll, get a little exercise before the next day's flight to Boston. But as I got closer to the coffee shop, the terms and conditions of that promise began to shift. If Max Bloemhof is there, I said as silently as I might a prayer, I will go in and talk to him.

When I arrived at the café, I spotted my neighbor Andrew sitting with his laptop by the window. He was working on a dissertation about the upper-class Victorian gentleman's attempt at constructing masculinity through fashion—a topic that had sounded legitimate, even interesting, when he'd told me about it, but that would seem completely preposterous to anyone back home in the Mojave. In the cozy armchair was Lena, working on her food blog while her blueberry scone sat untouched. And next to her was a kid whose name I had never learned because he always wore headphones and never looked up from his drafting notebook. I stood behind the window, my eyes traveling from table to table, looking for Max. Finally, I spotted his jacket at an empty table under the gilded wall clock. He always liked that spot, because it was farthest from the bustle of the ordering line. In a few quick steps, I went through the front door and was standing at his table. The clinking of a cup behind me made me turn, but instead of Max coming to the table, along came his wife, Evelyn.

They had been married seventeen years. Their oldest son's age, plus eight months. The marriage had been a mistake, Max had often told me, something he'd been forced into when he realized Evelyn was pregnant. They were both Dutch, both visiting professors in a small college in Texas, both unhappy that they had ended up in one of the most conservative states in the country. But less than a year later, his book *Before Night Comes* was published. It won the National Book Critics Circle Award and became a bestseller. Evelyn landed a tenure-track job at the San Francisco Art Institute. They bought a house. Their daughter was born. Whenever Max told me this story, he made it sound as though one event had led to the next, without his having played much of a role in what happened.

Evelyn's hair was longer now, and she was wearing a chunky turquoise necklace that verged on gaudy, but otherwise she had the same professorial look she had about her the only other time we had met, at a reading in San Francisco nearly a year before. The bookstore was crowded that night, so I hadn't seen her until after I'd put my hand on Max's arm and leaned in to say hello. She'd fixed her hazel eyes on me and I immediately withdrew my hand. Max did the introductions and made some small talk, but very quickly he maneuvered her through the crowd to the front row, leaving me behind. Now Evelyn was at his table, carrying his cup of Earl Grey tea and a plate of pastries. "You," she said.

"I—"

Words failed me. I had wanted to see Max to find out if he still stirred feelings in me, but instead Evelyn had appeared. She set the tea on the table and considered me for a moment, a half smile on her face, before she reached back and slapped me, hitting me so hard that my ears rang. Everyone turned to look.

"Stay away from us," she said.

Without a word, I turned around and left. All the way back to my apartment, my hands inside the pockets of my hoodie were balled into fists. At home, I went straight to the storage closet in the hallway and pulled out my suitcase. With an efficiency that came from years of practice, I started packing, carefully avoiding my reflection in the mirror above the dresser. Never before had I felt more alone.

Maryam

Ramadan was difficult that year—not because of its many deprivations or because it fell in the middle of the summer, when the days were long, but because I missed my husband so much. Yet the fast had a healing effect on me, too, each sunrise and sunset restoring a little more of my peace, so that, by the time Eid arrived, I finally gathered up the courage to take care of something I had been dreading. I started in the garage, thinking it would be easy to discard the transistor radio missing its knobs or the boxes overflowing with old magazines, but these immediately brought back memories of the donut shop, with the two of us listening to music, flipping through *Newsweek* and *Time,* looking for news of home.

From the garage, I moved to the bathroom. The medicine cabinet revealed eye drops my husband had been prescribed after his cataract surgery, tubes of heating cream he used to rub on his knees when they bothered him, a container of Calcibronat, which he said was the only thing that worked on his headaches. In the bottom drawer, I found an empty jar of Vicks VapoRub, its label translucent with grease, and the hot-water bottle he slipped under his blanket whenever the temperature dropped below fifty. There were so many pills and cures and ointments, useless protections against the inevitable—the Surat Al-Imran teaches us that every soul shall have a taste of death, and the life of this world is only the comfort of deception.

In the hallway closet, I found my husband's work shoes, the soles still caked with dirt, the gray slippers he wore around the house, and his hiking boots with the frayed laces. In the bedroom, I pushed open the accordion doors of the closet, ran my hand along the row of clothes hanging from the rod, and examined each jacket, each shirt and pair of pants, as if it could imprint itself in my memory under an intense enough gaze.

I set aside any items that might interest my daughters, put the clothes and shoes that could be donated to charity in Hefty bags, and then sat on the sofa with my hands in my lap, watching the cat groom itself in a patch of sunlight. The house was quieter than I had ever known it. Memories of long-gone years kept visiting me, bringing with them joy and pain all at once, and several moments passed before I got up to wash myself and unroll my prayer mat. I don't know how I managed that difficult day, but I did, which made having to do it all over again, a few weeks later, and in a place I despised, almost unendurable.

I had tried talking Nora out of living in the cabin in Joshua Tree where Driss brought the other woman, but my daughter was deaf to all the hints I dropped. My poor, gullible daughter. What would she have said if I had told her that her father had betrayed the trust I had placed in him? Maybe she wouldn't have believed me. To her, he could only be a hero, he could never be a man of flesh and blood, full of the same weaknesses and capable of the same mistakes as other men.

The sound of my tires as I pulled up to the cabin chased a family of desert quail from the front yard, and they ran to hide under the creosote bush. I dragged the trash bins that had been left near the mailbox to the kitchen door before I went inside. It surprised me to find that everything looked as if my daughter had just stepped out and might return at any moment, because she had left a half-empty glass of water on the counter, a pair of socks under the coffee table, sheet music on the piano. The piano! I had forgotten it was here, and now I realized I would have to call the movers from Riverside to have it returned to the house. What about the wooden chandelier? And this new rug? I called her on her cell phone to ask her, but she brushed me off. "Do whatever you like," she said. She was in Boston, she was too busy to talk to me.

I pulled a trash bag from the kitchen drawer and furiously emptied the fridge of milk, expired eggs, bread that had turned green. I found myself imagining the two of them at the kitchen table, or sitting on the sofa, or listening to the record player. When I asked Nora about the young man she'd brought here, to this place I wanted so desperately to forget, she didn't even try to deny it. But why him? I asked. Look at Salma, I told her, she's married, has two children, and lives a respectable life. But my younger daughter had lost her way. As I cleared out the rest of her things from the cabin, I murmured a prayer for her, as I had so many times in the past, only this time I prayed for more than her health, more than her safety, more than her happiness. I prayed for her greedily, for the thing I had given up years ago and never found again.

Home.

Nora

The pleasure of my company was requested, the invitation in my welcome packet said, at a cocktail reception held in honor of the featured composers. The party was funded by wealthy donors, and from all available evidence it was mostly donors who were milling about the ballroom that night, in designer tuxedos and satin gowns. My plane had arrived two hours late and I hadn't had anything to eat, but by the time I made it to the buffet the only offerings left were a few shrimp swimming in an unidentifiable sauce and asparagus drying under the bright lights of the chandeliers. Disappointed, I picked up a glass of champagne from a passing waiter and stepped outside. The terrace was less crowded, it turned out, and I found myself standing next to an elderly couple. "It's much cooler out here, isn't it?" the wife said.

"Mercifully," I said. It was also more humid than I expected, the air threatening a thunderstorm, and I wished I had remembered to pack an umbrella. I would have to see if any of the stores near my hotel carried any. Again, I searched the crowd, looking for one of the other five composers, or at least someone from the festival staff, but I saw only unfamiliar faces.

"First time at Silverwood?" the wife asked.

"Yes," I said, relieved to have some company. "How about you?"

"Oh, we're old-timers." She smiled warmly at me. Pinned to the neckline of her evening dress was a white ribbon, presumably a charitable cause she supported. "My husband and I have been coming here since 1989. It's one of our favorite things to do; we look forward to it all year long. We've made a lot of friends here."

"That's wonderful."

"And who are you with?" her husband asked.

"Sorry?"

"You must be one of the composers' guests?"

"I *am* one of the composers."

"Oh." He glanced at his wife as if he needed help in coping with this odd situation, then pulled out a folded program from his pocket and looked through it. "You must be, uh, how do you say your name?"

"Guerraoui."

"And what does the N. stand for?"

"Nora."

"I'm David Ford," he said, shaking my hand vigorously. "This is my wife, Liz."

The Fords made small talk for a few minutes before moving away, but my experience with them left a bad taste in my mouth. So it was with a great deal of trepidation that, the following morning, I met with Geri Turner and Roy Gilmore, the bass player and drummer who would be performing with me at the end of the week. Each of us worked in different styles, but Geri and Roy were so easy to work with that by the end of our first rehearsal I felt as though I had played with them many times before. I remember looking up from the piano and catching Geri's eye as she was about to start her solo, or the little nod that Roy gave as I started mine.

Still, the pleasure I derived from playing with these musicians was too often overshadowed by my experiences outside of rehearsal. A security guard stopped me as I tried to go into the venue on my first morning, asking me to show my ID and tell him what business I had in the building. Standing in the middle of the café one day, trying to decide on lunch, I was handed a tray of dirty dishes by an attendee who assumed I was part of the help staff. Another time, a music critic talked to me for a good fifteen minutes before I realized that he thought I was Tahira Khan, one of the publicists at the festival, a woman with whom the only thing I had in common was the color of my skin. Everything else about us was different: she was taller, heavier, prettier, and she even spoke with a British accent. For years, I had wanted to be included in one of these prestigious venues, and now that I had finally been admitted into one, I felt out of place.

I was caught between the contradictory urges of running away from Silverwood and proving myself to all the David Fords in attendance. My rehearsal week brought about an anxiety the like of which I had never known before, and by the time the day of my performance arrived I was seriously contemplating calling in sick. I had been out and about every day, so I knew I couldn't claim to have the flu, but I could easily have complained of food poisoning. Maybe from shellfish. Or deviled eggs. I was in my hotel room, frantically searching for the festival director's phone number, when my mother called. She wanted to tell me that she was clearing out the cabin and locking it up until probate closed in October, at which time it would be sold along with the restaurant. She would take care of moving my old piano back, she said, but did I want to keep the antique chandelier I'd bought? Or could she just leave it there for whoever bought the place?

"I can't really talk right now, Mom. I'm in Boston."

"What are you doing in Boston?"

"I'm featured at Silverwood."

"Silver-what?"

"Silverwood. It's a very big deal."

"So you want to leave the chandelier here?"

"Whatever you like."

She gave a sigh of exasperation.

"What is it now?" I asked. Standing at the window, I saw that clouds were gathering for an afternoon thunderstorm, and the sunlight had dimmed. In the street below, a car raced to make it before the red light and another one honked as it waited to turn. It struck me how much I disliked the noise of big cities, how unsuited I was to them. At heart, I was a desert creature.

"You left everything," she said accusingly.

"I don't understand. Isn't that what you wanted? You wanted to sell the restaurant, and I said it was fine. Now you want to clear out the cabin, and I'm telling you that's fine, too. I'm *agreeing* with you."

"I never said I wanted you to leave."

Even after I'd declared defeat and walked away from my mother's fights, she wanted to drag me into a new one. I was speechless, my mind reeling for a retort that would put an end to the conflict between

us, but coming up with nothing. And she must have sensed an opening, because she pressed on. "You always run away, Nora. When it gets
difficult, you run away. I did this, too, when I was your age."

When she was my age, she had moved to a new home, a new country, a new continent. She had meant to change the course of her life,
but she'd changed my sister's and mine, too. How different would
things have been for us if she had stayed? Maybe I would've had the
ordinary life I had always wanted. I would've felt that I belonged somewhere. I wouldn't have been taught, by textbooks, the newspapers, and
the movies, to see myself once through my own eyes and another time
through the eyes of others. I wouldn't have wanted so badly to fit in
and, paradoxically, to stand out.

I could go on like this forever, imagining the other world that might
have been. Then it occurred to me that my mother, too, had been
imagining a world that might have been: a nice house on the western
side of Casablanca, a husband who taught philosophy at the university,
one daughter a dentist and the other a doctor, both married to men
who were comme il faut, neither greasy account books nor dog-eared
music sheets in sight. She'd spent years trying to mold me into someone she could be proud of, but I had been so busy breaking out of that
mold that I hadn't noticed all the ways in which I was already like her.
My blindness to cheating. My running away when things got tough.

It was there, standing at the hotel-room window talking to my
mother, that I made up my mind to go onstage that night. I can't say
that I wasn't intimidated. The venue, the audience, the acoustics—
all these were on a grander scale than I had been accustomed to in
California. Walking across the stage to the piano, I had to resort to the
technique I'd been taught in middle school: pretend you're playing for
only one person.

Jeremy

It's hard for me to describe the weeks that followed. My heart was broken. What else is there to say? No one had told me that love could crack you open, make you bare your deepest self, then disappear and leave you defenseless. Years have passed since, and yet I haven't forgotten that feeling. At the time, I tried to drink it away. My insomnia came back, worse than before. Some nights, I would spend hours looking for traces of Nora online, either on Facebook or on one of the music sites she visited, or else I'd scroll through my phone for the few pictures I had of us. My favorite was a selfie we'd taken at Willow Hole, our faces flushed from the long hike, our eyes squinting in the sunlight, our arms around each other. It was like looking through a forgotten history, trying to convince myself that it had really happened the way I remembered it. What we had built together was so frail that it had collapsed at the first sign of trouble. I tried to tell myself that maybe it was stronger, all she needed was a little time, but as the days passed I found it harder to believe this—she'd met all my attempts to talk to her with a tenacious silence.

The only thing that kept me going during those tough days was work. Vasco had unexpectedly lost two deputies, one to a police department in the San Diego area and the other to early retirement, and when he asked me to take on a few more shifts in August I'd gladly said yes. One morning, while I was nursing a hangover, I decided to drive down to the Starbucks in Yucca Valley for an iced coffee. It was ninety-five degrees in the shade that day, and the temperature was still expected to rise to one hundred and two. I forced myself to keep my eyes on the highway as I passed the Pantry—a realtor's FOR SALE sign had appeared outside the restaurant some weeks earlier, and I was trying not to think about what this meant in the long run. So I didn't see the red GMC truck trying to exit the parking lot from the side of the bowling alley, and I had to hit the brakes hard to make room for it. At the wheel was A.J.

The GMC was a late-model truck, with chrome door handles, gleaming paint, and high-performance tires, like those I'd been wanting to buy for my Jeep. On one side of the back window was a yellow decal that said SUPPORT OUR TROOPS, and on the other was a red, round sticker with the logo of the bowling alley. Still, for all the bells and whistles on his truck, A.J. didn't take good care of it. Black smoke came out of the tailpipe, which meant the engine was probably burning too much fuel. A.J. must have spotted my cruiser in the rearview mirror because he had his hands at ten and two on the steering wheel and he drove just a couple of miles under the speed limit. After another quarter mile, he turned on his signal and changed into the right lane, but I didn't pass. I changed lanes too, and continued to follow at a distance. I have to admit, I was enjoying making him sweat a little.

Of course, excessive muffler smoke was a minor offense, and besides, it was a job for the Highway Patrol, not the Sheriff's Department. But why not practice a little interagency cooperation? I turned on my siren lights and pulled the GMC over. The license plate check returned only routine information. The truck was a 2012 model, registered to a Helen D. Baker. A.J.'s wife, presumably. Their address was on Sunnyslope Drive, the kind of neighborhood where homes had a circular drive ringed with trees and a stone path around the back that led to a deck and a hot tub. Everything always came up roses for this guy. Even back in high school, his performance on the wrestling team regularly earned him easy grades or reprieves from the punishment he should've received for his bullying. I stepped out of the cruiser, approached the truck from the passenger side, and knocked on the window.

It lowered with an angry hiss. "Is there a problem, Officer?"

"Morning. Your muffler's letting out excessive smoke. I need your license, registration, and insurance."

"It is?" A.J. glanced at his side-view mirror and unbuckled his seat belt.

My hand tightened on the weapon in my holster. "Stay in your seat."

"Sorry, Officer. I'll get that muffler fixed. I hadn't noticed it was doing that."

"License, registration, and insurance."

A.J. locked eyes with me and suddenly I felt aware that I needed a haircut, my sunglasses were cheap knockoffs, I had sweat stains on my shirt. It was like looking at myself in the mirror of a gas-station bathroom: it picked up every fault, every blemish. A.J.'s gaze shifted to the name tag on my uniform, and a look of relief fell across his face. "Gorecki. Jeremy Gorecki? We went to high school together, man. Don't you remember me? I'm A.J. Baker."

"Sir. License, registration, insurance."

"You were on the baseball team. You guys won regionals one year."

"For the last time, license, registration, insurance."

He leaned across the passenger side to reach into the glove compartment. His arm had a tattoo of intertwined roses and on his ring finger he wore a patterned gold band. "I'm pretty sure we had some classes together," he said, pulling out his registration and insurance. "Biology, I think it was. Or maybe algebra."

I took the paper slips from him. "I need your license, too."

"Like I said, man. I'll get that muffler looked at right away."

"License."

"I don't have it on me right now."

"What's your date of birth?"

A.J. leaned back in his seat and stared at the road. He said something between his teeth that I didn't catch. A complaint or a curse. The jolt of satisfaction I'd gotten after pulling him over had already vanished, and all I could feel now was the pounding on my temples and along my brows. I wanted to write him a ticket as quickly as possible so I could go get my coffee. "What was that?" I asked.

"March 8, 1985."

"All right. Wait here," I said. I went back to the cruiser, cranked up the air conditioning, and drank from the lukewarm water bottle that was wedged in the cup holder. A.J. was smoking a cigarette, which made me crave one, too, but I'd left my pack in my locker at work. I propped the registration and insurance against my laptop monitor and typed in the birth date A.J. had given me. No records. My hangover had dulled my thinking, and it took me a minute to realize that I'd entered his nickname into the computer system. But A.J.'s legal name was Anderson. I typed that instead and the license immediately came up. SUSPENDED. Nine months ago. DUI. It had to have been a major accident or a second offense for the suspension to be as long as it was. Did he have a substance abuse problem? I wouldn't have guessed it. He always seemed like he had his act together. Or maybe he just managed to avoid getting caught. Well, not this time. I picked up the water bottle again, but found it empty. My tongue felt as dry and heavy as a brick. I stepped out of the cruiser into the blazing heat. Far ahead, the midday sun had turned the horizon into a liquid haze. I tried to follow protocol—I reminded A.J. why he'd been pulled over, told him what the license check revealed, why he was now under arrest—but from the first, A.J. had to make things difficult. "Come on, man," he said. "It's just a muffler."

"Step out of the vehicle. Move slowly. Keep your hands where I can see them."

"I can get it fixed today. Come on."

"Turn around and put your hands behind your back."

"My suspension is up in two weeks. Two weeks, Gorecki."

I read him his rights and cuffed him. "Spread your legs, I have to pat you down."

"How am I going to tell my wife about this? She's been waiting for me to get my license back, and now this. It's not fair, Gorecki."

"Do you have anything in your truck I should know about? Drugs? Weapons?"

"No. Why are you doing this to me?"

"I'm just doing my job."

"Fuck off, Jabba—"

I yanked on his cuffs so hard that the word dissolved into a cry of pain, then dragged him to the cruiser and shoved him into the backseat. A car slowed as it drove past, the driver craning his neck for a good look. At the tire shop down the road, an inflatable sky dancer waved his orange arms maniacally. I took a deep breath. Don't let him get to you, I told myself. Stay calm. I got into the driver's seat and called my dispatcher to ask for a tow truck. The cruiser had been idling a while, and now it reeked of sweat and whatever the hell the officer who'd driven it the day before had been eating. I shifted in my seat, tried to find a comfortable position, but the weight of my bulletproof vest and the angle of my belt made it impossible. My head was pounding.

By the time we got to the jail, A.J. had calmed down, though he still wasn't cooperative. Three times he asked for his phone call, and Sergeant Lomeli told him they'd get to it as soon as they were done. "You can't get bailed until you get booked, and you can't get booked until we finish here, understand?"

A.J. sniffed.

"Are you on any medications?" I asked.

"I need my inhaler. I got one in the glove compartment, but you towed my truck."

"We'll get you an inhaler," I said. "Any other tats beside the one on your arm?"

"Got one on my back and one on my right shoulder."

"Take off your shirt."

"Why?"

"Why do you think? I have to check, motherfucker."

A.J. took off his shirt. In high school, he had been a gangly kid, but now his shoulders were broad, his biceps defined, and his waist as narrow as a swimmer's, a look I couldn't have achieved no matter how much I worked out. Not that I worked out much these days, anyway. On A.J.'s back was an elaborate vine, a full-color tat that must have taken several sessions under the needle to complete, but it was the simpler design on the shoulder that made me pause. "What's this?"

"It's a cross."

"Not just any cross. It's Celtic. Why'd you get it?"

"Because I'm a Christian, asshole. Or is that against the law now?"

"Guess what?" Lomeli said from behind the counter. "Phone lines just went down."

Never get on Lomeli's bad side was a lesson that meth heads, prostitutes, petty thieves, and other regulars at the jail knew by heart. It was time for A.J. to learn it, too. Now he'd have to wait until the end of the day to place his call.

I signed off on the paperwork and left, walking across the lot to the police station to get some Tylenol from my desk. Cheerful voices rose from the common area. Fran, my favorite dispatcher, was about to retire and someone had put together a party for her. When I came forward to say hello, my voice was weak, as though it came from somewhere far away. I drank two glasses of lemonade before moving to the buffet, where I piled my plate with lasagna and grilled zucchini and breaded cheese sticks. That first plate I ate standing, barely listening to the chatter around me. After I filled a second plate, I looked around the room and noticed Murphy talking to Coleman, leaning very close to her, as if he were sharing juicy office gossip or confiding a secret. Coleman saw me watching, sat up straighter, and waved me over.

Coleman

Two reckless drivers in one family. What were the odds of that? Pretty good, my husband might say. A chip off the old block. The apple doesn't fall far from the tree. Like father, like son. But I didn't put much stock in Ray's folk wisdom, and I didn't like that Gorecki was A.J.'s arresting officer. His involvement could give the appearance of police vindictiveness against the Baker family, maybe even create problems for the prosecution of the hit-and-run. So I took the short walk from the station to the jail and asked Lomeli for the arrest paperwork. He set aside the romance novel he was reading and laid out the forms on the counter, Gorecki hovering nervously over my shoulder the entire time. "What's wrong?" he asked me.

"You got him for excessive muffler smoke? That's a fix-it ticket."

"And I was *going* to give him a ticket, then I found out about his suspended license."

"You're telling me this has nothing to do with your girlfriend?"

"It doesn't. And that's over now, anyway."

"Uh-huh." I was about to give Lomeli the paperwork back when I noticed that A.J.'s address was listed as 8500 Sunnyslope Drive. That was his parents' address, too. I remembered suddenly that when I'd met with them, their daughter-in-law was in the living room, watching *Days of Our Lives,* her feet propped up on the ottoman. It was possible to trace from these details the outline of a different story. Maybe the Bakers were getting older, and A.J. had moved in to help them out, take them to their doctors' appointments or keep track of their medications. Or it could be that A.J. had fallen on hard times himself, and that was why he'd moved in with them until he could get back on his feet. What had that been like? It couldn't have been easy, living with your folks when you were already married and pushing thirty. Had it led to his drinking and, later, to his DUI? Or was the DUI the reason he had moved back home in the first place? "Where is he now?" I asked.

"B-8," Lomeli said, and pressed a button to unlock the door.

I went down the hallway, with Gorecki still following behind me. Light from the cell windows fell in sharp lines across the concrete floors, and a faint smell of bleach hung in the air. Hearing our footsteps, A.J. sat up on his cot. I noticed the surprise in his eyes when he saw me, without a uniform but with a detective's badge tucked into my belt. His gaze traveled to Gorecki, as if to blame him for this new turn of events, and then he lay back on the cot and stared at the ceiling. "Hello, A.J.," I said. "Is it all right if I call you A.J.?"

He didn't reply. Down the hall, a door closed in a clatter of metal.

"Do you need anything? A sandwich or some coffee?" He was still ignoring me, and I realized that Gorecki's presence wasn't helping. "We have that buffet upstairs today, don't we? Can you go get him a plate?"

"I'm not his fucking maid. They'll bring him something tonight."

I didn't need to ask if Gorecki knew the guy—everything about his bad attitude suggested it. He stood next to me with his hands on his hips, waiting to see what I was going to do next. The summer sun had darkened his skin, but there were gray hollows under his eyes. "That's a long time from now," I said. "I'm sure he could use a snack."

"You're wasting your time," A.J. said. "I'm not talking."

"Well, we're not talking," I said. "We're just saying hello."

"You can say hello to my lawyer. When I get my call."

Gorecki turned to me. *See?* his eyes said. *An asshole, like I told you.* But that only made me more curious about the story I was starting to piece together.

"Go get A.J. something to eat," I said, my tone making it clear that this was an order. I waited until after he'd walked off, then turned back to the cell. "All right, it's just the two of us now. Maybe we can straighten this whole thing out quickly, get you back home to your family. You're living with them, right?"

A.J. sucked on his teeth. It could've meant *What's it to you, lady?* or *Yeah, I live with them, and it fucking sucks* or something else altogether.

"Listen," I said. "Don't be so hard on yourself. These things happen. My uncle is a Baptist preacher—straightest guy you've ever met. One time at Christmas, my aunt forgot to get glaze for the ham and he decided to make a quick run to the store, even though he'd had a drink while he was waiting for dinner. Ended up with a DUI. It happens. And a suspended license, that's just rough, man. You have to get from place to place and you can never find a ride. It's just bad luck. I get it."

A grunt. "You don't get it."

"What don't I get? Your license was suspended, right? Like I said, that's tough. Especially for nine months. Now you have to ask people for rides or borrow your mom's car just to get around."

"You're wasting your time," he said, and shifted to his side, facing the wall. He was a tall guy, like his father, and his feet dangled over the cot. "Anyway, I'm not talking to a nigger."

He'd said the word under his breath, but I heard it all the same. Down the hallway, the metal door clattered as it closed behind Gorecki. I was alone. And I was nine years old again. Or eleven. Or fourteen. It didn't matter, it hurt the same every time. The only thing different was who said it, and what I did. Ran away from the playground in tears. Reported it to the teacher. Got into a fistfight on the stairwell and ended up with three stitches on my eyebrow. And always, always, trying to remove the sting of the insult, but feeling like it was too late, it had already poisoned me. My thoughts flitted to my son; that morning, he'd ridden his bicycle to school with Brandon, and waved me off when I said to be careful when he crossed Yucca Trail. "Don't worry, Mom!" But I worried about him all the time. That was what being a mom was all about.

With both hands, I grabbed the metal bars of the cell. "What did you just say to me?"

Silence. He was waiting for me to leave.

"Hey. I'm talking to you."

When he sensed that I was still standing at the cell door, he shifted on his cot again and sat up to face me. He spoke slowly and clearly, enunciating each word. "I said—I'm not talking to a fucking nigger. Did you hear me this time?"

My hands tightened on the bars. I thought about what Nora Guerraoui had told me, and what I had said in return: that what happened to her in high school many years ago wasn't relevant to the hit-and-run case. But I'd been wrong. The present could never be untethered from the past, you couldn't understand one without the other. "I heard," I said, and turned around and left. At the front office, I asked Lomeli to give me a little time, because I needed to look into something.

Twenty minutes later, when I pulled up to the house on Sunnyslope Drive, I found Helen Baker outside, pulling up the red flag on her mailbox. She was a tall woman, with thin lips untouched by makeup and graying hair that she wore in a high ponytail, like a gym teacher. With her hand, she shielded her eyes from the sun as she watched me step out of the cruiser and walk up to her. Her dogs, a pair of collies, stood at her feet, panting heavily in the heat. "Afternoon, Mrs. Baker," I said. I put out my hand, and right away the two collies came to smell it. "Such handsome dogs. What are their names?"

"This one here is Loyal," she said, almost reluctantly. Her tremors seemed worse than the other time I had seen her, when I'd come to interview her husband about the hit-and-run. "And that one is Royal."

"My son's been asking me for a dog, but I wasn't sure what breed would be best."

"Well, you can't go wrong with collies."

"So you recommend them?" I rubbed Royal's chin—or was it Loyal?—and it stretched its neck with obvious pleasure. The other dog let out a plaintive yelp. "Trouble is, my son is really set on having a chocolate lab. You know how boys are. They get an idea in their heads, and it's impossible to get it out."

"What's this about?" she asked.

I looked beyond her at the house, baking in the afternoon heat. The garage door was open, and the spaces inside were empty. "Does your son have a car, Mrs. Baker?"

"Not right now," she said after a moment of hesitation. "Why do you ask?"

"I was just wondering, you know. I didn't see any bus stops on the way over here. If A.J. doesn't have a car, how does he get around? Does he borrow yours?"

She put her hand on the mailbox, as if to steady herself. One of her dogs nuzzled up to her, asking to be petted, but she ignored it. She was watching me, trying to decide what she should say next.

"Maybe he borrowed your husband's car, too. Back in April."

"It was just an accident," she pleaded. "That's all it was."

We were both mothers, she seemed to be saying, didn't I understand how natural it was to want to protect a son? I scratched the scar on my eyebrow with a thumbnail, an old habit I fell back into from time to time. In my head, I'd arranged the pieces of this case one way, but I saw clearly now that they fit together in a different way. Of course, it was natural for Mrs. Baker to want to protect her son. But who would protect others from him?

Anderson

I became a father late in life. I'd always wanted to have a son, and when it finally happened, after fifteen years, I was surprised by how different it was from what I expected. It was even better than in my wildest dreams. I remember the summer A.J. was born, how I would sit on the couch with him curled up on my chest, sleeping, drooling all over my shirt. He was a happy baby, an easy baby. Slept through the night by the time he was three months old, got through his teething without too much fuss or trouble. Every time I try to unspool the past and pick out the specific moment when things went wrong for him, I fail. I can never find it. Maybe it was when Helen started coddling him, and I didn't put my foot down. Maybe it was when he was on the playground, and stuck to himself instead of playing with the other kids. Or maybe it was years later, in high school, when he turned into a bully. It's hard to love a bully, but Lord knows I did, with all my heart.

I tried to help him. He didn't listen to me, though, at least not when it mattered. Like when he wanted to start his doggie-daycare business, I told him straightaway that the timing wasn't right, what with the recession and all, but he thought I was just stingy, that I didn't want to lend him the $50,000 he was asking for, and he got his mom to pressure me into giving it to him. He lost it all, of course. I think that caused him a lot of embarrassment. And some anger, too, because of the way he lost it. He would get into nasty fights with his wife, and go out drinking, which is how he ended up with a DUI. We never talked back then; I found out about all this later, from his mother. So when he called me late one night, I was shocked. I'd just come home from work, and I was cracking open a beer when my phone rang. "What's wrong?" I asked. I thought it was an emergency—that's how unusual it was for me to hear from him directly.

"Nothing's wrong, Dad."

He didn't say anything else, didn't ask how I was doing, or why he was calling. Maybe he had tried to reach Helen, but she was in Kansas City that weekend for her niece's funeral. Whenever she was away from home, she would leave me instructions on the fridge about what I should eat and how to heat it up. She wrote in beautiful cursive, and I remember staring at the plans she had for me that night. *Tuesday: baked ziti. Set oven to 350 and heat for 15 minutes.* I walked out of the kitchen and crossed the living room, where the collies were sleeping, and stepped out into the backyard with my beer. It was a clear night. "The stars are out tonight," I said, just to fill the silence.

"I was thinking . . ." he said, and got quiet again.

I sat on a lawn chair, not caring that it was covered with dust and sand, and took a sip from my Budweiser. "How's Annette?" I asked. "Everything okay between you two?"

"We're okay. It's not that."

"What is it?"

"I sold my store sign today."

I should describe this sign, because A.J. built it himself. He's always had an artistic streak—he can draw almost anything—so when he opened his doggie-daycare business, he put a lot of heart into the signage. He built a five-foot collie out of painted steel, with a bone in its mouth that glowed at night, and mounted it on the roof of the building. It caught the eye, and his customers always talked about it when they came in, it made for a conversation starter. I knew what that sign meant to him, and I was surprised that he'd parted with it. "Who'd you sell it to?" I asked.

"Some guy who wants to melt it. Got forty bucks for it."

"Well, that's good." I was trying to sound encouraging, though of course forty bucks was a drop in the bucket of money he owed to the bank.

"Dad," he said, "what do I do now?"

He sounded so scared, it reminded me of the time he was four years old and the doors to the elevator in our hotel in Las Vegas closed behind him and we got separated. It took us twenty minutes of riding up and down that damn elevator before we found him. He was crying, and holding on to his crotch to keep from wetting himself. Afterward, he held Helen's hand all day, he wouldn't let go.

I took a sip from my beer and wondered if he really cared what I had to say. He'd never before asked my opinion about anything, but as the silence stretched I realized he was serious. "Why don't you come back home?" I said. "You could work for me, save on your bills, get back on your feet."

"And you would be okay with that?"

"Of course, I'm okay with that. You're my son."

He moved back in with us later that spring, along with his wife, his daughter, her hamster, and his collies. Overnight the house got smaller and busier and louder. Much louder. It took a little getting used to. Annette managed to find a job at a title company in Palm Springs, and A.J. came to work for me, but they were still behind on their credit cards and some of their bills. It wasn't easy, is what I'm trying to say. We were all under a lot of pressure, both at home and at work. Still, for the first time in our lives, A.J. and I spent entire days together. We talked a lot, he would ask me all sorts of questions about the business. It made me feel like we finally had a connection.

Of course, he shouldn't've been driving that night. But Helen couldn't drive much, on account of her tremors, and our daughter-in-law wanted nothing to do with the bowling alley. That didn't leave us with much choice, if we wanted to run our business. And I can tell you, he only took the car a few times, when there was no one who could drive him. What happened with the guy next door was just an accident. It wasn't A.J.'s fault, but I knew with his record they'd make it seem like it was. All I know is that my son isn't a bad guy. At heart, he's a good kid. I wish I could close the gap between the way things used to be and the way they are now. Maybe that's why I'm trying to tell this story.

A.J.

A couple of days after my arrest, someone tipped off a reporter and she went through my social media accounts, clipped a couple of comments and quotes out of context, and turned me into a brute. The readers of the *Desert Sun* ate it up, of course. It's funny, everyone goes on and on about celebrating diverse cultures, but the minute you bring up white culture, the oh-so-enlightened liberals turn on you and call you names. Someone sent a letter to the editor calling me a racist, which is what they call anyone who's a straight white man these days. Everyone else can be proud of their heritage, but not me?

What was infuriating to me was that after I posted bail and came out, some people started acting like I was a monster, a creature with horns and fangs. But I wasn't. I was just like them: I loved my family, played with my dogs, bought lottery tickets whenever I filled up at the gas station, then spent days fantasizing about what I'd do if I won millions of dollars. If anything set me apart from everyone else, it was only that I took charge of myself. When I graduated from college, for example, the country was in the middle of the worst recession it had seen in a century, but I didn't sit back and play the victim, the way so many others do all day long. No, I borrowed some money from my folks and started my own business in Irvine, a doggie daycare.

Of course, my dad wasn't thrilled about lending me money. He was tightfisted and didn't think dogs made for a good investment, but my mom talked him into it. And he turned out to be wrong, because my business did very well. Paws & Claws, it was called. Aside from daycare, I offered all kinds of other services, like grooming and kenneling. By the end of my first year, I'd already built a solid client base from the tech start-ups in the area, programmers who worked long hours and didn't have time to walk their dogs or play with them every day. I married my college girlfriend, Annette, and we had a baby girl. Everything was going well. We were happy. I didn't realize this until almost three years later, when it was all taken away from me.

That day, I was bringing two golden retrievers and a husky back from their afternoon walk when one of my newer clients jumped out of her car and came running toward me. Her name was Grace Chin. The husky started barking at her—that's how aggressive this woman came across—and I had to restrain him just so I could hear her. Not that it mattered, because I could hardly make out what she was saying, her English was so bad. But I figured she wanted to pick up Peanut, her Jack Russell terrier, which she'd boarded with me over the weekend. "Just give me a minute," I told her. I had to get the big dogs inside safely. Her Lexus had been left idling on the pavement, with the emergency lights on, and I remember having a bad feeling about it; it was almost as if I could tell that something was about to go down. I took the two golden retrievers and the husky inside, got them off their leashes in their pen, and went back to get the Jack Russell. Behind me, the gate bell jingled, and I knew that Grace Chin had come inside.

I want to stress that I followed all the laws and regulations when I set up my business. I'm certain that Peanut must have had some prior condition, because there was nothing in what I'd done that could have caused him to die. I gave him the same food and the same water I gave him every day, so it wasn't anything I did that could've made him sick. But he wasn't moving, not even after I called his name, and just as I realized something wasn't right, that Chin-Chong lady started pestering me. "What you did to my dog?" she asked. "What you did?"

"I didn't do anything," I said. I petted Peanut, and I swear he moved. "See?" I said.

She walked around the counter, completely disregarding the sign that said MANAGEMENT ONLY, and came to stand next to me. When she cooed to him, he didn't move. Then she tried to pick him up, and he was limp. The scream she let out would've made you think someone was flaying her alive. Even before the vet could figure out what exactly had caused the death, she'd told everyone at her work that I'd killed Peanut. She was a database engineer, she knew most of my other clients, so of course I lost a lot of business. And then, with the lawsuit, I couldn't keep up, financially. I've spent many sleepless nights going over the events of that day, and I still can't figure out how the Jack Russell terrier died. It wasn't the food or water, I was sure of it. Maybe he ate something when I took him for a walk. Whatever it was, it wasn't my fault. But it didn't matter, I started bleeding clients left and right. I couldn't believe it—this woman came into my country, could barely speak my language, and then sued *me* for negligence.

It didn't make sense to keep my business, at least not in the Irvine area, but I didn't have the money to start it up somewhere else. And my mom's symptoms were getting worse, so I ended up moving back home. I figured I might as well get used to running the bowling alley, since it would come to me someday. My dad was seventy-eight at the time, well past retirement age, but he didn't want to retire, so it was one of those situations where I just had to wait, even though I had so many ideas about the business. We needed to turn the concession stand into a full snack bar, buy new game consoles, get better music for our theme nights, put up better signage, things like that. Whenever I brought up these ideas with him, he'd say it would cost money, and he'd already given me all his savings to start my business. My failed business.

What happened to the guy next door was an accident. I didn't mean for him to die. It was really dark out and I didn't see him until it was too late. I mean, why would I want to kill him?

Driss

I think I mentioned before that business had slowed down that winter. Two new restaurants had opened a couple of miles west on the highway, and although one was a sandwich shop and the other a café that served only pastries and cookies, I was worried about the competition. Forty percent of my revenue comes from tourists, people who only stop here on their way to the national park or a concert in the desert, so I was considering a few changes. I wanted to drop the corn hash and fried cheese sticks from the menu, add new salads and fruit smoothies, replace the vinyl flooring in the entrance, maybe look into that alcohol license. And, more urgently, because the highway runs fast and I only have one chance to grab the attention of tourists, install a new sign.

The old sign, which I inherited from the previous owner, was made of planked wood, with the words THE PANTRY painted in white over a green background. It was a handsome marquee, but its colors had long ago faded and its right side was occasionally obstructed from view by a palo verde tree on the sidewalk. In the spring, when the palo verde bloomed with yellow flowers that overhung the sign, it seemed as if I were advertising that my business was THE PAN or sometimes THE PA. Even without this springtime interference, it was easy to miss at night, because there are so few lights on the highway. The owner of the hardware store two blocks from my restaurant had understood this years ago, and put up a neon sign.

One night in February, working at the counter while Rafi mopped the floors, I sketched out a new design on a piece of paper. I kept the planked wood, because I wanted the sign to remain familiar to my customers, but I made it bigger—eight feet by seven, much larger than the old one—and I changed the colors to red and white for higher contrast. I decided to hang it higher, so it wouldn't be obscured by the blooming palo verde, and for good measure I added a curved arrow over it, made of metal and dotted with lightbulbs. It was Beatrice who gave me the idea of the lighted arrow; she said it would give the marquee a classic look that would be perfect for a diner like mine.

I took my design to a local sign shop early the next morning. I couldn't shake the feeling that I was on the brink of change, that I had finally taken the first step in an adventure I had dreamed about for years without ever daring it. Aside from the plans I had for the restaurant, I had plans with Beatrice, which meant that I had to have an excruciatingly difficult conversation with Maryam. Every morning I woke up telling myself this was the day I would tell her, and every evening I came home and pushed it back another day. So that entire winter felt at once rife with danger and ripe with possibility, contradictory feelings that I hadn't experienced with such intensity since I was a young man.

It took only four days for the sign to be made but another six weeks to get the permits approved. The installation was scheduled for April 28, and when the shop told me it would send a truck for the job, I said to come early in the morning, before the bowling arcade opened. But they didn't listen, or maybe they were too busy that day. The truck didn't make it to the restaurant until nearly eleven in the morning, and the crane blocked part of the parking lot. I had to move my car to the south side of Chemehuevi to make room for customers. It took an hour to remove the old sign and hoist the new one up, and while my energies were consumed with making sure that people could safely come in and out of the lot, and that the contractor followed my instructions, Baker's son stood outside the bowling arcade, watching us.

After the truck left, I stepped back to admire my new sign. It had come out even better than I expected and, pleased with my work, I felt energized to take on another little project. The pendant lamps that hung over the leather booths dated back to 1959, when the diner had first opened, and although they were made of beautiful cream glass, they were so dim that they made the place look ghostly at night. I decided to upgrade the lightbulbs to 75 watts—bright enough to see the menu, but still intimate enough for a cozy meal. So that night, I told Marty to go home and that I would close up.

I locked the front doors and brought out the bulbs from the storage room. With only the pale light of the counter to see by, I went from table to table, changing the old lights with the new. Then I flipped the switch on, and the row of booths came into view. I stepped out into the parking lot, to see how the diner looked from outside. The whole place was so bright and inviting that I was half-tempted to leave the lights on all night. From the corner of my eye, I saw Baker's son stepping out of the arcade. He paused next to his father's Crown Vic and observed my restaurant for a minute, as if he had a stake in it, too. He used to be a lanky, shifty-eyed boy, but now that he was a man, his frame had filled out and he had a direct gaze. Almost too direct. Again, that feeling of being watched came over me.

Still, it was a good day's work, and as I left the diner and locked the doors behind me, I was filled with hope about the future. I'm doing it, I thought, I'm finally doing it. Tonight, I would tell Maryam about Beatrice and me; I would delay it no longer. Jiggling my keys in my hand, I walked to my car.

Jeremy

I was walking down a hallway that had recently been sprayed with graffiti, blue and yellow scribblings whose shapes I couldn't quite make out. A tall crate partly blocked my way and as I rounded it, three of them came upon me. I fired, killing one and injuring the other two. Then the doorbell rang. I pressed Pause, my rifle frozen in the center of the screen, and checked my score. Just four points behind Damien85, a Canadian gamer I'd been trying to beat for weeks. Taking out my wallet, I went to the front door, trying to remember whether the lamb masala was $14 or $16. But it wasn't the delivery guy, it was Nora. My heart lurched.

I stuffed the money back into my wallet and stepped aside. She came in, a faint scent of perfume trailing behind her. No makeup on her face. That silver necklace around her neck. And in her hands, I noticed now, a brown shopping bag with my hiking shoes and hats and clothes poking out of it, all the little things I'd left at her cabin. So this was it, then. We'd arrived at the fork in the road, the place where love ends. For weeks, I'd braced myself for this moment, and yet it had come and found me unprepared. "You can just leave that right there," I said, raising my chin toward the nearest corner.

But I wasn't ready to return the dress that hung in my closet, the dress into which I'd buried my face until I could no longer detect her scent. I wanted to keep the enameled pillbox that held her vitamin supplements, and that still sat where she'd left it on the bathroom counter. I couldn't give up her copy of *The Fire Next Time* on my bedside table, the margins filled with notes sometimes so long that they spilled out over the edges and onto the next page. Signs that she had been here. Signs that she'd shared her life with me for a little while. She put down the paper bag and took in the mess in my living room: a first-person shooter game on television, frozen at the moment when blood spattered the screen; the pile of clothes over the couch where I slept, or tried to sleep, most nights; the bottles of beer and whiskey; textbooks and notebooks tossed under the coffee table, gathering dust. Then she fixed her eyes on me. "How are you?" she asked.

"Never been better."

I was trying to provoke her, but she ignored my sarcasm altogether. After a moment, she said, "I heard from Detective Coleman."

So this was why she'd come. Just this, nothing else.

"I can't believe A.J. killed my dad, then let his father take the fall for him." She shook her head in disbelief. "And we would never have known if not for that traffic stop."

"I had no idea it would lead to this," I said with a shrug. It hadn't occurred to me simply because I didn't know what it was like to have a father like Anderson Baker, who would have sacrificed anything to keep his son safe.

"Either way, thank you, Jeremy."

I gave a quick nod of acknowledgment. Still, the sound of my name on her lips brought fresh pain. Go, I thought. Go. Make it quick. The doorbell rang again. Relieved at the interruption, I went to answer. It was Joe, the delivery guy. I'd been ordering from the Indian place two or three times a week, and there were days when Joe was the only person I talked to that I wasn't working with or trying to put in jail. "Hey, man," he said cheerfully, handing me the paper bag with the receipt stapled to it, the total highlighted in yellow marker. "It's $21 even. Samosas were half off tonight."

I took the bills from my wallet again and quickly counted out $25. "Is that your girlfriend?" he asked, glancing over my shoulder. "What?"

Joe broke into a smile. "Your girlfriend? She's cute."

I handed him the money and took the brown bag, kicking the door closed with one leg. The smell of warm naan and garlic and lamb wafted from the bag, but I didn't feel hungry anymore. I set the food on the kitchen counter, and when I turned around, I found Nora in the doorway. To be this close to her was unbearable. A knot formed in my throat and I had to swallow hard before I could speak. My words came out halfway between a cry and a question. "You just left."

She came to stand against the counter, across from me. "I thought everything that happened before was going to happen again. Only with me, instead of my dad."

"I told you, I would never let Fierro hurt you."

"That's not something you can promise."

"So you leave? You don't call, you don't write, you just disappear. It's like I meant nothing to you, like I was just a crutch you got rid of when you didn't need it anymore. You just moved on."

"I didn't. That's what I'm trying to tell you. I'm just as broken as before."

All I'd wanted was to take care of her, and somehow I had managed to do the opposite. "I fucked up," I said. "I know I fucked up."

She touched my arm, and in that instant the memories came back in a flood. How she'd leaned into me the first time I'd kissed her, out there in the desert. How she'd pressed her lips against my skin when I'd told her about Fletcher. The Neruda poem she'd slipped into the pocket of my jeans while I was in the shower one morning and that I'd found when I was fumbling for my keys later, in the parking lot of the Stater Brothers. I'd stood beside my car with the ten-pound ice bag I'd just bought melting in the sun, and read it again and again. *I love you as the plant that doesn't bloom but carries / the light of those flowers, hidden, within itself.* It was the closest she'd ever come to telling me she loved me. The few weeks I'd had with her were the barometer against which the rest of my life was measured. A moment earlier, I'd been so angry with her I'd wanted her to leave, and now I felt light-headed with longing. "I miss you," I whispered.

"I miss you, too," she said.

Love was made of echoes like this, and now that I could hear them, I knew we could figure it out, find a way forward together. I opened my arms and she stepped into them, her body fitting so perfectly against mine it was as if she had never left. All we needed to do was to keep talking.

Nora

We left Oakland on a drizzly morning in September. The lock on the back of the U-Haul truck rattled as we drove down the narrow streets of my neighborhood, but the sound was drowned out once we reached the freeway. I had done this drive many times before, though never at the wheel of a truck and never with my mother, who had a mortal fear of accidents and frequently asked me to slow down. In the glove compartment, she found a map of California, candy wrappers, an old magazine—things left behind by strangers. She leafed idly through the magazine, then put it back and looked out of the window. We passed vineyards, citrus groves, industrial feedlots whose smell lasted for miles, signs that blamed Congress for the drought, billboards that advertised restaurants at the next exit. Sometime in the afternoon, my mother pulled out the magazine again and started reading me clues from the crossword puzzle in the back. *Haunting spirit,* five letters. *Elephant's strong suit,* six letters.

Late at night, we finally reached the desert. As soon as we took the exit for the 62, my mother turned on the radio and looked for KDGL on the dial. "Claudia Corbett is about to start," she said, raising the volume. An elderly man was calling to say that he was worried about his son, who had a well-paying job with a mortgage company in Denver, but was always struggling with money. "No matter how much he makes," the caller said, "he always spends more. I don't get it." I expected Claudia to suggest that the son cut up his credit cards and go on a strict debt-payment plan, but instead she began to ask questions about his childhood and upbringing, confident that the root of his financial problems would be found there. My mother listened raptly.

She loved this talk show, and it came to me that there was a voyeuristic element to it: this show broke open the door between public and private, a door she kept scrupulously closed in her own life. I waited until the episode had ended before I turned off the radio. "I need to tell you something, Mom," I said. "About Dad."

"What is it?"

How to go about this, except bluntly? I had waited long enough, I needed to stop carrying my father's secret. "He was having an affair," I said.

I let out the breath I'd been holding and waited for the uncomfortable questions that I knew would follow—what was I talking about and it wasn't possible and how would I know something like this anyway. It wasn't easy to accept that the man we loved had done terrible things, because love itself is a singling out of one person over countless others. My mother turned away from me and stared at the road ahead. We were driving through a dark wilderness of creosote, mesquite, and yerba santa, guarded on all sides by mountains. It took another moment for the truth to dawn on me. My hands tightened on the steering wheel. "You knew?" I said. "You never said anything."

"Why would I say? This was between us."

So she had seen the ugly face my father kept hidden behind a mask, and yet she still loved him. All my life, I had found her to be uncompromising, sometimes even unforgiving, and it stunned me to discover this side of her now—in a moving truck. A brown, furtive shape crossed the road; I lifted my foot off the accelerator. "Who is she?" I asked.

I could see how difficult it was for her to say the name, but after a slow, uneasy moment, she did. "Beatrice Newland." The name rang no bells for me, and held no meaning. But speaking it seemed to have released something in my mother, because her voice was deep with emotion now. "She's so young. She looks about your age."

How tawdry, I thought, until I remembered my time with Max. "Why did you stay with him, then?" I asked. I was still trying to reconcile the mother I had always known with the woman sitting beside me now.

"I was sure it would pass, I just had to wait. We spent thirty-seven

years together, you know, and to throw all that away for that woman—
I couldn't do it."

"What about after he died?" I asked. "Why didn't you say something then?"

"Talking about it wasn't going to change what already happened. It wasn't going to turn him into someone different."

"I see." And I did. But even though my mind agreed, my heart rebelled. She had never been this gentle or patient or understanding with me. If she was capable of this kind of love, why not with me? Why did she fight so hard to mold me into someone else? All I ever wanted was for her to take me as I was. By then, we were coming out of the valley, and the road narrowed as it rose through the canyon. One of my ears popped. An irksome feeling. "Mom," I said after a moment, "you never even asked me about Silverwood."

"I did. You said it was a big festival."

"And you weren't curious to find out more? Or ask me what piece I played or anything?"

She turned to look at me. "I don't understand that stuff."

"It's *music.* It's not supposed to be understood. It's supposed to be enjoyed."

"Oh, Nora," she said, and reached across the seat divider to touch my arm. "That's not what I meant. I *like* your music. I just meant, I don't understand festivals and competitions and grants and things like that. That's all." The road dipped and flattened, and after a little while we reached the first grove of Joshua trees. "So what was Silverwood like?" she asked.

Maybe something had finally shifted between us. By talking to her about the secret she had kept hidden for so long, I had begun to chip away at her other defenses. She had to let go of her fantasies about me, and accept the fact that I was only a musician, I would always be just that, and nothing more. Now that she seemed willing to listen, I began to tell her about my time in Boston, the drummer and bass player I had met, the plans we had made, the good things I had learned, and the bad ones, too.

Afterward, I lowered the window and rested my elbow on the sill. The air was warm and dry. Soon, the Santa Ana winds would begin to blow through the passes, bringing with them fury and fire. How often had I lain in bed, dreaming of leaving the desert someday? This place had been filled with quarrels and recriminations, and it would be a while yet before they ended. I still had to face A.J. in a courtroom. Three days from now, when the time came for his preliminary hearing, I would watch in disgust as he walked out, a free man on bail. But there would be other times, over the next few months, and one day I would finally have a chance to speak, tell the judge and the jury about my father, and honor his memory in this small way. At every court date, A.J.'s lawyer, an attorney from Orange County who specialized in hit-and-run cases, would file motions or ask for continuances, and it would not be until three and a half years later, when I was pregnant with my first child, that A.J. would finally be convicted of manslaughter and sentenced to five years in prison.

And I would still be here. The desert was home, however much I had tried to run away from it. Home was wide-open spaces, pristine light, silence that wasn't quite silence. Home, above all, was the family who loved me. Only now, after my father's death, did I come to understand that love was not a tame or passive creature, but a rebellious beast, messy and unpredictable, capacious and forgiving, and that it would deliver me from grief and carry me out of the darkness.

Acknowledgments

I am grateful to many people and organizations for their support during the writing of this book. I would like to acknowledge, in particular, the City of Santa Monica for an artist grant; the Yaddo Corporation for a stay at its colony; and the John Simon Guggenheim Foundation for a fellowship. Thank you to my editor, Erroll McDonald, who gave me astute comments and patient encouragement. Thank you to my agent, Ellen Levine, who offered early notes and unstinting support. Josefine Kals, Michiko Clark, and Kimberly Burns, my publicists, make miracles happen. Nicholas Thomson at Pantheon Books and Martha Wydysh at Trident Media worked very hard on this project at every stage. Miriam Feuerle, Hannah Scott, and Andrew Wetzel at Lyceum Agency have been steadfast advocates of my work. Special thanks to Alexis Kirschbaum, Rachel Wilkie, and Ros Ellis at Bloomsbury UK. I am indebted to the park rangers at the Joshua Tree National Park for their expertise on fauna and flora in the Mojave and to the officers of the San Bernardino County Sheriff's Department for answering my many queries. Thank you to Dana Boldt and Gavin Huntley-Fenner for help with legal and logistical questions. Thank you to my early readers: Scott Martelle, Maaza Mengiste, Souad Sedlik, and Jane Smiley. Thank you, most of all, to Alexander Yera.

A NOTE ABOUT THE AUTHOR

Laila Lalami is the author of *Hope and Other Dangerous Pursuits; Secret Son;* and *The Moor's Account,* which won the American Book Award, the Arab-American Book Award, and the Hurston/Wright Legacy Award, and was a finalist for the Pulitzer Prize. *The Moor's Account* was also on the Man Booker Prize longlist and on several best books of the year lists, including *The Wall Street Journal, Kirkus Reviews,* and NPR. Her essays have appeared in the *Los Angeles Times, The Washington Post, The Nation, Harper's Magazine, The Guardian,* and *The New York Times.* She is the recipient of a British Council Fellowship, a Fulbright Fellowship, and a Guggenheim Fellowship, and is currently a professor of creative writing at the University of California at Riverside. She lives in Los Angeles.

A NOTE ON THE TYPE

This book was set in Caledonia, a typeface designed by W. A. Dwiggins (1880–1956). It belongs to the family of printing types called "modern face" by printers—a term used to mark the change in style of the type letters that occurred around 1800. Caledonia borders on the general design of Scotch Roman but it is more freely drawn than that letter. This version of Caledonia was adapted by David Berlow in 1979.

TYPESET BY SCRIBE, PHILADELPHIA, PENNSYLVANIA

PRINTED AND BOUND BY BERRYVILLE GRAPHICS, BERRYVILLE, VIRGINIA

DESIGNED BY IRIS WEINSTEIN